MW00640337

To Nancy,
One of my favorite ladies.

SCRIBE

Antiquity Theft in the Maya Ruins

LINDA LINDHOLM

Linda Lindholm.

Glue Pot Press

Cover and Interior Design: Max Marbles & Linda Lindholm
Publisher: Glue Pot Press
First Edition
Printed in U.S.A

ISBN-10:
0-9831616-3-1
ISBN-13:
978-0-9831616-3-9

ACKNOWLEDGMENTS

I would like to express my thanks to Joanna van der Gracht de Rosado, Max Lindholm, Margie Alexy, Lee Christie, Jorge Rosado, Dora Lee Eldred, Kathleen Brown Werner, Alexander J. Werner, Andrew S. Brown, George McClellan, Mhaire Merryman, Greg Casini and Mike Hill for their assistance and inspiration.

CHAPTER 1

Edzna, Campeche
1560 A.D.

According to the Maya, time is not linear. They believe the flow of life to be circular and repetitive. What happened before shall happen again.

Mayan scribe and astronomer, Ko'h Dzib, worked alone. For almost one *katun*, twenty years, he'd created charts to keep track of the movements of Venus, Mars, the stars and the moon. A long room with its stone roof for protection from the elements held much of his life work. He gazed over the adjacent wall filled with numbers, tables and computations indicating the short and long calendar counts spanning thousands of years.

Ko'h knew from daily calculations which deity was overseeing the heavens at certain times and could predict the appearance of a full moon or eclipse years in advance. His astronomical record keeping was used to advise his cousin the king on matters such as propitious days for planting crops or war making.

But today, his hands and arms were covered in thick limestone white wash. He splashed the stucco solution on the wall to cover over a portrait of the sovereign ruler in all his finery. He reluctantly took another look at the back wall and hesitated.

Tears of grief followed the deep creases in his face. The royal scribe knew that, like the earlier burial of his precious books, he must also hide the workshop writings or his family would be in grave danger from the invaders. Since his wife had died and his brother-in-law Nim Ao fell fighting the white demons, he was the one responsible for his daughter Itz and his sister Yaxche.

He took a deep breath. Using his large shell ink holder as a scoop, he tossed on the last bit of the thickened gritty limestone mixture and plastered over an entire lifetime of mathematical records and predictions.

Ko'h returned to his sister's home near the main plaza to purify and prepare for what was to come. He donned his finest clothing, clasped jade and red coral jewels around his neck, wrists and through his earlobes. He draped a resplendent cloak of colorful feathers around his shoulders. Offerings to his gods asked for guidance and forgiveness. Directing the copal smoke, he prayed to the east, the direction of the wind and Kukulkan, the feathered serpent. Finally he dipped a turkey feather quill in his carved conch paint pot and used *sabak*, soot ink to write one of his characteristic fine-lined stylized poems on accordion-folded bark paper. As he dropped another amber colored lump of incense into the clay burner, he heard the approach of men in clanging metal suits coming up the stone steps.

Tiny bells on the doorway curtain jingled as a hairy hand reached in to rip aside the covering. Spanish soldiers entered his room with swords drawn. The stench of their unwashed bodies stung his nostrils. Their presence offended and frightened him. Ko'h had seen the foreign soldiers and their rampant callousness in action. He found that unlimited power in the hands of limited people usually led to cruelty.

Without a word, a tall white man looped a rope around the scribe's neck and quickly bound his wrists. Keeping it taut, he forced his Maya prisoner's arms up and yanked them up between the shoulders. A second soldier bashed Ko'h on the side of his head with the hilt of a sword.

Ko'h buckled in pain and gasped for breath, but did not shame himself by crying out. Not yet. The once noble scrivener was led away, dizzy and struggling to walk upright.

Boar-skin drums thundered and whistles shrieked and echoed across the main plaza to summon the people. In Ko'h's befuddled daze, he was not clear if those ancient sounds signaling sacrifice were in his mind or actually happening. He knew a hundred eyes watched him from inside the rooms and buildings that lined the causeway.

Spanish soldiers dragged him to the old sun-god temple. Their black-clad priest followed, chanting strange incantations and carrying a large ivory cross against his breast. His thin-lipped mouth reminded Ko'h of a viper's, with a tongue that flicked in and out.

The recent invaders favored public spectacles and ceremonies to display their power over the conquered Maya people and instill fear. Last moon cycle, Edzna's young queen was strangled in front of her followers. The *ah'hau* king was sent in chains to the five-hill city of T'Ho, a place the Spaniard leader had renamed Merida. Across the land, the true peoples' sacred temples were torn away and their stones used to build the churches, walls and homes for the white newcomers.

Ko'h had been targeted for public humiliation. Not only because he was of royal lineage and high rank, but scribes like him, empowered by their education, were considered indispensable to the community, as well as its leaders. Members of the elite group of communicators were persecuted and executed as dangerous. Scribes could preserve the ancient stories and were considered a threat to the new order and Christendom. To the Spanish, the old Maya religion was deemed blasphemous to the god brought across the seas with them.

The colonial soldier who bound him, spit on Ko'h. The priest put aside his ivory cross, crumpled painted bark papers in the scribe's face and yelled, "Pagan! Why do you continue to write demonic incantations?" He threw Ko'h's carefully recorded and illustrated medicinal formulas gathered from great healers into a brazier, oblivious to the wisdom lost. In the name of noble purposes the foreign men committed unspeakable acts to hold on to their newly gained power through force and fear.

The soldiers ripped Ko'h's cloak off his shoulders and stomped the treasured feather mantle into matted piles. They threw his other carved stone adornments to their companions.

"What, no gold or real jewels?" they shouted.

Ko'h didn't understand their words, but he knew the precious gifts of his shaman father meant nothing to them.

People of Edzna, who had been forcefully gathered to observe, stood helpless. The king's son, Tepal, skulked around the edges, looking afraid and unwilling to challenge his scribe's tormenters. Ko'h stood before the jeering strangers of no color, wearing only his loincloth. He was grateful his daughter had fled to safety in another village weeks before.

The priest stood inches from the scribe. There was complete silence as the two men faced each other. Copoya lowered his eyes to the ground. He could not stand to look at the bare crudity of an ugly soul in the hollow smirk of this supposedly holy man. Christians of the time held all other creeds and forms of worship in infinite contempt.

The padre ordered two large armed men to come closer. They held iron pinchers and used them to pull out the scribe's thumb and forefinger nails from both hands. The agony was beyond his endurance. Ko'h bit his tongue. Foam and blood flecked on his lips and leaked from the corner of his mouth.

An unflinching cruel man took Ko'h's bleeding fingers and snapped each one of them back, tearing the ligaments at the joints. Another withdrew a filleting knife and cut the fatty pads of flesh off the scribe's fingers to the bone. Blood gushed out of greatly disfigured hands in a slow rhythm. These vicious acts broke him, both in body and in the eyes of the crowd gathered in the plaza. A low wailing rose from the shocked and saddened observers.

Throughout the agony, Ko'h drifted in and out of consciousness. He had visions of his deceased mother standing next to a woman with golden hair. He saw himself as a young boy running around the platform. Babies wrapped in shawls on their mothers' backs looked up at him with familiar earth-brown eyes. He could not grasp or separate the past, present and future cycle hallucinations circling through his head. The carved sun-god stone faces helplessly watched the bitter bane of Ko'h. Without humans feeding the deities with their worship, the gods did not have the strength to help.

Two soldiers eager to participate in the spectacle, came unseen from behind and simultaneously smacked the back of the scribe's head and right leg with wooden staffs. Ko'h's chest heaved, his face creased, wet with blood and tears. All strength and pride lost, he crumpled into a heap at their feet. Satisfied that he was finished, the Spanish left him on the stone platform to die.

CHAPTER 2

Edzna, Campeche
1560 A.D.

Ko'h could not feel his life force, yet knew he had not died. He was too depleted to move. Terrible pain racked his body. Darkness came over him like a slow black wave. He exhaled and waited for it to finish him. Voices faded in and out. Some said to stay, some said to come. One voice, more insistent than the other, softly begged him to open his eyes. He could not. He saw a flickering light on the other side of his eyelids and sensed a strong presence beside him.

Yaxche, shadowed by torchlight, knelt beside her brother on a reed mat. The dark haired noblewoman stroked his head with a damp cloth from a bowl of cool water in her lap. She whispered encouragement as she wiped away blood from his face and hair. She soaked his mangled hands in herbal numbing solutions. She gently opened his lips and trickled liquid into his mouth. Her potion made him relax and lessened the pain. He felt parts of his body being jolted as she worked on his deformed hands. His injured leg was braced and immobile.

His semi-conscious state and the anesthetic affect of the medicines she administered kept him still. This had allowed her to cleanse and massage his bloody hands back into more natural positions. She sutured his wounds with her own long strands of hair. To treat and close his flesh wounds and seal damaged blood vessels, she applied resin from the *ek balam* shrub and bark of the *bakalche* tree. She splinted and covered his fingertips in bandages over a plaster blend of cooling leaves, burned feathers, honey and tobacco.

Yaxche was a *x xiu*, a woman who knows how to use medicinal plants. She came from a long line of traditional healers. Her holistic approach placed great emphasis on the connection between mind and body. Her training in the art of *pul yah* could take pain away directly from the point of origin. Yaxche understood how the physical world and the spiritual world overlapped.

She kept the ritualistic traditions of her ancestors alive. Prayers, offerings, dance, chants, burning of copal incense and ritual drinking of alcoholic *balche* proved to have a significant impact on healing and recovery. She fasted and, using the sharpened edge of a sacred crystal *sastun*, made a sacrifice of her own blood to the goddess Ixchel.

The air was kept pure with a mixture of marigold, cedar and rue herb water poured over hot rocks. Ko'h lay in her sleeping room, which was warm from steam and incense smoke. Yet her brother still shivered with fever chills. His *ch'ulel*, divine life energy force, ebbed and flowed. She fought to keep him in the earthly realm.

"It has passed," she comforted the bruised and battered Ko'h. He turned his face to the wall.

"It would have been better to let me die," he sobbed. "I am broken beyond repair. I am no longer the person I used to be. I am no one."

"Your dignity can be mocked and compromised, but it can never be taken from you," Yaxche replied.

She'd nursed her brother's bodily wounds, but his psychological damage tested her healing abilities. Injuries could be treated. Mental attitudes toward life and living were so intertwined with physical being that imbalance could change the course. His injuries were grave. She knew he could allow himself to die. She hoped his will to live was strong enough to keep him from the underworld.

As she dabbed his feverish forehead with a cloth soaked in lavender water, she said nine prayers to overcome the pain and shame in his broken heart. She struggled to replace sadness and rejection with healing and peace. Yaxche treated her brother with a blend of religion and science, everything she could think of to heal both the body and soul. His health and life depended on balance.

Ko'h awoke briefly on the second day and looked down at his tortured hands bound tightly in loom-woven cloth wraps. He could smell the pungent antiseptic herbs and see the moist compress seeping with his blood. He sipped the honey mixture his sister held to his lips. She convinced him to take bitter tasting medicines by mixing them with cacao chocolate and dried maize paste. For a short while the treatment reduced the throbbing in his head, hands and leg. But he would wake later with pain so intense that she was forced to administer stronger psychoactive drugs with a leather enema sack for more rapid absorption and quicker relief.

The devil's trumpet plants Yaxche used contained hyoscyamine and scopolamine to relieve the pain and nausea. The nightshade substances not only numbed his entire body, but also induced communication with the gods. His thoughts in the trance-like drug-induced dream state were scattered. He visited spiritual realms inhabited by long-gone ancestors and by spirits yet-to-be-born.

Yaxche continued her tireless efforts. She could only do so much to save her brother. His struggle between the two realms tipped back and forth. Healing had to come from within him, as well as from her skills as a physician. In his weakened mental and physical state, she feared she would lose the battle, so sent for his daughter Itz. With his only child at his side, Ko'h might be compelled to live.

CHAPTER 3

Edzna, Campeche
1560 A.D.

The complex remedies of Yaxche helped Ko'h only to a point. Rituals and natural medicines gradually restored his shattered body, but his mind fought their healing powers. He was deathly ill with wounds and fever. He debated and pleaded with his gods. He used his bandaged hands to scoop a jade stone into his mouth as payment for his underworld journey.

"I demand you take me!" he screamed to the spirits. Ko'h would rather enter a realm unknown to him than remain in the strange world of the Spanish conquistadors and their sadistic priests. If he could have held an obsidian knife in his useless hands, he would have quickly ended his life. There was a reason they called such razor sharp blades, the 'hand of god'.

"I no longer have a purpose or place," he cried out to his sister. "Nothing's left. My memory only spins tortuous threads to remind me of all my losses. They killed me in front of my people. Everyone thinks me dead," he argued.

It was true. Everyone thought the scribe died. Yaxche's son had carried the limp body of Ko'h back to her home under darkness on a moonless night. Drops of his royal blood fell at the base of the sun-god's temple, but it was not enough to empower the god on Ko'h's behalf. The nephew left flowers and burned bee's wax candles in the spot where his uncle fell. Rituals one would do for a departed spirit.

"Just let me go. I am through."

"No," answered Yaxche firmly. "You are not finished yet. Life's web will hold you here until your fate is fulfilled."

She turned to refill his jug and helped him sip a bit more herbal potion mixed with thin corn gruel. "Itz will be here by nightfall. Your daughter is part of your legacy, still part of your life purpose," she added.

"I don't want her to see me broken and shamed." He turned his face to hide the agony tearing at his heart. Ko'h drifted off into another dream state. This time the potions did not take him into audience with his gods, but transported him back to a joyful time when his wife ran to greet him after a trip. She fell into his arms and kissed his face.

It seemed so real. Ko'h's cheeks were moist and warm with touch. Through his glazed eyes he saw her dark hair and the warm glow of amber stones around her neck.

"Perhaps I have died and my beloved late wife is with me again," he sighed and he reached out his arms.

When his heavy blue-veined eyelids opened, it was Itz, his daughter. Their tears mingled. She was grown up now, a full *katun* of twenty years. Looking so much like her mother that it brought both sorrow and joy to his heart. She had the same blue-black hair and always wore her deceased mother's amber pendant with the lily border setting.

In honor of her mother, Itz underwent the pain of having her face marked with permanent raised beaded dots. Small round scars curled in a fluid circle from the corners of her mouth up to her cheekbones to symbolize elegant speech and song.

Her mother had been a gifted singer, famous as far away as the

Toltec lands. Itz had heard stories, but had no clear memories of the beautiful mother who died within two years of her birth.

Although never discussed, Ko'h believed that Itz had the raised scaring put on her face to distract from a deep tear shaped gouge left under her right eye, inflicted on her in youth by angry blows from Prince Tepal, second son of the king.

Itz could barely contain her horror at seeing the dramatic changes in her once strong father. He appeared gaunt, and bore a distant haunted look. Yaxche warned her about his fatalistic mental state, but not about the physical manifestations of a mortal soul longing for release. She propped him up on fresh straw mats and covered him with hand-woven blankets to stave off the chills he continued to suffer.

"Fear made his heart go cold and the fevers are trying to restore the balance," her aunt told her.

"Father, I am here with you. I will help care for you until we go to a safer place," Itz comforted him.

"Your smile gladdens me. But know that I am dying. I have surrendered. I am ready for my journey to the ancestors."

"No, your fever will only kill what needs to die within you to repair your soul. Your ills remind you of the eternal piece of you, the part of your spirit that refuses to quit. You must not die. I need you alive and healthy again," she pleaded.

Itz massaged Yaxche's sweet smelling poultice onto her father's shoulders and arms. Ko'h breathed in the floral scents and relaxed into an intoxicated euphoric sleep. He felt a sensation throughout his system and connection to those who cared for him deeply. It went beyond unconditional love of family to union with his Maya people and all he held sacred.

Itz visited with her aunt in the other room. "How selfish of me. I should not speak of my own needs," she scolded herself. "I am afraid of being left alone. He keeps talking about joining gods and ancestors."

"We live in a world where Earth is not separate from Heaven and where the Creation is not separate from the Creators. Matter and Spirit infuse each other. After treating the body, it is wiser to stay out of the way. Your father will process and embrace his fear until the terror subsides. Truths will become self evident," Yaxche addressed her niece's concerns.

Itz lit crystalized nuggets of healing copal incense in an elongated ceramic brazier topped with the carved face of Itzamna, the creator god. She placed the smoking burner on a shelf near her sleeping father and left the room.

He drifted between hazy dreams and moments of clarity. He focused on the brazier's features with its timeless eyes and enchanting soul. Watching the waning embers behind the ancient face, he soared to the eternal place where his forefather's souls dwelled in grace and spirits ran free. He bowed to them in reverence. He wanted to stay where past and present seemed to occupy the same space and time. He felt welcome in their realm, but knew that for now his visit was over. Without words they instructed the scribe to resume his frail mortal body and return to all things temporal and human.

"I will forever move in different forms down through the ages, again and again," he realized.

He was called to endure for the good of others. His ancestors and gods expected service as a sacred act. They indelibly imprinted a new meaning, a greater purpose on Ko'h's heart.

CHAPTER 4

Edzna, Campeche
Present Day

"Archaeology is a dirty business," said Hannah as she wiped at the damp locks of strawberry-blonde hair poking out from under her sweat stained canvas hat. She couldn't see the muddy smudge it left over her right eye.

"In more ways than one," groused Roberto Oc, the Maya co-director of Edzna, their site excavation in southeast Mexico. He recalled a meter-deep hole gouged into an ancient temple platform they'd encountered that morning. Looters had obviously plundered another ancient building near the edge of the archaeological zone.

Hannah's right arm trembled with exhaustion as she swung her machete through the bright green hell of the Yucatan jungle. This particular part of the trail was beset by morass, liano tangles and long-leaved growths that could cut like knives. Creeping, clutching foliage and unrelenting clouds of insects surrounded them.

The late morning air shimmered hot. Enervating jungle heat was immediate. High humidity fell over her like a steamy wet sauna. There seemed barely enough air to breathe. Hannah found little relief in the faint breezes that passed through the forest.

"Books and movies don't show you this part? Never warn you

about the hardships and dangers involved in field work, do they?" Roberto teased.

"Archaeo-romantics read National Geographic and wistfully say how they always wanted to be archaeologists. If they only knew the other sides to this so-called glamorous profession," she groaned, pressing the front of her shirt to absorb trickles of perspiration.

As trying as the environment and hard work might be, archaeologist Dr. Hannah Char still thrived in the field. She felt the same thrill she always did while excavating a site and never grew weary of being part of rediscovering history. It was not the possibility of long-lost treasures that kept her coming back; it was the challenge. She was an expert at piecing together clues and solving the old mysteries. Hannah pitted herself against the jungle and forced it to surrender its secrets. She was passionate about discovering the stories behind the artifacts she uncovered.

For her it was a heightened sense of stepping back in time. But such an overused phrase was not sufficient to describe the sensation. Hannah's feeling was more one of being grabbed and yanked back into the past.

This field season had been the best yet in proving her theory that forbidden Mayan books, burned by overzealous Spanish priests, were reproduced on ceramic pottery. Using breakthroughs in deciphering writing codes, she had uncovered fragments of sequenced stories. Experience and instincts convinced her that the dig still held undisturbed ancient wisdom forgotten by the world.

"I can't imagine doing anything else," she said to Roberto. "It's worth any difficulty when we find exciting new evidence like the canal system we confirmed today."

Hannah remembered how their morning survey at the far edge of their site revealed walled waterways and cornerstones of a fortress not seen for over five hundred years.

"We are rarely rewarded with those Indiana Jones moments, are we Roberto?"

His answer was cut off by deep droning thump, thump, thumps

approaching from the distance. Through a narrow opening in the treetops, Hannah and Roberto saw a camouflaged military-type helicopter. It was painted shades of green to make it difficult to spot from below or above against the jungle canopy. The chopper accelerated skyward, a bulging load dangling underneath.

With a quick look they realized the helicopter carried a huge carved stone and plaster object. The giant grimacing face of a sun-god stared down at them through the tangled mesh of rope and canvas.

"No! A statue from the temple," Hannah screamed. Her head shook back and forth in disbelief. She froze in place, unable to believe what her eyes had seen. Shock left her unable to speak of the unspeakable.

"*Cabrones*," cursed Roberto, shaking his clenched fist at the departing aircraft. He smelled fuel fumes as it disappeared. They spun around and hurried back toward their work compound. Each silently dreaded, for their own reasons, what they might find at their ancient Maya site.

CHAPTER 5

Edzna, Campeche
Present Day

Bursting through the green wall of jungle surrounding the archaeological ruins, Hannah and Roberto approached the wide main plaza. A handful of site-workers huddled on the carved temple steps murmuring to each other. Roberto's eyes swept the area, immediately seeking his mother, Mari.

"Madre?" called her son. "Where is Dona Mari?" he asked.

A man pointed toward a hut in the site compound. Mari Oc, the *curandera*, healer and camp coordinator could tell them what had happened in their absence.

Roberto pushed through the rough-woven sisal door and hurried inside. Mari squatted on her heels tending an injured young man. The relieved director stood behind his mother and gently patted her shoulder; both to reassure that she was alright and let her know that he was back. Roberto was a calm and spiritual Maya man who usually feared nothing in this world or the next. But possible harm to his family or friends sent him into a hard, protective mode.

Smoke from copal resin hazed the one room shelter. The mixed bite of bitter medicinal herbs and sweet honey from Mari's beehives filled the air. She pressed a small fish totem above the man's injury "to nibble away the evil in his cut," she explained.

"How is he?" Hannah inquired as she entered the hut. She wanted her site workers to be cared for like extended family. Even a minor injury or infection in the jungle, far away from medical facilities, could prove fatal.

"He tried to stop the theives, but they beat him. He's got a concussion and abrasions," Mari replied. She pressed an herbal salve on his shoulder wound and finished with wrapped gauze around the abrasions. The man held half of a sour orange to a goose egg bump on his head and sucked on the salted other half.

"What just occurred here?" Roberto asked his mother.

The man nodded a weak greeting and interjected, "I was the only one near the temple. I wanted to protect Kin, but couldn't fight four of them. When they saw me, they hit me with their guns and a wooden post."

Mari turned away from her patient for a moment, "Roberto, Hannah, you need to go to the Temple of the Masks. I'll meet you there."

"Yes, we'll go see what is left of it," Roberto fumed.

CHAPTER 6

Edzna, Campeche
Present Day

Shock sent chills and nausea through Hannah's body. She walked with her head bent and her hands in her pockets to stop the trembling. Roberto mumbled curses or prayers. Hannah couldn't tell which.

She hurried to keep up with his pace along an ancient causeway. They passed an imposing five-story structure and entered what was little more than a parting between the trees. They trudged along a dank foot trail. Birds scolded them from the treetops. Ahead Hannah saw a rocky mound and courtyard through the foliage. Her stomach tightened with dread.

Roberto came to a dead halt in the desolate plaza. He stared at the chaos and destruction of irreplaceable, one-of-a-kind carvings in front of the temple's tiered platform. Limestone fragments, chunks of stucco and other bits of debris at his feet stood as silent witnesses, evidence of the crime.

The structure's north façade, once decorated with hieroglyphic symbol stones and a large pair of magnificently carved and painted faces, was now a pile of rubble. Before the raid, two well-preserved stucco heads of young Maya king-gods, wearing distinctive flanged crowns of royalty, flanked the staircase. They had elaborate earplugs, exaggerated lips and the haughty brows of true lords. The pair, still colored with red and blue mineral paint, were among the finest humanized depictions of *Kinich Ahau,* the bulging-eyed sun god. *Kin* was the center of the Maya universe and calendar.

The movements of the sun were particularluy critical to the ancient Mayas. The male deity, called Father Sun, was the ruler of space and time. The sun-faced lord was connected with ruling lineages and identified with the Corn God, as a symbol of renewal and fertility. Represented as the K'in glyph, the sun god had a Roman nose, crossed eyes with square pupils and knotched teeth.

The carved statues were not just extraordinary works of art; they were priceless to science. The temple and façade had been buried and hidden on purpose by the Mayans, over a thousand years before. Maya archaeologists, like Hannah, called this process a 'termination ritual', a ceremonial closing of a sacred building. The original classical era inhabitants of Edzna knew its importance even then and wanted to protect it.

Now in contrast, conspicuous by its gaping absence, the better-preserved stone and stucco image from the right was completely gone. The vandalized structure exhaled a tragic sense of loss.

Feeling as empty as the ragged hole in front of her, Hannah ran her fingertips over the rough stone. She could feel sadness through the walls. Powerful rock saws had ripped the divine noble from his post overlooking the plaza. The temple's stone guard was no longer at his duty station.

Roberto yelled to the sky and the long-gone aircraft. "How dare you raid our heritage and sell to the highest bidders." He needed to vent the frustration and anger of such a travesty.

Hannah's face flushed in outrage. She and her team worked for weeks, exhausted themselves to excavate the landmark find. In less than an hour, vandals with rock saws and spikes ravaged the temple. All her efforts had been reduced to dust. An irreplaceable piece of Maya civilization was lost to scientific research and history. Every month more sites were being desecrated by looters than methodically excavated by archaeologists. She paced around the perimeter taking photographs of the damage, looking for any clues or traces of evidence.

"They came in with a helicopter," she said, still in disbelief at their audacity. "Oh, Berto, Will this ever end? How do we stop it?" Hannah sighed and swept her arm toward the ruined temple.

He answered with a scowl. His face, like dark leather, tightened, the nostrils in his large hooked nose flared, and jaw muscles clenched. The rock-hard expression made him appear much older than his forty-seven years.

Roberto approached the work crew hovering at the perimeter. Following the degrading of their ancestors' building, men gathered to expose the guilty, if they could. They would confide in Roberto or Mari, but give nothing to the police or other outsiders. Maya society often excluded the state or church. Now, in this case, they would close ranks again.

The *campesino,* local workers from around the area would listen to Roberto, not only because his family had served as elders and shamans for longer than anyone could remember, but also because he made the choice to return and live among them, as one of them. This earned him a great deal of respect in the pueblos.

Hannah and Mari joined Roberto as he spoke with the workers in the shade of a neem tree. Mari worried her son might be overly distressed to calmly discuss the invasion. Her fears were relieved when she saw him pat the men's backs and offer comfort rather than confrontation.

"It's best to let us question them. You understand?" Mari asked.

In response, Hannah stepped far aside and did not speak. She was accepted and beloved by Mari and Roberto, but a North American woman could not expect the others' confidence. Sometimes, as she approached villagers, she would hear, '*He cu tal dzul*, a white person is coming'.

Being a full head taller than most Mayas, and having red hair and fair freckled skin separated her genetically. But the connection

Hannah felt for the people of the Yucatan and their ways went beyond that. Even though she looked physically different, there existed within her a certain deep familiarity. Yet, over the years, Hannah learned to put ego aside and gracefully accept their ingrained hesitations about including a stranger.

Worried workers approached Roberto, their *maestro*, supervisor. From a distance Hannah heard sharp and excited noises, over and over. The men sounded like frightened geese,

"What happened?" Roberto asked them. The small group fell silent. Their hands were held out, palms up, and their shoulders shrugged. Most looked at the ground. The men's pleading eyes wanted answers too. How could Roberto explain who and why to them when he was not even on site when the theft occurred?

Roberto succeeded in getting no more information than he could already deduce from an examination of the ruined temple façade. The workers had been occupied far away from the Temple of the Masks at the time of the heist.

"Didn't you hear the noise?" he inquired.

Several said they thought the booming sounds were far away thunder. Each expressed complete ignorance of the sordid affair and slipped into the forest after questioning. The injured man was the only one to check out the disturbance. His curiosity almost got him killed.

"Do you think someone was bribed to report when everyone would conveniently be somewhere else?" asked Hannah, as they walked back to the compound.

"Little doubt," responded Roberto.

"Who among our crew would inform such big-time looters about the recent finds?" she asked. "Such personal betrayal seems unthinkable to me."

"An invasion that sophisticated required planning, time and privacy. Whoever pulled this off had to know we'd be gone today and the site practically vacant. Unscrupulous thieves probably used a mix of rewards and intimidation to get someone to help them," Roberto further fleshed out her theory.

"Can we figure out who?" she asked.

"A local informant would have nothing further to gain and lots to lose if he identified the looters. Besides, criminals don't report other criminals," said Roberto. "We'll go through the personnel lists and see if any patterns or clues show up. Anything we find will be part of the reports to the Mexican National Institute of Anthropology and History (INAH), as well as other related agencies with initials. We need to construct an inventory of losses for the police."

"Oh, no," Hannah groaned. "What a waste of time to involve local police. They may appear long on concern, but they are short on actions. They will do nothing."

"You are probably right," agreed Roberto.

"Even INAH is too underfunded to investigate or prosecute," Hannah complained. She had faced this before.

"We should make it public and clear that whoever buys the sun-god mask will be arrested and prosecuted to the fullest extent of the law…" she began.

"Hannah, you know that's pushing it. There are too few enforceable laws on trading in stolen artifacts," he replied cynically. "All your efforts in that direction are futile."

Hannah growled in frustration, but did not contradict his outrageous statement. Outrageous because it was true.

"At least I'll report to groups who post lists of stolen art and artifacts. Come on Berto, we can do that much."

As soon as they got back to camp, Roberto saw Hannah writing something down on her tablet. Every day Hannah wrote up a list of ten tasks she would accomplish before going to sleep. For anyone else, getting two or three of the items done would constitute a successful day's work.

"I'll add registering the loss to today's things to do," she sighed deeply.

"Hannah, your list is meant to be a helpful reminder, not the Ten Commandments," Mari chided. "After today's events, it is okay to put some of it off until another day."

"Dr. Sarra, our INAH Museum Director, is coming here for an inspection tomorrow. He'll demand a report first," Roberto added. "He's almost as meticulous and a stickler for procedure as you."

"He could shut us down over this incident," Hannah fretted. "The only silver lining to this dark cloud, it is that they only flew away with a temple carving, not my pottery discoveries," Hannah said.

As soon as she completed that sentence, she gasped. "Oh no, do you think they got into our storage lab too?" She took off in a running dash toward the expedition field camp.

CHAPTER 7

Edzna, Campeche
Present Day

Hannah's heart hammered in her chest as she approached the storage sheds the archaeology team used as laboratories that season. She groped around inside her work shirt to extract the two keys she hung from a braided silk cord. At a distance she saw that the blue wooden door to the laboratory shed was damaged and possibly breached. Her hands fumbled as she removed the broken heavy-duty padlock off the latch. She stumbled inside.

Dappled light filtered through the shuttered windows and edges of the palm-thatched roof. It was just bright enough for Hannah to see that nothing seemed ransacked or out of place. The most useful and marketable item in camp, the gas generator, still stood on its pallet inside the front door. Her computer and camera cases were visible through plastic crates. Common thieves would have gone for those items. At least for a moment she felt a sense of fleeting peace. So this looting was not an ordinary theft. They were probably after something she valued more.

Hannah threw open the wooden window coverings for more light, to allow a closer inventory of her most irreplaceable discoveries. She rushed to check the secured cabinet for three ancient ceramic pottery pieces. They were vital proof, keys to moving forward on her new theory. She pulled the stubborn cabinet drawer open. It resisted until it slid forward with a screeching sound.

"*Oh, please, please,*" prayed Hannah. "*Let everything be intact.*"

A week before, she had carefully packed two polychrome cylinder vases and one effigy incense burner in separate wooden crates. She slowly lifted the first crate's lid and soft covering to find the largest painted vase resting safely in its bed of cotton batting. The piece was banded with classic glyphs. In the center panel, featured the bas-relief of an aristocratic Maya scribe at his writing table. He helped quell her worries with his deep almond-shaped eyes and large lips, open as if greeting her.

The artist had not spared detail in the incising and rendering. His image was so realistic. The writing instrument in the scholar's hand was slightly bent, due to the pressure exerted in his painting or recording. A lively rabbit figure, the symbol of writing, further confirmed the subject was a scribe. Hannah admired the exceptional skill of the vase's unknown artist.

She sighed with relief. It was like seeing a long lost friend. Other vital items laid in their places, undisturbed, awaiting transport to the security of the National Anthropology Museum in Mexico City.

"*Thank goodness Director Sarra is coming tomorrow to take them back to a safe place, away from the greedy hands of the grave robbers,*" she thought.

Numerous similarly unique items from this season's dig had already been sent ahead for study and display at the museums in Mexico's capital city and their sister museum in Los Angeles, California.

Hannah had painstakingly uncovered the three latest ceramic treasures from Structure 15 near the main ceremonial plaza. She nicknamed the area Platform of the Knives because she and her team found so many flint and obsidian blades there. The two hundred and fifty foot long platform contained twenty residential rooms with vaulted ceilings.

This platform structure was one of her favorite areas in Edzna's two and a half square mile zone. She often went there to eat lunch, make notes and think things over. On especially hot sweltering humid nights it offered a comfortable place to hang her hammock and sleep under the stars.

Once Hannah knew her treasures were safe, she again put them under lock and key. She decided to visit the main temple where she could be alone to calm her nerves and process the day's events.

Encroaching jungle around the main plaza was regularly cleared, so she easily reached the base of Edzna's partially restored acropolis. Supported on an enormous man-made platform, stacked rooms soared up for five stories. A filigree-like roof comb crowned the monument. Bridged by a broad stairway, each stone step was covered in hieroglyphic symbols. Carved stone blocks, unique in the world, captured the lives of gods and kings in various forms. The temple's ornate detailing harmonized with the foliage that still partially engulfed it.

Looking up, Hannah observed the rock and stucco patched façade. The huge pyramid never ceased to amaze her. Roofs caved in years ago, leaving only walls in many places. Occasional hardwood lintels, barely holding back the carved doorways, remained on some rooms, added strength to upper entryways. Doors led to dark and narrow compartments, sheltered by corbelled ceilings.

Plaster coatings and figures had been eroded away by rains of innumerable autumns and creeping vegetation. Low growing vines twined unabated over the backside and terraces of the mostly crumbled pyramid. Tendrils reaching toward the sun were consumed by it. Seedlings took hold between the rocks. Expanding roots levered loose limestone blocks, weakening the structure and scattering sections of the temple walls in great dejected heaps around the acropolis. At one time the ancient Maya conquered the land, but now nature reigned.

Hannah zigzagged around rubble up to ascend the steep stairs. She took deep breaths and moved slowly because heights scared her. Reaching the top level, she gratefully leaned against a rough rock wall in the shadow of the towering roof-comb.

In the classic period, Edzna extended for several square kilometers. Its crowning glory, the acropolis stood ten meters high and measured a hundred meters on all sides. Only a small part of the thriving Maya city, which six hundred years before held at least thirty thousand citizens, was cleared. Each dry season site workers cut back trails to key locations and exposed the plazas. Archaeologists reconstructed the fronts of major pyramids, but chaotic vegetation still claimed the sides and backs. Labor to maintain open spaces to live and work was daunting. Most of the jungle forest around the ruins was yet undisturbed and unexplored.

From where Hannah sat, the structures of the Far West Group and covered mounds beyond it, three kilometers away, could be seen clearly. Temples and residences were abandoned; their patrons disappeared into the forest hundreds of years ago. Below her, a millennium of urban debris spread randomly. The full extent of Edzna was swallowed up by tropical jungle that hid the once mighty city's features. The green blanketed past only increased the mystery for historians and anthropologists.

One and three quarters of a century before, John Lloyd Stephens and artist Frederick Catherwood, chronicled numerous Maya ruins in two illustrated volumes. *Incidents of Travel in the Yucatan (1843),* was Hannah's favorite series. Stephens described one city as laying before him 'like a shattered ship in the midst of an ocean of green, with masts gone, crew perished and none to tell from whence she came or how long she had been on her journey'. Hannah often referred to their accounts. The text and images rang true and always taught her something new about the ruins, the land, and about herself.

From atop Edzna's main temple, the cloudless blue sky dominated the bright green world below. Being simultaneously rooted in the past and in communion with the present gave Hannah the perspective she needed. She had no idea how long she'd been up on the temple pyramid. As the sun lowered in the sky, she worked her way down the carved steps. She turned her back on the ancient city where gods and kings turned to stone. She returned to camp, ready to strategize better defenses to protect Edzna's remaining treasures.

CHAPTER 8

Edzna, Campeche
Present Day

After Hannah's time on the temple crest, she approached the compound's living quarters. The savory aroma coming from the cooking lean-to structure behind Mari's house drew her near.

"Mari, your stew smells fantastic. *Venado*, deer, right? I definitely need some of your comfort food right now." The rich smell of corncakes on the griddle held a tinge of the grinding stone. Mari's familiar foods connected the two women. It would nourish them both in body and soul.

"*Bix a bel*, how does it go with you?" Mari inquired. She often used Mayan language with Hannah to share lessons and feelings.

"I am beyond exhausted by this morning's survey work and then the horror of these last few hours," Hannah said.

She dropped like a dead weight onto a wooden seat placed near the cooking hearth. When sitting the 5'8" archaeologist came to eye level with the rounded 4'10" Mayan woman who was like a mother to her. A traditional white *huilpil* dress with colorful hand-embroidered flower borders complimented Mari's smooth dark-skin and graying hair. Her serene smile showed off the gap between her front teeth. She insisted Hannah rest a while as they talked. Mari enjoyed the company as she prepared the afternoon meal using foods from her dooryard garden.

"True evil came here today," Hannah shuddered.

"Nature doesn't recognize good and evil. It only reacts to balance and imbalance," responded Mari. "Don't let those thieves throw you off center. How they misbehave is their destiny. How you respond is yours."

"I feel furious and helpless at the same time. I want to stop assaults against sacred sites," Hannah said, balling her hands into fists. Mari merely glanced up from making tortillas.

The first slight smile of the afternoon crossed Hannah's lips. "I know, from your look, you're about to tell me that I can't fight a jaguar with my bare hands. I need to use my brain and make a plan."

Mari patted Hannah in her nurturing way. She handed her a clay cup filled with hot frothy chocolate. Pepper and cinnamon tickled her nose and pleased her palate. It probably contained a pinch of calming herbs and a sprinkle of chia seed for strength. *Curanderas*, angel healers like Mari, are found in all sizes, shapes and nationalities.

"Don't take this theft so personally, *hija*. My daughter, their actions were for reasons other than attacking you. People aren't against you, they are just out for themselves."

"But, Mari, looting affects me personally and professionally." Hannah frowned. Her firmly set jaw and narrowed eyes left no doubt. She was visualizing what she would do to the invaders if she caught them.

"Behind all anger is fear. What are you so afraid of my dear?" asked Mari.

The basic question snapped Hannah back from her vengeful thoughts and softened her features. "I am afraid this robbery will hurt my professional reputation and chances to work on ruins. If the authorities blame me, I might lose permits to dig or funding," she admitted.

"My theory of sacred books being transferred onto pottery is about to break through. This season I found and translated hieroglyphic codes on a series of ceramic styles never before seen. I need more proof. I'm so close. I can't stop or disappoint people because some vermin stole the evidence or drove me away."

"As important as this seems right now, you are not loved or respected just because of your work. It does not define you as a person. What else frightens you?" nudged Mari.

"For over a decade I've dedicated myself to archaeology, with all its isolation and hardship. I gave up the so-called normal life and relationships. I don't want my sacrifice and suffering to be for nothing." Hannah's mind drifted to thoughts of personal roads not taken and past losses. Briny evidence of her regrets leaked out the corners of her eyes.

Hannah hugged her dear friend's small compact frame. "Thank you for listening to me."

"God might be relieved of his heaviest burden, if we would listen to one another thinking out loud."

Mari squatted on the packed dirt floor next to Hannah and took the archaeologist's wringing hands into hers. "There is a deeper fear inside you." She knowingly searched Hannah's forest green eyes and waited.

"Only you would understand this," Hannah said. She moved closer and confided to her friend in hushed tones. "Mari, I want to let the world know who the Maya were and what happened in cities built by the old ones. In the pottery I have worked on, myths, astrology and medicines from the ancient books are depicted in a new way, using clay to tell the story." Hannah looked around to be sure no one else was listening to her unspoken motivation.

"It sounds unscientific and not my usual analytical self, but I feel like I could be a living gate, a conduit for the people of the past."

Mari nodded with empathy. Mari's almond eyes twinkled and her cheeks creased into a knowing smile. "This is *malob*, good. It explains the intuitive sixth sense you have about the ruins and ways of the ancients. Your path is difficult because of your high calling. I will help you learn to listen," Mari promised.

"I rely on my education, logic and experiences. But sometimes deep inside, I feel like I have a long-dormant but fragmented memory. It's like trying to recall a vague dream. I'm here for a reason. That is why I am fearful Mari. I can't just stand by while tomb robbers steal the clues I need to find the long-lost messages and solve the mysteries."

"There are those who wish the sacred words of the Maya never come to light," Mari warned. She stirred the pot of stew with a worn wooden spoon and pondered.

For countless millennia the Aj k'uhuum, shamans had been keepers of the holy books and rituals. Mayas believed that if it were not for their stewardship of the Earth through ceremony and prayer, certain gateways to their collective destiny would be lost forever.

"In the 1500s the Spanish conquistadors and their priests burned all but four of the original bark and deerskin books written in Mayan hieroglyphics. They killed those who created or protected them. Obviously, some force is still willing to destroy and kill to keep the ancient knowledge hidden," Mari said.

CHAPTER 9

Edzna, Campeche
Present Day

After the excitement of the antiquity thieves' raid, the Edzna archaeology team began settling back into camp routine. Roberto joined Hannah and Mari at the rough-hewn wooden table in the side yard, half-hidden beneath vermillion branches of the flamboyant tree. Mari served an afternoon meal of venison stew with squash and piping hot handmade corn tortillas. Despite the disappointing upsets of the day, they all found comfort and pleasure in one another's company and kindness.

"Your delicious food tells me that I am nowhere but home," Roberto complimented his mother. "*Dios bootic*, thank you."

Mari's house, kitchen shed and garden were the heart of the larger compound of dwellings and storehouses that served the archaeologists. She grew golden squash, tomatoes, green beans, corn, dark green and red peppers. Mint, rosemary, camomille, herba buena, and ojo santa herbs grew profusely in pots around her home. Three beehives produced about a gallon of honey each month. Fruit trees provided an abundant supply of limes, mangos, and bananas. The papayas clustered like giant green pears at the top of their stalks. The garden provided nourishment and healing. Mari served as expedition cook, medico healer and mother to all.

Hannah thought back seven years to when she first met Roberto. His scholarly career and countless site excavations he supervised around the Yucatan impressed her. He brushed away her praises by saying, "I was too restless to teach, not interested in farming, and my temperament was not suited to government, so I became an archaeologist." He was compelled to use his skills to preserve history in his homeland.

Her modest co-director was one of the few who left the quiet seclusion of his Maya pueblo to attend university. He published internationally acclaimed books, and taught archaeology at UNAM and her alma mater in California. He was proud to be Maya. He preferred life in his village, rather than the offered tenure at a large university. He bridged two worlds, equally fitting and not quiet fitting in both.

Roberto had uncanny insights and perceptions that worked mysteriously below in his subconscious. Sometimes they helped him and sometimes they disconcerted him. But he learned never to ignore them.

Roberto would ask, "Did you know that those *muuls*, mounds of old stones, once were magnificent temples, ball courts, palaces, observatories and marketplaces?" when he taught in classrooms or to his workers. His ability to explain Maya history made his own people aware and proud of their lost heritage.

There were forty-five Maya *campesinos*, day laborers, including masons and occasional artists or graduate students who worked with directors Hannah and Roberto.

The survey and excavation group had four to five months, generally January through May, to get their work done before the start of the rainy season. The team did as much as they could with what money, time and personnel were available. The wet and dry seasons set limits. If not for climate considerations, Hannah knew she'd work fulltime for a lifetime and never completely explore a site. Once the rains started, the workmen returned to their own pueblos and fields.

Hannah, Mari, Roberto and a few key workers lived on site during field season, in simple practical huts called *na*, built in the traditional Yucatan way. The oval shaped foundations were limestone. Rounded at both ends, the sidewalls were made of stucco plaster over interlaced poles. When dry, the *na* was painted a glaring white. Huts were topped with tight-thatched guano-palm pitched roofs. Shelters made of nature rearranged. The functional home design, immortalized in stone friezes at Uxmal and other sites, had changed little in two thousand years.

Two opposite doors provided cross ventilation and light. Local Maya Indians painted their doors blue. They believed evil spirits would think it was the blue cloak of the Virgin Mary hung over their passage way and move on. Hammocks hung from ropes and hooks on the main posts or rafters. One or two chairs, a table, a trunk for storage and kerosene lanterns were often the only furnishings. The promise of sufficient food and a hammock beneath a mosquito net seemed like high living in this part of the world. The key was simplicity, utility and working with nature, rather than trying to fight it. Fieldwork as a shovel bum could be tedious, boring, lonely and located in dangerous places and less than ideal conditions.

Like all archaeological sites in the jungle, teams of machete-wielding workers were hired to whack back profuse vegetation. Without the crew's continued clearing efforts, the ruins would be engulfed again in a few years, as many ancient cities had been.

Work in Edzna's archaeological zone started soon after dawn when the temperature was the coolest. By six a.m., dozens of workers sifted through the jungle screen and appeared from hidden trails. They came by foot, bicycle or packed standing up in the back of old trucks driven in from Noyache, Hontun, Lubna, Tixmucuy, or Bolonchen-Cahuich---villages within kilometers, places that appeared on few maps.

"Communities are a system of defined roles and relationships. Outsiders and any kind of innovation are perceived as threats to that order," Roberto reminded Hannah when she felt excluded because of her origin or gender. He became her symbolic chaperone, her male uncle who traditionally served as a shield, go-between, and voice.

Roberto assigned daily tasks to the workers, because culturally men were not familiar or comfortable with a woman giving orders. At times, Hannah turned to her co-director and stated what needed to be done. The staff would hear and move away to complete their duties without him repeating the instructions. But if she directly ordered a man face-to-face to go do a job, it embarrassed him and was not acceptable in their *machismo,* male controlled worldview.

"Mexicans, like other paternalistic societies, don't encourage or tolerate strong women," Mari would tell her.

Hannah did not take it personally that locals were unaccustomed to a *dzul*, white stranger, especially a woman scientist. In their society, there's no tradition for a scholarly female. In fact when she'd first arrived at the site, village women brushed up against her to see if she had breasts and was really female at all.

"Don't expect your own level of motivation or competence from our helpers," Roberto told her when she expressed frustration at workers' attitudes of subservience or lack of innovation when the men waited for orders to start the simplest tasks. Her patient guide pointed out how generations of Maya served as slaves under their own cacique leaders and later hacienda owners. "Any native who took initiative didn't last long."

"*Do whatever it takes to get it done. Just play the game,*" Hannah said to remind herself. "*It doesn't matter who assumes the authority role or gets the credit, it only matters that we complete our work,*" She breathed patience in and breathed frustration out as a common practice.

Each day Roberto distributed tools. Everyone received an Edzna branded machete and a shorter curved *coa* blade. Noticeability no shovels were issued until clearing was completed and back dirt rubble needed to be moved into the jungle.

Hannah found that Maya workers had their own way of doing things and different body motor habits. She bought and demonstrated how wheelbarrows could carry more dirt than bags on their backs held by forehead tumplines. Her workers murmured admiration and immediately resumed using baskets or bags across their shoulders and backs. Hannah shrugged in resignation. It would be okay because they always got the job done somehow.

During that long field season in Edzna, the workers and leaders had found a balance and functioned well. The archaeological zone and living compound had been a self-contained little world, pretty much unplugged from civilization and secure---Until the afternoon of the raid.

CHAPTER 10

Edzna, Campeche
Present Day

As Mari served the meal, she addressed the topic weighing on all three of their minds. Without betraying confidences shared by Hannah, Mari needed to discuss the impact of the robbery and how to protect the ancient city and those she loved from harm. She knew from experience that helping others brought her calmness. If she succumbed to anxiety, she felt self-centered.

"Should we hire more guards?" asked Mari.

"No," Roberto answered quickly. "It would be impossible to guard everything in an archaeological zone as large as this one. Besides these latest thieves are bold and vicious.

"Not just locals who take old stone to use for house foundations or walls. Or, like last month, when you caught a couple of local teens pot hunting behind the ball court," said Mari.

"In that case, I gave them a serious talk and arranged other ways for them to make an honest peso in the village," he recalled. "I try to be kind. People are fighting a battle to stay alive. Their families can't eat old rocks or henequen fiber. Museums mean nothing to hungry people."

"Young people have little to no sense of what happened in their history," commiserated Mari. "Even when you ask people living next to overgrown mounds, 'Who built these'? The answer is invariably, "*Quien sabe*, who knows?"

"This is why we hire local crews. They need to earn honest money. They learn the importance of saving the past and become loyal. If you see a rich *campesino*, you are looking at a thief," Roberto said.

"Berto, when you questioned the workers and point blank asked who raided and destroyed the Temple of the Masks, I watched their faces and body language for any flicker of reaction to give me a lead or clue. There was none. Not that we expected them to know much, if anything," said Hannah.

"We are dealing with a sinister gang of professional artifact thieves, not the same petty vandalism that's always gone on," he observed.

"Usually it is some guy buying local looted objects for a very small amount of money," contributed Mari. "Those who dig up the artifacts probably get less than one percent of the actual market value." She touched her fingertips to her elbow to indicate that looters dealt with stingy dealers.

"But to a farmer or laborer, even a small sum might be a good deal for one night of searching and shoveling," admitted Roberto.

"Wouldn't dealers have a hard time selling a well-known and identifiable item like Edzna's stucco sun-god mask?" Mari asked.

"Not at all. Unscrupulous private collectors are lined up in the USA, Japan, England and other capitals of wealth," said her son.

"Illicit trade in antiquities is the third highest-grossing criminal activity worldwide, after narcotics and weapon trafficking. Art crime is popular with organized cartels because it is so lucrative. Interpol reckons that between five and seven billion dollars change hands in the art underworld every year," said Hannah. "War-torn countries' military terrorists excavate and sell their own cultural property to buy bombs and bullets," she added and frowned.

Mari let out a loud whistle of distain. "Plunder is as ancient as warfare. Francisco Montejo, the Spaniard conquistador, built the Cathedral and his mansion in Merida with stones ripped from the T'ho Maya pyramids. In their lust for gold and treasures, the first looters stole and destroyed national treasures."

"In truth, thieves don't have to sell a major piece," Hannah sighed. "Only five percent of stolen objects are ever recovered." She had to realistically accept that the temple mask would probably never show up on the market or be returned.

The sobering facts left everyone feeling a futile sadness. Roberto excused himself and walked over to the stone-lined well, fetching water to wash up and provide for the dog, turkey and a pig rutting in the back. He needed to lower the bucket even deeper than the day before. Toward the end of the dry season the water table always dropped. Some of the neighboring village wells had already gone dry and they were bringing in water from nearby towns. Soon farmers would burn their fields and pray to Yuum Chaac for rain and a bountiful harvest.

The smell of boiling chocolate with *canela*-cinnamon and honey passed by him on the breeze, and drew him back to Mari and Hannah for dessert under the tree.

"Water or the lack of it remains the curse of this land," he told them on his return from the well. "Having no above-ground rivers, Yucatan's natural water resources are hidden and people have to work for it."

Getting back to the subject of the theft and how to defend their site, Mari continued, "The young man who was beaten said there were four men. He told me the raiders all carried guns and moved with military precision. They knew exactly what they were after, removed it and escaped quickly in the helicopter," related Mari.

Roberto stood deep in thought, rigid with intensity. To Hannah, he had always been a source of permanence, like the stones of the pyramids, rising above the jungle canopy. Berto, as only she was allowed to call him, taught her invaluable lessons about the interconnections of land and history. The Mayans would label him *kam*, strong. He carried a manly, but mild countenance.

"I'm afraid we need to arm ourselves from now on for protection," he told them. "Hannah, start wearing your holstered 38mm. Mother, I will clean the rifle and leave it here with you in the house." Mari stood on a *canche* three-legged stool, reached up into the hut's rafters and retrieved the family's old hunting rifle.

"I hate that it has come to this, but we need to be prepared for the worst," admitted Hannah.

She'd worn a gun at times in the past, as defense against animal predators, but it seemed that now the most dangerous creature in the jungle was man. She knew how to use her .38mm, but the only time it ever came out of its holster was to clean it, or for target practice on the firing range.

"I never played cowboys and Indians. But here I am, armed and ready to defend our territory," she said and spun her gun barrel.

"As futile as it may seem, I don't want the crime against our site to be ignored." Hannah said. "Director Sarra can take my reports to INAH when he leaves here tomorrow after his site visit. I'm sure he will help us make it difficult for those smugglers to sell Edzna's sun-god mask." She left her friends and went to the laboratory office to prepare the necessary paperwork.

CHAPTER 11

Edzna, Campeche
Present Day

The sun was still below the horizon when Hannah opened her eyes. A narrow pink strip silhouetted the compound huts against the sky. The warmth came before the true light.

A hand-made cotton hammock, that she fondly called 'mother's arms', wrapped around her. Protected by a diaphanous tent of mosquito netting, it looked like a cocoon with a beautiful butterfly ready to emerge. She occasionally stuck out a foot, pushing against the wall or the cool floor, to set the hammock in motion. Swinging through the air like a pendulum created a peaceful place for morning meditations before the rest of the camp came to life.

"This is the day. Maybe the site will be closed down. Maybe I get fired. We're at a turning point. At the mercy of whatever Dr. Sarra decides."

Samuel Sarra was only twelve years Hannah's senior, but already held the high-ranking position of director at INAH and overseer of the National Museum's excavation permit section. He excelled at his private Catholic schools and as a double history and anthropology major at the National University. But everyone knew his high position was primarily due to his vast wealth and many connections. In Mexico, hiring was largely based on who you knew or what secrets you possessed. Society and business accepted the *personalismo* factor of using family and personal friends for advancement. 'That is what family is for', would be said without any embarrassment. In Sarra's case, people called him the 'helicopter' because he rose so quickly through the ranks.

The sun jumped up, and began to fill the sky with its brilliance. The whole jungle came alive, every tree and creature. One minute there was silence, and the next it was noisy. Dogs ran around barking and looking for something to eat. Workers shouted in the plaza ruins beyond the trees. A symphony of sounds filled Hannah's world. She especially enjoyed the wind ensemble of birds around her hut. Any location without songbirds was like food without seasoning.

She swung out of her hammock ready to face whatever the day might bring. She opened the windows for any outside light.

One of the first rules of living in the jungle was never walk around barefooted in the dark or put your hand in a place where you could not see. Darkness or hidden recesses invited centipedes, spiders, snakes and scorpions. These were lessons Hannah learned the hard way. She had been stung when a scorpion lurking in a shirt stabbed her with its poisonous barb.

Turning her clothes inside out and giving them a good shake, Hannah shivered at the memory of the searing sting. To her scorpions were like lobsters, wasps and her worst nightmares combined into one cruel joke by nature.

Even when she was back in cities, nothing could induce her to reach into a dark container or under a piece of furniture without the automatic precaution of a look beforehand. Wherever Hannah was, she habitually shook out her footwear each morning. A dark freckle on the third toe of her right foot had been intinctively swatted dozens of times, thinking it was a bug. Jungle rules apply to man or animal. Simply, 'don't be surprised; the alert and quick will survive, the slow die'.

"*Note to self: Buy stock in Columbia sportswear, REI, and Ex Officio when I get back*," Hannah said with a smile regarding her wardrobe selection for fieldwork. Everything she wore was functional, quick-drying, and unisex, except for her secret indulgence in lace underwear. She pulled on a pair of olive green zip-off pants, a ribbed flesh-toned tank top and a white, vented long-sleeved shirt. Hannah decided to leave her freshly washed hair down around her shoulders today, instead of braiding it as she often did for convenience and coolness.

Following Roberto's advice, she topped off her practical tropical outfit, by strapping on the heavy 38mm. For comfort she slid the holstered gun around, to rest in the small of her back. The over shirt covered the weapon from sight. She knew how to use it and was ready to do so.

The sun stood three fists off the horizon when Hannah walked over to Mari's outdoor dining table. Her friend was gathering dark green chaya and herbs. Mari believed in doing garden work while the sunrise dew lay on the leaves. Instead of medicine, the healer would prescribe a draught of morning air to anyone who was feeling down or worried.

Hannah inhaled deeply and went over to help pick chilies, careful to avoid stinging juices that could make her hands prickle and swell. She was pleased to see Mari harvesting some dark amber honey from her *melipona* stingless-bees' hive. Not only was the golden liquid delicious, it was one of nature's best preventatives for disease. On site, they used honey as both an anti-viral and antibiotic to treat wounds. It acted as a curative and as a regenerative food.

Within the hour, Hannah and Roberto heard vehicles approaching. The rugged gravel road leading into the Edzna archaeological zone was laid down over chicle sap gatherers' trails. The packed earth around the compound rippled with heat waves. The oncoming cars shimmered in mirage. Moving images floated and dissolved and finally burst through into clear view.

A dull black Land Rover, carrying two equally dark looking armed guards, led the convoy. The director's gold Jaguar rode in the middle, escorted by a jeep in the rear. The jeep's roof rack carried stacks of supplies for the camp. The packages were a promising sign that the team might get to continue excavations a while longer.

The lead vehicle sped into the compound clearing and did a quick recon of the common area before braking in front of the expedition storehouse. Armed escort guards, with their black military-style cargo pants and t-shirts, shiny lace-up boots and proverbial sunglasses, jumped out first to check the immediate surroundings.

Roberto, immaculately dressed in the traditional Yucatan white guayabera shirt and white trousers, stepped forward to open the door of the director's car.

"*Dzub u man kin*, too many days have gone by," Roberto said giving Dr. Samuel Sarra a formal welcome. The INAH director only nodded without comment, not wanting to admit that he remembered any of the Mayan language his grandmother taught him. The director ignored what he perceived as a public insult. He wished Roberto and others would not remind him how his family's pure Spanish blood had been tainted by an Indio woman two generations back. Nothing about the man openly bespoke any Maya world connection.

Dr. Sarra beamed a dazzling smile and walked directly toward Hannah. His mannerisms and features were as refined as an aristocrat. He was six feet tall, with dark hair and steel-gray eyes. His chin was strong, cleft and resolute. Attractive people have a certain commanding presence, and he was one of them. His tailored European safari clothes and alligator boots completed the picture. She extended her hand in greeting, but he took her shoulders in an embrace and kissed each cheek in turn.

A balding older man emerged from the back seat of the Jag, finishing a call on his cell phone. Perhaps he'd lost the signal because he pounded it on the palm of his hand. The director introduced him to Hannah, "My old friend from San Gabriel Church, Father William Batz, decided to accompany me on our tour of Edzna today."

Dr. Sarra's friend had dressed in light blue linen shorts and open-toed sandals, not really appropriate for exploring remote jungle ruins. After the revolution, the Mexican government passed laws that priests could not wear their cassocks or clerical collars in public, but to see a Catholic priest casually dressed always made Hannah do a double take. However, robes or no robes, the holy fathers were recognized by their flock. They remained cloaked in pompous and superior attitudes.

"William Rudolph James Edward Batz," he rattled off and offered her a clammy limp hand. He was short but pulled himself stiffly erect to appear taller.

Hannah looked directly into his eyes. They were so intensely black that it was impossible to tell where the pupils stopped and the irises started. Animal eyes. His features were razor sharp, hawk-like. Father Bill Batz flicked her hand away and walked beside the director, without looking back.

Mari chuckled into her arm and whispered to Hannah, "The padre seems to think names are important. My cousin Luis says that names, like prayers, build spiritual ladders that lead to heaven. With enough names, one like him could simply rise, rise…" She held her arms up to the sky and rolled her earth-brown eyes.

"Don't make me laugh," Hannah said. "This is a serious visit. A lot depends on Dr. Sarra's decisions about our site and work. He has all the control."

"Oh yes, el Doctor Director is aware of his position and personal status. He wears it like an expensive cologne."

"Power is intoxicating," sighed Hannah, following his movements with her eyes.

Mari shook her head back and forth in a worrisome way. She walked over to supervise the unloading of expedition supplies from the second black jeep's rooftop. There were dozens of boxes and bags packed with food staples. The fresh goods like oranges from the citrus groves of Campeche, shiny green coastal coconuts, and fuel for the generator were a welcome sight. Bountiful provisions they brought indicated that the excavation team would not be shut down before the rainy season. Hannah sighed with relief at the promises the care packages signaled.

She threw back her shoulders, stood tall and dismissed her

previous feelings of dread. If there was ever a time she needed to be strong and be perceived in command, it was now. The best way to control her future was to create it.

As if Sarra sensed Hannah's readiness to begin, he turned back and gently took her arm. They walked to the long table and handmade wooden chairs set up in front of the laboratory storeroom.

"Before we go over the usual updates, tell me about the raid here yesterday," he requested.

She and Roberto succinctly reported details of the looters' invasion and damages suffered to the temple and the worker. Hannah handed Sarra documents and photographs to file with the proper authorities upon his return. She had stayed up late the night before to be sure everything was as perfect as she could make it.

"I'll send these files via email to you, as well as others when I secure an Internet connection. Local police say they will be here tomorrow to investigate, but we don't hold out much hope for an appearance or assistance. When someone around here tells you '*manana*' it doesn't always mean tomorrow."

"What about the latest ceramic finds? Were they disturbed?" he inquired with an intensity not noted before.

"The laboratory door was bashed, but the thieves must have been interrupted because they didn't get into the storage cases to steal my pottery."

"Your pottery?" he teased, with eyebrows raised.

"I guess I am a bit possessive," she blushed. "Archaeologists, especially Yucatologists, get personally attached to their ruins."

Hannah corrected herself, "I meant to say, the extraordinary polychrome pieces found at the Structure 15 complex. Two weeks ago I sent you rollout drawings and photographs, full of new hieroglyphs." Hannah's voice rose in excitement. "Thank goodness they weren't taken."

Dr. Sarra patted her hand in a gesture that was half-consoling and half-caressing. He left his hand on top of hers a bit longer than necessary. "*Gracias a Dios*, Thank God you are unharmed, my dear. I will personally make sure these pre-Columbian pieces get where they belong."

CHAPTER 12

Edzna, Campeche
Present Day

Director Sarra waved a round-up gesture to the archaeology team members and his armed escorts. "I want to see the Temple of the Masks and assess the damage for myself," he ordered as he rose from the table.

"How far away is this temple? Do I have to go? This heat and humidity are on the raw side of stifling," complained Father Batz as he used his fingers to comb over the few strands left of his receding hairline.

"Accompany us, Bill. This ruin is a treasure chest. Hannah and Roberto's work here is very important. You should see for yourself where all the jewels are found."

The group walked single file along a *sacbe,* ancient stone causeway Hannah discovered last season. Bright sun burned off the morning mist. They crossed the grassy park-like main plaza. Edzna's towering pyramid cast a long morning shadow over their path as the group hiked between vine-covered trees. Beams of sunlight, filled with swirling insects, cut through the canopy. The air smelled like a blend of earth and rotting leaves. Roots wrangled with the rocky limestone soil to claim their space.

Those with field experience paid close attention when walking in the jungle, not only to avoid tripping on roots, but also to sidestep army ants or to keep a lookout for camouflaged snakes. Hannah learned to watch for glistening brown twigs that were actually strands of interlocked ticks pulsating with hunger, waiting for a host to brush against them.

The director, archaeologists, and priest were accompanied by Sarra's ever-present bodyguards from the convoy. Their eyes constantly darted around the jungle, putting Hannah more on edge than giving her comfort.

"Sadly, people of means or position feel they need to engage security to discourage kidnappers or assassins. Ransoms are just another source of funds for cartel operations. Lives are treated as collateral," Roberto reminded her

"Living in fear is never worth it. It's too high a price to pay for luxury in a gilded cage. Freedom and peace of mind goes with a sparse way of life," Hannah whispered back to her companion.

She and Roberto carried an insulated cooler with fresh water and fruit for their site crew. The muscular escorts did not offer to help. They needed to be hands free for weapons and keep all their attention on the surroundings.

At the scene of the robbery, Dr. Sarra halted and studied the temple area. Several *campesino* workers stopped nearby clearing efforts, wandered over, and stood in a curious knot a few meters away, watching the newcomers. Hannah waved in their direction and indicated the renewed water supply. A stocky man hauled it back to the thirsty men.

Sarra's gaze followed her motions and he stood facing the small group. The workers made a slight bow and touched their foreheads in deference to him. Their decorous unsmiling nods showed no expressions. Out of habit, the laborers hid their thoughts behind simple courteous gestures. He took in the homage as a given right and made no effort to acknowledge the greetings. He turned back to the plaza and continued his appraisal.

Batz, sweating and fidgeting, paced. He absently rubbed his hand across his shirtfront to feel the crucifix beneath. Eventually, he sat on the carved stone steps and drained his water bottle in one continuous glug. Like the hawkish bird he resembled, he squawked loud orders to the guards and continued to mumble complaints.

Director Sarra walked slowly around the grassy plaza in front of the Temple of the Masks. A gaping hole and rubble scarred the temple façade. Hannah rested her hand on the cornerstone, a square block hewn from a limestone quarry a thousand years ago. One lonely sun-god face gazed out, waiting in vain for the feather clad priests and worshippers to return.

Hannah noticed something new. Remnants of a burned beeswax candle and dried flowers rested on the back wall. During the night Maya workers must have come to chant prayers to placate the gods whose temple had been invaded. She silently added her apologies and condolences to the offerings.

"Do you have any idea who did this? What evidence were you able to gather? How much did your witness see?" Sarra wanted to know.

"*Kaz ik tu betah,* they came in on an evil wind," said Roberto. Then solemnly added, "No ideas who the *pinche cabrones* are and no solid clues." Lack of information about this case did not seem to surprise or upset the pragmatic director.

"The sun-god mask is gone forever," Sarra continued. "But you must press on with your work. You've been remarkably productive and I want that to continue." He assured Hannah and Roberto that excavations would not be closed down before the rains began.

Although the sun was climbing higher, Dr. Sarra continued his field survey of Edzna, inspecting their excavations in progress. He validated the importance and exciting nature of their work.

"Any turn of your spade could reveal long lost clues and rich treasures of Maya kings."

He actually seemed to understand how compelling it was to believe that the next trowel of soil or overturned stone could be a winner, like a gambler throwing dice. Archaeology was likewise a chancy numbers game and just as addictive.

"There is no cure for curiosity," she replied. "Archaeologists love the thrill of a good find."

Hannah was relieved to move the discussions beyond the tragic incident of the theft and focus on other successes of the dig. Sarra proposed ideas on tasks. An opinion from Sarra was not to be taken as a suggestion. Hannah admired his insights, experience and intelligence. He walked next to her, continuing their exchange, as the group returned to the living quarters for refreshments. Roberto had to put his big dog, Oso, in his hut because it kept growling at Father Batz.

Mari prepared her special cacao chocolate 'drink of the gods' made from beans she cultivated in the shade nearby. She'd whisked it together with pure sweet honey. Today it was poured over ice that came with the director's generous supplies.

"No thank you, I don't care for chocolate," Sarra said and brushed aside the mug of cacao mixture with a hint of repulsion. "Bring something from the car for me," he ordered his guard. The escorts were allowed nothing while on duty.

Batz snatched the refreshing iced drink from Mari's hand and rapidly downed the liquid. "God bless you," he said.

"I didn't sneeze," the impish Maya woman replied.

The archaeology team leaders sat around the table discussing plans for the remaining weeks until the field season ended. Like the sun's gravity attracts and holds the planets in orbit, the director's friend Batz hovered near his side, as he had the entire visit, seeking attention. But Dr. Sarra was too busy pouring over the site map with Roberto and Hannah, pinpointing locations of the latest discovery of ancient water canals, to notice the growing frustration of his companion.

After a while, the agitated Father Batz, his clothes plastered to his body with perspiration, insisted in a loud voice, "Let's go back now. I need a strong drink, a swim, and a nap, in that order."

He yanked on the director's shoulder. Sarra looked up at him sternly and didn't answer right away. "Wait in the car," he said. Batz roughly shoved Roberto out of his way and stomped off in a huff, kicking at the red earth.

"Raging is a case of arrested development," Hannah noted to Mari.

"Batz's words are all alike; they mean 'what about me'. There are always people like him looking for conflict," whispered Mari. "The battle he's fighting isn't with us, it's with himself," she said quietly to Hannah.

Roberto grimaced at the behavior of the priest.

"As a rule, is your companion always so unhappy?" he asked Dr. Sarra as they finished and rose from their seats.

"Sometimes, he isn't easy to be around. But he has his uses," was the vague reply.

"Oh, I almost forgot," said Sarra, tapping his forehead. "A photo-journalist reporter out of New York contacted my office. He wants to do an article about Maya ruins and such. I granted him permission to interview you and take a few pictures."

"Okay, but I hope he doesn't mind talking while we work. I don't have time for an ink-stained media hound right now," Hannah said.

"My secretary said he sounded English or Australian. What a foolish profession. Tramping around places like this and war zones reporting stories is not for me," declared Sarra.

Mari gifted Dr. Sarra with a kilo jar of her finest dark honey. Bits of honeycomb floated in the liquid gold. Hannah hand-carried three crates loaded with her precious ceramic vases out to the waiting car. After they secured them in the trunk of the Jaguar, the director took Hannah aside.

"You look radiant Hannah. Time in the field agrees with you."

He pulled her behind the rounded edge of the hut out of everyone's sight.

"Dr. Sarra, I…" Hannah stammered, shocked and flattered at this unexpected personal attention.

"You must call me Sam," He put his arm around her, took a handful of her curly red hair to turn her face up close to his and consumed her with his eyes. "I want to see you the minute you return to Mexico City. I can make life very pleasant for you." His actions left Hannah expecting a kiss, but it did not happen.

Dr. Sarra walked back to the car and put his foot up on the bumper. He beckoned one of his men with a raised eyebrow and a half-inch movement of his head. Without a word, a guard rushed over to clean dust off the director's boots and pick away sticker burrs from his pants cuff.

Father Bill was in the Jag's air-conditioned back seat with the laminated wooden tray down, drowning his displeasures in a double martini. Dr. Sarra, waved a quick regal farewell to the expedition crew through the tinted window and told his driver, "To the hacienda, pronto." His armed caravan sped away in a cloud of dust and gravel. Mari's gift jar of honey was left on the table.

CHAPTER 13

Edzna, Campeche
Present Day

"How could you?" Batz pouted to Sarra as they sped over bubbling hot tarmac to the director's old family estate. "I was miserable in that inferno. We spent hours in your dusty old ruins with those filthy peons staring at me. Most disgusting of all, you couldn't keep your eyes or hands off that woman."

"You knew I would be on site all morning when you asked to come along," he reminded the priest. "Each of us does what we have to in order to get the job done. Hannah Char has this uncanny intuition and luck at finding valuable artifacts and structures. We need her. Those old ruins are a deep well of resources. That is how the museum procures its inventory and assures our income."

"Yea, your precious museum," smirked the sulky priest.

"We picked up three outstanding ceramic pieces today, didn't we?" Sarra said to end the conversation.

Back at the Edzna archaeological site, Hannah, Roberto and Mari chatted and reviewed the director's visit as they tidied up the common area. Mari didn't say a word about the rejected or forgotten honey and just returned it to the cooking shed shelf.

Raw emotions of yesterday's theft and previous uncertainty about their work being continued reflected on their faces. But soon they started smiling and singing. Roberto swept his mother into a few turn-around steps of the traditional jarana dance. The elderly lady's youthful zest and quick fluid movements belied her gray hair and wrinkles. Roberto danced and sang and laughed. He was one of those people whose laughter was contagious and usually funnier than his jokes.

"Yes!" Hannah pumped her fist into the air. "We have permits, supplies and obviously renewed energy," she winked at her dancing friends. "We'll focus on getting as much done as we can until the rains come. Now time is our greatest enemy."

After the evening meal, Roberto fed and played catch with his rescued street dogs over by his dwelling.

"What was going on between you and Dr. Sarra today?" Mari asked when she got Hannah alone.

"His personal attentions were as big a surprise to me as the raid," confessed wide-eyed Hannah. "I won't take his fond words and actions of today seriously."

Hannah had lived and worked in Mexico long enough to know how Latino men's romantic gestures, flattery, and promises were all quite enthralling, but never to be taken too literally.

"Let's chalk it up to the heat," she sighed. "*Mixbaah*, nothing, it was nothing."

"Perhaps," whispered Mari. "Human hearts can be like wild animals. That's why ribs are called cages."

"Next time I see him in the capital city, he will be back in his element with high society. No doubt, I'll be ignored and treated once again like one of his lackey museum assistants."

"Our Dr. Sarra has a history of acting superior and lording over people. His grandfather was a hacienda owner here in the Yucatan with tens of thousands of hectares of henequen fields."

Hacienda estates were working self-contained villages. Like the old southern plantations in the United States, they had fabulous wealth flooding in from their fields. Henequen sisal plants were called 'green gold' for a good reason. Before plastics products took over, tough sisal fibers from the Yucatan were the world's primary source for ropes, bags, and industry. Vast fortunes were made on the backs of Maya laborers. People cut prickly spears of henequen in over hundred-degree heat.

La *Casta Divina*, The Divine Caste, the hacienda owners called themselves. Families, like the Sarras, built palatial chateau homes along the Paseo de Montejo or Avenida Colon in Merida and equally sumptuous estates in Mexico City. Silver-plated carriages of the multi-millionaire entrepenueral landowners lined the Paseo.

"My ancestors were slaves with no freedom. Many died." Mari's eyes were misty by the time she finished recalling stories her own grandmother told her of days in the henequen fields. "Just be careful, Hannah. Always look beyond attractive surfaces. What mattered most then and still today, to competitive wealthy people like our director, is owning more of and the best of everything. This compulsion is in his blood," cautioned Mari.

"I've seen my fair share of suffering in the world caused by attachment and greed. I'll continue to live simply and naturally. I won't let myself get hooked by illusions. Mari, thank you for caring."

"Nothing goes into a coffin but your dusty used up shell. Your friends and family are your treasures, your estate," said Mari.

"You are right. I won't waste my short turn around the sun chasing material stuff that doesn't fit in the box." Hannah said.

Mari still worried. She didn't want Hannah to become one more prized acquisition of a hacienda lord.

CHAPTER 14

Edzna, Campeche
Present Day

True to her word, Hannah put the powerful director's visit behind her and returned to her inch-by-inch, stone-by-stone excavations. The technical side of archaeology demanded patience and control. Organization and rules had been drilled into Hannah at school and through experience. She found success in routine and discipline.

Roberto good naturedly teased her about being such a list-making perfectionist. He noted that even her doodles were linear, columns, and boxes.

"Remember that order is the fantasy of men, the law of nature is chaos," he said.

Fieldwork was slowly teaching her to be more flexible. She tried new techniques and equipment. But in most cases, Hannah found that even a big shovel did too much damage. The trowel and whiskbroom were her most often used tools of the trade. Trained archaeologists cringe at the very thought of treasure hunting criminals who desecrate ruins by using bulldozers or dynamite.

In the heat of the afternoon, Hannah sat under a shady tree with two teenaged Maya sifters. No one called them assistants. They were called sifters or diggers for a reason. Every scoop of soil removed from its location went through wire mesh screens. Once the dirt was removed, any man-made materials were placed in precisely numbered quadrant level bags marked with exactly where they were excavated.

Hannah set up an assembly line to clean pieces of pottery, write a location code on the finds with black ink and return them to the original labeled level bag.

"Couldn't we just dig temples or work on big whole pots?" fussed the older sifter, as he swished around another soil-encrusted item in the bucket of water.

"Sounds like you think of archaeology like they show it in the movies. Just remember that every temple Indiana Jones ever entered ended up totally destroyed," she exclaimed. "You've also seen movies and TV shows about police detectives and criminal forensics haven't you?" she asked the boys. They nodded yes.

"Well, we are dirt detectives. All these bits and pieces are our clues. The archaeological site is the crime scene, with scientific investigators gathering evidence to solve the mystery. Even the smallest detail can crack the case," Hannah explained in a way the boys could relate to and enjoy. They began to look at each piece of material with respect for its potential importance.

"If you are going to tell the story of your people, you must use your investigator's skills. Careless excavation or neglecting proper classifications will destroy the record forever," she said when one mislabeled a group of potsherds.

"Context is vitally important. An artifact's significance could be lost if not carefully labeled to preserve the exact location where it was found. Think of the soil levels, like layers of a cake. Each level or layer is marked by width, height and depth to place items in their 3-D space," Hannah explained using familiar images.

"The site itself gets destroyed by excavation. Once something is removed from the original spot, an archaeologist could never be certain where it was found to authenticate it without proper labeling," Hannah instructed.

Hannah and her team worked hard to assure that scientific techniques and strict documentation was maintained. If a worker or field technician came across a larger piece of pottery, painted stucco, carved stones or bones, they would stop digging and call the supervisors. Worthwhile discoveries were photographed in place and carefully removed by Hannah or Roberto. The context or the exact archaeological find-spot, the provenance, was an essential standard to Hannah, never to be compromised.

'Beautiful, but dumb' is what she called an object that couldn't be traced to its exact place of discovery. Hannah told her helpers, "They might look good, but they tell us nothing."

"Your ancestors left you these clues. They're telling you their ageless stories. Pieces like this are the only voice they have left," she said and showed them a pottery bowl edge she'd just cleaned.

"This Mayan glyph *jaay* means clay bowl. The *u* glyph before it is possessive. *U*-tu means 'it is his'. These symbols are for *ich,* chili and squash ingredients, then a noble's name. The message reads, 'This is nobleman X's clay bowl for chili and squash."

"I just cleaned a cup with realistic drawings of honey bees," the younger exclaimed, showing off his discovery. That started a friendly competition between the teens to find hidden clues in the smallest of details.

Hannah wanted workers to learn proper excavation techniques. Locals needed to be part of preserving their own history and making it come alive. Educating indigenous people about the past might stop some from vandalizing and plundering.

To work in sacred sites was to awaken a greater respect for the earth and accelerate a unity and harmony between people, cultures and religions. Ancient people who created the sites, artifacts and writings wanted others to discover and remember important truths.

CHAPTER 15

Edzna, Campeche
1560 A.D.

The wounded Maya scribe awoke with his head and heart filled with a new purpose.

"Itz, come quickly. Bring your bark paper and quill!" shouted Ko'h from his room.

She grabbed a candle and ran from next door. Yaxche followed close behind, thinking her brother was hallucinating again. They were stunned. Ko'h stood, leaning on the entrance stones of the small room, awaiting their arrival. His eyes shown bright and excitement behind them replaced the blank stare of earlier that day.

"We will work together to record the true history of our people. I remember many ancient texts and experiences. The invaders will not annihilate us. They want to bury us, but they have not realized that we are seeds."

Itz stood frozen, not answering or moving to gather writing materials. She knew how to write the things her father wanted transcribed, but to see him back from the edge of death and despair to being animated and full of inspiration was a shock.

As a child, Itz tagged along and helped with her father's work as a scribe and other court activities. She learned languages, reading, writing and painting while participating in Ko'h's role as court scribe and diplomat.

Gender and age never limited the learning patterns of Itz and her royal cousins. Interaction with adults was important to their hands-on training. Children's activities were often an emulation of mature work happening around them. Observation and practice developed her skills and survival instincts. Expected community participation meant Itz was frequently given meaningful responsibilities. She possessed a talent for drawing and painting. She'd been respected as a capable scribe assistant and contributor since as young as five.

"What exactly are we going to do, Father?" she asked, curious about his renewed energy and purpose.

"The Spanish take away ancient books and smash inscribed stones. They attempt to silence scribes like me or anyone who supports Maya ways or power," he explained.

"Writing and art represent tools of persuasion and authority," contributed Yaxche.

"Destroying people's ability to communicate is a powerful and symbolic act," Itz agreed. "Where do we start?"

"We will make duplicate records of our mathematics, astronomy, history, philosophy and medicines. Foreigners may not know it or be willing to accept it, but Mayans have developed and refined knowledge needed to survive. Information we preserve will be discovered someday and help the world. I saw this through the gods' eyes," he said solemnly.

Ko'h leaned on his daughter's arm and limped outside for the first time in days. Beaming with excitement at his new mission, his laughter echoed off the limestone city walls and great forest trees. An outburst of birds answered him before the wind carried it away.

"We will leave Edzna so we can work without interference or discovery as long as possible. You know the inquisitors will target and search for us. Become like us or perish, they preach. They fear us as much as they hate us. Killing Maya people who can't work or pay tribute is treated as an incidental inconvenience," he grimaced, both from pain and disgust.

"I'll prepare travel and household supplies," offered Yaxche. "You can leave tomorrow after nightfall. The moon is a thin smile and few travel on the white causeway this time of year." Ko'h was weak, so he would ride in a covered litter carried by her son Etz'nab and his strong friends. They could be trusted not to disclose the persons or destination of the small convey.

"We have a sacred mission worth living and even dying for. That is more than most have," he concluded and they agreed. Itz, Ko'h and Yaxche planned and prepared for the challenges ahead.

Itz gathered her father's surviving quills made of reeds, maguey thorns and bone splinters from small birds. She packed carved couch shell paint pots to be used as ink holders and his favorite black ink made of coal base. She put in her thicker paintbrushes of animal hair and vials of brilliant symbolic colors of red, yellow, black and bright turquoise blue formulated from plant and animal products. Fig tree bark, *kop*, flattened and covered with a fine stucco lime gesso paste was the first item packed into their scribe bundles. Maguey papers, deerskin leather leafs and cotton cloth would also serve as canvases for the accordion folding-screen text writings. At the last moment she included her pottery carving tools and tied the package tightly with leather cords. Their possessions stood stacked by the side door.

Just then, Yaxche's son Etz'nab rushed into the room, his face beaded with perspiration and creased with worry. "We must leave immediately." He wrapped his uncle Ko'h in blankets and shoved bundles closer to the doorway.

"Soldiers are searching the houses. They are only a few buildings away. Come with us now," he whispered hoarsely,

Sounds of leather boots pounding down the stone causeway filled the air. Itz gazed around the room. They could only take what was ready and absolutely necessary. She scooped medicine pots and bandages within reach into her carry bag.

The back room was full of evidence that her aunt cared for an ill or wounded person. Anyone who assisted the occupation forces' enemies was considered equally guilty. Yaxche was in grave danger. From looks on their faces, the same thoughts must have gone through Etz'nab and Yaxche's mind. Three of Etz'nab's friends followed him into the room to help with the escape.

"You there," pointing at the youngest one, "Lie down on the sleeping platform mat and stay behind to play the patient. Here, eat a hot chili. You'll look sick and feverish enough to fool the Spanish soldiers," Yaxche ordered.

"How did the enemy know? Who among us would send killers after their royal scribe?" asked Yaxche. Images of a jaguar tattooed man with jet black eyes passed through her mind. "Only Prince Tepal would harbor such hatred for our family and curry favor with the captors by betrayal," she nodded, answering her own questions.

Etz'nab easily lifted the cloaked Ko'h into his arms. He ducked under the carved door lintel and headed through the dark side corridor. He ran down the back steps to a waiting covered litter sedan chair. He gently placed his uncle inside. Bundles they were able to grab on the way out were placed around him for support. A wooden box containing a multi-colored jade pectoral cape was placed at his feet. Precious stone pieces could be sold individually to support them in their exile.

Ko'h pulled the crude plaited reed curtains around rough-hewn wooden sticks to shield himself from view. In better days, his private palanquin had been constructed of the finest polished mahogany wood and decorated with multicolored gems and feathers. But this humble box slung between green sapling poles was a welcome mode of transportation.

With one young warrior left behind, Itz hoisted the fourth corner pole of the carrying platform onto her shoulder. Although tall for a woman, she was shorter than the others, so she needed to reach up to carry her share of the load. She made no complaint. Adrenaline coursed through her veins. Her heart leapt as they scurried away into the darkness, away from their deadly predators.

From a shadowed corner of the marketplace columns, a hidden figure with squinting black eyes followed the small band going east. He raised a conch shell to his lips to sound the alarm; then lowered it. He smirked, showing canines filed into points, and thought of his own plans for Itz. Prince Tepal decided he would wait a while longer.

CHAPTER 16

1560 A.D.
Yucatan

Shrouded in darkness, the scribe's small band trekked through the night, to escape the invaders' steely grasp. Panic prickled Itz's skin and made her heart pound against her rib cage. Her shoulder muscles and stomach tightened and went cold. When they entered the jungle cover, the thumping in her chest to return to a more regular beat.

Their mission was dangerous but important enough to take whatever risks were necessary. Recording the knowledge stored in her father's memory gave him a renewed will to live. She knew the challenge would change her own destiny, as long as she survived under such life-threatening circumstances.

The jungle's sea of darkness unmoored Itz. To keep her mind off the pressing burden of the enclosed chair carrying her injured father and their few possessions, Itz softly hummed sacred tunes. She busied her mind with a review of what items they'd salvaged when they escaped the ancient city.

Much was left behind. She was relieved that at the last moment Aunt Yaxche wrapped and pressed her precious book of medicinal cures into a traveling bag. When the smelly soldiers with their big boots and rattling sabers searched, at least her aunt would not be punished for holding such a forbidden item. Itz promised the four-meter long accordion-fan record of medicinal plants and formulas would be the first copied and preserved on clay and deerskin.

Itz felt encouraged and strengthened by her brave young cousin Etz'nab. His early warning and knowledge of the terrain saved their lives. He guided them through networks of raised fields and retaining walls formed around ancient canals. In the past, enormous wetland basins around their city were converted into gardens and water reservoirs. The group avoided the main causeways out of town because he knew the crisscrossing paths of the old irrigation systems. He got them away quickly and unseen.

Etz'nab, marching ahead with his long shiny ebony hair and confident manner, reminded Itz of better days when they played around the palace courtyards and chased colored birds through the forest. Like many, he now toiled in disguise as a subservient *milpa* corn field farmer by day. At night he met with his peers in secret to honor the old gods and hone his fighting skills.

Etz'nab was a fighter from birth. As the midwife severed his umbilical cord, he grabbed the sharp flint blade and cut his tiny palm. He wore the deep long scar as a sign of the knife he would carry as a leader. His once-handsome tall bronze body bore new disfiguring flaws. He carried deep-pitted pockmarks across his slanted forehead from small pox brought to their land by foreigners.

When anyone referred to his scars, he responded, "My survival makes me a lucky one. Countless numbers did not recover from the curse. Entire villages died of pox or fevers. They were left abandoned in a matter of days."

His mind recalled unutterable pain as though he saw it happen in front of him again. As he remembered thousands of victims who fell to diseases or oppressors' indifferent swords, a wave of revulsion swept over him.

"Tonight we are taking a different route because I heard that the next village has an outbreak of fever," he told his companions.

"Disease and death do not discriminate between the old, young, rich or poor. Many innocents took the journey to the unknown," Ko'h said.

Itz' warrior cousin represented a population who learned to accept death as a daily fact of life. He now took a sorrowful but fatalistic approach to it. That shift in world-view came as a great defeat to a culture as accomplished and proud as the Maya.

Tragically the Spanish prevented Maya healers with their array of medicines from saving their own people. They dismissed ancient cures and rituals as abominations.

"When my mother offered her help, those ignorant newcomers called her medicines 'vomit of the idols'," Etz'nab swore.

In addition to disease, the death and violence that fell on Itz's people in the name of religious salvation was tragic beyond belief. The beloved plumed serpent of the Maya, *Kukulkan*, was a bearded wise man who brought great wisdom and prosperity, along with concepts of peace and love. Sailing east, he left their lands promising to return and rid the world of evil. Ironically a new evil came across the eastern seas from Spain.

Itz recalled strange cosmic signs, like the comet her father showed her. Some people believed the Spanish leader named Hernando Cortez was the returning *Kukulkan* or Aztec god *Quetzalcoatl*.

"His armor appeared like overlapping scales of a serpent and his helmet bloomed with feathers on top. His ships came from the east. Was he the plumed serpent?" she discussed the ideas with her wise father.

"Invaders talk about a baby god who grew up to be called Jesus. They say he embodies love and wisdom. Is Jesus the foreign name for *Kukulkan*?" Itz asked. "His Mother Mary reminds me of our moon goddess *Ixchel*," she rationalized. "If the white men love and worship the peaceful child god and his sacred mother, how could they be so cruel?"

Itz had boundless faith in the good in people. She wanted to believe that the worst was over. Her father and cousin knew better.

Etz'nab walked steadily on little known causeways through the jungle. The tiny group moved so quietly it did not interrupt croaking frog rhythms in the ditches or the birds' pecking for food. When it was certain they weren't followed, they stopped under a silk-cotton *ceiba* tree and put down their heavy loads. Itz lifted her head skyward and murmured a prayer to the leafy cross of a tree.

"I know you support the heavens and symbolize life itself. Shelter us from harm, mother tree. See us safely on our way and we will spread your words of wisdom." Beyond the treetop she saw patches of dark infinity, alive with bright stars her father tracked and recorded for a lifetime. He taught her that stars represented things eternal and divine.

Ko'h leaned out of his covered chair in time to see a meteor shower of shooting stars. "The gods are throwing down their cigar butts," he observed, his voice crackled like dried fall leaves. Itz knew the old stories of how hunters in the woods at night would smoke cigars to frighten off evil spirits of the underworld, like the Hero Twin Brothers.

She took out gourd canteens and gave everyone long drinks of water mixed with chia seeds for endurance and hydration. Her cousin's friends assisting in the trek, although obviously tired, continued bearing extra loads without comment or complaint. No one would sleep until they reached the small village sanctuary.

The sun set orange hot in the western sky as the exhausted band approached their final destination. They walked by several well-tended corn and squash fields. Tradition allowed travelers to take what they needed for food from the first three rows, so the young men gathered ears of corn and a handful of beans for later. No more than necessary.

The weary group stumbled forward through a tall corbel-arched limestone entry structure. At one time the capstone announced the pueblo name in bold glyphs. The symbols had been chipped and chiseled away. Now the identity was a mystery to all who entered.

Their new home would be in a small village, no different than scores of other villages spread throughout the land. Perhaps forty buildings, some stone, but mostly typical oval huts with pole walls and thatched roofs, dotted the landscape. Humble homes lay scattered throughout the trees. A narrow path led to an underground cave where the communal *cenote,* well was found.

Sounds of the evening meal tortillas being slapped into shape filled the air. Babies fussed and dogs thumped the ground in perpetual scratching. Men carried firewood home on their shoulders or held in place by tumplines over slanted foreheads. They silently nodded a hesitant, but friendly greeting. Little knots of curious children and women stood in doorways of the huts and watched as the strangers walked past.

An older man, with the subtle aura and markings of a leader, fell in step with them. He and Etz'nab conferred for a moment about the prearranged safe house and wall of silence to be maintained by the villagers. He led Etz'nab's exhausted troupe to a modest stone building at the end of a plaza.

The litter bearers helped Ko'h up the steps and onto a sleeping platform. Itz gave him a cup of corn gruel with medicinal herbs for his pain. His face smiled at his caring daughter, but his eyes winced as he stretched himself out to sleep at last. The two bearers also curled up in the courtyard for a few hours of rest before heading back to Edzna.

Etz'nab and Itz walked around to inspect the new living arrangements. Colorful painted carvings of hummingbirds on the interior stucco walls caught Itz's eye. That coincidence brought a sense of belonging, since 'Hummingbird' was her grandmother's nickname for Itz, because of her flitting about showing beauty and sweetness to others.

"This home belonged to a noble family taken to the capital city of T'ho as guests, or rather captives of the invaders. They will never return," the village man lowered his eyes and shook his head in sadness as he explained.

Built on top of a slight stone platform, the structure contained five rooms and a spacious open-sided area for cooking, raised gardening troughs and stick pens for animals. A skinny caged turkey loudly scolded them for entering his territory, but grew quiet when Itz scattered corn seeds within his reach.

“This will serve us well as a home and workshop.”

A long grassy plaza graced the front of the house. A *stelae*, a freestanding stone column that once marked a monarch’s rule or important occasion, was crushed into bits, then intentionally scattered around the plaza. Overshadowing the open space was a ten-meter tall pyramid in ruin. Although deserted and overgrown for eons, it too had been ravished by the conquistadors, bent on destroying old religious buildings and pillaging for building blocks.

From what Etz’nab had observed, the Spaniards were amazed at the sheer grandeur of the Maya architectural and other achievements.

“Our ancestors accomplished all this,” her cousin waved his arm in a broad stroke across the plaza view. “My swords are of obsidian and theirs are of steel. Before the Spanish came, our metal works were limited to the creation of art and jewelry. Yet, the conquerors melted down our finest artworks and razed the grand carved stone temples.”

“They tear our identity and culture to shreds. I don’t understand their need to lay waste and ignore ancient wisdoms,” Itz added. She felt deep pain over these destructive acts against her homeland.

“How can I see what is facing me when I am blinded by tears?” she said. Etz’nab put his arm around his exhausted cousin as she wept. “Our past is like a piece of my father’s paper all crumpled into a wad. No matter how much we try to press and straighten it out, it can never return to its original true form.”

Itz inhaled deeply and pulled back her shoulders with renewed determination. “Well, we can’t go forward by looking back. This time, with its sorrows is mine to make better.”

Etz’nab comforted her further and said, “Fate provided you the gifts to keep history and traditions alive.” He reminded her, “One or two people can accomplish unbelievable things.”

"I thank the universe for my talents, my family and for all the good things in my life and future that I do not know about yet," she said.

Itz said a doleful goodbye to her cousin who decided to go alone to Coba before returning home. The two young warriors who aided in the bold escape set out in the opposite direction back to Edzna. Itz never knew that she was the last one to see them alive. They were attacked just as they reached their final destination. A certain party had tried to get information out of them.

After everyone was gone and her father slept, Itz sat on the rough stone stair step overlooking the small plaza courtyard. She spread out her arms at its openness. She could never see too much of the blue sky. When she felt dispirited, the vast sky gave her security from the threat of harm or loss.

She accepted this village without a name as their new home and workplace. It was here she and her father would stay in seclusion and preserve the ageless stories and knowledge. There was no choice about whether to be involved. Her heart expanded with commitment and beat rapidly in anticipation of the task ahead. How long they could live and work without detection was another question.

CHAPTER 17

1561 A.D.
Yucatan

"Pain engraves a deep memory. Revenge, bitterness and rage are poisons that destroy those who harbor them," counseled Itz's father. Together they discussed how to get through the past and take up the work ahead. "At least we can save our people's stories."

"Ashes do not turn back into firewood. I know there are things we can not restore or change," acknowledged Itz.

Her father still loved a world that no longer existed. But the book project gave his life a purpose. The old scribe wanted the world to know how the Maya had mastered the rain forests and why they watched the skies.

"We will weave a connection, an invisible thread, between our own time and the future," he said to assure her their efforts would be worth the risk.

"If I do not live to finish this task, let these writings mark my life. Please guide the right person to find and use this knowledge for good. *Yuum bootic tech*, thank you," he prayed privately to a pantheon of gods.

Committed to her task, Itz had a compass by which to travel, a means to overcome the negative thoughts that might niggle at her mind. Goals and ideals became propulsive forces, as true as the rains falling from afternoon clouds. Success depended on the faith and strength of the woman promising it.

Itz lived with her quiet hopes and labors, recording word pictures on pieces of bark paper and deerskin when available. She believed her incised and painted ceramics would last longer than fragile written texts. Pottery could be used right under the nose of the invaders, even on church altars if mixed with Christian symbols.

To her frustration, she did not always have the right clays or sources for materials. She mixed available ingredients, making sure not to spoil precious clay pottery batches with too much dilution.

"If I want it thinner, I add laughter. Deep thought tends to produce thicker clay," she told her father.

Itz believed that a potter's mind set affected the outcome and that creations needed a spiritual aspect. She always left a piece of herself in her work. Pottery became a lesson in patience as she took her works step-by-slow step.

"Creations in life cannot be hurried if they are to last," she said.

Raw red clays were gathered from the Puuc hills or the cave edges near her new village's well. Formulas had to be mixed thoroughly and wedged to force out as much air as possible. She made temper from sand, ashes or by crushing shells or broken pottery pieces with a large mortar and pestle.

Kneading established the consistency she liked to work with. A smooth basalt hand-held rolling pin gave a uniform thickness to clay pieces. She shaped vessels with a combination of coiling and pinching. Ko'h called her ropes of clay '*gusanos*', worms. Smoothed even surfaced finishes created by her slip-wet hands provided palates for paintings to come.

Experienced fingertips and palms served as her principle tools. Itz shaped pieces into a particular vase, cup, bowl or platter form according to its purpose. Tall cylindrical vessels proved best suited to her task of reproducing codices. During the clay's pliable times, handles or decorative devices were added. A charred fire-hardened sharp stick acted to incise glyphs, bands, panels and patterns on the pliable surface. Additional fluting or impressions were created with wooden paddles and edges of seashells. Occasionally, if Itz's finger pressed too hard against the bottom of a piece, it left a faint print. She used her stylus stick to form a lily symbol.

Once the ceramic object dried to leather hardness, it was ready for firing. Itz had a gift for burnishing the surface of her wares. She rubbed the pottery with a piece of wood or stone to produce a polished finish that survived firing in her pit kiln.

Painting pottery was the highlight of her day. Itz fashioned her own brushes from hair and feathers. Paint formulas were more difficult. She longed for her chromatic palette of more than thirty different colors she was forced to leave behind when they fled.

"I have a list of items needed to prepare the paper surfaces and make my paints," she told her father. "First, more deerskin and copal sap. When Etz'nab returns, I want him to bring me sak tu'lum white clay; ch'oh indigo plants for true blues and bark of chukum to darken my blue and green tones; tzeltal knate root for yellow and chante wood for my red pigments."

Ko'h's eyebrows went up when he saw the list of supplies needed to create their texts and pottery reproductions. "Is that all?"

"I also require cochinilla insects, purpura patula sea clams, axin oil, cinnabar mineral and the resin of the sapote tree, if we are going to do this right," she added without hesitation.

"Well, at least your list contains thirteen items, a very lucky number. We can use all the gods' blessings we can get."

"When the gods created the world, they created it from four colors: Red, black, white and yellow, the colors of corn kernels and of men. The goddess Ixchel ground kernels on her stone and a single *masa* cornmeal of humankind was created," Ko'h sang an old poem to her as she worked in the courtyard.

Month after month, the crippled scribe dictated and corrected as his daughter reproduced hieroglyphic texts, mathematics, astronomy and formulas on paper, skins and her incised painted pottery. The plan was to seal completed writings in wax and place them in secret places until the world was made right or ready to accept their truths.

Flexing his hands in frustration, Ko'h longed to hold a quill between his fingers again and feel the flow of ink onto the smooth white clay guesso coated paper. Still unable to grasp or make a fist, he used both scarred hands like paddles to bring a cup or morsels of food to his mouth. What he suffered no longer mattered to him. His physical strength was never what it had been, but his mind stayed sharp. He worked beside Itz from sunrise to dusk every day. He was impressed with her exquisite calligraphy skills in ink, charcoal and paints.

Each dawn he sat in meditation to welcome the sun god. Offerings and chanted prayers petitioned to release the old cycle and to get rejuvenation and guidance for the new one. Copal incense smoke left the morning air pungent and heavy.

Passionate and absorbed hours were spent dictating astronomy charts of the planet rotation periods, equinoxes and calendars. Ko'h had dedicated decades of his life documenting the Milky Way tree of life and Venus' appearances. He was saddened that he'd been forced to cover his precise calculations in Edzna to avoid discovery. As he remembered, Itz recorded his observations of the sky's five cycles of 584 days, the time between observations of Venus to Earth. It turned out to be exactly the same as eight years of 365 days each on the Spanish calendar.

Ko'h recalled folklore tales and royal lineages. His deep laughter rumbled off the courtyard stonewalls as he remembered incidents of now-petty city-state politics, ancient myths, and *pok a pok* ballgames played as a youth. Joy filled his eyes when he recollected more difficult mathematical formulas and calendar calculations.

Itz and Ko'h adapted to the small village way of life. He wore calf-length white cotton tunic shirt and the rough rope sandals of a humble laborer. Gone were the days of jade adornments and downy feather cloaks. Itz enjoyed loose white *huipil* shift dresses she embroidered with colorful flowers on the neckline and hem.

They ate corn, beans and squash from a home garden she rescued and nurtured back into production. Itz's favorite staple was *pozol*, maize paste sweetened with some of Yaxche's dark honey. Mixed with water, it served as both food and drink. Occasionally they bartered some of her simple hand thrown pottery bowls or plates for salt, meat and other items.

Trying to avoid harm proved more dangerous than just facing it. There were always those who would kill without a second thought to keep the folded folio pages or tales recorded on Itz's books and pots from coming to light.

Nothing was done that might attract attention. Few travelers came by way of the trails around the isolated pueblo. The secluded village's inhabitants displayed a distrustful curiosity when a stranger passed through. Itz and her father were warned to stay inside their home. The locals called the two scribes' structure Akab-Dzib, meaning House of Obscure Writing. They did not know or ask what went on inside the compound. In one small alcove, Itz painted an inner chamber wall with a likeness of her scribe father sitting on a raised platform studying one of her vases incised with hieroglyphic inscriptions.

Once a month Etz'nab came with news and supplies he and his mother gathered to keep the codices project going. He and Itz wrapped finished books in skins and sealed them in stone boxes. The final touch included applying coats of bee's wax over the container to keep out ever-present jungle insects and moisture. Pure wax harvested from Yaxche's hives in hollow logs on the edge of the forest proved to be best. Wooden boxes were wax-dipped many times in order to survive deep wet underground grottos and secret alcoves.

Itz went with Etz'nab on regular trips to bury special pieces far in the back of caves or in sacred rooms of remote citadels that slept in silence. The old abandoned structures' intertwining decorations resembled the jumbled green vegetation that engulfed them. The cousins dug caches and piled rocks stone-by-stone over the treasures. Someone walking a few feet away would not know what was hidden within reach. No maps or directions existed to say where the books were placed, except the ones in their heads.

One occasion Itz brought her charcoals to sketch glyphs and portraits on walls of abandoned buildings, hoping people's spirits would be raised. It was a secret reward for those faithful souls visiting the old sites. Etz'nab dipped his hand in red paint and mud slurry and pressed it against the ceiling or wall. You could tell it was uniquely his by the gash scar across the palm. Red sun symbols invoked the spirit of Itzamna, the celestial hand of the creator god. The cousins sat on stone pyramid steps sharing a meal.

"Once thousands of men, women and children gathered at these temples to celebrate and offer tributes to the gods. Marketplaces and plazas teemed with life. Now the crowd has shrunk to us two," said Etz'nab.

"What happens to gods when no one is left to worship them?" Itz whispered to her cousin.

As if to contradict her, a flock of bright parrots crashed about in the treetops.

"You stand corrected. Birds with their brilliant feathers, like the iridescent plumage in a high priest's headdress, still pay homage to the gods."

A night monkey, *kin kajou*, howled his warning of nightfall. Itz and Etz'nab jumped up and ran through the pathless jungle to return to her house and father. The sun dropped behind the rubble pyramid to throw its last rays. Torchlight flickered on the old city walls, like ancient spirits dancing. It grew dark beneath the trees. Fireflies pricked the night around them. With darkness came a host of living creatures, crawling through the growth to hunt and be hunted.

"Watch out Xtabay doesn't get you," Itz teased.

"When I see a pretty girl in the forest and she starts chanted for me to follow her into the bush, I turn the other way and flee. I've heard that sometimes men are lured off the path by a beautiful spirit. She turns into a tree with thorny branches and strangles them. Lost forever. Not me," smiled her handsome warrior cousin.

"There you two are at last. I was beginning to worry. It wasn't like you to be out after dark Itz. You are usually punctual as a star," said her father. His words seemed held apart with relief and scolding.

When it was time to return to Edzna, Ko'h gave packets of letters to Etz'nab to hand-carry to friends and noble relatives. They were unsigned, but those receiving them recognized his style and knew the author by message content.

Deliveries often went unfulfilled because many of those souls were missing or dead. The nephew never mentioned those particular letters to Ko'h. They both knew what no reply meant. Silence and sad news left the noble scribe demoralized. Bouts of nostalgia stirred up unwelcome pangs of longing. Plunging back into the past and remembering times of strength, love and laughter would make him cry. Grief's unrelenting physical pain surprised Ko'h.

Less than a week after his last visit, Etz'nab tapped on their door lintel in the middle of the night. Fearing the worse, Ko'h and Itz rose from their sleeping platforms and dressed in haste. Etz'nab stood with his head down, feet together, arms folded across his chest and his fingertips tucked under his forearms, a posture of childlike humbleness.

"What news brings you back so soon, Etz'nab? Tell me," a fearful Ko'h demanded.

"I was talking to a merchant from Zaci, the town the Spaniards now call Valladolid after one of their villages over the seas. He swears that the Franciscan Father De Landa is on a rampage. Our noble elders and priests decided to call a secret meeting near Mani to discuss how to handle the crisis."

"*Yan in bin*, I must go," Ko'h declared in a firm way, leaving no room for argument. "Our written texts of recorded wisdom can serve as invaluable guides for those gathering," said the scribe.

CHAPTER 18

Edzna, Campeche
Present Day

Roberto and the site itself reminded Hannah at every turn that people are connected by symbols. Carved and painted messages cover Edzna's great buildings, stone monuments, and other artifacts. The ancient Maya were a literate people. Hieroglyph writings often concerned dates and calendar markings.

Early archaeologist and scholars believed the ancients were philosophers and abstract thinkers concerned with time and mathematics rather than war. Discoveries determined that the rulers of the Maya city-states were kings, priestly mathematicians, and deity all in one. Like the pharaohs of Egypt, Maya kings were earthly incarnates of their gods. But they were also humans who fought battles over dynastic succession, love and property, like leaders since the beginning of time.

Without the use of metallurgy or the wheel, ordinary subjects supported the building of great cities connected by vast roadway systems. Hannah worked to uncover the everyday lives of royals, philosophers, artists and average citizens.

Countless threads in the ancient culture's fabric were already forever lost. Discovering remaining objects, allowed their artifacts to speak for the people who created them. It was an alien tongue, but it was the only voice they had left. Hannah worked hard to uncover information before it was destroyed by nature or man.

Whenever people brushed off Maya civilization or its descendants as primitives, Hannah asked them if they were defining 'primitive' in Robert Redfield's terms, "enduring isolation and homogeneity."

Even Europe's Middle Ages and into the Renassance were marked by these qualities. But both worlds' civilazations built monuments and developed written languages. Eventually both turned outward.

"While our own European ancestors struggled through the Dark Ages, the Maya built great ceremonial centers to honor their deities and govern the citizens" Hannah reminded them.

City-states, similar to Athens and Sparta, were home to accomplished architects, astronomers, mathematicians and scientists. The Maya were intellectuals, the Greeks of the New World, for over two millennia. A brilliant civilization, in an area the size of Texas, developed, flourished and declined before the Old World even knew it existed.

Millions of full-blooded Mayan speaking people still populate and thrive where their ancestors lived for thousands of years. Subsistence lifestyles have changed little since pre-conquest times. Modern Maya who live in the countryside could probably give up everything the invaders brought from the New World, with the possible exceptions of steel machetes, chickens and Coca Cola, without missing any of it.

Roberto showing the occasional visitor *stelae*, free-standing stone monuments, would explain, "Mayan written history did not begin in 1492 with Christopher Columbus. It began before the birth of Christ, with the first Maya ruler who decided to have his name and deeds carved on a stone."

Hannah gained notoriety publishing popular articles about Maya astronomers who, for almost three thousand years, charted the course of stars and planets with cunning precision.

"The Mayan calendar, carried out four decimal points, is more accurate that the one we use today," she wrote. "Three different calendars interconnected, like mechanical gears."

Hannah envisioned the endless parade of number named gods eternally walking with their burdens of time in careful mathematical sequences.

"Ancient calendars looked at cycles instead of lines back and forth. The Maya did not construct calendars to put time in artificial boxes or linear forms," she explained the differences. "They created circular calendars to record and predict. Even today, there exists a deep belief in cycles of time exists and that cycles repeat themselves. The ancients accepted the earth's natural rhythms, instead of trying to harness them." Circles of time can pose a new idea for a modern age, time conscious Western society that live by linear concepts and clocks.

Hannah's greatest passion was for Mayan books and writings. Pre-Columbian scribes compiled codices or books that combined pictures and hieroglyphic writing on folded sheets of bark or deerskin. They recorded lineages, myths, special events, astronomy, medicines and calendars. Ceremonial centers contained priceless libraries of wisdom accumulated over the centuries.

All but four of the Mayan codex ancient texts were burned in the 1500s by the conquistadors and Catholic priests. They called the hand-written and painted books 'devil-worshipping pagan relics.'

Hannah and other scholars grieved to imagine those tragic bonfire scenes, equivalent to the Romans burning the great library in Alexandria. Lifetime works of great scholars went up in flames. No one really knows what all was lost. Crusaders and terrorists inflict a wound on all humanity that is felt long after the religions and causes of the barbarians are forgotten.

CHAPTER 19

Edzna, Campeche
Present Day

Edzna's possibilities drove Hannah, not guarantees. She worked tirelessly to reconstruct the Maya history as best she could from rare and broken man-made clues.

Wilting afternoon heat of a cloudless day writhed around Hannah. Like the workers, she took a mid-day break to eat and rest. Rather than return to the compound, Hannah often strung an old hammock up on site in a shaded temple room or structure for siesta. Structure 15 was her favorite spot.

The structure complex stood on a man-made platform seventy meters long and twenty-five meters wide. It contained several inter-connected rooms. A little room in an obscure corner of the rambling complex was her chosen rest area. Rock walls around the *tarima*, sleeping platform provided solid anchor points for hammock ropes.

As she lay swinging, trying to catch a breeze, she noticed that where her foot tapped the plaster cap on the platform it sounded hollow. Her gaze also fell on a stone at the bottom of the back wall. For the first time, in the opaque light, she noticed something geometric carved on a limestone block. A bold letter X was clearly carved on the stone. Crossed bars were commonly used in buildings as a symbol of the snake, like diamond back rattlers, so it hadn't seemed significant before.

Hannah jumped up to check out the anomalies. She used her pocketknife to clean the surface and chip through an inch of crumbling plaster encasing the sleeping shelf. "*How strange*," she thought. "*There are no coincidences.*"

"Berto, I know a dozen other things need my attention, but I have a certain feeling about the Structure 15 front room. I want to do a test pit," Hannah informed her co-director.

"Trust your instincts," was his only reply, knowing her gut usually led to discoveries.

Hannah photographed and measured of the meter-high *tarima* shelf set wall to wall at the end of the room. Her project site was an eight by six meter residential room with an ordinary stone and stucco covered sleeping platform against the back wall. Hannah set up grid markers before she chipped away the center third of the stucco plaster seal on top of the platform. Loose rock rubble filled its interior. Nothing unusual, so she planned to take it to floor level to determine if the platform shelf was a later addition to the room.

Hannah lifted out heavier stones and screen sifted the removed dirt. A few small pieces of broken ceramics resulted. After a full day of excavating, she was within centimeters of room floor level. Before dark she jogged back to camp with her paper level bags.

After dinner, she and Roberto cleaned and labeled an array of common bits and pieces. Ceramic shards are the most abundant artifact recovered from sites. They can reveal key information about artistic expression, economic systems, religious rituals, cooking and traditions. But most of the time they are just ordinary broken potshards.

"I'm not real impressed with your latest finds. I think the room and platform served you better as a bed," Roberto teased.

"I'll go to floor level and then fill it in if nothing worthwhile shows up. But thanks for the vote of confidence," she poked back.

The morning earth steamed as the sun rose. Hannah walked to work alone. She triple-checked her depth measurements, because instead of reaching floor level plaster in the next section, she found more rubble and rough stones. She used her whiskbroom to scoop up another dustpan full of gravel and dirt. The next layer of rocks flattened out and as she cleaned around the edges she noticed dirt sifting through cracks.

Startled, Hannah stared down at five polished border stones forming a perfect pentagon shaped opening. She used the camera tripod because her hands shook excitedly as she photographed the half-meter wide 'home plate'.

"*If I am going to see what this hidden cache holds, I'd better have room to move around,*" thought Hannah.

The rest of the day she removed remaining plaster and gritty fill from the sleeping shelf. The platform's three stone high outer retaining wall and edge cap were left in place. She preserved an offering niche in the outer wall center.

"I thought you were filling in your test pit today, not bringing back more random stuff," Roberto chided when he saw her return with additional level bags of pieces to be cleaned and labeled.

"Come. Let me show you why I continued to dig," she said quietly as if sharing an important secret.

Together they walked over, climbed up the broad front staircase, and turned right into the room. Roberto examined the unusual opening.

"It is probably just an old *chultun*, stone lined reservoir for water storage. See what they dropped in before filling it to the rim and capping it off. Check out this compartment to satisfy your curiosity, but I'll need your help soon on another key building," said her co-director.

Hannah, undisturbed by Roberto's passé attitude, worked from can see dawn to can't see dusk. She carefully scoped and sifted the debris. As usual, every six inches had its level bag of fragments. The first half-meter finds in the opening yielded little. Hannah lay flat out on her stomach with her head and arms reaching in the hole to dig. Tight fitting stones lined the inside neck of the bottle-shaped reservoir and widened as it went down. As Roberto said, it appeared to be a typical water storage tank.

"*Maybe I'll get some everyday ware or marker water bearing ceramics out of this*," Hannah consoled herself.

While shutting down for the night, she couldn't find the words to explain why she felt an overwhelming need to continue. Her experience and professional training should have dismissed this unproductive exercise for other priorities long before now.

By noon the next day, Hannah was sitting lotus style inside the bottleneck. Not even the top of her strawberry-blonde head showed above the opening of the cramped space. At mid-day meal, she asked one of the older workers to follow her back to help.

"Arriba, up," she shouted and held the filled bucket over her head for him to grab and screen. Hannah wore her old canvas hat as protection from dirt and pebbles tumbling down from above. Within a few hours, she could stand up inside. Roberto built her a crude stick ladder. It got hoisted out after her descent to make room for the bucket and digging. She wore a flashlight headband like a miner to supplement the narrow beam of outside sunlight from above. In the heat of the day, steamy heavy air inside the old well shaft became unbearable. Hannah emerged dizzy and soaked in perspiration.

Plastered solid walls of the *chultun* water reservoir continued downward. Outside the ground level of the main plaza was only another meter down, so Hannah continued the difficult task of breaking up the packed earth and sending rubble-filled buckets topside.

During analysis in the lab at midday break, she noted, "Berto, all the dirt is the same color, not various color levels that occur when a tank is layered gradually. These ceramic pieces come from the same stylistic era, not spanning a long period of time."

He agreed with her analysis.

"This well was filled in all at one time. Why would folks pack a perfectly good water source with tons of debris if not to hid something of importance?" she puzzled.

She could see his curiosity being aroused. He was changing his mind about this side project being a fool's errand.

At the end of the next day, she was about to call it quits in the never ending deep well, when her trowel scraped over large cap rocks covering the entire well bottom. One by one she measured, photographed and lifted them out with the assistance of her helper. As she tipped over the last stone, the dirt sprang alive with writhing movements. Hannah recoiled and scurried her way out of the old well in seconds.

"Like a popped cork," Roberto kidded with her, standing at the top of the hole.

"You're as pale as a ghost. What's the matter?" he asked.

"V-v-viper!" she managed to squeak out. "I think I'm all right," she assured them. If the poisonous snake bit her, those would have been her last words.

Roberto hung over the pit opening squinting down at the dimly lit floor. "There it is. Bring me the ladder."

"You are not going down there," Hannah burst forward, grabbing his arm.

"No, I am going to use the poles to crush it." Roberto stabbed at the snake time after time. It went under a stone and he pounded on that for a while. But when overturned, the hardy reptile was not even fazed. A couple of times he hit the serpent directly but loose soil padded the blows. As suddenly as the deadly menace appeared, there was no trace of it. They combed the dirt with long poles to locate it again. No movement.

"Maybe it went through a hole in the wall," suggested the frightened worker.

But Hannah knew the stone walls were plastered over with thick stucco and so solid she couldn't wedge her knife blade between the double fist-sized rocks. Her helper looked over his shoulder and jerked his head with a 'come on let's go' gesture, hoping she'd give up on the old well.

"Bring me a flaming torch. We'll smoke the thing out," she ordered. She threw burning branches and green leaves into the pit and waited. When the bundles reduced to embers, she stirred the soil again and again. Still no sign of the snake.

"I didn't imagine I saw something, did I? The heat and all, you know?" she asked with a smile.

"No more than I imagined I struck it," Roberto laughed.

"I have to get back to work," she said seriously.

Both Roberto and the worker stood dumbstruck. They looked at each other in unspoken agreement to physically stop Hannah if she went for the ladder. As a stall tactic, until he could talk some sense into her, Roberto announced, "I have one last plan." He went to camp and brought back two big fat cigars.

"I'll light these stinky things and let them burn overnight in the bottom. Tomorrow we'll review our options."

Hannah agreed. "Berto, you usually know what you're doing." She didn't want to climb back into the pit until it was safe. "Archaeology doesn't need any more martyrs," she said.

That night in camp Roberto retold the Mayan legend about cigars from a story in the Quiche Maya *Popol Vuh*, book of counsel.

"Two brothers, expert ballplayers, are challenged to a match in the underworld," he began. "They lose the contest and are sacrificed, decapitated," he emphasized with a dramatic horizontal hand cut across his throat. "As the death god's maiden daughter walked by, one of the severed heads spit into her hand and she became pregnant. She was expelled to this mortal world and gave birth to twin boys, Hunahpu and Xbalanque. They grew up to be masters at the ritual ballgame. The death gods of Xibalba sent the brothers a challenge to play. The Hero Twins took an epic journey through the realms of hell. One of their trials was the impossible task of keeping cigars lit all night."

"Like ours," inserted Hannah.

"Yes, but they fooled the guards and affixed fireflies to the ends of the cigars. They won the ballgame and achieved immortality. When they ascended from the underworld they took their places in the heavens as the sun and moon," finished Roberto and sat back from the table.

"That is why you see night hunters smoking cigars. It is so the Lords of the Night will not harm them," he whispered, trying to sound real spooky.

The next morning the cigars were burned to ash. No sign of life, or death, as it were, stirred below in the test pit. Nevertheless, Roberto insisted that Hannah leave Structure 15 and assist him in analysis of the northeastern El Temazcal rooms. She agreed but felt even more drawn to the dangerous chultun than before.

Over the next week, their new excavations on the main temple showed an annex room. It had been closed off in Late Classic times and converted into a steam bath. Cleansing rituals took place before ceremonies. Small drain holes in the floor and foundation depressions showed where builders braced up large sections to hold earthen jars of hot water.

"The Greeks and Romans had no monopoly on running water, plumbing and public bath works," said Hannah.

When daylight faded, Hannah collected her tools and sketchpads. She and Roberto cautiously climbed down the steep narrow pyramid steps. She fought back waves of vertigo.

"Not a good phobia for an archaeologist working among ruins filled with towering structures," she shared.

Some nights she experienced heart-pounding dreams about heights and falling down stone steps. Lately her dreams featured the deep chultun. Structure 15 drew her back, and this time she would not be dissuaded.

CHAPTER 20

Edzna, Campeche
Present Day

"I am going back in the well pit today," Hannah announced at breakfast. Roberto, not surprised, cautiously agreed, but insisted on being there to help. Her previous Maya helper came down with a sudden cold, probably caused by superstition, and couldn't assist on the Structure 15 excavation.

Those first few minutes inside the dark humid chaltun were sheer psychological terror. Every time a piece of clothing rubbed against her skin, Hannah jerked, her heart pounded. Sweat ran into her eyes and trickled down her back in a steady flow. She didn't lean back against the wall for support like she generally did before. The small of her back locked into twitching spasms.

Slowly, but surely, the next few centimeters of samples went up and out in buckets tied on a rope. Roberto called her out for a lunch and rest break. As she pushed to stand upright, her palm pressed over a small hard object.

"One last sample from level twenty-one," Hannah said, and stuck the piece in her shirt pocket. She climbed up to fresh air and sunshine. Roberto secured the opening with a thatch cover and they returned to camp.

Dizzy from the work and the heat, it wasn't until after mid-day meal and a siesta Hannah remembered the unlabeled sample in her pocket. She photographed, and brought it into the light for closer inspection. A hardened ball of wax wrapped with remnants of the rough fibers from centuries before rested in her hand.

She brought it to Mari who melted the old wax away in a pot over the open fire. They preserved the wax and fibrous materials. Inside the hard wax ball was a small phalange.

"*Dios mio*, My god, it's a human finger bone," Hannah exclaimed.

She turned the little bone between her own fingers. She laced the key silk cord through it and put the important item around her neck, inside her shirt. For some reason it seemed the right thing to do. She wore the new talisman comfortably and had no more fears about working in the test pit.

Within the day, Hannah cleared the remaining dirt from the bottle-shaped reservoir's much wider spaced base. Whisking away the last bits of rubble and soil, revealed a long rectangular stone. One end was wedged under the wall. She called for a bucket of water and carefully sponged off the surface.

Fine yellow-white limestone that sculptors reserved for their most sacred works, showed evidence of etched carvings in pristine condition. Hannah ran her fingers over the symbols in silence.

"Berto, I'm coming up."

He passed the ladder down to Hannah. Her wobbly knees took her to the surface. She leaned against the structure wall, pressing against a piece of smooth cool plaster for relief. Her hands felt clammy until she stroked the bone amulet hung between her breasts. It gave her calm strength. She told Roberto of her newest discovery.

He climbed down to conduct his own inspection. "You are right. It looks like we have a carved altar. Good work, Hannah." He beamed and patted her on the back.

"Now the real work begins," she claimed and bit her lower lip. Her eyes gleamed in anticipation. "I'm eager to get started," she said with a voice trembling with exhilaration. She ran back to the compound for her camera, close-up lens, and other necessary tools.

Hannah returned quickly and descended into the dim confines of the well. Only a faint glimmer of light penetrated the small opening above. Roberto sent down a second lantern for extra light. She knelt in the dust to clean, photograph, and measure the mysterious stone altar. She took additional old-fashioned rubbings on rice paper, one of her favorite ways to copy ancient artwork. Hannah drilled a tiny hole in the top corner to get a test plug of the composition and thickness of the slab. She crawled around down there for hours, not caring about the heat or growing darkness.

Finally Roberto tempted her to the surface with cold drinks, food and promises of an interesting evening review and analysis of her photographs. They double secured the thatch cover and carried her equipment back to the camp laboratory.

Using her rice paper rubbings and photographs, she and Roberto created a composition copy of the altar on her tabletop. They began deciphering symbols and glyphs. They started with an easily recognizable up-ended frog or birth glyph, followed by various date inscriptions that they would translate and compute later. They also noted astronomy signs that appeared in the upper corner.

"Xaman Ek, North Star," Hannah wrote down, then translated the *ya-el,* parentage statement symbol for 'child of'. Next she and Roberto figured the mother's name to be 'Lady Yaxche'.

"That's Green Tree or Tree of Life, isn't it?" confirmed Hannah.

"Yes, and look at the paternal name, 'Lord Nim-Ac'. Here is the known classic symbol for the city of Edzna," he said. "This last glyph was barely readable, almost hidden under the chultun wall…"

"That's the shell-fist symbol for death," Hannah translated. Goosebumps raised hairs on her arms. She grabbed her drilled sample and ejected it into a glass plug. Three centimeters of yellow-white stone shavings ended with a thin red layer.

"Red, color of the rising sun and renewal of eternal life. It's red mercuric oxide, cinnabar pigment." she whispered, "It was powdered over remains to preserve and act as a symbol of the sacred energy of blood." Hannah looked at the photographs again. She pulled out her talisman bone.

"Lady Yaxche's finger, an ancient Maya mourning custom. The mother wanted something of herself to accompany her dead child before she ordered the well filled in. The noble child, Xaman Ek, North Star, was buried and her tomb concealed under the palace," Hannah shared her thought process out loud. "All the pieces fit together."

"Berto, This carved stone isn't an altar. It's the lid of a sarcophagus." Waving her hands in wild excitement, Hannah declared, "We have a royal burial!"

CHAPTER 21

Edzna, Campeche
Present Day

"Here we go again---rich in artifacts and poor in time and protection," said Hannah to Roberto. "What rotten luck to find such a potential treasure just as we have to close up the site for rainy season."

The two archaeologists stayed in the laboratory later than usual discussing their evidence and conclusions about the Structure 15 burial discovery.

"We can't continue to work in an old bottle well. To get to the carved stone sarcophagus lid and excavate properly, we'd need a wide trench into the platform from the north side. To do it right would be a long-term project. Excavations, guards, preservation, analysis…" Roberto said, already calculating equipment and manpower in his experienced supervisor's head.

"That's more time, permits and money than we have allotted or may be able to get." Hannah's brow furrowed. "More importantly, even a hint of something this rare would bring out the worst of the grave robbers. The entire site and all our lives could be in danger."

"Thieves would get that stone palace wall out of their way with a stick or two of dynamite," Roberto concurred.

Hannah put her hand to her heart in despair over the desecration that would surely take place if word got out. They continued talking in hushed tones over breakfast.

"No one but you and I know about North Star's grave. Let's keep it that way," advised Berto.

"Not reporting this find to Dr. Sarra and INAH would be breaking the rules I've always followed to the letter," Hannah sighed. "I was always afraid that if I broke a rule, I might start breaking others, one-by-one like firecrackers exploding," she confessed. Yet, something deep inside told her to listen to her friend and to wait.

"Some situations require breaking rules, or the rules break you," said Roberto. "All acts are divided into two kinds, commission or omission. Anyone inquiring will be left merely uninformed on the matter, not misinformed," said Roberto to help with her decision.

"It's only omission then," Hannah confirmed his intent.

"We still don't know who helped the last thieves. If we want to save this child's grave, we can't tell anyone or stop to ask permission. We'll ask for forgiveness later," he said.

"Okay. Let's keep this total quiet. We'll protect this discovery until we can excavate it properly and provide North Star the honor she deserves," Hannah decided. Roberto nodded in agreement.

They gathered the necessary tools and walked to the well in silent understanding of what needed to be done. Hannah climbed down inside the chamber and tenderly traced over the glyphs with her fingertips one last time. She covered North Star's carved stone with sturdy linen cloth. She leaned against the smooth stucco wall for a moment of prayer and reflection before ascending the ladder.

She and Roberto refilled the chultun hole with several meters of available dirt from the sift pile. They replaced the thatched palm pentagon entrance cover with a rough-hewn wooden one. It took most of the morning to refill the sleeping platform with its original limestone rocks and rubble. A new gritty plaster layer over the top sealed the end platform. To the unknowing eye, the room appeared the same as before her intuition pulled her to the site.

Rejoining the work crew at the south side of the acropolis, Roberto simply told the others, "Maestra Hannah hit bedrock. There will be no more time wasted on that activity." After all, many excavations ended without anything noteworthy being found.

They chuckled behind their hands at her folly. Hannah shrugged, cast her eyes modestly downward, and hung her head meekly in false shame. She picked up a shovel and removed a tree sapling that had taken root almost overnight in a staircase. It signaled a new direction.

"Back to work, amigos," Roberto shouted to everyone. They continued as if nothing of importance had happened.

Hannah took her afternoon break under a tree near the main acropolis platform. She was alone and it was unusually quiet. Hannah closed her eyes, remembering that at one time Edzna was a thriving center, teeming with thousands of people. Vivid images of the proud city as it once stood flooded over her. Buildings were covered with brightly painted plaster frescos. Stately processions of priests in fanciful costumes and headdresses of flowing quetzal feathers ascended the lofty pyramid. She envisioned the white causeway, leading to the main plaza filled with retainers carrying canopied palanquins, burdened porters, warriors, musicians, and citizens. Marketplaces overflowed with merchants hawking imported wares to eager customers. She could almost hear the hum of commerce and life.

The Maya world, governed by rites of time, was one of polarity. Like her own, filled with war and peace, wealth and poverty, fertility and death---the world always existed in tandem.

CHAPTER 22

Mani, Yucatan
July 1562

Itz, her father and Etz'nab trekked through the summer heat to a village near Mani for the Maya leaders' congress.

"What occured in the past will happen again. Nothing can exist without time and space, two aspects of the same divinity," Ko'h told Itz of his firm belief. "Our Maya elders have continued their work in secret."

The time-keepers fulfilled contracts with the gods to honor their names and keep their days, tracking cycles of heavenly liquid time. Using stellar patterns and rigorous mathematical computations, they predicted recurrent actions of the gods and men. Now these men and other leaders would convene a meeting to make decisions about their people's futures.

"Our honored day-keepers will remind everyone that time is divine and eternally flowing," continued Ko'h. "They track the moon, sun, Venus, Mars, and other heavenly bodies of the celestial caiman milky way. History repeats itself and the holy seers can guide us to the right decisions."

"But father, there may be others not so holy at this meeting. Many men converted to the foreigners' thinking. Countless innocents died because the guilty lurk among us," Itz expressed her fears aloud. "They will try to convince you and others to follow them." A shiver of premonition shook her body and soul.

"I do not trust the Spanish. Ambitious persons infiltrate our ranks, traitors who think only of their own gain or power. Like Prince Tepal, who now works with their priests to turn people away from the traditional ways," added Etz'nab.

Ko'h nodded, deep in thought about the upcoming conference. "I have many questions. Should we embrace additional edicts of the invaders or is it time to defy them?"

"Can we survive as a true people, as a faith, if they continue to enslave and convert us?" asked Itz.

"Is there a way to compromise and live together?" questioned Ko'h, as he limped to the meeting spot with assistance from his daughter and nephew. He needed Itz by his side at the conference. She would use her keen eyes to observe and her skillful hands to transcribe the events.

"My warriors and I are ready to fight the white demons," Etz'nab informed his uncle and shook his fist to the sky for emphasis. "Give us the word. We will gather and drive them from our lands or perish trying."

"We do not want either our youth or our truth to die," answered Ko'h.

Maya elders, priests and nobles gathered in a small village on the road to Mani, the former capital of the Maya Tutul Xiu family dynasty. The congregation took over a week to assemble. They had to be covert, careful not to draw the attention of Spanish overseers or others not part of the city-state leadership inner circles. Even though they received the news late, Itz, Ko'h and Etz'nab were not the last to arrive.

According to custom, participants consulted their day-keeper priests for auspicious dates and observed rituals. Preparations and arrival took more than travel time to set the scene for the upcoming discussions and decisions.

Priests and members of royal lineages practiced purification rites in anticipation of the tribunal. Some shed their own blood to seek visions and answers from the gods and ancestors.

Since Ko'h's own southern kingdom king had been held captive and killed in T'ho, the second son, Prince Tepal came to town early to attend the conference. He boldly arrived in a jaguar-skin covered litter chair and cape to match his jaguar tattooed upper arms and torso. Dark ink rosette markings were administered when he was a member of the priesthood.

As second sons were often known to do when they had no clear role in the succession line, he became a priest. Subjects whispered that his father witnessed diabolic signs in him as a young child that he hoped the priests could exorcize or contain. Tepal's coming of age readings by hired and pre-briefed soothsayers predicted that he must enter the priesthood as his calling and forego any authority role in governance of his father's kingdom.

Tepal hated the harsh fetters of priestly duties. However, as a recent Catholic convert of Spanish priest Diego De Landa, he learned to appreciate what tremendous powers priests could hold over the population.

De Landa represented Queen Isabella, the Inquisition and the conquistadors. When freed by the death of his father and other family members, Tepal immediately left the Maya priesthood. He befriended the Spaniard, donned Spanish garb and took up the title of *cacique*, overseer of lands. It was believed he disclosed information to the occupying forces to get rid of all persons who kept him bound to his monastic temple duties. By order of the Bishop in Merida, southern kingdom high priests and his father were tortured and burned alive in the main plaza in T'ho.

"It was necessary to save their souls," said Tepal without emotion when the topic came up.

Tepal studied and admired the fairer-skinned conquistadors. They welcomed him into their ranks after he converted and in exchange he provided them valuable information and tribute produced by his people. His nobility and position became a tool to be used for mutual gain. If he received a portion of the tributes and additional spoils for his insider reporting and actions, so be it. He hungered for recognition and companionship.

Diego De Landa let Tepal participate in secret inquisitor methods of questioning and punishing infidels. He proved to be a fast learner. Tepal admired Christians for their dominance and control of the weak. Imitating his mentors, cruelty became both his weapon and pleasure. The malicious churchmen did not regret their abuse of the local population, rather they regretted any feelings of loss of control and impotence.

A few days before the main assembly of elders and nobles met, and before Ko'h and his party arrived, Tepal set the stage to implement his plan. He had a scheme in mind to bring hesitant natives into the fold. To be visible to the public as an elite noble making special gestures of piety on their behalf was part of his plot to rule.

Accompanied by Cimi, a Maya priest from his former order, Tepal marched up the steep stone steps of an old temple. He paused, turned around and made sure the crowd of people at the pyramid base and courtyard got a long look at him about to exercise his privileged connection to the gods. He raised both his arms high, as if to bless the gathering. He held up a bowl with an open cloth bundle of ritual paraphernalia such as the whip-like tail of a stingray and other bloodletting lancets and obsidian perforators. Allowing people to see his instruments of auto-sacrifice induced awe and fear, as he intended. His headdress contained the symbolic water lily. It showed wealth and status and was indicative of the visionary trip he was about to make between the physical and spiritual worlds. His people believed that a connection with the sacred was essential to existence of a natural order in the world.

Once the prince felt that his presence had been duly noted by enough people, he dropped his cape at the entrance and bowed under the carved lintel to perform the rituals expected of him.

Tepal and his assistant had fasted for two days. He and Cimi took a steam bath for ritual cleansing. While in the heated chamber, they drank deep cups of alcoholic brew mixed with lime and powered nicotine-rich tobacco.

"That demonstration went just as I had planned out there," smiled Tepal. "What theater! Those dumb spotted dogs are in sore need of shows of strength and leadership." He removed his heavy carved headdress and loincloth to stretch out naked on the stone bench.

An attendant in the dark corner sprinkled water over hot rocks. Evaporating droplets hissed and steamed up the enclosed room. Sweat poured down Tepal's muscled back and chest and ran between his legs. Cimi used moss and a soft balsa wood stick to scrap the dust of the world off his master. He had been enamored with Tepal since he first entered the priesthood. The older man would do anything just to be near his beloved prince.

"Joy fills me to see you back practicing the old ways. I thought I lost you to the invaders' religion and priesthood," Cimi said.

"Oh Cimi, their worship rituals are not unlike yours, just different faces on the idols. I think of their cross as our four directions for water, wind, earth and sky when I pray with them."

"They worship half gods with wine and bread. Real gods demand blood," Cimi declared. "After your conversion, you looked dedicated to the Spaniards' new teachings and richer lifestyle. I was afraid you left me behind," he whined.

"You will always be my brother. Yet, in Friar Diego I have found a father, one who loves me, unlike my own. He even calls me 'son'," beamed Tepal. "I can appear to practice the new religion and also follow our traditions. Whichever serves my purposes at the time."

Steamy heat and honeyed *balche* drink made both men lightheaded. Cimi leaned back against the wall and sipped in short shallow breathes. He knew what would soon be asked of him. He felt honored to again be chosen.

Tepal looked through his bundle of items for the bloodletting rituals. He inspected various objects like shark's teeth, stingray spines, bones, and jade, all sharpened to draw sacred blood. He brought spoons, bowls and bark-papers to collect the offerings, hallucinogenic substances and incense to burn and carry their sacrifices to the gods.

He decided not to use the stingray spine on Cimi this time. Last year it caused an infection in his leg where an area of flesh and muscle decayed. His assistant would forever walk with a limp from that bloodletting technique.

Tepal tested the sharpness of one prismatic obsidian blade. A mere touch sliced his finger and blood trickled down his arm. This tool pleased him. Not to waste his precious fluid, he blotted the red drops on paper scrolls. Their blood soaked papers would later be burned. The smoke would transfer their offerings. When a giant serpent manifested in the rising spirals of smoke, it was then that communication with spirits and ancestors was possible.

Tepal's choice of a perforator was a jade needle used to pierce the genitals and tongue. He got aroused just thinking of what was ahead. He took another long drink of alcohol to calm himself. The container he chose to collect his blood was unusual. It was a conch shell used by scribes to hold their writing inks and colors.

"This scribe's inkwell and the lily on my headdress, like the lily scar on her cheek, will remind me of Itz while I am in my ecstasy and dreamlike state," silently mused Tepal.

His loins tightened at the thoughts. Tepal did not dare share these fantasies with Cimi because he would become jealous and uncooperative. He needed Cimi's blood mixed with his to open the gateways to spiritual realms. Dialogue with the old gods demanded suffering and blood sacrifice. Tepal would be sure that Cimi bore the greater burden of that demand.

"Let's proceed with our ceremonies, brother," Tepal called to the Maya priest. He held out a hand to help him up and wrapped his arm around him. Cimi trembled at the caring touch. He lowered his eyes; long dark eyelashes on his cheeks held back tears of love.

Cimi rinsed them both with cool clear water and wiped down their bodies with sweet-smelling leaves. They gathered the cloth bundles of sacrificial objects and went through a narrow interior passageway into a secluded back room at the top of the temple. Cimi lit two small torches, giving the stone room another world shadowy feel. He placed copal and dried toad venom in a bowl to smolder. Blue-gray spirals of smoke burned the back of his throat, but its intoxicating affects would ease pain and help erase disturbing memories.

Meanwhile Tepal mixed a liquid concoction. He took the favored jade needle and pierced his earlobes to add drops of blood to the mixture. He saw that his personal gesture greatly pleased Cimi, who longingly sighed and smiled.

Pouring the potion into a soft leather bladder, Tepal tightened a band around a thin nozzle. All was ready. Ritual enemas contained psycho-active solutions that brought men to a trace-like state and supernatural visions. His former priests taught Tepal this useful formula and effective internal means of rapid absorption.

Each placed their blood gathering bowls filled with bark paper in front of them. Knowing what was expected, Cimi lay down on a long woven paper mat and turned on his side.

"Do you desire to visit the gods, Cimi? Remember and tell me everything you see in your dream state."

"Oh, yes, dear one. I'll help you renew your divine energy, my lord. I am ready."

Tepal cut an x on top of his hand, one that would show later in public, indicating probable other sacrifices. He used warm blood that ran to his fingers to lubricate Cimi. He inserted the smooth wooden enema nozzle deep inside and pressed the leather sac several times to release the magic fluids. He squeezed every drop out with a slow circular twisting motion before withdrawing. Gratitude was obvious on his friend's face and in the erection he was rewarded for his numbing formula application.

Tepal's left hand remained wet with blood from the cut. He reached over and stroked Cimi's penis with his moistened palm. Cimi arched his back and moaned with desire. His organ tip was split halfway down into two pieces caused by previous cutting mutilations. Tepal, serving as his past partner in other religious sacrifice rituals, had himself inflicted this unnatural condition on the priest.

The potent enema solution was working. Cimi's head and eyes rolled around. He murmured, "Now, Tepal, Tepal …" His mind flooded with chemicals whisked him far away.

"Not yet my friend, not yet." He cupped the priest's testicles and slowly stroked his scarred genitals.

Tepal tested the drugs effects by raking a shark's tooth over Cimi's buttocks. He bled but did not flinch. His phallus remained erect and clear liquid drops formed on the tip. Tepal equally engorged, hovered on the edge of climax.

Tepal drew out the razor sharp obsidian from his basket. He held it firmly in his right hand. He wrapped his fingers around the base of Cimi's penis and positioned it over the largest bowl. He pumped faster and faster. Just as the dreaming man shot powerful gushes of semen, the prince used the obsidian blade to cut clean through the tip lengthwise. The flesh severed into four tassel-like quarters. Copious blood spurted into the container. Cimi opened his mouth to scream, but only a rush of foul air came out. He curled up and passed out on the mat.

Tepal could wait no longer. Excited, he used a carved bone to nick a raised vein on his own shaft. He screamed her name, "Itz", and instantly exploded into his scribe's bowl. Blood and life seeds mingled, covering the paper scrolls that would be offered to pacify the gods.

CHAPTER 23

Mani, Yucatan
1562 A.D.

Ko'h rose from his wooden stool and walked slowly to the edge of the stone platform to open the meeting of the Maya leaders.

"Although our lives have been filled with suffering, they are also filled with overcoming it. The future is up to us, not fate," said Ko'h to the auspicious gathering of stalwart men and women.

"We have become sedated people. We must be more aware of what's wrong, and aware of what's right. All of you came here to decide what needs to change and what should never change. Once we make our joint decisions, the universe will move in the direction of our choices," Ko'h began the talks.

Those assembled in the ceremonial plaza nodded in agreement with the noble scribe. Many heads turned when he first arrived and took a seat on the tiered platform reserved for those of authority. They'd heard he was dead, killed by Spaniards two year before. Even though his step was unsteady and his disfigured hands trembled, their hearts were lifted by his esteemed presence. Ko'h's opening words echoed their beliefs and encouraged citizen participation.

Tepal strode into the meeting late. He glared over the crowd standing and seated in the grassy courtyard. Itz was relieved she'd set up her low writing table in the shadow of a tree behind the platform where he could not readily see her. Even after years, being close to him turned her skin clammy with dread. She wanted to leave, but knew her father relied on her insights and event recording notes.

Prince Tepal, with a jaguar pelt cloak and iridescent quetzal feathers woven through his long back hair, drew all eyes in his direction. He came with every intention of running the meeting and getting the results he desired. Looking like a powerful lord of the past, he interrupted Ko'h's remarks and began speaking.

"We were a fragmented people when the Spanish arrived, squabbling city-states who never built an empire. After the fall of Mayapan kingdom, the Cocom and Xiu families continued to fight. Mighty white warriors arrived to unify and save us. They want to share the wisdom of their ways and their powerful god. We must give up old superstitions and live a better life under their rule," he began his monologue.

Tepal held his wounded hand up close to his torn ear for emphasis. "During my recent sacrifice and vision quest, noble ancestors and the green-mouthed serpent god coming from the rising smoke spoke to me."

Intake of breath and looks of awe came from the audience, just as he anticipated. Cimi and others planted throughout scattered groups followed orders to prompt responses and shout out agreement with his points on cue.

"The gods instructed me to embrace the new era and guide my people into a new age," he lied about an altered-state vision he never had.

An elder frowned and shifted uncomfortably on his woven mat. He turned his wrinkled walnut-brown face toward Tepal.

"Your words are less than half truths. In reality, our twenty separate independent provinces and the bitter Xiu and Cocom city-states' feud hindered conquest by the foreigners because there was no central political authority to be overthrown. Maya achievements have been intellectual, not political."

Another *cacique*, noble overseer on the platform added, "Spanish leaders took advantage of fragmentation and pre-existing rivalries between the states to divide us. When the powerful Mayan Xiu lord of Mani converted to Christianity, he united his forces with the Spanish and their hired Mexican Indian allies to violently put down remaining Maya resistance along with his own Cocom enemies."

"Tepal, when you tell half-truths, be sure you tell the right half," the elder scolded. The crowd agreed more with the elders' renditions of history.

A former *sajal*, military warlord walked to the front, waved Tepal to sit, and spoke, "We faced horrific weapons and dishonorable tactics meeting the outsiders in warfare. They fight to kill and subjugate everyone, claiming economic and moral justifications. The devils slaughter women and children and burn towns, sanctioning it under the umbrella of war. The Maya way is not killing innocents. Our fighters were trained to capture and humiliate elite leaders. The concept of surrendering an entire army or state is not familiar to us," the veteran said.

Another added, "Spanish aliens will never understand that wars are not primarily based on material gains, but upon honor and dignity."

"Conquerors like the Montejo family, who came here looking for precious metals were sorely disappointed in our land's other resources. Our treasures were wisdom and knowledge, not gold or silver," noted Ko'h.

An old crone from the back called out, "Never forget deaths from diseases. My entire family line died from pestilence brought from far away. How dare they call that plague, *mayacimil*, 'easy death', when entire villages perish in days with pox pustules rotting on stenching bodies."

People in the crowd grimaced at remembrance of losses suffered by every town and family. Over eighty percent of the Maya people had succumbed to diseases and other hardships.

Tepal positioned himself to rise and address these issues but a wizen hand on his shoulder held him firmly down.

"Perhaps your misunderstandings come from youth and no memory of the tragic events and situations of which we speak," whispered the oldest member of the leaders' group to the prince. "Listen to the people."

A bent over farmer with straw hat in hand said, "We are forced to tear down ancient temples and use the stones to build Christian homes, city walls and cathedrals. We survived many generations, tending our fields in the countryside. But they rounded us up and made us live in new colonial grid towns. To be sure we didn't return to our villages, soldiers burned our homes and cut down all the trees and crops. We are dying in the new settlements without gardens to grow corn or squash and no freedom to hunt. We labor under the whip for Spaniard's projects and to pay tribute while our own families starve."

"Round ups to concentrated towns to be supervised by Spanish civil, religious and military authorities is not working," agreed the committee of elders. "We must address this." In the background Itz was recording all the points made.

The audience chanted, "We are slaves, we are slaves." The rhythm of the message carried voices to a loud roar.

Tepal nodded subtly to Cimi to identify the instigators and speakers. They would be punished and pay for their audacity later. Tepal's hands tightened into fists in his lap and shook with fury. He was losing control over the meeting, over the emotions of the crowd. He did not want them to remember the bad or think too much. Something brewed behind Tepal's dark eyes, the eyes of someone without limits.

Counsel members shook their heads in sympathy to the gathered citizens. "People need more freedom of where they live, the work they do and to practice their traditional ways," the sage counsel concurred.

"The old ways include our religion too," shouted a bystander. "We should not strengthen the chains of their priestly powers with which they continue to evilly fetter our people."

"Tutul Xiu, lord of Mani converted and was baptized as a Catholic. Our brother goes by the new name of Melchor. He sent word to encourage his new religion," another counsel member said.

Tepal saw his chance to regain their attention and jumped up. "Christian practices like prayer, lighting wax candles and incense, keeping statues and altars, chanting, rituals, and sacred places for worship are familiar to us. New religious practices don't represent big change. You will learn to love the mother goddess and her baby son of peace," he said.

"Where was this loving goddess when my wife, a village healer, was dragged from our home by armed hirelings and killed as a heretic?" a man shouted.

"My husband was strung up by his neck, with my young son hung under him on his still twitching leg," another anguished cry rose.

"Why do black robed inquisition priests torture us to confess sins we have not committed?" an elder on the platform asked. "Even Lord Tutul Xiu's cousins and member of royal families have been taken away in chains, never to be seen again," he reminded them. "No one is safe."

"How can the Spanish preach peace, love and charity when they are the cruelest of masters and treat all but a few nobles who convert as less than humans?" a crippled woman cried.

"*This gathering must be controlled and the discussion limited*," fretted Tepal. He had a personal interest in the outcome and gave no thought of how concession would impact the future of others. For him it was a matter of how they would submit, not whether.

While finding the dissent of the people difficult, Tepal also found that it invigorated him. He stood up and said, "Those are past grievances. Father De Landa loves and accepts the Maya. He thinks of you as his children. He learned our language and studies ancient writings. That's why he wants you to gather your books and bring the old scripts to him. He wishes to know more," Tepal argued.

A man with a bruised face and eyes swollen almost shut from a recent beating, spoke out, "The soldiers search everywhere. They loot temples, comb through deep caves and raid homes to take our books and destroy every altar and deity representation they see. That doesn't sound like love and acceptance to me."

"My subjects, your future under the Spanish governor and as Christians will be better," Tepal countered. "That is all you need to know and accept."

Many in the assembly smirked and booed out loud. Tepal could not contain his anger and looks of disgust. He did not tolerate disagreement with his words or ideas. "Forget the past. Just wait, trust, and cooperate," he insisted.

Ko'h stood up shakily and said, "Forgetting is painful. Waiting is painful. But not knowing what our enemies are going to do next can be the most agonizing," he warned and continued, "One does not make important decisions alone, they should come through discussion," Ko'h reminded all present, hoping to move on to a more productive debate of the issues.

"Tepal, we have a wise experienced counsel assembled here of elders and nobles. We will take time to talk about each issue and find real solutions. Listen to everyone's experiences," the scribe said, waving his broken hand out over the crowd, "Heed the sage advice of your people and their principals."

"I already know what will be said. I don't want to hear it," answered the petulant Prince Tepal.

"It is best for us to follow the Spanish ways. Remember, gods speak through me," Tepal shouted to the gathered crowd. He roughly pushed Ko'h back to his seat. "Be quite old man. You disgust me, trembling like a coward."

"I must speak the truth even if my body and voice shake," boldly answered Ko'h. "If we act too quickly, we will have more and different problems and have to start all over again."

The eldest counselor firmly told Tepal, "We will not advise people to declare loyalty or convert before we deliberate and make unified decisions. Unwise choices are followed by great moral regrets."

Tepal ignored the statesmen. He figured the audience could not hear what men on the platform were saying. He turned his back on the council and stood at the front edge of the stone platform to loudly address the assembled crowd.

"I have decided. Pledge loyalty and cooperate with the Spanish lords," Tepal stated in a resounding deep voice. Cimi and other shills shouted words of agreements and prompted the some others in the crowd into half-hearted cheers.

"Convert to the holy Catholic religion and forsake other practices. To show good faith, all books and religious images will be turned over to the priests immediately at the Franciscan church in Mani," Tepal continued. "Refuse and you will be punished severely. If you flee, you'd better go far away, like the Itza cowards who ran south to Tayasal in Peten, now quivering in their island city. They too shall fall for their disobedience and heresy."

Wooden trumpets and conch shell horns blasted from somewhere in the back to signal the end of the meeting.

"Go and do as you have been told," announced Tepal to the audience, and gave a dismissive wave of his arm.

"But we have not finished our business here," an elder leader protested.

"There will be no further discussion. This assembly is over," proclaimed Tepal.

The confused crowd stood in shock for a moment and then dissipated listlessly away from the plaza. The elder counsel could not believe how quickly the unilateral decision and pronouncement was made by Tepal. Dazed, they meekly gathered their belongings and blended into the remaining few gathered below the platform.

CHAPTER 24

Mani, Yucatan
1562 A.D.

The assembly of elder leaders had been ended unexpectedly and abruptly by Tepal's bold orders. Ko'h and the other council members were in shock. Itz helped her father down the steps and sat beside him on a bench in the shade.

As she crammed her writing utensils and notes into a carry bag, she said, "That selfish, cruel, arrogant man! He does not understand or care about us."

Itz's father touched her arm to interrupt her tirade. Although he agreed, he was alarmed at such sharp language in public and the depth of her anger. Ko'h was aware of the possible consequences of the lifelong conflict between his daughter and the prince. She almost lost her life twice because of his mood swings.

"My dear, you must be careful how you handle sharp knives and fools," her father warned.

Luckily, Tepal and his cohorts were at a distance, congratulating each other on the victory. They hadn't heard the disdain and open rebellion in her voice. That situation soon changed. The prince rounded the corner of the platform and headed straight for Ko'h and Itz.

"I am delighted to see you Itz," he cooed, as his gaze slowly swept over her from head to toe. "Where have you been hiding all this time?" Tepal turned his back and purposefully ignored Ko'h as if the scribe were invisible to him. He would not allow another word about his decree.

Cimi limped up and stood behind Tepal. One of Yaxche's former apprentices, a short stocky girl with crossed eyes, walked up and grabbed Tepal's hand in a possessive gesture. Itz recognized the long woven brocade dress, braided leather sandals that the girl wore as possessions she left behind when they had to escape. Itz's mother's amber necklace with silver border lily edges hung around her neck. The smooth honey-colored stone in the jewelry had been Itz's protective amulet used for focusing spiritual vibrations. The simple girl, who failed in herbal training, had no idea of its history, strength or purpose. What a shameful waste.

Tepal reached over and touched the deep inverted scar on Itz's cheek. She recoiled like she'd been burned. It flooded her with memories of the day when Tepal, in one of his temper tantrums, grabbed a ragged piece of wood and struck her so hard that she fell to the ground unconscious. In his irrational frenzy, he would have hit her again if Etz'nab had not pushed him to the ground. To touch a royal that way was a punishable offense, so her cousin had to go into hiding until the ruler forgave the incident.

As children growing up together, if Tepal did not get his way he flew into manic fits, which often ended in cruelty to animals or those weaker who could not defend themselves. Itz tried to avoid him without insulting the regal personage, but he would seek her out. He enjoyed teasing her above all others. Even after he was taken into the priesthood, he roamed freely, and showed up at her doorstep or suddenly beside her in the forest as she gathered herbs or drew pictures. He seemed lonely and she tried to be friendly. She hoped he would change.

When they came of age, his attentions became lustful, not romantic or amorous, just testing his newfound sexual powers. One day when she walked alone gathering fruit, he surprised her and pinned her arms from behind. His free hand pushed away the maiden shell she wore on a rope around her waist. He grabbed roughly between her legs. He groped around, seemingly shocked at female anatomy, missing parts like his.

"Stop Tepal! You are hurting me."

"Pain and pleasure go together, my love," he panted.

"I am not your love."

"Someday you will be my wife, Itz," he crowed.

"We are not fated to marry Tepal. Our birth star charts are complete opposites," she said, relieved that it was a trusted fact. "You are studying to be an astrologer priest and know that."

"I am no ordinary priest. I am no ordinary man. I have the power to order new readings, readings that will bind us to one another."

"Tepal, as children we had lessons and played together. That is all and it is over. I don't want your attentions," Itz told him firmly.

"Then why do you send me secret signals like wearing a lily in your hair?" he asked.

"What are you talking about?" she asked in surprise, tearing the flower from behind her ear.

"Don't play coy. You asked for this," Tepal said and squeezed her breast until she cried out.

"I swear I will never be bound to you. Leave me alone," Itz shouted and slapped his face.

"If I cannot have you, no one else will," screamed the frustrated man-child, as he stomped away.

The next day, tattooed priests with their reeking, blood soaked robes and human bone necklaces arrived at her home to take her away. It was no coincidence she'd been chosen as a sacrifice to Chac, the rain god. Itz screamed for her father and aunt, but no one was around to save her. Temple wardens roughly bathed and painted her with a bright blue combination of indigo, clay minerals and copal tree sap paste. They forced vile tasting liquid down her throat to quiet and sedate her. Huge jade and copper ornaments were placed around her neck, wrists and ankles to act as weights. The stone necklaces were so heavy they required counterweights down her back. Such massive ornamentation would sink her body into the dark recesses of the *cenote* well after the priests ripped her beating heart out before her still living eyes. She would serve as fertility offering and reside in Chac's palace in the underworld.

"It is the greatest of honors," dark monks repeated as if to make her accept this grisly fate.

Two acolytes carried Itz up the temple steps. She was too dizzy to stand. Her head spun from the drugs and terror that she would never descend the stairs alive. Four priests grabbed her arms and legs to place her prone across the stone altar pillar. Her thumping heartbeat matched the drumbeats from the plaza. To the side a priest blew a high-pitched clear flute seven times. Seven was to open an invisible pathway between the realms of creation and spirit. Death produced a lively show for the worshippers below.

Tepal stood behind the main group of his grizzly brotherhood. "You should be honored," he mouthed to her. By the light of the blazing torches, she saw his wicked sharp-toothed grin.

As the high priest raised the long obsidian blade over her heaving chest, action stopped mid-thrust. He touched her scarred cheek. A look of disgust crossed his hardened face.

"This will not do. She has imperfections. Chac's brides must be perfect in every way. Remove her and bring me the next maiden." He flung Itz aside. Her head smacked the hard stone floor. Itz woke up in her aunt's caring arms. She scrubbed and scrubbed to get the loathsome sticky blue paint off her skin.

Tepal was crestfallen and furious. It was his past actions that made her an unsuitable offering. He ran from the temple and went down the back stairs. The unsuccessful sacrifice attempt was the last time Itz had seen Tepal until he paraded into the elders' gathering near Mani. In her heart, usually filled with love and compassion, there was a dark recessed place, filled with loathing for the prince and all he stood for.

CHAPTER 25

Mani, Yucatan
July 1562 A.D.

After the futile meeting of the elders, Ko'h fumed and ranted against Tepal's order to surrender written records to the Spanish priests in Mani.

"No! We will not turn over our works to the Catholic friars. Itz, you and I will produce more books and pottery to tell the Maya story," swore a determined Ko'h.

In sympathy, her father addressed an unspoken fear, "I know this is a life that you did not imagine or choose. Spanish zealots pledge to destroy hieroglyphic books and all who possess them. Reproducing texts is an extraordinary risk and sacrifice for one so young. I am very proud of you, dear daughter."

"What we do is defiant against powerful invaders, but it is right. It's not hard to make a decision once you know where your values lay," she responded.

"The Maya seem drained by apathy and only interested in living day-by-day. Are you willing to give up a normal life to preserve the old knowledge?" he asked, wanting her to make her own decision.

Itz answered with a courageous, "Yes, I want to continue our work. My choices are not easy, but who wants to be ordinary anyway?" She laughed to cover her trepidation.

Out of the blue, an idea hit Ko'h's heart in one beat of his pulse and stayed.

"Before we return to the village, we'll go into Mani to see and hear Father De Landa's words for ourselves. He issued orders for people to come to his big church to listen to plans for the future."

"Are you sure? There will be priests, soldiers and others around who might recognize you," asked Itz.

"I'm not sure, but for some reason I feel drawn. I will go to Mani."

People trustingly brought their precious folding book codices and objects of worship to the village friars and directly to their superior, Father Diego De Landa, in the town of Mani as ordered. Mercenary soldiers searched and collected items from across the land. The cavernous sanctuary structure and square in front of the Franciscan church overflowed with ancient statues, stone carvings, paintings, pottery and hieroglyphic recordings of history, beliefs, medicine and astronomy.

Despite the fact that most large ceremonial centers from classic times were abandoned and in decline, the Maya continued in the same social structure. They used their original language and still practiced the nature-linked religion after the arrival of the Spanish. Certain day-keepers, scribes and other specialists, to stay in touch with the gods, created codices and could read the old symbols.

Stationed on the Yucatan peninsula for years with the mandate to convert and educate the heathens in the ways of Christianity, Father De Landa undertook a study of local society and customs. He spoke the Mayan language and read it tolerably well. Out of curiosity about the foreign writing system and beliefs, he gathered all the codices he could find. With the help of interpreters, he tried to decipher the strange pictogram hieroglyphs and ideograms painted on sacred items. Assistants read and gave interpretations that varied in accordance with their understanding and areas of specialty. Converts, like Tepal, were richly rewarded for bringing in books and finding scribes and translators for the strange folded painted bark papers.

Codex book pages used horizontal and vertical lines to separate the texts and thick red frames dividing the long sheets into several squares. Inside the frames were glyphs related to subjects like agriculture, medicine, astronomy, history or prophecies. Not only everyday, but also spiritual worlds, took on life in the colorful pages and surfaces of pottery.

Diego De Landa was a good Roman Catholic. He believed that there was but one God, and anyone who worshipped other gods committed a mortal sin. De Landa's god was a jealous god who could never be just another personage in a pantheon. Like other men of his time, ingrained intolerance justified immoral acts and atrocities in his Christian religion's name. Forced conversion, slavery, killings, and the suppression and elimination of other religions were zealots' way of life. Inquisition, questioning under torture, was only one method to assure his flock contained only the truly faithful. Conquerors needed to establish their identity and establish strict order to maintain control. People become slaves whenever religion and swords are in partnership.

"Walk with me, Brother Juan Guillermo," a nervous and gaunt De Landa requested of the convert Tepal. "Do you think the Indios are bringing all their idolatrous writing and paintings to us as ordered?"

"Yes, Father. More ancient items than I ever imagined are stacked around the church here in Mani. Local people and soldiers carry in additional articles every hour. My efforts on your behalf have been successful." Tepal stood near De Landa, his eyes fixed on his master, like a dog, hoping for a treat or fond pat on the head.

"From what you and others tell me, heretical Maya underground networks of priests, jealous of the power of our one true Catholic Church, attempt to draw people back to their old heathen ways," said De Landa.

He, like many in his Franciscan order, believed that they were bound to convert as many souls as they could. That eliminating pagan practices and evil would usher in the Second Coming of Christ much sooner. Caught up in his own brooding thoughts, the priest announced, "I shall expose and destroy this evil. We will be forgiven in killing sinners if it will save the overall community."

"I helped you root out many satanic idol worshippers," Tepal reminded him. "Heretics questioned by our inquisitors confessed that magic and witchcraft continue to be practiced. Mayans bow in church to our Christ and saints, but whisper names of their old gods." Tepal paused for effect. "Just yesterday we found evidence of human sacrifice in caves near Chichen Itza," he said, purposefully fueling the priest's fury.

"I have been betrayed," De Landa sobbed. He pounded his fists on his concave chest, above the cassock cowl. Veins stood out on his neck and forehead. "After all I have done to help these misguided lost souls," he said in anguish. Fury and pain were a habit, now a part of his nature.

"Idol worship and sacrifice! Is my life's work a complete failure? My children have turned their backs on me," he lamented, truly saddened by the violations.

De Landa's angular face glazed with sudden sweat. Like a wave washing over, it went blank and became hard as a stone mask. He flinched with a fleeting idea at a faint clue to his angst.

"Written language is the key to preserving their religion," he deduced aloud. "So, we shall destroy this evil tree at its root."

De Landa went on the attack. "Guards, gather those known to practice ancient traditions and bring them to me by mid-week," the red-faced priest ordered. Franciscan brothers and Spanish military reinforcements scoured the towns and countryside for any additional hidden idols and practitioners of idolatry. Those observed practicing any ancient traditions, even offering prayers to protectors of the hearth or cornfield, were brought to Mani. People, who only heard of Christianity within the generation, would be punished as infidels in public for mere traces of indigenous beliefs.

Mani, the capital of the Mayan Xiu dynasty, previously ruled the western part of the Yucatan peninsula. When the Xiu lord and his subjects converted to Christianity, the Franciscans celebrated one of their greatest successes. They built a magnificent church on top of the former Maya ceremonial pyramid. People were herded to the plaza in front of the new Catholic Church in Mani.

The day was Wednesday, July 12, 1562 on the Spanish linear calendar. Diego De Landa, in an insatiable obsession for exorcising idolatry, brought the full force of the Inquisition down on the masses trembling in the plaza. Hundreds of Maya were questioned and many died under torture. Dozens were flogged to death or committed suicide during the process. Nobles, scribes, shamans and others who had assisted the friars in text readings and translations were cruelly eliminated to destroy the ancient knowledge and leadership. Blood covered the church floor and courtyard stones.

CHAPTER 26

Mani, Yucatan
July 12, 1562

"It was a mistake to come here," Itz whispered to Ko'h.

As they entered the town of Mani, she and her father blended into the populous in their course-woven clothes and downcast eyes of common workers. Dust of the white limestone road, begrimed their shifts and sandals. Foreign soldiers herded reluctant citizens along with the butts of their swords and spears. Events quickly unfolded unpredictably, unfairly. New arrivals were startled by the terrifying blood-curdling screams of people being interrogated.

De Landa dispensed with the usual formal procedures and documentation that accompanied his home country inquisition questionings. He insisted that a papal bull, *Exponi nobis*, justified his actions. His interrogations used levels of physical abuse and torture upon the Maya that were excessive. Scores were subjected to examination under a technique called hoisting. In hoisting, the victim's hands were bound and looped over an extended line that was then raised. The entire body was suspended in air while lashes were applied to the back. Often stone weights were tied to the ankles.

"Father, Etz'nab told us there was a crown fiat from the Spanish king and queen, that exempted indigenous Maya people from the authority of the Inquisition. Even though insulting, they said we were 'too childish' to be culpable for heresy. Yet, De Landa's Christian priests silently obey him to torture and slay us."

"Religious crusaders far from home do as they wish," he answered. "Their fear of us is the source of their cruelty. Torturers are cowards who know fear and use it."

"No matter what the Christians promised to get people to listen, we can't trust this enemy to honor our peoples' beliefs and heritage. But, I'm afraid it is too late to leave," he said.

"Do you see Tepal?" asked Itz.

"Perhaps he fell victim to his own ambition along with other false converts and text readers," said Ko'h."Greed and power poison his soul. He's returned to a world of atrocities and marched his own people into bloodshed and misery. He must have foreseen this pending desecration."

Itz looked around for her childhood enemy, and was relieved not to run into the turncoat. Tepal was always one to have an excuse or quick way out when trouble brewed.

Citizens and visitors to Mani were forcibly assembled in front of the main church to witness De Landa's scourge of heresy and idolatry. The sun beat down. No water or food was available to sustain the people. Thirst was written on their pinched faces. Horrified by gross acts of the inquisitors, some tried to run and find refuse in the forests or caves. Soldiers brought them back, shamed them by cutting off their hair and hung them in trees around town as examples.

Converts' fervent prayers to Virgin Mary and Jesus went unanswered. It seemed that God stayed out of sight, ashamed of the inhumanity his followers were promoting in his name.

Father De Landa stood on the top step of the church entrance and looked out over the gathering. His smoldering black eyes studied the scene with an unreadable expression. Deep lines cupping his mouth were indelible and harsh. Itz had never seen a man look so dangerous. For several minutes he did not speak. Then he began.

"These images ands idols are falsehoods and works of the devil," he spat out as he pointed to piles of art and effigies around the church.

Itz and Ko'h saw figurines of the gentle goddess of childbirth and weaving, the young corn maize prince, along with copious paintings of flowers, medicinal plants, animals like the mighty jaguar and colorful birds of their land. There were representations of *Kukulkan*, the embodiment of divine love and wisdom. Some incense burners were decorated with wrinkled old man faces, but they were not demons.

"Father, these art works are not evil or any threat to Christians. Why would agricultural, gestation cycles or studies of the stars frighten the Spanish? We have much to teach them. Our books explain old miracles and reveal new ones," said a confused Itz.

"What they do not know, they fear. What one fears, one destroys," he stuttered with sad awareness. "What the mad priest said is hollow, base and untrue," declared Ko'h. Any vague hope the scribe had for understanding or unity with the conquistadors quickly faded to regret.

"The Christian god is the one and only sacred being!" the priest screamed at the top of his lungs.

"Father, an infinite god like theirs should be able to protect himself without going into partnership with sadistic priests."

De Landa raised his hand and beckoned over clusters of priests and troops. "Smash these demon idols to hell," he commanded.

The cruel and grim master stood above the chaos, chanting to himself with his hungry gaunt mouth. Vast collections of ceramics, stone statues, woven fabrics, paintings and carved wooden items from over the centuries were condemned in one order to be systematically destroyed. It took the workers until mid-afternoon to club, cut and crush the thousands of images and other religious objects. Shards and shreds were thrown into a huge pile.

“Bring me a torch,” shouted De Landa.

Soldiers added sticks of wood and pitch to the giant mound of smashed objects in the center of the square. Pieces of clay arms, bodies and faces of old gods from homes and temples lay in looking up and reaching out of the jumbled disarray. De Landa’s eyes glowed red as he lit his great bonfire.

“You will stop the worship of idols. You will stop the sacrifice of children. You will crawl humbled to the one true god, the god of mercy.”

“What mercy?” someone in the hoard shouted out. “The dead you have sacrificed cannot bend their knee. Your cruel god demands more blood than any of ours ever did.” The protester nodded in the direction of a pile of corpses.

“Burn the bodies,” De Landa screamed, to get rid of the evidence just pointed out to him. The wiry priest paced rapidly around the fires, carried away by the excitement of fulfilling his mantic mission to eradicate heresy.

Mangled corpses left blood-smeared trails along the courtyard stones as indifferent hirelings carelessly dragged them by arms, legs or hair toward the waiting flames. Heads with empty eyes and mouths frozen in agony bumped along the pavers. Right in front of Itz, a dead child’s face rolled to one side, her jaw dropped open in a mute scream for help.

The priests and their minions did not appear fazed by the holocaust they inflicted on the innocent people or the irreplaceable cultural losses. Additional ranks of guards drank and laughed around the edges of the plaza. Standing far aside from his comrades, one foreign man shook his head back and forth in disbelief as he incredulously observed the events. Itz saw tears swell in his eyes before he pulled down a cassock covering to hide his face from view and left the nightmare scene.

Birds dove and screamed over the smoke-filled plaza. “*Dzoch Ah Pech*, the night bird of death is here. He walks among us,” whispered a wizen old woman. Soon even the birds closed their eyes and sat silently in the tree branches after the last of the bodies were thrown on the bonfire.

"We are being selected out of history. This is an unforgiveable crime," pronounced Itz to all within hearing range. "Making us fearful can force obedience, but it can never change our hearts."

Willing new converts to Christianity discovered too late that the priests who taught them about the exemplary qualities of the new god could be as implacable and cruel as any warrior on a battlefield. Maya and other indigenous mothers around Mexico, tired of blood sacrifice, had turned to the Madonna and child. Jesus was appealing and Mother Mary vaguely reminded them of the goddess *Ixchel.*

"The Virgin's followers betray her. They have no compassion for life," said a mother with babe at her breast. "Will the agony of our dead increase the power of your god?" she shouted at the oppressors.

Itz, coughed and choked on the acrid smoke of burning flesh. She cried out in grievous moans. She'd never witnessed such a hecatomb of human suffering and sacrifice.

"*Lajel, lajel*, death, death," the crowd sobbed in unison. Sounds of grief echoed and crawled around the plaza walls. People fell to the ground in shock. A shroud of ash and shame covered everyone.

Ko'h leaned heavily on his daughter, both to comfort her and to support himself. This display was more than he could stand. A leaden weariness descended upon him. There were no words for the depth of despair his heart and soul experienced at the infamous scene of destruction playing out before him. He cringed at the foreboding terror that it stirred.

"Occupation has made cowards of us. Our sin was not idolatry. It was to stay silent for so long," he spoke softly to the crowd.

Flames leapt up behind De Landa as he addressed the gathering.

"I have read your writings and studied many books in these strange characters of yours. I find that Mayan manuscripts contain nothing but superstitions and falsehoods of the devil."

He turned to his fellow priests. "Bring the Mayan books out of the church. Throw them into the fire as well. We shall stop sin and abomination here and now. Burn them all!" the fanatic screamed.

"No!" roared the crowd. Made bold by their own fears and suddenly unafraid of the repercussions, people surged forward to stop the parade of priests as they brought forth age-old precious writings. Anguished cries and shrieks of revolt soon died among the heavy thud of blows. Soldiers savagely beat the protestors back. Burly guards grabbed the woman who protested the betrayal of the Virgin and flung her and the baby into the bonfire.

Unable to reach the porters with their treasures, the Maya crowd could only watch. They stood helplessly sobbing and swaying like the rhythmic waves of the sea.

Stacks of paper scrolls, deerskin folders bound in wooden covers, and paintings on bark, were thrown unceremoniously into the roaring flames. Centuries of ancient knowledge in volumes of texts perished forever in a single fire. Franciscans monks, led by their superior, sang their foreign church songs and smiled at their auto-de-fe handiwork of burning the strange and indecipherable symbols.

"Destroying a conquered peoples' ability to communicate is intoxicating," said De Landa to his minions. "Today's powerful acts prove an important and visible way of maintain control over the masses."

Destruction and cruelty, like other vices, required no motive or justification outside itself that infamous day. Like the death of Cain, men once again killed others over the question of who stood closer to God.

Stunned, Copoya prayed, "In your upward flight like a lark with no song, let smoke rise from this flame and ask the gods to pardon all people. The Spanish madmen do not understand what they are destroying. Forgive their ignorance and fear. Help us through this darkest of times."

He hoped that a holy hummingbird would carry his prayers to the gods. Scalding tears rolled down and fell to the parched ground. His eyes reflected the emptiness of the ages.

"Rooted in stupidity, indifference or greed, the consequences are the same---the devastation of our past," responded furious Itz.

"Attempting to convert souls, those superstitious fools ignored our wisdom and condemned mankind to ignorance by torching entire libraries," mourned Ko'h.

Apart from the shock of seeing precious books burned before her, Itz was stunned and mesmerized by the scene before her. She could not stop staring into the flames. To break the spell, Itz turned to hide her face in her father's chest. She could no longer bear to watch destruction of what they held sacred. Ko'h was not at her side. She frantically searched the crowd for him. Had the soldiers seen the elderly scribe and snatched him away?

"Father, where are you?" she cried out in panic. Itz found her answer in an audible gasp of the gathered crowd.

Ko'h had broken through the ring of guards and rushed toward the backside of the fire. He grabbed books out of the flames and tossed them aside, out of harm's way. Saving as many as he could, he was unaware of the blaze igniting the bottom of his thin shift.

A staggering drunken soldier came up behind Ko'h. With a mighty thrust he drove a double-headed spear through the scholar's back. The force of the blow sent the scribe face first into the roaring conflagration. In his last strong agony, the dying warrior of truth lay eternally still. Books removed from the fire were thrown back in on top of the dead scholar. Ko'h's life was not all that was lost in the struggle against oppression. Humanity itself had been betrayed, profaned, and plundered that July afternoon in Mani.

Later in his journal entry about the large number of idol and book burnings that day, De Landa boasted, 'We burned them all, which the Maya regretted to an amazing degree, and which caused them much affliction.' As a second thought and seemingly without remorse, he noted that 'Several died by a visitation of God'. The shameless man rejoiced in his viciousness.

CHAPTER 27

Edzna, Campeche
Present Day

Dr. Hannah Char sat at her field laboratory workbench looking through a magnifying glass to examine burnt bone fragments found in Structure 15. She lamented how the ancient engineers, philosophers, scribes, astronomers, and physicians had been silenced over the centuries. Every site has a story. Maya spirits whispered their truths. She wanted to establish a dialogue between civilizations, showing the extent to which human beings are linked. The connections may be invisible but they exist. The departed were waiting for someone like her to find time capsule messages and tell the world. She poured over recently discovered pottery shards. Small bits of evidence teased her.

"Archaeology reminds me of the jigsaw puzzles I did as a child," she said to Roberto.

"But in these cases, not all the pieces are there and you can't cheat and look at the box cover for the big picture," he replied.

"Will I ever discover how to interpret the past and bring yesterday's stories into our lives today?"

"As mystical as it sounds, for us to learn the truth, we must approach the ruins with intuition as well as a shovel. As we both stress to the workers, improper excavations of materials would destroy the record for all time. We just have to take our time and do the job correctly."

Outside the laboratory, rains fell unchecked from the darkened sky and quenched the parched jungles thirst. Yucatan's rainy season was getting an early start. Constant downpour released scents from the forest flowers and wet earth to mingle with the fragrant wood smoke from Mari's cook fire.

Rains would soon make jungle growth so thick and impenetrable that clearing or excavation efforts would be impossible. Wild field grasses would grow shoulder high and tropical forest paths become obscured. Not to mention dangerous slippery ruins steps that resembled cascading waterfalls in a downpour. Stone building walls, when saturated, could turn into landslides in an instant.

If a hurricane struck the peninsula directly, huge trees fell, mowed down as if trampled by a running giant. Local Maya would take refuse in underground caves until the most severe storms passed. There were valid reasons not to continue fieldwork during the summer through autumn wet season, but almost half a year away from the ruins were difficult for one so dedicated to finding answers to age-old questions.

Hannah worked all morning in the laboratory. She finished reports and packed up for the expedition's season end. The dark overcast morning, a portent of the rainy months to soon fall upon the land, reflected her somber mood. A tight knot of dread grew in her stomach. She didn't look forward to returning to work in the city at INAH headquarters during the off-season. Hannah thrived in the field, not the office.

When the rains let up, she jogged over to the Temple of the Masks to see how the thatched roof and sidings protecting the remaining plaster temple sun-god mask weathered the storm. The archaeologists would be leaving and she wanted to be sure it was secure until next season. Since the theft of the temple façade, the team had been extremely vigilant and cautious, yet she saw nothing more to alarm her.

Walking through the main plaza, Hannah stopped and watched colorful birds overhead. They circled, soared and descended, similar to her alternating thoughts. The day's edgy tension began to ebb and she felt calmer than she had for a long time.

She strolled through her ancient city and tuned into the sense of place and energy. She settled cross-legged on the palace steps, closed her eyes, steadied her breathing and meditated. Mari taught her that to divine the true substance and nature of things, a chattering mind and open eyes were more of a hindrance than help.

She sat quietly, completely still on the stone steps. Nothing moved around her, only a soft breeze that wafted through her golden-red hair. In the overwhelming jungle, she remained a little apart, as if she had a space of her very own.

That was how he found her. The dark stranger stepped silently out of the opposite temple, bowing his head as he passed under the low carved door lintel. The building's overhang provided shade, a cool refuse from jungle heat steaming off the stones after the recent rain. He leaned half- turned, against the wall and just waited and watched her.

Hannah sat in the filtered sunlight, looking calm and regal. In his life he'd never perceived such an instant profound sense of familiarity and connectedness. A startling thought shocked through his system---that choices and events in both their lives led them to this exact same place at the exact same time for a reason.

At that moment Hannah turned and their eyes riveted on each other. They silently gazed across the courtyard. She felt as if she looked at him through a camera, with the lens zoomed in all the way. The time span was probably no more than the split second between shutter opening and closing, but it seemed an eternity. Click.

Hannah averted her eyes and rose to meet the stranger. She sensed no danger. He remembered his manners and walked over to join her on the stone steps.

"Dr. Char, I presume? I am Joseph Comouche, here to interview you and your team. You were told of my coming, weren't you?" he said formally as he approached her.

Up close, the dark haired reporter was several inches taller than Hannah and athletically lean. His warm skin tones suggested Mediterranean origins. His features bordered on the edge of handsome. Words like rugged and strong came to her mind. When he offered his hand to shake, she saw that his fingers were long and elegant, but had a roughness that only hard work and outdoor activities produce.

"Please call me Hannah," she stammered, finding her voice.

Hannah was Joseph's favorite name. At least it was now. He was getting an internal grip on the odd flash he'd experienced before.

Hannah self-consciously brushed back her hair and tucked it into her worn hat. Under an even tan, he noticed a scattering of beige freckles across the bridge of her nose. Her forest green eyes sparkled in the mottled jungle light. This woman was not the dumpy academic archaeologist he was expecting to find hidden in these remote ruins. This lady struck him as lovely.

"I have permission from your institute director, Dr. Sarra. I want to hear more about your discoveries and the antiquity thefts that occurred recently," Joseph said to resume his professionalism.

"Yes, Dr. Samuel Sarra, my boss. Did you interview our INAH Director in Mexico City?"

"Not really. He's a busy man. Couldn't give me any of his time, but the secretary handed me a press packet and color photograph of him as she hurried me out."

"Busy and modest too," quipped Hannah.

They both began to laugh. Hannah quickly stifled herself. "Seriously, Dr. Sarra is a remarkable man, top-notch in the field." She did not want to seem disloyal or have negative comments put in a magazine article.

"*Any lapse might appear in print. Keep to the facts and don't say anything sensational,*" she reminded herself in a low whisper and changed the subject.

"How long will you be our guest? Do you have time for me to show you around the archaeological zone and get into the realities of working an important site?" she inquired as she guided him back toward the camp compound.

"Is this considered an important site?" he asked.

Hannah looked up in earnest surprise, "There are no unimportant sites, only uninspired archaeologists. Researchers could spend entire careers digging and unraveling the mysteries of one place such as this."

"I could never be an archaeologist," he said. "I didn't even like to hunt for Easter eggs when I was a lad."

"Excavation can challenge you mentally and physically in ways you can not even imagine."

She excitedly talked to Joseph about Edzna and her profession as they walked along. There was nothing quite like the spark in a person's eye when discussions turn to something they are passionate about. He noticed every nuance of expression, every shift of her chin or eyes. Joseph saw dedication for her chosen field in her face and heard it in her tone.

"*Her work seems to be her calling and also her sanctuary from something. She's experienced pain and fear in her life. What?*" he pondered and tapped a finger on his upper lip.

"*Meraki,*" he said, almost to himself.

"What is that?" Hannah questioned.

"*Meraki* is a Greek word. There is no equivalent in English, but it describes how someone does their job with soul, creativity and love. It's when you leave a piece of yourself in your work."

Hannah was shocked at his quick assessment and recognition of her devotion to archaeology.

"We are both investigators, detectives digging around for the truth, rather than pulling down a high salary," he said.

To cover feelings of being so transparent to a stranger, Hannah fell back on old archaeology jokes.

"Archaeology is the only job where you start at the top and work your way down."

"Your work is groundbreaking," he retorted.

"We want to have our archaic and eat it too," she countered.

"How much carbon dating should someone do before they are ready for carbon marriage?"

They both groaned and agreed not to exchange anymore corny, junior high school type humor for the time being.

"I was told your team was headed back in a few days. If it is alright with you, I will stay to explore a bit, get my story and ride back into civilization with you when you pull up stakes," he answered regarding her earlier question about his timeframe.

"That's fine with me. Let's get you settled in. You can meet Roberto, my co-director and Mari, chief of operations, cook and much more. They are the real heart and soul of this field expedition."

Joseph adjusted a weather-beaten backpack against his broad athletic shoulders and picked up the pace. As they neared the compound, a charcoal grill whiff of cooking meat filled the air with appetizing aromas.

"Smells like something delicious roasting on the barbie already."

She liked his clipped British sort of accent. Dr. Sarra had said the reporter was from Australia or somewhere. Hannah wished she'd paid more attention.

Introductions were made. Joseph claimed his assigned hammock gratefully and deposited his things in the extra hut next to

Roberto's. Around the dinner table, he chatted openly with the expedition members, using a combination of Spanish and English. His Spanish vocabulary was sufficient, but occasionally his conjugation of verb tenses and inversion of phrases were deuces wild in a poker game. Using his poor Spanish with a fluent confidence made it sound better.

Roberto's big furry dog, Oso, who never paid much attention other than to growl at strangers, curled up at Joseph's feet wagging his tail while getting his share of inclusion in the conversation.

"What is that you are saying to my dog?" asked Roberto.

"Oh, it's old Italian. I speak to animals, especially dogs, birds and horses this way. I figure if it worked for St. Francis, it might work for me," he grinned sheepishly. "My father is originally from Pescara, Italy, part of the De Cesare line. Even though he's lived in New Zealand most of his life and married to my very English Kiwi mother for almost thirty-five years, he often speaks Italian at home. I like to try new languages, to feel the differences roll around my mouth."

"Really?" asked Mari with a mischievous smile. She taught Joseph a couple of Mayan words. "Here's a phrase you will like and use, *co'oten hanal*; it means 'come eat'."

Everyone chuckled at his attempts to click the sounds. His voice was low and soothing, while his laughter rang singingly through the forest.

"Mayan has a gentle rhythm to it that our rigid Anglo words don't allow," he noted. He taught them all to say *'Kia Ora'*, the Maori greeting for hello.

Hannah felt more like an observer that evening over dinner, as Joseph chatted mostly with the others. When he told stories and joked around with Roberto and Mari, it was obvious his mind was sharp. The more they talked the more she noticed a gentle modesty about him. His quick humor and intelligence was evident, but he wasn't a show off, not by any means.

Joseph expressed great appreciation for Mari's home-cooked meal and helped her prepare a fresh fruit and honey dessert. She let him have a piece of honeycomb to chew afterward as a treat. He looked happy as a little boy getting to lick a bowl after the cake mix was poured into baking pans.

Joseph shared some of his background in journalism. Turned out he had not only newspaper and magazine articles to his credit, but also books, including an excellent historical study of Alaskan Indian carvings.

"Perhaps he could be relied upon to produce an accurate account of work being done in Maya archaeology and problems with antiquity theft," Hannah whispered to Roberto.

With a long sigh, Joseph touched sadly on his times working embedded as a war correspondent covering military action in Iraq and Afghanistan. He stopped talking and fell silent for a moment in contemplation.

"In life, there are more experiences than you would imagine for which there are no words," he said. Everyone in the small circle individually knew the truth of his statement and nodded in silent agreement.

"We don't change the past by dwelling there. We heal by living fully in the present," said Mari to lighten the mood.

They moved on to other topics. By the end of the evening, Roberto had given Joseph the Maya nickname of *Tem Chen*, deep well. It suited him.

As the hour grew late, Joseph stood up and politely offered Hannah the crook of his outreached arm. "May I escort you to your chambers?" She looped her arm through his and rested a hand on his forearm. He casually placed his hand over hers, the very proper hand of a protective male.

"*Can she feel my elevated heart rate? Obviously not, based on her cool demeanor,*" he decided. "*Hannah is nothing but professional. I am here for a story. There is obviously no personal interest on her part,*" he scolded himself. "*We will do the site inspection and interview and I will never see her again.*" Joseph nodded in discipline and determination. His mind was made up, but it forgot to tell his heart about the decision. All this internal chatter ran through his brain as they walked in silence the twenty meters to her oval thatched casita.

"Good night, milady. See you in the morning for an escorted tour of your jungle wonderland." He turned, clicked his dusty boot heels like a soldier and walked away. He fetched a bucket of water and entered his own abode without looking back. Hannah heard him inside his hut splashing and washing himself and perhaps his clothes. He was humming and quietly whistling musical pieces from Phantom of the Opera. There was a certain joy and comfort in the vagabond reporter's presence in camp.

CHAPTER 28

Edzna, Campeche
Present Day

Diffused early morning light came through the open doorway and woke Hannah. Before she opened her eyes she smiled, looking forward to the day ahead. She took a little extra time getting ready. Wearing her favorite green print cotton shirt and khaki cargo pants, she emerged from the hut. She put on a big smile because Mari taught her that her day would go the way the corners of her mouth turned.

Mari and her new garden volunteer Joseph were already in the yard picking oranges and avocados from nearby trees for breakfast. A black and white turkey, that would probably be their last camp dinner, strutted and fanned its way in and out of huts at will.

"Good morning," he waved. "Let's get an early start so the light will be better for my photographs. A really tasty chocolate drink is waiting for you on the table. We'll join you in a moment," he shouted across the way and threw her a dimpled smile.

Obviously the journalist knew something about exploring in the wild. He came prepared with good boots, broad sun hat, plenty of water and provisions in his backpack and a telescoping red-strapped hiking stick that he also used as a tripod.

Before they left the main site, Hannah checked on the progress of closing down excavations. Grid units in the plaza and atop mounds, which before were covered with meshed plastic roof tarps on poles to protect workers from the brutal sun, now remained secured with those same heavy plastic sheets and anchored down with rocks and dirt. Coverings over test pit openings and a permanent guard living in the camp might safeguard and preserve some of the work until next year.

"Good, the local staff took the latest finds back to the lab," Hannah noted. The crew had packed up and returned to the compound to clean and label the artifacts with site codes.

"I keep impeccable records of location and strata where we find everything. In a few hours the last of it will be boxed up and ready to take to the regional INAH center and museum in Merida." She explained more of their procedures to Joseph.

"Mexican anthropologists are happiest when they have final control and recovered objects don't leave their country. Too much has gone missing over the years,"

Joseph leaned over and picked up a pottery shard from the side of the pathway. "Look, it has part of a handle and some painting on the inside," he said. He was thrilled to touch something handmade that was hidden for so long. He put it back down where he found it, saying in a soft voice, "Don't worry, I wasn't going to take it. I have too many broken fragments in my life already."

'That clay piece you just held probably came from a previous site clearing. My first season here, we cleaned trees and rubble off the plaza and long building that faced the main pyramid. Dirt and debris were carted far down the trail. Two seasons ago, indications of something significant appeared in our old dump area, so we removed the huge piles and dug around. Guess what we found? A major temple fronted with a pair of stone sun god masks. Go figure," Hannah laughed at the memory.

"I have heard the old axiom that the best part of a site is often under your back dirt," he said. "I suppose you just proved it true."

"It's estimated that ancient people in the Yucatan peninsula numbered over a million. There are enough ruins and artifacts to keep an army of archaeologists busy well into the future," Hannah shared. "Let me show you the main five-story pyramid and then we'll go see where the looting took place."

On their excursion through the ruins, Joseph clamored all over the place taking pictures. He asked lots of questions about architectural and art styles, historical events, and the season's best artifact finds.

"Did the Maya perform human sacrifice?"

"On occasions like dedication of a major temple or to gift their gods with a defeated warlord or king's blood. Nothing like the Aztecs of Central Mexico, who believed they had to offer copious human blood daily to be sure the sun would rise every morning."

"I suppose when people couldn't figure out where the sun went at night or what caused lunar eclipses, that's how religions got created," said Joseph.

The brief pleasant morning cloud cover was quickly burned away. From horizon to horizon the cloudless sky was the same tint of blue. Relentless tropical sunlight filled the air, with an unremitting golden flood. Everything cowered beneath its hot rays.

"Good thing I got the best lit shots I needed early on. This kind of undiffused, pure light turns every reflective surface into glares, painful to look at and harder to capture on film," he commented as he packed his equipment and stowed it in his daypack.

As they approached Edzna's towering acropolis, Joseph exclaimed, "Wow, the last time I saw a place this regal and spectacular, I had to cross a castle moat."

Together they climbed to the top of the steep pyramid. "Instead of constructing a stair wide enough to accommodate an average sized shoe, the Maya made their stone steps so narrow you need to turn your foot sideways to climb upward," Hannah cautioned.

She inched along the slope in a crablike way, aggressively pushing her feet into each carved stone niche for a foothold. She leaned in and used her arms to pull herself up the high risers. About half way, she felt small pebbles sliding under the heel of her left foot and a shower of gravel went tumbling down the side toward the jungle. Drops of nervous perspiration puddled between her breasts and rolled down her back.

Hannah tried desperately not to look down. She breathed deeply and swallowed hard to control her terror of heights, not wanting to expose this personal weakness to Joseph.

Shaking from anxiety and exertion, Hannah finally negotiated the last stretch. She collapsed on the top platform and lay flat out. Her trembling muscles felt like they would not yet support her to stand.

"How do you do this all the time?" exclaimed Joseph as he rolled over the top edge and crawled to the wall.

"I could barely keep my knees from whacking my chin on those steep bloody steps," he surprisingly echoed her own silent complaints. "My pounding heart could leap out of its own volition. No need for those ancient priests to cut it away," he joked. His humble reference to his own difficulties of climbing made Hannah feel better and braver. They took a minute to catch their breath.

"I counted. There were one hundred and eight steps to the top. Is that a significant number?"

"Oh, yes, it is very significant," Hannah leaned in with a secretive whisper, "That is how many steps they needed to reach the top."

Joseph's easy grin let her know that he appreciated her dry sense of humor. They sat and looked out over the flat landscape, a sea of undulating greens. The crowns of tall trees formed an unbroken forest of jungle canopy. It was more arresting than Joseph could have supposed. Each was thinking of the eons of history hidden at their feet.

"You know more lost cities and pyramids have been discovered in the Yucatan than in Egypt. Maya traditions and rituals survived over three thousand years. So much has been destroyed since the conquest and more is yet to be found," sighed Hannah.

"This temple we are leaning against is over twelve hundred years old," she said and pointed up at faded streaks of red, blue and green paint on the roofline where they sat.

"Speaking of age, when is your birthday?" he asked.

"I reach the big three-zero, thirty, on August 14th of this year."

"You have got to be kidding. That is my exact birthdate and year too," wide-eyed Joseph exclaimed. "Maybe we were twins, separated at birth," he smirked.

"Not very likely," laughed Hannah, holding her fair skinned and freckled arm up next to his dark complexion and hair. "Such opposites."

"Well, surely we are at least opposite sides of the same coin," he offered, turning a Mexican peso over between his fingers.

"Obviously you're the sunny side, *sol*, and I am the eagle side, *aguila*," he decided. "*Aguila and Sol.*"

Overhead the sun, in complete command, made the air dizzying with scorching heat. For a while they leaned against the cooler rocks and rested on the shady side of the pyramid crest. They shared an orange and drank water from a gourd canteen they passed back and forth. An unusual familiarity, trust and comfort flowed between them, like they were long time friends. Joseph sensed it, but didn't mention anything, for fear the closeness would evaporate or be awkward if Hannah did not feel the same.

After an easier climb zigzag down the main structure staircase, Hannah led Joseph to the temple where the looters had stolen the large limestone and plaster sun god mask. Sweeps of tree branches and bushy shrubs silently occupied and defended their territories, almost obscuring the narrow pathway to the plaza. Hundreds of different plant species fought for room. After a big rain, weeds and grasses grew rapidly in whatever crevices and cracks they could find. The jungle always tried to take back its own.

Hannah could not visit the sacked and vandalized spot without cringing and being flooded with red-hot anger at the invasion.

"What a nightmare to see a helicopter fly over, loaded with our priceless find," she lamented. "I felt personally violated," she responded to his unspoken question. "I don't know what more I could have done to prevent it. It's beyond frustrating."

He inspected where thieves hacked away at the temple face to remove the huge ancient god mask. Plunderers left chunks of plaster and carved stone remnants around the area. Sloppy hurried work. The vandalism took its toll on the temple, more so than time and nature. He jotted notes and snapped multiple photographs.

"Who knew of the treasures? Do you trust your own crew? Did the hypothetical robbers take anything else from your excavation?" he asked in rapid-fire succession.

Hannah's nostrils flared, "They are not hypothetical just because they haven't been caught yet," she replied in rancor. "Authorities shrug their shoulders, saying it's impossible to pursue such cases unless we catch them red-handed. Cutting through all the bureaucratic nonsense is like an Alice in Wonderland nightmare. There has to be some way to stop such plundering of the past."

"If consumers thought about stolen artifacts like they do poached elephant ivory, then we'd see some changes. Thefts of these types leave the sources destroyed. Let's see if we can shine some media light on the cockroaches and make them scatter," Joseph offered.

"You do understand," Hannah cried out. "Please write about this art heist. Use Edzna's robbery as an example of lost heritage and criminal greed. It could change public perception."

For the first time since the theft, she believed there was hope. She may never recover the ancient mask, but other looters might have a harder time selling or pawning their ill-gotten artifacts.

CHAPTER 29

Edzna, Campeche
Present Day

Hannah guided Joseph toward the outskirts of the archaeology zone. All around was the dangerous, waiting jungle. They left the main complex and took a winding path that led into dense vegetation. Vines hung down and connected branches like the rigging of a ship. Where they walked was more of a notion, rather than a true trail. Elusive potpourri of acrid odors, decaying wood and other scents that defied classification filled their nostrils. Myriads of unseen insects vibrated loudly, having undecipherable conversations in the undergrowth.

"I'm taking you to see a special discovery, but you have to stay on the footpath," warned Hannah. "This type of jungle gets so tangled that you can get lost even a few meters off course."

They walked on, submerged in the shadows of overhead tree branches. The leafy canopy spared them the sun's direct heat, but also sealed in humidity. Sweat trickled down their brows and shirts stuck to their backs. The ground itself seemed to perspire.

"Even though they didn't use the wheel, the ancient Maya had a complex highway system through these forests at one time. They built raised roads called *sacbes*. *Sac* is Mayan for white and *be* means road. The roadways were coated with marl, white lime cement. Sometimes builders added mica or other shiny reflective materials so people could travel at night in the dark. We've found evidence of roads that were five meters wide and went hundreds of kilometers in all directions," Hannah lectured on a favorite topics.

"You describe them as if you walked the great causeways yourself. I sure wish some of those raised plaster roads were available right now," he jested wistfully.

Rustling sounds in the nearby underbrush caused Joseph to freeze in place. Broad leafy branches parted and exposed an iridescent blue-green iguana out scrounging for food. It curtseyed up and down, inflated its wrinkled neck pouch and then scurried away.

"That scaly dragon thing was longer than my arm," exclaimed Joseph. He closed in on Hannah and heeded her advice about staying close and out of the brush. He put his trust in her knowledge of the terrain and sense of direction.

"Snakes three times or more your height live in these parts. But it's tiny vipers, like the fer-de-lance, that can stop your heart before you hit the ground," Hannah added, true, but with a teasing air.

Joseph received her information on the subject with raised eyebrows and facial expressions that read, 'Get out of here'. But figured she would not tease about a serious thing as deadly reptiles.

They continued through the jungle. Walls of green fought them continuously.

"Stay out and go back to where humans belong," Joseph mimicked plant voices. The unremitting sameness of flora blurred into a tunnel. The cover was absolute, pure jungle.

"This is how Moses and his tribe must have felt, walking between the green waves of the parted sea, not knowing whether the water would overwhelm them or not," Joseph tried to insert some humor into their foreboding trek. Here and there beams of sunlight peeked through narrow openings in the jungle canopy. He pushed aside an overhanging branch with his walking stick and was showered with dead leaves and other arboreal ammunition.

Hannah pointed out an old zapote tree with zigzag grooves cut into the bark to harvest *chicle*, chewing gum sap. "Chiclero gatherers climb the trees with spurs, like linemen climbing telephone poles, cut v-shaped gashes into the bark with machetes and bleed thick milky white gum out into bags. Any miscalculation can be fatal."

"For over a century, chicle sap was the base ingredient for chewing gum. Zapote trees only produce the gummy substance during the rainy season, so those hardy souls spend the absolute worst part of the year in this jungle. Many die after pathetically short lives and some lose their noses and ears to repeated and infected insect bites," she described hardships.

"And we thought we had it rough. Ours are such first world problems, nothing like pure jungle survival that others faced and still encounter today," sympathized Joseph. "Some of my own greatest lessons in humility came from nature."

"I wanted to bring you to this outlier part of the archaeological zone to show you a remarkable *stelae*, stone column we just found."

"Maya archaeologists call such large carved panels, stone trees, or *te tun*. Mari says there is no fruit on a banner stone tree, but we will be picking at this one a long time for information," Hannah said.

"Are there many of those big stone memorials around?" he asked.

"Places like Calakmul have plazas filled with multiple *stelae*, virtual forests of stone trees. A shaman once told me the figures are men, magicians who volunteered to be frozen in time. Someday those holy and divine essences will come alive again when the world is ready for Maya truths," she said solemnly. "I plan to make this *steale* and the plaza complex where it's erected my main focus in next year's excavation," she told Joseph.

To the untrained eye the jungle floor seemed cumbered with rocky piles smothered in green and large vine-tangled mounds from which trees towered upward. Right in front of them, half concealed in the foliage, stood large stone blocks of an old building spilling from a mound of earth split open by tree roots. Dense green growth had buried man's handiwork.

"My prize is right around here on the other side," she announced. "Okay, there it is."

Joseph merely saw a ridge bump snared in vines and covered with a frenzy of plants.

"Wow, we hid it to protect it until next year, but the jungle did an even better job of deeply embedding it. I almost missed it myself."

Hannah reached forward and parted the gnarled vine curtain. She tore aside vegetation that covered the solid column. Joseph planted his trekking pole in soft dirt nearby and helped her partially clear the stonework monument that lay tilted on its side, pulled down by long invading roots.

A once proud figure, with a face portrayed in life-like accuracy, stared out in sadness at his now desolate city. Larger than life, a male figure carved in bas-relief on a seven-foot stone canvas, stood resplendent in an elaborate feather headdress half his body size.

His torso was covered with ornately woven fabrics and a jaguar pelt cloak that hung to the ground, its tail twisting around his sandaled feet. He wore rows of jade bead collar necklaces. Both wrists were cuffed with oversized bracelets. The crook of his arm supported a baton symbolic of power. The carvings were deep and rich. Unspoiled details of the headdress feathers were particularly fine.

The noble face, in left profile and uplifted hand portrayed a sense of frozen movement, as if caught in a photograph. But it was the distinct individual facial features and parted lips that held Hannah and Joseph spell bound and silently studying the figure set against a painted bright red background.

"He appears ready to speak," whispered an awestruck Joseph.

"That's exactly what I said when I first saw him," she agreed.

"It took a lot of digging, cursing, lifting and propping to get this monumental stone even this far up. I was totally covered in red mud. Never thought I'd be able to wash the clay out of my hair.

"Does he have a name or date?" asked Joseph, trying to take his mind off visions of Hannah in a shower.

"I nicknamed him 'Big Red' because there are thick layers of original red paint on all four sides. We plotted him in relation to nearby structure mounds, photographed, and drew what we can see so far of the stone from every angle. I can't wait to get back and work on this area next season," Hannah explained. Her face beamed with smiles and bright eyes.

"These hieroglyphs on the side panels and front are threatened by slow amnesia of erosion, but we'll definitely be working on his true identity. Mayans, obsessed by time and dedicated to themes of its passage, dated this *stelae* with number glyphs and symbols, so we will be able to place him in a timeframe."

"How can you make sense of these round cornered symbols?"

"Most hieroglyphic script is laid out in a grid like a chest board. It is read left to right, top to bottom, in exactly paired columns. The symbols are based on both meanings and sound signs. This museum-quality specimen will yield lots of evidence, probably a combination of history and propaganda," she said.

"Gosh, your job is like Bones, C.S.I. and Laura Croft all in one," Joseph laughed. "To top it off, you work everyday in a place where humans were not meant to survive. That takes dedication and perseverance. I have a new appreciation for archaeology that you'll see in print," he said, as he took photographs of the stony proud dignitary in his feathered headdress.

"Gracias, Tem Chen," Hannah accepted the compliment. "Now we need to completely cover this fellow up so the wrong folks don't stumble across him. Then head back to camp."

They left Big Red peeking between camouflage branches, awaiting her return.

"We will go back a different way, a shortcut to make it quicker. The vegetation is especially thick along here," stated Hannah as she pushed and cut a way through the creepers.

"You don't say," said Joseph, noting the screen of constantly growing plants brushing along his body at every turn. Just the shades of green alone made him slightly dizzy. Even the most mundane plants glowed with an unusual intensity. He waded in a sea of leaves that lapped at his boots. A finely sculpted stone, a treasure that lay half-buried in the middle of the trail, caused him to stumble. All around him giant tree trunks with buttress roots gripped ancient building blocks like octopi.

"The jungle is not aggressive and does not attack like a savage animal. It is just masses of indifferent life, furiously growing like it's on speed and silently swallowing you whole," he said to Hannah.

"All this abundant life goes on without regard for humans. If a plant is stepped on, eaten or slashed away, another will rapidly take its place. There would be no change to the natural order of things," she answered, impressed with his insights.

The path degenerated into little more than a game trail, so Hannah used her machete more often. Her swinging rhythm went back and forth like a symphony conductor bringing the wind section into a rousing finale. They trekked on. Conversation dwindled to an occasional observation or question. Joseph stopped and fell back a bit trying for an accurate satellite fix or GPS reading. It was useless. Overhead cover was too thick, and electronic coverage too thin.

Despite generous applications of insect repellent, buzzing entourages of mosquitoes and other aberrant insects grew worse. Batting the swarms away did little good.

"Let's take a break under this tree," Hannah suggested.

Joseph took out a couple of cigarettes.

"I didn't know you smoked," said Hannah.

"Never have and never will. But there are other practical uses for them," he said as he tore open the papers and rubbed tobacco on Hannah's arms and neck. Then applied the same old campers' remedy to himself.

"That should keep away some of those bugs who seemed to have escaped from a science fiction movie."

"We'll be back on a local road that leads to the compound soon," Hannah said, trying to keep doubt out of her voice and assure herself that she'd taken the right path when they left the ancient statue. She'd made this hike many times, but a freshly broken branch caused her to pause and wonder if she'd strayed too far afield or gone in a circle in the trackless forest.

Jungle light turned from yellow white to a more golden glow. Hannah realized the sun rapidly headed west. She began calculating daylight left and amount of water they carried. She rolled a pebble around in her mouth to stave off thirst. She reviewed in her head how to make vine sleeping slings to keep them off the ground at night, away from devouring army ants and other night predators.

"*I'm not lost, just taking the scenic route*," she silently chided herself.

Then focusing on the path again, she realized she could not hear or see Joseph behind her.

"Are you there? Are you on the trail?" she called out. "Answer back."

"Marco-Polo. Aguila to your Sol," he chimed in from farther behind. She stood still waiting.

"Aguila---Sol, Aguila---Sol," they bounced back and forth until he came into sight.

"Stay close and do not lose sight of me again. The path is your lifeline, like an air tube that connects the diver to the surface. If it is broken…"

"If I got off the trail, couldn't I just call for help?"

"Ten paces away to either side, you can get lost and vanish. Shouting even at a short distance is of no use because thick vegetation muffles and screens the sound of your voice. When you step into the brush, it closes very quickly and all directions become the same," she warned.

Hannah pressed forward with Joseph close behind. The trail took a barely perceptible gradient upward. She recalled this familiar part of the way back. She turned and nodded to Joseph to indicate the end of their jungle trek. A fallow field with a partially uncovered mound appeared to their left. The air smelled of smoke from the farmer's slash burning.

Hannah sighed in relief. The emerald wall opened and the two wanderers stood on a rutted road at the edge of the pathless woods.

"Well, we made it," Hannah announced unnecessarily, smiling as if nothing unusual had happened. *Hopefully, Joseph never suspected my moments of hesitation and disorientation*, she thought, not forgetting that he was a writer here to evaluate and report.

After feelings of being lost in the vivid capsule called a tropical rain forest, Joseph was relieved to see the narrow opening to the road and feel safe again. When they emerged from the overgrowth, he subdued his impulse to kiss the ground. His spirits soared like a bright kite into the open blue sky above him.

Joseph crossed himself and shouted, "Hail Mary, blessed are thou!" He stacked up three or four rocks, bowed dramatically and said, "I erect a shrine to celebrate our deliverance."

He smiled broadly, grabbed both Hannah's hands to join in a little victory gig dance. It was amazing how quickly theatrics and laughter dissolved the tension.

They fell into a cadence step and continued moving east toward the camp compound. It was the last night of the archaeology season and Hannah had to prepare herself physically and emotionally for the departure.

CHAPTER 30

Edzna, Campeche
Present Day

Farewells often come in waves. People always moved on in a profession like archaeology, especially seasonal fieldwork excavations that lasted approximately January through May. Just the nature of her chosen field. Hannah was determined she'd handle the last evening in camp with a certain amount of efficiency and bravery. She'd miss the intense work, but mostly miss the good times with Roberto, Mari and the workers. They became, as the Maya would say, *iiches*, great friends. Goodbyes and going forward had created new challenges. But they also made Hannah face the only challenge that truly belonged to her, that of solitude.

Mari cleared out her hut and the supply shed, giving most of the provisions to the remaining guard. What wouldn't be used in the off-season was distributed to local workers before they returned to their villages. A bag of rice or a metal pot could make a life or death difference to an indigenous family who subsided on next to nothing, living day-to-day like birds.

Functioning as their own social welfare service agency, Mexican friends and families helped each other out. Whether it was food, jobs or health issues, they depended on others. No matter what level of society, extended family was everything.

Mari's abandoned garden would become home to wild bees and butterflies. Hannah and Roberto made sure the diggers and masons had their earned pay and a bit more for all the hard work and sacrifices made by the team.

The last night in camp, the foursome feasted on Mari's gourmet camp meal. Hannah was right; the strutting turkey was nowhere to be seen. Pavo pibil, fowl roasted with herbs and vegetables in banana leaves, was appreciated by all.

"I'm as full as a ranch dog," said Roberto, patting his rounded stomach. After dinner he and Hannah completed a final pack of the four-wheel drive vehicle they would take out first thing in the morning. Everything was covered with a waterproof canvas tarp and secured with ratcheting tie-downs.

"Listen," said Mari, putting her hand to her ear. "Hear the motmot bluebird's voice? Big rains are coming."

"Also the toads' plaintive cries of 'buoooh' come from the forest," said her son. "The noise can be deafening, but it is welcomed as a sign that replenishing rains are coming."

By dusk, thick charcoal-colored thunderhead clouds filled the eastern skies and claps of thunder rumbled through the air. As predicted by nature's creatures, the sky opened up and drenched the compound in a warm but soaking downpour. This was no mere rain shower. The storm, a powerful pounding roar, filled the evening air with cubic masses of falling water. Hard tropical rain drummed the roof like rapidly tapping fingers.

Hannah, Mari, Roberto and Joseph gathered in Mari's large hut. Various sized and aged stools and chairs, with nothing in common but their rickety condition, were scattered around the patio. Hannah and Joseph chose to swing in the hammocks.

"Old man Chac, the rain god saying it is time to go," commented Roberto.

"This is why digging has to stop," he pointed skyward. "We need to return before the back roads wash out or turn into muddy mires. Even if we stayed, our excavations would come to a halt. Heavy rains would force us to retreat early every afternoon and spend the next morning bailing out the pits," he said to Joseph. But he nodded in Hannah's direction, as if he still needed to convince her why she must leave her site and work elsewhere for a while.

"Time, it turns out, is more difficult to budget than money. It feels wonderful to complete such a productive season. But my pleasure is also mixed with an ache of absence, a void where all my fieldwork used to be," said Hannah to conclude the topic.

"Hey, Tem Chen, on a scale of one to Lord of the Rings, how far did Hannah make you walk today?" Mari kidded their guest.

"A lot farther than I am used to and into incredible places even Frodo would balk at. Everything about this place is intense---the colors, heat, tastes, and rain," Joseph said, holding his hand under the roof's overflow stream.

Roberto laughed in agreement and said good night. He ran through the downpour to his hut to prepare for the next day's journey.

Joseph and Hannah took seats in suspended woven hammocks under Mari's larger veranda. They fell into a gentle swaying pace, like the hammock maker's shuttle passing in and out, to and fro across the warp.

For a while Hannah fell into a pattern of swinging toward Mari's cascading red flower hanging basket, touching the flowers and swinging back.

"You are like a hummingbird," Joseph declared at the sight.

The night air was cooler and fragrant from the now intermittent rain. Hannah saw bats weaving back and forth soundlessly between the compound huts. They were swift and erratic against the dark sky. As lights went out she only sensed them as movements across the courtyard.

Joseph was a man with special charms that drew people to him. Hannah liked being the sole focus of his attention for a short while. They talked about their lives and dreams. Joseph shared stories about trekking in Turkey, being chased by a rogue elephant in

India, and getting caught in a typhoon in the South Pacific.

"My life is based on a true story. Born and raised in New Zealand," he started. "There are about 40 million sheep and four million people, who are allowed to roam free. I have a great family. I am the oldest. I have four brothers and one sister. My dad tells people he has 'all girls but five'." Joseph's lips curved into a wide infectious smile, showing off his dimples.

"Mum and Dad worked hard in their printing business to provide us with food, shelter and decent educations. My youngest brother Gino stepped in to help run the family firm. He does a super job. Thank goodness. I was free to follow my dream of being a photojournalist. I was never one to work at an office desk day in and day out. I need to have a varied life, not a flat one. Mundane and ordinary are lethal."

"What are two things you could not live without?" Hannah asked.

"Books and horses," he replied quickly. My family lives in the countryside and I get to train and ride regularly when I am home. I'm curious and love the written word and storytelling."

"Tell me about your writing work."

"I am first an observer. I watch from the margins and fringes. I can't get too involved personally in what I research or it would ruin my objectivity. After I study, ask questions and listen. I can tell the world what I have found. I love the thrill of discovery. By writing I live the experiences twice."

"We are alike in that respect. We're both detectives, interested in finding the truth: who, what, why, when and how," commented Hannah. "It is exciting to find something created by people of a great and vanished civilization, that was covered centuries ago and lain unseen since. What other occupation offers moments like those? I try to tell tales to forge connections between the past and our own times. My news tidbits are just a little older than yours."

Little lights of amusement and respect gleamed in his eyes and she smiled in recognition. Mari told her once that 'you don't make friends, you recognize them'.

"My life has been quite different than yours," Hannah started. "My mother died soon after I was born. I don't have a single recollection of her; only what my dad told me and by making up my own stories from a few faded photographs. My father Max pretty much raised me by himself. He is a librarian and book restoration specialist at a major university in California. So I grew up as an only child in a huge city. I took refuge and joy in the books surrounding me. I was always the girl who talked about books the way other girls talked about rock stars."

"What were your favorite books?" he asked.

"Probably read all the Nancy Drew adventure books as a child. I even organized a Mystery Club. I loved solving puzzles with Nancy and her friends George and Bess. But when I read *Incidents of Travel in the Yucatan* by John Lloyd Stephens and Frederick Catherwood, I knew I would become an archaeologist and focus on the Maya civilization. I have several versions of their two illustrated volumes, both hardback and softback. Not first editions from 1843, of course, but many others. I usually go for assignments in the Yucatan to dig. Sort of my Trevi Fountain, I always return."

"I worked several years at the Los Angeles Country Museum of Natural History," Hannah continued. "Competitive, but some of my best times ever. As you know, in the academic world, professors have to publish or perish. It's the same in archaeology and museumology, we must publish, have exhibits and constantly write grant proposals to get funding to continue our work."

Hannah looked deep into Joseph's eyes as she spoke. She had almost forgotten what it felt like to sit with a man and just talk. Better yet, to have him pay attention to her and really listen.

"*He recognizes me, the me under all these external things I use to label myself,*" she thought gratefully. She'd missed having a boyfriend, but this would all end tomorrow. She accepted that Joseph was a professional doing his job. "*He probably views this time together for what it is; two ships connecting in the night, nothing more,*" she tried to convince herself. Her mind waivered between interest and sadness, and then interest again. She was not certain which she should feel.

That short night there was room for nothing but truth between them.

"I can see we both live lives of isolation and wrestle with inner questions," commented Hannah.

"Both of us sacrifice a lot to seek so intangible a thing as meaningful work. Luckily, we are passionate about what we do. I feel sorry for blokes who dread to go to work and do jobs just for money. To labor for any reason other than love is prostitution."

"Most people live and die in the same corner. Writers get to travel and work all over the world, while scholars usually dedicate a lifetime to one area of study," Hannah added, comparing their diverse fields.

"It is okay to live a life that others don't understand. However, I've been thinking that it's time to explore other avenues. Our lives shouldn't be either-or. Better to have a combination of what we need personally and what can serve our vocations," Joseph shared.

"One of my biggest challenges is distinguishing between passion and addiction to work," Hannah said.

"Passion completes and addiction depletes," he answered. "I know from personal experience.

"*Hannah is an amazing woman, but for some reason she's chosen a solitary journey. She has something in her past that is shaping her life. I don't know what it is, but I know it can't be ignored,*" Joseph thought.

He asked more questions about the site, the robbery and excavating the red statue. Hannah responded factually, and tried not to say anything too controversial that might appear in print. She spoke with open admiration about INAH Director Sarra, as her mentor and key to her future.

Mari heard them whispering and laughing out on her veranda. From a lifetime of experience she knew that threads of intimacy were spun through humor. Bit by bit they tested uncharted waters and shared secrets. If asked they would have said Hannah was still answering questions about archaeology for the article and they were just becoming better acquainted. Whether they realized it or not, the connections they forged were far stronger than a brief encounter. Mari smiled at this joining of spirits. The only problem she could see for them came in the form of one museum director who was used to getting whatever he wanted.

As tired as Hannah and Joseph were, neither wanted to break the evening's spell and call it quits. They stayed suspended together in a space where neither consequence nor time mattered. Finally, they left the porch to the somber embraces of the night, and stumbled off to their respective huts to catch some sleep before the next day's drive back to the city.

CHAPTER 31

Edzna, Campeche
Present Day

"*Co'oneex*, Let's go!" shouted Roberto as he put the expedition's old Jeep in gear. The windshield wipers gave an unexpected and inadvertent salute. With transmission grinding and a few bronco lurches, the team of four roared onto the overgrown passageway.

Hannah looked back. There was a brillant rainbow over the site. It was taken as an apology for angry skies of the night before. She kissed her fingertip and held it up to the window glass in farewell.

Although evenly loaded, the vehicle bounced all over the rutted gravel road. Joseph and Hannah made for additional ballast sitting in the backseat. The narrow pot-holed lane winding through the jungle made the journey tedious. At times the four-wheel vehicle moved so slowly through the chlorophyllic grasp that it appeared to be grazing between the trees.

Joseph mimed closing an invisible curtain and zipping it up to separate them from Mari and Roberto in the front. He held up four fingers before her eyes. "Four hours," he silently mouthed. She knew he was referring to how much time left before they went separate directions. His blue eyes pierced and held hers with an unreadable expression.

They shared more details about family, work and ambitions. Hannah's eyes grew heavy with exhaustion and her head began to nod forward to her chest.

"It's the late night and rocking car, not the company," she tried weakly to excuse her sleepiness. Joseph smiled sympathetically and patted his shoulder, indicating that she should rest a while in more comfort. She slowly folded herself against his broad chest and his arm moved around to steady her. She smelled sunshine and citrus soap in his white cotton shirt. She felt safe. She heard him whisper her name as she fell asleep.

Although his body craved rest too, his mind couldn't stop. He watched Hannah. Light through the window caught the golden highlights of her hair, framing her head like a glowing halo. Her face was calm, but as she went into a deeper sleep and began to dream, he saw furrows of worry crease her forehead. Strong yearnings stirred within Joseph. He wanted to protect and lift the burdens from this precious person. Even though he knew that kind of thinking was dangerous, he put his cheek against the crown of her head, in half kiss and half comfort.

"*If I told her about this surreal connection I feel, she would probably go all rational and scientific on me,*" he chuckled to himself. "*She has not done or said one thing to indicate that she might be interested in returning my sentiments. Silence and restraint are the best ways to deal with my feelings for now.*" Joseph felt the muffling weight of self-doubt for the first time in a long time.

The dirty expedition jeep pulled up to the air terminal in Merida less than the two required hours before Joseph's plane was due to leave. While Roberto and Hannah got his pack untangled from the cargo on top, Joseph watched Hannah.

Mari caught him staring, so he leaned over to her and shyly admitted, "Wanting to get close to a person is not an emotion I'm used to. I am the one usually being pursued. Hannah clearly is not of the same mind," he lamented.

"Your destinies are more closely affixed to each other than you might believe," said Mari. "Give it time."

Joseph tapped his black covered passport against his palm and addressed the three new friends before him. "Thanks for the hospitality and interviews. Time at your archaeology site has been an eye-opener in so many ways. I am headed to New York to write this article and then off to wherever I'm needed next." Joseph gave quick goodbye hugs to everyone.

He looked down at the pavement to find the right last words to say to Hannah. Finding nothing that wouldn't give him away, he turned and walked away.

Before Hannah had a chance to utter a farewell, Joseph was gone. She watched him stride across the wide sidewalk and disappear into the airport terminal. She expected her new acquaintance to leave after his assignment was over, but what she didn't expect was how final his departure felt. It was like she would never see him again.

The trio drove into Merida's historic center where Mari and Roberto owned an older colonial house four blocks from the main plaza. The stone and stucco building had been home to the Oc family for seven generations. It was simple, but always a welcoming oasis for friends.

Hannah and Roberto took the last shipment of artifact boxes to the Merida INAH offices. Their site records and prized discoveries were turned in as required by law and ethics. They knew from prior experience, most crates were unceremoniously placed in the institute's huge storage warehouse to be dealt with later, if ever.

Hannah would spend the next six months in Mexico City at INAH Headquarters or the Anthropology Museum. Her personal time was marked for researching and documenting mid-1600 era pottery that she believed were reproductions of long lost codex books. The lady dirt detective was investigating a case of great importance to her and to Maya history.

CHAPTER 32

July 1562
Mani, Yucatan

Diego De Landa's bonfire of Mayan books and humans blazed with unearthly intensity. Itz's father had just sacrificed his life in a futile attempt to save their people's heritage. He was murdered for trying to pull ancient texts from the flames.

Itz stood in a daze, shaking from the nightmare she witnessed. Her soul was mad with pain and rage. Old friends of Ko'h grabbed her by the arms and whisked her out of Mani to the roadway as quickly as they could. Two promised to stay behind to retrieve the charred bones of the honorable scribe and take them to her aunt Yaxche in Edzna. Itz couldn't look at their faces as they murmured words too incredulous to comprehend. They did not look directly at her either, shattered in grief.

Alone, she stumbled along the narrow white path across the kilometers to their remote village. Vivid memories of burning relics and bodies played before her eyes over and over again. Her thoughts went out of the world to somewhere utterly dreamlike as she wandered. Twice she leaned over the edge of the causeway to vomit up her disgust.

"Father," she screamed to the silent gray sky. Bird and monkey cries told her the day was fading. Daylight extinguished itself without apology.

She reached home as a cold moon sank between the dark clouds. The sky had opened up and water hammered down. Drenching rains soaked her to the skin. She didn't care enough to cover her head. She walked right through tea-colored puddles and along muddy paths. The downpour washed the dust of many days from the jungle plants and roadway plaster.

"Nothing could wash away this stench of death," Itz cried.

She shook her long wet hair vigorously and twisted her clothes to wring out water and mud before entering the dark house. Itz fell exhausted onto her sleeping platform and curled up in the pallet blankets. The chilling wetness of her dress did not faze her.

Unrelenting rain pounded down on the thatched roof, cooling the night air. Cascades of water ran down the stairs and flooded the plaza. Strong winds banged her door coverings, and rapidly blew inside like a bold guest. A flicking reed torch was her only companion. She looked through the window into the dark night.

"*Let it keep on pounding the empty steps all night. I have no place to go and no one else is coming home.*"

Heartsick, arrows of grief and terror overcame her. The path between fear and hate is a short one. Fury rose within Itz like the head of a cornered snake. Anger became her prayer and her protest. It gave her a sense of being in charge of life. Outrage temporarily served as a protection against the emptiness and helplessness that clawed at her.

"*Superstitious fool. Burning scholars and libraries. De Landa's attempt to save our souls has set the world back centuries and condemned humanity to ignorance,*" she fumed.

Days passed slowly. There was little energy or order in her life. She often forgot to brush her hair or eat. She avoided looking into the pyrite mirror. Seeing earth brown eyes that looked like her father's sent her into uncontrolled sobbing.

Several mornings Itz woke up anxious to talk with her father about a new idea. It took a moment for her to remember that he was gone. Impulses that had become habitual were frustrated and stopped cold by reality. It amazed her how absence and silence could be so loud and so painful.

She discovered that sorrow and grief were really love that gathered up inside and had nowhere to go. All the love she had for her father but could no longer give him sat in the hollow part of her chest and spilled out of the corners of her eyes.

Itz took her pitcher to the well and stood wondering how she got there and why she came that way. Heightened by seclusion and solitude, sadness hit with double force. Her world fragmented like shards of a broken clay pot. Try as she might, she could not put it back together.

Yaxche arrived as soon as she received the tragic news of her brother's death. Her son, Etz'nab, guided her to the village hideaway. Itz fell like an orphaned child into her aunt's comforting arms. The wise healer knew that no words could mend her broken niece. Being close and listening were the best remedy.

"Events in Mani unfolded so fast. The lies, horror and slaughter," she sobbed. "I felt helpless. Now I am lost. I can't live in the same world as my father's murderers."

Something more than fear and worst than anger reflected in Itz's eyes.

"An evil wind, *kaz ik tu betah*, surely swept through," whispered Yaxche. "Don't let wild thoughts rule you."

"Your father died bravely for what he believed," added Etz'nab, crossing his arms in respect for his brave uncle. "Ko'h stayed with us years longer than the oppressors intended."

"My scholarly brother taught you well. You are ready to carry on without him," Yaxche assured her trembling niece.

"Sorrow and wrath burn up my judgment and my life. Those strangers who are not us, *dz'ulu'ob*, have taken over our world and destroyed everything and everyone in their way. I am afraid."

"Obviously, fear does not halt death, but it has the power to stop life if you let it," advised Yaxche. "The earth longs to feel your bare feet and the winds delights in caressing your long hair. Get up and go out again."

Itz rose to bathe and prepare a meal for her guests. "The only way out of grief is through it. The best way to honor my father is to finish our works and preserve ancient truths. Like my books, I have to turn the folded page and press forward."

Itz lit beeswax candles and placed fresh flowers around the *canche*, low wooden stool where her father had sat and chatted with her only weeks before. The candle's light flickered on the back wall, as if it were the dancing shadow spirit of the departed scribe.

"Now I understand why our words for love and pain have the same *yah* sounds. There is never one without the other. My dear father is gone and I cannot follow. I will never forget the past, but my purpose is here and now," announced a revitalized Itz, much to her family's relief.

Determined to continue her project right away, Itz organized the center courtyard workspace and sorted the supplies that her aunt and cousin brought with them. Yaxche and Etz'nab started their tearful goodbyes.

"Hundreds of men from around the area have been conscripted by the Catholic friars for a work project in Izamal. If I don't report this week, there will be consequences. As usual with the Spanish, we have no choice."

"I will accompany merchants to town and come to see you at the work camp before the moon is full," promised Itz.

"Bring your delicious tamales and some frothy chocolate drink," her cousin requested with a boyish smile. He and his mother waved as they walked through the town arch and away into the jungle foliage. Itz smiled when she heard him practice bird whistles long after he was out of sight.

CHAPTER 33

1562 A.D.
Yucatan

Itz rose with the lemony morning sun. For the first time in ages, she noticed the bright red color and fragrance of the bougainvillea that spread ruffled arms up and over the courtyard wall. She breathed in undiluted morning air. A green ringed iguana lumbered over and cocked its dragon-like head back and forth at her. He hissed and shook his leather jowls until she threw him pumpkin seeds from her breakfast tray. Satisfied, he scurried away to a high rock to bask in the direct sun.

Itz liked a certain amount of ritual and organized routine in her work. She took out her favorite animal hair and bird feather brushes and lined them on top of low tables on either side of her. She used several different conch shell and gourd containers for her inks and paints.

Black paint was made from charcoal or manganese oxides. She created her special blue paints from indigo leaves and *anil* plants, clay minerals and copal, *pom*. By heating them together, she could achieve a beautiful brilliant *kaan* sky and turquoise water-colored pigments that stayed true.

"*Did the sky just sigh with envy at the gorgeous blue I took out of my pottery kiln pit?*" Itz laughed proudly as she put a finished platter on the shelf.

She mixed various organic hues of green to use in pictures of trees and young corn maize. Orange-reds came from iron-rich clays she found in the caves, as well as ground hematite. The orange paint in her largest shell bowl glowed hot and intense.

Her richest red colors came from cochineal insects that lived on the back of *nopal* cactus leaves.

"*To look at the white powdery beetles, who would think that when crushed it would yield a royal purple hue that I turn into red paint*," said Itz.

She remembered when her aunt showed her how the red from cochineal could be used as paint, dye, cosmetics or medicine for intestinal ailments.

Purples came from a *caracol* or sea snail found at the coast. Her vibrant yellows were created with ground turmeric roots from Chiapas to the west. Additionally, her paint box contained salmon colors from rock lichens and browns from crushed cooked nuts.

She mixed certain paints with mica to make them glow in the sun. Like the mica mixed in temple stuccos to give the sacred sites a lustrous dazzling appearance. Stucco was prepared with an organic adhesive from the local *holol* tree, mixed with burned limestone and *sascab*, a natural occurring mineral that did not need to be burned. The outer layer was a finer ground limestone with barita, finer than the sascab.

Itz made clay slips from a mixture of minerals and colored clays. Preparing thin quicklime, she added finely ground mineral pigments that would dissolve in firing to create rich greens and blues. Other potters used mostly black, red and cream, but Itz wanted her pieces to be as lifelike as possible. To increase durability, whenever she could get it, she would mix volcanic ash with her clay.

In spite of the catastrophic life experiences that had struck and overwhelmed Itz's soul, she found that art reminded her that she still had a soul.

On many of her ceramic vessels, to honor her father, she would include a scribe somewhere on the piece. She'd place the symbol of writing, a rabbit transcribing the scenes she portrayed on the pottery. She drew *juun* glyph symbols for books or the symbol *ah tz'ibob*, for one who paints. Many times Itz would sign her work with an inverted lily symbol or leave her thumb imprint.

For ages, scribes and artists were commissioned to create special pieces to be used as funerary offerings, gifts between rulers, dedication markers, and ceremonial cups for foods or cacao drinks. Itz fondly remembered royal collections of art at her uncle's palace.

"*I know my work is as fine, but such artistic pieces would draw too much attention. I will continue to create and paint pottery that passes on information, yet something subtle enough we can wave under the noses of the invaders.*"

Occasionally, when her hands were tired from holding a writing quill or paintbrush, Itz would put her fingers back into cool slippery clay. For diversion she formed statuettes of noble women or men standing tall or seated in dignified postures. Her figures wore elaborate tunics and woven skirts. They were adorned with sumptuous jeweled necklaces, bracelets and earrings. Sometimes she would construct detachable headdresses decorated with flowers and exotic feathers.

Her favorite piece was one where the lady's hair has been stylishly cut back from her intentionally slanted forehead, with long braids interwoven with ribbons, flowing down the back. The noble clay woman carried a bobbin of yarn to offer to the goddess of weaving in her left hand and a woven fan, the symbol of a high-ranking noble in her right.

Itz had fun reproducing the traditional designs of the *huipil* dresses with borders of flowers or *quechquemitl* yokes of her countrywomen, as well as the finery for royal models. She embellished her works with designs featuring jaguars, birds, fish, or owls. She depicted handmade figurines with such fidelity, it seemed they had returned from the dead.

But her most important task was recording medicinal formulas, mathematics, myths and histories of her people. She first made the plates, vases, cups and other ceramic vessels. Then set about painting them with a series of long-remembered book topics. Destroyed books lived again in a more durable form of clay.

She spent weeks copying Chame style, centuries old works. Cylindrical vases bore distinctive black and white chevron motif bands painted around the rim and base. She applied bright white and strong red and black palette to distinctive yellow to yellow-orange backgrounds. Continuous scenes wrapped around the cylinder.

Itz knew that no seed in the warm earth ever experienced being a tall tree with wind blowing through its branches and no caterpillar ever saw its colorful butterfly wings or felt the exhilaration of flight, but she recognized the possible invisible connections. She visualized the impact her artwork could have on unseen others, and that helped draw her creativity forth.

CHAPTER 34

1562 A.D.
Izamal, Yucatan

People only see what they expect to see. Itz walked by old acquaintances unrecognized. Her black hair with its bluish highlights, now fell in long braids with bangs. A hand-woven headscarf hid her facial markings and scar. She traveled about freely as a simple peasant, trekking the roads and forest paths with pottery wrapped in a *rebozo* shawl to look like a sleeping child slung over her back. She passed by invisible to the soldiers who didn't suspect that a shuffling subservient female carried hieroglyphic books and pottery to be secreted away for the future.

Itz completed her tedious recording of the books of ancient knowledge her father dictated months before. She created several copies of her aunt Yaxche's medicinal journals, memorizing many natural healing techniques as she worked. She carefully wrapped her reproductions in animal hides, sealed with wax and concealed them in caves and behind walls and under floors in deserted temples and homes. She said she would do this text work and she'd kept her promises.

Now Itz's work focused on pottery creations. In addition to figurines and polychrome vases, she developed a line of plain wares for household use. Stoneware pottery sales funded her works and gave her reasons to visit other locations unnoticed as a market merchant.

On one occasion she sold a large platter decorated with corn plants to a Spanish missionary. Her cousin Etz'nab laughed hysterically as he told her about seeing her creation on the new church's altar. Little did the foreigners know the border designs were stylized symbols of Yum Kax, the god of good corn, who represented both strength and life. Other Maya recognized the symbols, smiled to themselves, but said nothing.

It took weeks to develop and create a series of ceramic dishes with a new design she thought would appeal to the Spanish. Once again she took a Mayan hieroglyphic symbol and disguised it into a repetitive design. This time her choice was the symbol *juun* for book. It was an oval with three lines diagonally across the center with a band of glyphs and two dots on each side of the lines. When elongated and a slight twist added, it took on the appearance of rope encircling the edges.

"The Spanish love their ropes," Itz explained the pattern to her cousin. "They use them for ships, horses, binding and hanging."

The irony of the word *book, book, book* repeated over and over on their tables was her intention. Itz created entire sets of cups, plates and bowls with the *juun* symbol made to look like rope borders.

She couldn't stop herself from spitting into each batch of the clay and paint mixtures. "*Curse you white demons. May you be poisoned with my venom of hate. I pray you leave our lands.*"

Itz decided to accompany village merchants to Izamal, a town being built by forced laborers, including her cousin. She packed up ceramic dishes for sale and enough supplies to stay a while. Two young load bearers helped her carry the goods to market.

Farmers and other vendors carrying various products on their backs held by a strap braced by the forehead, trudged in single file along the old white roads. Near one of the new grid and plat towns where the government forced natives to live, she saw burned buildings and fields where villages once thrived. The Spanish cut down the trees and polluted drinking waters so residents would not return to their former homes.

The pure Spanish lived in the three walled cities of Merida, Valladolid and Campeche. Their hired indigenous allies from around central Mexico lived outside their towns to serve as household help and protection from rebellious or marauding natives. Various old nobility of the Maya, *caciques*, were allowed to own land and oversee their area subjects in exchange for payment of tribute, such as cloth, salt, corn and slaves. Francisco Montejo, the founder of Merida, included slaves in his tax submissions to the Governor of Cuba.

Many villagers were relocated to pre-planned towns that centered about a large church, plaza and government buildings. The church and administrators believed this was the best way to supervise and control the Indian masses. Tributes were collected in these centralized locations.

Priests from the Old World were accustomed to populations in concentrated areas, not spread throughout the jungles. Friars felt they would be unable to save souls and oversee their converted flocks if they had to administer to hundreds of small remote compounds instead of one large center. Salvation, taxes and safety were how they rationalized the repatriation of entire populations to sterile new towns.

"Where are the fruit groves or the *milpa* corn and vegetable fields? Can't the fools see this experiment will fail? Thousands die of starvation and disease. Do they even care?" a tired old man walking next to her asked as they trudged into the settlement called Izamal.

Itz took her ceramic goods to the merchants' area. She swayed to the sweet hum of life found in the marketplace. Under palm thatched stalls or spread out on blankets, bright and fragrant jumbles of items tempted buyers.

Vast arrays of lemons, beans, squash, multi-colored corns, sweet potatoes, onions, strange fruits and stranger vegetables filled the senses. Wild turkeys hung by their legs like upside down flower bouquets. Pigs, iguanas and other livestock awaited their fate.

Caged chattering monkeys and colorful plumed birds speaking Mayan filled in any lull in the buzz of commerce. Popular booths sold tortillas, cloth, pots, baskets and useful everyday items, while others in the shadows sold mysterious sweets and alcoholic beverages like *balche* and wines.

Itz set up a three-sided palm covered lean-to and spread out her pottery for sale. She sat upon a low wooden stool and zealously bargained, bartered and chatted with throngs of browsers, buyers and other sellers. A young Indian boy was sent to locate her cousin and somehow informed him that she was in town.

Etz'nab found Itz sleeping on a ground mat in the lean-to among her remaining pottery. It had been a successful day. Her plan worked. Several foreigners or their household servants purchased dishes with the *huun* book symbols. Strange how an inside joke brought her such joy and revenge.

"Wake up Itz. I only have a few moments," Etz'nab gently shook her shoulders. She sat up and embraced her cousin. He involuntarily winced and stiffened as she touched his back. Spots darkened where blood soaked through and crusted on the thin fabric of his tunic.

"What have they done to you?" Her eyes burned with shock and fury.

"It is nothing compared to some," he replied, embarrassed to have his painful condition discovered.

"The overseers say we are too slow and lazy. Their solution is the whip. They are not the ones in the heat and dust of construction, carrying big rocks for grand buildings."

"How did you get away from the workers' camp?"

"You know a rabbit like me can always find a back door or friend to let me through a crack in the wall. I must return soon or they will punish the others. We can meet in three days while the white men are at church services. Come back behind the church, outside where they allow us to listen."

Itz rummaged through her cloth bundle to hand him the tamales he'd requested and salve to relieve pain and keep his wounds from getting infected.

"Take this. It is one of your mother's remedies. I will make more for you and the other workers before Sunday." She hated to see him return to the barbarians' forced labor camp confines.

The next day Itz caught sight of her cousin and other laborers as they carried unimaginably heavy loads up the steps of a house being built for the new governor. Backs bent and muscles tensed with every step under their burdens. The conquistadors used stones they removed from nearby ancient pyramids. Many still had temple engravings and bits of colorful plaster and painted designs. Marked pieces were turned inward during construction, so only the plain chiseled rock sides were exposed.

Hundreds of men slaved in the heat. They groaned under stone weights. Lungs gasped for air and stomachs growled. Itz did not see any sign of water or food for the spent and feeble workers. Those who collapsed were taken away, most never seen again.

"*The conquerors dispense suffering without reason, otherwise they would not be feared or obeyed,*" thought Itz. She saw De Landa once through the church doorway, with his hands raised in prayer, appealing to his 'most mericiful God'---hands that were crimson with the blood of innocents. He and his kind terrified her.

On Sunday Itz joined her cousin for Mass behind the huge stone church. Standing next to Etz'nab, she took his hand in hers and covered the action with her shawl. His fingers were calloused and raw. Yet she felt a strong connection of energy flow. It encouraged her. His courage was contagious. Since he was being brave with his life, it helped her become more daring with her own.

After services, workers were allowed to visit with their families and friends under the trees by the church. Guards kept watchful eyes out for desertion or any items they might want to confiscate for themselves. The natives only had a few hours before returning to their grueling tasks, because of a vague fear that they would become dangerous and defiant if they had time to rest and reflect.

Etz'nab told her about the work they were doing. "Maya engineers among us want to build the structure with rounded corners and facing certain directions, so not to bruise the feathers of the wind god. We explained that it helped capture the breezes to reduce heat, capture light and stand against big storms. Foreigners still want to square corners and few windows, like what they left behind in Spain or wherever they are from across the seas. If they can't adjust to the jungle, they will learn the hard way."

"How long are you in service before they let you return home?" asked Itz. Her cousin gave her a sideways look of disbelief.

"I've never seen anyone go home yet, except wrapped in a shroud. We are beasts of burden to them. They have too much work for us to do to let us go."

"Have any men escaped?" she whispered.

"Very few. Most are hunted down and come back tied on poles like slaughtered deer," he lamented, remembering with a wince those poor tortured souls.

Etz'nab sat up straight and stole a wide glance around for large ears that might overhear what he was about to say.

"The overseers do what they do because they don't have the power over us that they'd like. Their meanness springs from weakness. But, cruelty plays against them. Fear leads to anger and anger leads to hate. Many here grow stronger in their willingness to rise up. Soon we will break free in numbers too large to find. Then regroup and fight to protect our people," he shared.

Such news both pleased and dismayed Itz. She knew that if Etz'nab lived through an escape, his life would be a rebel warrior's existence on the run. He saw the conflicting emotions on her face.

"I have learned many new things here. One particular friendship readied and changed me. Here comes Miguel now," said Etz'nab rising to warmly greet the man who inspired him.

CHAPTER 35

Izamal, Yucatan
1562 A.D.

Itz saw a simple man in the despised robes of a priest. He was on the north side of thirty. The monk stood shorter than other Spaniards, but taller than most Maya men. His core frame was thin, but he had muscular broad shoulders and strong legs. A weathered nut-brown complexion suggested hours of working in the sun like a common laborer. As he drew closer she noticed how unusual his eyes were, even for a foreigner. They contained gold flecks like a sunstone and reflected light like certain stones do when wet.

"My new friend, talks of us as 'Indios', not mistaken for natives from a land the Spanish were seeking called Hindustan or India, but because he believes we are 'in dios', in god or god within us," her cousin added with pride. "We call him Ajaw Nocxit, one of Kukulkan's names, because he is an ocean of wisdom and healer."

Miguel pulled back the cowl of his friar's robe and greeted them with an easy smile and good humor. When Itz first met him, she felt she had seen him before. She couldn't understand or explain why he seemed a familiar acquaintance.

They were joined by more than just a moment in time. Some deep fragment of memory stirred. She didn't let her puzzling thoughts bother her because she knew that some questions have no answers. Itz found comfort in her Maya view of a circular world in which history repeats itself in recurring patterns. All things come and go, if only so they can be repeated later in time.

Miguel carried two baskets of provisions with him. He handed out corn tortillas and fried fish bits to those in the courtyard. Father De Landa stepped forward from the shadows.

"What are you doing?" he demanded in a hoarse growl.

"I am feeding the hungry," answered Brother Miguel.

"That is a waste on these idol worshipers."

"No act of kindness is ever wasted. It is loving to do something for someone who can never repay you."

"Pray for them instead," the priest's superior snapped.

"First you pray for the poor, then you feed them. That is how prayer works," countered Brother Miguel.

De Landa's scowling tree trunk face glared at Miguel for a beat before he stomped off to discuss this latest insubordination with fellow clergy. In their circles even a suspicion could be deemed cause for condemnation.

"It seems that Father Diego keeps tripping over truth right in front of him. But he just picks himself up and rushes away as if nothing has happened," he smiled.

The next day, after Itz finished in the marketplace, she came by the worksite to speak with her cousin and hopefully slip him some food. Brother Miguel was in line with the workers, carrying wooden beams up the ramp. After he deposited the load and started back down he saw her. He walked over to the bench where she sat. She handed him a water-filled gourd. He poured a trickle over his head and drank a long draft. She took a bucket of water to the other men. Guards stepped forward to stop her, but a nod from Miguel halted them by their posts.

"I weep sorely for your people. I respect the compassion in you first of all. The measure of civilized behavior is caring for others. Indios seem born with kindness and recognition of a common humanity," he said. He looked at Itz with a calm acceptance that she'd never felt from a total stranger.

"I am not worthy of your praise," she bowed her head and turned away, thinking of her deep fury at those who killed her father.

"I am full of hatred over the injustices put upon my people. I don't like this rock of anger inside me. Will your god condemn me for my feelings?"

"No, you are punished by your anger, not for it. When we hold thoughts of violence or hatred, we contribute to the wounding of the world. We rob ourselves of a heaven on earth," Miguel answered.

"You will learn, grow and get through these difficult times. When you plant seeds of love, it is you that blossoms," he said. "Itz, if your compassion doesn't also include yourself, it is incomplete."

They sat under the broad shade of a sacred cieba tree and visited. He mostly observed and did not speak. In those first exchanges, he watched Itz's eyes and listened to her emotional stories and expressions, taking an inventory of her being. Miguel was a man who read souls. He nodded and his smiling face beamed at her like someone pleased with the reading.

"I feel like you already know everything there is to know about me, even without words," she admitted her vulnerability. Although disconcerting, having someone connect at a very profound level created a warm coming home sensation.

Even though knowledge of writing and art were forbidden for natives, she trusted him enough to show him her recent drawings done on bark paper.

"Your art and presence are a gift to myself and others," he said with a soft earnest voice. "This world needs your knowledge, your skills and your light," he told Itz, with the kindest expression she'd ever seen.

"But I am just a simple woman," she replied modestly.

"Women hold up half the sky," he answered. "Females are really the stronger and wiser beings. They make up over fifty percent of the population and they take care of the other half of us. Women should be respected and honored for their service, not made to feel inferior by society or a patriarchal religion. My mother, Maria, was a loving and courageous woman, just like you."

Itz's spirits and sorrows lifted as she conversed daily with Brother Miguel under the plaza tree. She'd never known someone who brought out the best in everyone he encountered. He projected an aura or magnetic draw that attracted the scattered filings of humanity around him.

"Do you have any of your drawing pencils and papers with you?" the holy brother asked one afternoon. When she produced several fig leaf sheets and a charcoal stick, he sketched the angelic face of a woman. Her bright eyes, like his, searched the viewer's very soul. A mouth, opened in a gentle smile, graced the page. It seemed the lady in the portrait was about to whisper a message of great importance.

"This is a likeness of my blessed mother. See how I turned the head slightly to the side to give it a more realistic dimensional look and put in highlights. I am sure you can add your own touch and make it better."

"May I draw you," Itz asked shyly from beneath lowered eyes and chin, as she withdrew a small paint pot shell and a bird feather quill. "I will practice the new technique you just showed me."

"This rugged thief in the night face?" he chuckled. As an answer he gave Itz a subtle nod of his chin and broad grin.

"I would be honored if you would use your pen of glory to commemorate our meeting and friendship."

It was hard to part ways and end their exciting exchanges. Itz continued to learn more from Brother Miguel. She decided to remain in Izamal as long as she could stay in the Spanish city safely.

CHAPTER 36

Izamal, Yucatan
1562 A.D.

Itz and Brother Miguel met beside the Izamal main church regularly for many weeks. He taught her about the other side of the world and different philosophies. He instructed her in Spanish language and how to write the difficult letters of European people. She found hieroglyphs easier by far. Miguel insisted she be prepared for the future, so she practiced hard.

She continued to perfect the artistic methods he showed her and added her own style and signature to each rendering.

"Here is a picture of your Saint Francis of Assisi," Itz showed him.

"Incredible. You captured his duality and personal struggles in his eyes and expression. Every saint has a past," he said in candor.

"And every sinner has a future, according to you," she retorted, happy to demonstrate how carefully she listened to his lessons. Miguel was like a saint, living in grace and extending it to others.

"Love comes natural to the human heart. No child is born hating others for their skin color or religion. These things are taught. If one can learn to hate, they can also learn to love. We are all brothers and sisters," Miguel told his growing group of followers.

Several weeks after her arrival, she spotted Miguel beside the church. Guards with their prisoners in tow and fellow priests gathered around him. They sat on cut palm fronds under a tree. He told fascinating tales and answered questions.

"Once there was a humble man called Jesus," he began another interesting story about a person in a time and place far away. When there was a lesson to be taught, Miguel told parables or wrote down stories that all could understand, rather than simply stating dogma. Itz sat at the edge of the gathering and secretly took notes. She loved his instructions and insights. He was the first foreigner she knew of who came bearing a pen in his hand rather than a sword.

Brother Miguel gave encouragement, warmth and blessings to those on a spiritual path. He showed Itz and others how to forgive trespasses.

"Don't drink the poison of hatred and think it will harm others. It only harms you," he counseled. "Holding on to your anger is like picking up a red hot cinder to throw at your enemy. You are the one who gets burned." He continued, "Your forgiveness doesn't erase or excuse their crimes, but you need to dissolve the emotional links of resentment that bind you to the wrongdoer. You deserve to be free and have peace of mind."

After the others left, Itz stayed behind to discuss her feelings with Brother Miguel.

"I try to forgive, but I seem to move like a tide, in and out of light and darkness," Itz admitted later when they sat alone.

"People are not all good or all bad," Miguel said. "In fact, good and evil are not complete opposites. They are intertwined with invisible cords and can't be separated."

"Just as being good is a choice, is being bad a choice?" she asked. "Can I defeat wickedness with good decisions and deeds?"

"Yes, light within is the power to choose more loving and positive actions. Right and truth, even temporarily defeated, are stronger than evil."

"It's my strength that the wicked seek. I refuse to let them extinguish the values I cherish," she pledged.

"Develop an open mind and heart Itz, so that no matter what happens you are standing at the center, the middle of the road. Everything that comes into that sacred space has come to teach you what you need to learn."

Through Miguel's teachings, Itz understood that serving and doing tasks like her art could be a sacred act because she chose to view it that way.

"It is not what you are doing, but your attitude and the dignity with which you do it that matters," he explained to those who felt crushed and subservient.

Itz memorized a few common prayers in the new language. She especially liked the ones to the Virgin Mother. If more Christians embodied benevolence and wisdom like Miguel, the world would be a better place. He told her to re-examine all she'd been told and then dismiss whatever insulted her soul. Itz incorporated some new beliefs and ways into her own.

A variety of people gathered regularly outside the church to listen to Brother Miguel.

"All faiths, religions and methods of worship that contribute to the betterment of humanity are holy," the good brother told his followers. He compared Maya theology with Christian beliefs and found many parallels.

"Jesus Christ giving his life is no unique event in history. Your own mythology speaks of the death and resurrection of twin brothers. Many have suffered martyrdom and death, given their lives willingly for humanity's sake so that others might be free," he taught. "Kukulkan, the feathered serpent, part snake, part bird, combined earth and sky. Jesus too combined heaven and earth. Your Hero Twins were born of a virgin mother just like Christ."

"Since there are more similarities than differences in our beliefs, why can't religion center on love and not worry about minor details?" asked a young monk.

"That would seem logical since there are as many ways to worship in god's universe as there are possible spokes from a central hub. No one path is the only way to the center," Miguel answered.

"My father taught me that the One Great Spirit takes many faces and guises," said Itz. "No lone form is superior to another and all spirits are to be respected," she added.

"Organized religions tend to hold on to strict beliefs. Spirituality is going beyond beliefs," he answered.

"Why isn't your religion more tolerant?" inquired an older woman.

"Despite the current rigid theology, churches do provide a communion between people. They can be a great force for good in the world. Heaven has no mouth, so it must speak through the actions of good men and women."

"Are you saying that salvation or redemption depends on our own actions?" someone asked.

"Yes. People need to believe in their own intrinsic value and sacredness, rather than a belief in the divinity of another person or the infallibility of church leaders. The role and obligation of the church is to love and serve all people."

"What blasphemy is this?" screamed an irate De Landa from the courtyard. He stormed up to Miguel and grabbed him roughly by his robe.

"We are here to save souls and redeem these heretics. If that is even possible with such heathens," the inquisitor said looking down his beak nose in disgust and hatred at the frightened crowd.

"Father De Landa," Miguel began gently, "Love has redemptive power within it. If you dislike people, you have no way to transform or to redeem them," he said to his infuriated superior.

"Love?" On his lips the word 'love' was full of contempt. "That is not the way I deal with infidels and idol worshippers," he threatened all within range of his dark scowling look.

"Heretics, as you called them, are rarely cured by persecution," Miguel offered.

"Salvation is not possible outside the Catholic Church," screamed De Landa. He shook the gentle brother once again, released his thick peasant finger grip and stomped away from the gathering.

Brother Miguel, looking more like Ajaw Nocxit at that moment, addressed the departing priest with a twinkle in his eye, "Diego, I guess you will continue to go about God's work in your own way, and I will go about it in the Savior's way."

"Guards, escort Brother Miguel to my office immediately," De Landa shouted over his shoulder.

Itz was shocked and frightened for her friend, the saintly priest. From behind a tree she watched Miguel taken away. Even being in the same town with De Landa, the book-burning fanatic gave her nightmares.

No one ever saw Miguel again. An old priest told her cousin that the good brother was transferred. However, given De Landa's reputation and personal fury, most believed that Miguel became another victim of his inquisition to purge dissidents from the rigid church ranks.

Itz read that Hernando Cortez, the Valley of Mexico's conquistador, gave orders to the Spanish to bury their dead at night and in secret so their enemies would believe them immortal. Maybe that was what happened to Brother Miguel.

Itz frantically asked around and could not find anyone willing to talk to her or provide reliable information. For the first time, she entered the large church structure that the Spanish forced her people to build with the stones of their own shattered pyramids. Smells of copal resin mixed with the foreigners' candles and incense. The Old Ones were still residing behind the altar and under the stones. Changing the shape of the building structure did not alter the essence and energy of the place.

Desperate for news of Brother Miguel, Itz drew on every ounce of courage to ask for an audience with De Landa. To both her dismay and relief, she was told he'd been sent back to Spain by Merida's bishop for questioning over some incidents.

The sudden and mysterious disappearance of Miguel, her dear friend and mentor, caused a deep disabling grief. She suffered like when she lost her father. Again the best way to get through the darkness was to take up her tools and honor their memories with dedicated works.

She knew that meeting Miguel was no accident. Their paths crossed for a reason. Brother Miguel told her the better part of the human spirit refuses to give up even in the face of annihilation. She was driven to rebuild.

Rumblings of rebellion started among the workers, so her cousin warned her to flee town quickly. Itz returned to her home complex in the remote village. She continued to re-create Maya knowledge on pottery and paintings. Adding to her efforts, she drew numerous Madonna portraits and themes from the priest's stories.

"*Maybe Brother Miguel was a saint, or simply enlightened. I don't care. I adored him and will preserve his memory,*" she decided.

Pink rays of dawn moved across the threshold. Itz looked out in surprise. She'd been up all night, working on a special vase to commemorate Brother Miguel in a realistic likeness. She held it up to the morning light to admire her work. Miguel's face glowed warm and real enough to touch. She used her newly acquired odd Spanish letters to tell of his disappearance at the hands of the conquistadors' priests.

Like ancient Maya knowledge, she believed that the stories of Miguel's wisdom and miraculous deeds deserved to be told.

CHAPTER 37

Izamal, Yucatan
1563 A.D.

"I shouldn't get angry with people I don't respect," Itz reminded herself as she returned from delivering an order of pottery to the monk's living quarters in Izamal. She used her visit to the religious compound to see if she could learn anything new about Brother Miguel's disappearance. People who had attended his talks and gatherings denied knowing him or being his friend. Their eyes shifted back and forth hoping no one was hearing her associate them with the missing priest.

"*He existed, he taught, he healed, and made a difference. Why would they feign ignorance and deny him?*" wondered Itz. Some would turn away when she approached, so she left the grand church without answers.

Itz crossed the wide enclosed courtyard and started down the stone staircase. She brushed pass two robed priests, one fair and the other dark. They were distracted, deep in conversation or prayer chants while they rotated their rosaries. She took in a sharp breath and pulled her shawl closer to her face when she recognized the darker friar as Tepal. Only a few more steps and she could disappear into milling market day crowds. Itz started walking with an exaggerated limp, pulling her foot behind as if it were crippled. Her worn peasant cloak dragged the ground in a clumsy manner.

Prince Tepal, called Brother Juan Guillermo by the Franciscans, broke stride. He halted in place for a moment and turned to confirm whom he thought he saw. He shook his head to clear it and watch closely until the hunched over limping figure blended among the other poor souls on the street.

Rapid footsteps approached behind her. The sound triggered a shiver of apprehension on the back of Itz's neck. Her trembling legs buckled from dread when she got around the corner out of sight. She kept expecting a jaguar-tattooed man to grab her and drag her back. It was not the chili being roasted over open flames at the vendors' booths that made her eyes tear up, it was sheer terror and frustration.

She dodged in and out of the market day crowds and made several turns and circles to be sure she was not followed. Itz knew she must leave Izamal immediately or face discovery.

"Thank you for your family's hospitality and your assistance with my ceramics," she told the kind fellow potter where she rented a tiny room and workspace. "I received news from my family and must leave right away," Itz explained as she bundled up her few possessions and art supplies.

"You understand these difficult times," she said and nodded in the direction of the monastery and church. "Please do not tell anyone of my stay here. It is for your safety as well as my own."

She left nothing of hers there except a tall stack of generic unpainted plates for additional payment. She would greatly miss the home atmosphere of young children playing in the yard and sisterly company of the potter's wife.

Itz stopped at the construction work site to explain her hasty departure and say farewell to her cousin, Etz'nab. She squeezed his rough sunburned hand through the wooden stick fence and slipped him another dark green jade piece from her father's collar to trade for food and other needs.

With adrenaline still rushing through her veins, Itz traveled halfway to her remote village before nightfall. After a restless few hours in a lean-to build on the causeway for long distance travelers, she arrived home in her hideaway the next evening.

Within a week of her return travelers passing through told tales of a frantic house-to-house search by the priests and soldiers in Izamal.

"The troops threw over marketplace stalls and stabbed swords through large baskets and blankets. Priests took people to question them in their cruel way. Who could they be after this time?" they puzzled.

Itz knew she was the most likely target of those searches if Tepal recognized her after all.

Staying away from Izamal was a must from then on. As an extra precaution, Itz packed up her dwelling and art supplies and moved far away to a safer location. She returned to the home of her ancestors in the Cupules-Talol kingdom. It had been the government seat of Ukit Kan L'ek Tok, known as the powerful Black Jaguar king. Thus his ancient city was called Ek Balam, Star or Black Jaguar.

In the shadow of the ruined acropolis, Itz found a serviceable stone structure inside the old city walls. Causeways, water wells and supply exchanges were available in the area to serve the hundred or so families of the Ixkunil pueblo. Itz fixed up the old building, planted a small garden plot and started over. The lady scribe continued her secret works.

She asked cacao traders who passed through southern parts of the territory to carry a small cup decorated with bees to her aunt. That was a coded signal for Yaxche to meet Itz in her new village near the ruins of the Ek Balam capital. Her cousin and aunt knew of this back-up location if Itz became endangered where she'd stayed before with her father.

Doomed splendor of her noble Maya ancestors lay covered in a dark tangle of jungle growth. Ages of magnificence and cultural grandeur went back over three thousand years. Great kingdoms rose only to fall in cascades of catastrophe, both man-made and natural.

"I realize that most of my people's ancient cities like this were deserted and reclaimed by vegetation before the Spanish arrived. But if the fools hadn't burned the books and killed our leaders, the histories and lessons of the past might have been known in detail. Lost cities and their treasures could have been found and thousands of years of accumulated knowledge rediscovered. What a pity." Itz thought as she looked out at hints of glory in Ek Balam.

She was proud that Maya civilization reached such improbable heights in a harsh and forbidding environment. Her forefathers mastered the dense rain forest challenges and built formidable cities with grand monuments to express the greatness of the rulers and awe the common population.

On her way to the corn fields near the well, she saw where early citizens adopted intensive methods of cultivation, using irrigation, terracing, composting, and raised silt gardens. They had coaxed enough sustenance from the land to feed thousands of people and support noble, artistic and religious classes. Evidence and usable remnants survived of stucco-paved causeways that crisscrossed the jungle lands and large cedar canoes still plied the rivers and seas exchanging merchandise over hundreds of miles.

In the past Ko'h told her tales of how, like political entities throughout history, the Maya had built and defended cities, traded for goods, made alliances and made wars. Eventually the powerful, but fragmented Yucatan peninsula city-states fought and destroyed each other. Conquered cities no longer rebuilt, they were deserted and ceased to exist.

People fled from the centers into the countryside. Those who lived in natural ways proved to be more lasting than the massive stone structures. Itz and her country neighbors led simple existences and yet wanted little more than they needed. In serving nature they created their own reward. They tried to live so the land could continue to feed their descendants when they were gone.

Common farming villages, like the Ixkunil pueblo, were built right beside and around the once grand city that resembled Biblical descriptions of Babylon. Everyday life in the small pueblo was lived in the shadows of towering pyramids. Like living next to a cemetery, the people of the village did not disturb the old ceremonial center. They held it in a kind of fearful superstition and respect reserved for the dead.

This was the way of the people where Itz lived on the edge of ancient Ek Balam. After hundreds of years, huge temples in the imperial centers now appeared as forest covered hills. Where once thousands walked the great causeways and celebrated with royalty in the broad plazas, only the jungle animals and plants reigned. The remote building where Itz took refuge was a short walk to the village and clear water *cenote* well called X'canche.

Old raised roadways ran around the area in several directions. An active trading center and marketplace thrived a day's walk away in the town of Nabalam, Mayan for 'mother jaguar'. It was here that Itz would travel on foot occasionally for news, additional supplies and to continue selling her pottery.

Nabalam was having a special festival next month. Gatherings were planned all over the territory. It was the end of a Maya calendar *katun,* a twenty-year cycle, which fortunately fell around the same time as the Catholic celebration of Easter. Unaware of the significance of this special ancient calendar event, the Spanish thought their new converts were excited about this holy season and celebrating Christ's resurrection.

Itz had decided not to attend the regional gathering. She wanted to remain hidden. It was still too dangerous for her to mingle openly in public places where the foreigners and their minions, like Tepal, might see her or discover her secret work.

CHAPTER 38

Mexico City
Present Day

"Museums hold many secrets and treasures that the public will never see," Hannah Char said from personal experience.

Hannah's fieldwork season in the Maya ruins came to an end when the heavy rains began. The National Institute of Anthropology and History, INAH, called her back to work at the National Museum of Anthropology in Mexico City.

Hannah still owned a two-bedroom apartment she shared with Paloma, a symphony musician. Between both Hannah's fieldwork and Paloma's concert tours to far corners of the globe, they hardly ever crossed paths

The first floor apartment had served as Hannah's home base for six years. A block off Paseo de Reforma in Lomas proved ideal for her. The front window looked out over huge trees and an old stone bridge she convinced herself had been there since the days of the Aztec empire. She passed through Chapultepec Park on her way to work. That path always lifted her spirits.

She enjoyed the museum's easily accessible location in the middle of the park right on Reforma. She could stroll over to the lake at lunchtime or visit one of the other nearby museums or the zoo.

Her favorite features of the Anthro Museum were the central courtyard and an umbrella roof water fountain supported by a single column. This mammoth structure represented a mythological ceiba tree. She occasionally got fooled into thinking it was raining outside when they turned on the waterworks that overflowed its top and fell into the interior wide-open space.

Museum collections had been gathered little by little over one hundred and seventy years. Without a doubt, much of the history, ethnography and pre-Hispanic art, would have been lost without the existence of the museum and national institute. The National Anthropology Museum transformed time into space. Set on almost twenty acres, over thirty thousand square meters of exhibition space displayed the finest examples of the country's archaeological and ethnographic materials. The entire top floor paid tribute to indigenous people of Mexico with exhibits of present day life in each cultural region of Middle America.

"Anthropology is not the study of ants," Hannah joked with first year students who came for classes every Wednesday afternoon.

"Anthropology is a science that involves the study of man in the broadest sense. The topic is divided onto two basic sections, physical-biological anthropology and cultural-social anthropology," she explained as she drew diagrams on the white board. "The first studies man's evolution over time and environmental adaptations. The second area of study focuses on cultural development, linguistics and human behavior when united in groups."

Museum visitors were delighted by the vast multi-leveled extent of the halls, murals, and facilities. They didn't expect to see libraries, lecture halls, auditoriums, restaurants, and such impressive, interactive displays and comprehensive exhibits. Most were pleasantly surprised at luxurious stone flooring and crystal clear glass cases with multi-language labels.

Like the Louvre in Paris, Mexico City's Anthropology Museum was not a place one could do justice to in a day. It bemused Hannah to observe those who rushed in just to see the original Aztec Stone of the Sun with its summoning presence, standing guard at the back of the Sala de Mexico. Sometimes they'd catch a glimpse of colossal Olmec heads or perhaps the replica sarcophagus lid from Lord Pacal's tomb in Palenque. Then they would leave like they were double-parked.

Cradled within the museum's lower floors, additional legendary treasures stayed hidden. Civilians rarely saw the professional centers for research, conservation and teaching. Under the main building, thousands of square meters were dedicated to laboratories, archives, workshops, classrooms, administration and storerooms. Various research departments operated out of the public eye.

Hannah sat at her assigned desk in the artifact analysis section of the underground beehive of activity. Papers and books decorated with tassels of bright post-it stickers spread across her work area beneath the harsh florescent lighting. Comforting, but pungent, smells of burnt coffee and acetone solution used to clean artifacts reassured her that she was right at home in a lab.

She plugged away on her computer. Focus and concentration had always been a strong point. She got lost in her work no matter where she was placed. Not for the first time that week, she worked right through lunch hour and ignored signs of fatigue.

Hannah dove deep into statistical research of pottery samples she'd excavated only a few months before. Looking at photographs and hand-written descriptions of a small offering bowl, she sighed and thought back to the exciting moment she discovered this particular incised piece at the base of Edzna's five-storied temple.

As a scientist, she understood why entering all the field notes into databases and doing statistical analysis were necessary. Yet, it seemed a waste of her talent to be constantly recording data like an accountant.

"*Just part of my job. I can do anything for five months,*" she encouraged herself to continue.

Hannah kicked off her leather heels and pulled one leg up under her skirt in the office chair. It took getting used to wearing business style clothes after months in loose, wash-and-wear field gear.

People who saw her dressed in a smart suit and high heels said, "I can't imagine you trudging through the jungles and dirty ruins with a gun on your hip."

"My friends at the archaeological sites chuckle at the thought of me wearing a tight skirt and hard pointy high-heeled shoes," she replied in turn.

Being in the city and working indoors for eight or more hours a day took its toll. Report compilations and grant proposals always required more effort and energy than expected. Analysis and paperwork were the mundane tedious sides of archaeology that most armchairs dreamers didn't think about. Competitions for permits and foundation grants were fierce. Well-qualified field professionals would consider selling their mothers to get articles published or receive funding for fieldwork or even to attend regional meetings.

An intern with an armload of papers cruised by Hannah's desk. "Director Sarra wants to see you in his office," he mumbled.

"The director is in town?" And he wants to see me?"

"Duh. Seems like…" the young student replied as he continued down the hall.

Hannah pushed back from her desk, straightened her beige pencil skirt and tucked in the new white silk blouse. She patted her hair into place and applied a quick swipe of tinted lip-gloss. Putting on her matching jacket and grabbing files containing her excavation results to date, she felt ready for the unexpected appointment.

The museum chief's stern secretary signaled her to go in. Hannah stopped for a moment outside the director's closed oak door. Uncertain whether her nervousness was due to reporting to a museum top superior or seeing Sam Sarra for the first time since she returned to the city, Hannah closed her eyes to gather confidence. She drew in a deep breath, tapped on the door and hearing a 'Yes' from beyond, turned the knob to enter.

Director Sarra's office was not as she imagined. It was sparse and empty as a monk's cell, bereft of personal details. Nothing adorned the walls. There was barely enough furniture to keep it from looking like a doctor's sterile waiting room.

Dr. Sarra rose from an aged brown leather chair and stood behind his well-worn dark mahogany desk. Longish blue-black hair framed his tanned face. When a lock fell over one of his lively steel-gray eyes, Hannah wanted to reach over and brush the stray back.

"Dr. Char," he said, waving his hand palm up to invite her to take a seat. "So very good to see you again." His voice was deep and robust. Their eyes locked and did not waiver.

Even though his manner this afternoon seemed formal, it was cordial, and the physical attraction she sensed at the archaeology site was still present. At least for her it was. Dr. Sarra represented her image of the epitome of masculine vigor. His demeanor looked assured and assertive, as only those born wealthy can pull off.

"How is analysis of the Edzna excavation progressing?" he asked.

"Very well. Other than the looting theft, this was our most successful field season." Hannah cringed internally. "*Why did I have to mention that fiasco at the beginning?*" she scolded herself.

To distract from her mistake, she hurriedly continued, "Patterns are presenting that only large samplings can reveal. We found several examples of Mixtec and Zapotec style incursions," she reported. Excitement rose in her voice.

Hannah shifted into her vocational master mode. She took a deep breath and readied to expound in colorful detail. Sarra put his hand up to stop her.

"Hannah," he smiled indulgently and began, "I trust you are well on your way to publishing a series of articles about unique finds. We look forward to hearing about the past season of prolific discoveries. I'll be reading your works for months. Details can wait until then."

Hannah absorbed what he said. She took his statements as off-handed compliments and assurance there'd be work ahead for her. She focused more on the fact that he called her by her first name.

And that perfect smile of his took her breath away. She sat in silence staring at him star-struck.

Dr. Sarra came around the desk and placed his hand lightly on her shoulder. "I know a superb restaurant nearby. Why don't we take a break from shop talk and have a late lunch?" he suggested.

"No," said Hannah.

Sarra's was taken aback only for a second. He looked at her speculatively and asked, "Why not?"

"Because I am right in the middle of something in my analysis. I need to get back to it."

"You're a woman of many surprises," he laughed out of astonishment and something else.

Hannah sat shocked wide-eyed at what she'd just done. She wanted to be in the company of Sam Sarra. "*Where did that refusal bubble up from*?" she asked herself. Her lip hurt where she bit it and swallowed back an urge to ask if she could reconsider and accept.

"Perhaps another time," she said, and fervently hoped that her rejection of his invitation would not make it the last one.

"Perhaps," said the man not used to being refused what he wanted, when he wanted it.

CHAPTER 39

Mexico City
Present Day

Hannah sat at her analysis lab desk. Her forehead rested in her palm. She thought of a dozen other ways she could have handled the meeting with Director Sarra. Reacting like a romantic teenager was not her style at all. She took a deep breath and pulled herself back into control.

She fiddled with books and papers piled high on her desk. The stack resembled a middle-eastern layered tell mound. Unable to concentrate on the work in front of her anymore, she gave up and took a break.

'I am going upstairs to see the new Maya exhibit pieces just in from Jaina Island," she told the lab secretary. She offered the information as a courtesy, although other staff members often slipped out for three hours lunches or came in late, if at all, without a word to co-workers.

"*My dad taught me to always be on time. And if you can't be on time, be early*," she remembered her early training in personal responsibility.

Once ensconced in a Mexican government or institution position, an employee's job was pretty secure. At quitting time, workers, swift as arrows, converged on the elevators and burst through revolving doors in escape. Hannah couldn't get accustomed to the attitude of 'do as little as you can for as much pay and power as you can get'.

"*Different cultural habits and expectations,*" she noted with a shake of her head. "*That work ethic and degree of low volition would never fly in my old museum,*" she said to herself as she walked into the main level floor Maya Hall on the left.

The new exhibits she sought were displayed in one of the less frequented side halls. Tour guides seldom led their charges this way, except as a shortcut to see the famous jade funeral mask of Lord Pacal from Palenque.

Hannah passed glass fronted display cases that reached from floor to ceiling of the wide main room. Pottery samples, weapons, tools, jewelry and other artifacts, dating from the sixth century, filled well-lighted displays. Accumulations of items were catalogued and described in detail in several languages.

There was beauty in each one of the specimens. Nothing detracted so much as the overcrowding of an exhibit. She remembered lessons well learned from work at the Los Angeles County Natural History Museum.

Ahead, on a low stone pedestal, covered by a crystal clear glass dome, stood the newest acquisition, an imposing ceramic figure of a Maya nobleman.

One foot in front of the other gave the appearance he was in mid-stride. The half meter tall statue captured a distinguished man in full regalia and a tall, feathered headdress. His realistic and expressive face grabbed Hannah's attention. Eyes of shiny black onyx and rock crystal stared at her so implacably that she shivered. She gazed at him with awe and a slight sense of recognition.

Hannah knelt down to examine this portraiture artifact more closely. The clay was beautifully hand-molded and painted in vibrant blue, yellow red and green colors. Fabric weaves and ornamental trims, the breastplate and other jewelry details were astonishing.

The artist who created this ceramic sculpture transcended limitations of technique. Delicately etched textures in the clothing, the puff of quetzal plumes, and details in the jade ornaments secured the essence. But it was the proud face, with its odd tattoos, slight smile and piercing eyes that riveted her to the spot.

She leaned in even closer, until her forehead touched the cool glass. The statue became imbued with life, swayed and turned before her eyes like a 3-D hologram. Hannah felt strangely overcome by a wave of familiarity. She studied the figure from head to toe.

"*I stitched those small copper bells onto your sandals. The green quetzal feathers in your headdress were from my father's favorite cloak*," her inner voice said in recollection.

Striking in their clarity, images and emotions touched her core awareness. An eerie, physical welling up of a sight, sound and smell experience, gave her a flashing momentary realization that she'd intimately known and loved this person from the far past. The indescribable nature of strong *deja vu* sensations evaporated as unexpectedly as they had come.

"Don't leave me!" she shouted.

Hannah collapsed on the floor in front of the case and wrapped her arms around the glass barrier between her and the figure. Recognition and connection was swallowed up and sealed tight. She would dare to see more, would actually follow that dangerous, disappearing, inbound road back if she could. She screamed in frustration.

Hannah sat on the cool stone floor, bent in half by sorrow. She leaned against the stone pedestal, and cried for the lost memory.

Dr. Sarra came bounding around the corner. He paused momentarily to see if she was physically hurt. But he could tell that something far deeper and more mysterious occurred in the narrow exhibit hall.

He helped her up and over to a bench by the wall. They sat in silence. He slipped his arm around her trembling shoulders and after a moment she relaxed against him.

"It seemed so real. My nobleman's statue, the connection and memories," Hannah sputtered and tried to explain what she herself could not understand.

"I know, I know," he soothed her.

Not wanting to lose her objective scientific view of life and her credibility, she said, "I guess my mind was just playing tricks."

"Maybe your unconscious desire for love," he suggested and tightened his possessive embrace.

"There was a flash of lives together. A firm sense it genuinely happened."

"You may have been to that place before, it was just in a different body, in another time. Soul mates in two historical eras perhaps? An unfortunate scrivener's error made by God," he shrugged.

"You do understand. You believe me. Right now, I just need to stay in the present and deal with one world at a time."

Hannah leaned into Sarra's chest and hugged him. "*Here's a man who shares a love of antiquities, believes in the possibility of other pasts and could provide me with unlimited opportunities to fulfill my life and career goals*," she mused.

"*It doesn't hurt that he's gorgeous and wealthy*," she thought as she looked up into his eyes.

"Shall we continue over dinner?" he proposed with a knowing smile.

CHAPTER 40

Mexico City
Present Day

After the unsettling episode in Maya Hall, Hannah began to relax over wine and dinner with the charming director. She didn't want to stare, but he was a handsome man, with a cleft chin and chiseled features. Sarra exuded ease and elegance. He had perfected the air of aristocratic grace to a fine art. His powerful presence overshadowed nearly everyone and everything he was around. She found Sam, as he insisted she call him, captivating.

Hannah reminded herself that it might not be a good idea to get involved with him, but that evening the attraction seemed to outweigh any possible risks in her mind. Swarms of butterflies in her stomach fluttered overtime. She worked hard to be on her best behavior and match his worldly conversation.

Sarra drove Hannah directly to her home after dinner. She wondered how he knew where she lived while in the city. He never asked for her address or directions. Like a gentleman, he walked her to the front door gate.

Sam Sarra leaned over and kissed her forehead. "To remove the remaining furrows of care from your mind," he said.

He turned from her and walked back to his waiting Jaguar. She watched his back recede down the long, dark sidewalk.

At the museum, Hannah was infused with optimism and had a renewed zest for her work. She was convinced that the strange connection to the Maya noble figurine came as a sign. She felt chosen to bring ancient messages to the modern world. Days patiently followed days, piled one on another like temple stones. She toiled over analysis of past digs and project proposals.

Hannah was working on a grant application to go back to Edzna. She wanted to double-check some of her accounts regarding worker wages. The administration office provided payroll ledger pages from her prior fieldwork.

"Where did all these new names come from?" she asked the finance officer. The payroll list in her hands indicated that sixty-five site workers had been paid. "I only had forty-five people employed at the ruins. I don't know any of these additional twenty named individuals."

"Oh, you know it works," the administrative clerk said with a flutter of her manicured nails. "You probably put a few ghosts on your pay requests and pocketed the money. Everyone does at each level."

"I never padded the payroll," Hannah huffed.

"Then you're a fool," the administrator said and grabbed the folder back.

Hannah spoke and corresponded regularly with Roberto and Mari about her progress on the site materials and submission of grant applications. They were all anxious to be reunited and back in the archaeological trenches.

"I am working hard and jumping through all the hoops, but don't know if and when INAH will issue permits or if there will be funding available to return to Edzna," Hannah worried aloud to her friends.

Mari showed special interest in the episode with the nobleman statue when Hannah's conscious mind remembered the past. Mari understood eyes staring through layers of lifetimes. Hannah experienced, for an unforgettable instant, that a soul clings to and longs for the purest memories of its previous life.

"There must be some scientific explanation. Was it real?" asked Hannah.

"Your question is the wrong one. No one can tell you that your experience was false," Mari replied.

"I know for a fact how I felt. It is real in that the vision has persuaded me to alter my motives and my behavior. Imaginary or not, I will act accordingly."

"It sounds like you are even more dedicated and excited about your work than ever. If that is possible."

"Mari, I wasn't frightened by the flash back. It felt comfortable, like being home, even for a moment. Afterward I was sad, lonely for the soul from the past, missing him. I wondered why I was in this modern era and not back in time with those I loved," Hannah tried to explain. "Guess I am needed here for some purpose."

"Comfort can be found in a circular world of recurring cycles of time. We Maya believe events repeat themselves in the same orderly manner as planets. All things have appointed times to end, if only so they may be repeated later," Mari assured her.

"I guess after all, a succession of lives is really no more startling than the miracle of birth or more preposterous than having one life," Hannah replied. Deja vu experience discussions with Mari made Hannah look forward to future collisions or overlaps with destiny.

CHAPTER 41

Mexico City
Present Day

For some reason, during their telephone conversations, Hannah was reluctant to tell Mari or Roberto much about seeing Sam Sarra away from the museum. She continued private dinners with the director and accompanied him to various social functions. Powerful and wealthy, like the star in his own movie, everything revolved around Sarra. People rearranged their schedules to accommodate him.

At first, being on his arm was a fantasy, a whirlwind of glamorous events and even more glamorous people. But the superficial glitter soon wore thin for Hannah. The Divine Caste that Mari had told her about was alive and continued their beliefs in superiority over their inferiors. They were indifferent to struggles of others. It became obvious that wealth didn't buy morals or integrity. Also, she observed that the rich had servants, and no real friends. Sarra's acquaintances were so poor; all they had was money.

Hannah frequently found the conversations and people in high society 'shallow as a pie pan', as her southern cousin would say. They weren't friendly, just talkative and exchanging cynicisms. Socialites seemed to find sound more manageable than silence. What irritated Hannah most was their cruel hostile sense of humor that tore others down, thinking it would build them up.

Sarra was often the center of attention in his wealthy circle. It was the allure of power. Envy tended to draw people closer. When Hannah was taken into Sam's universe, she became another asteroid fixed in orbit around him.

The handsome director used his compelling personal magnetism to his own advantage. Everything seemed to come easy for him. He acted destined to entitlement. His aura was admired, sought after and rewarded.

Hannah observed when he mingled and shook those outstretched hands, that his empty flat smile did not reach his eyes. Sarra was a closed book, with pages known only to him. People could merely see the cover and read the title. She watched him in his practiced poses and sensed a hidden past and something slightly dangerous.

Early on, Hannah had flashes of self-consciousness. Insecurity, disguised as mild-mannered doubt, whispered that she was not good enough to be the object of Sam's attention.

"*Why me when he could have a rich debutant or super model on his arm? I feel like a brown wren out of place in flocks of exotic birds. But a group fixated on female thinness is not about health or beauty, it's about female obedience*," she concluded. Most of the spoiled women she met were all about high shoes and high drama. What was too much for anybody else was never enough for them. They had no brims and never said when.

Yet she wondered sometimes, "*Am I truly wanted or just being settled for*?" Comparison could be the death of self-confidence.

Hannah, with her full lips, oval shaped face and bright eyes, believed she bordered on attractive. But not compared to her mother, who had been the beauty in the family. And everyone knew that good looks often skip a generation.

"The whole insecurity bit is ridiculous," she laughed as she shared these thoughts with her roommate, Paloma. "My self-image does not come from Dr. Sarra or his jet setter crowd."

Hannah finally truly accepted that she was her own kind of

beautiful and being herself was enough. She had a deeper fulfillment in her life, like a fine Belgian chocolate harboring a secret center. Confidence added to her natural prettiness. Hannah continued to think highly of herself because of the secret she'd discovered…'others take you at your own estimate.'

"Dr. Sarra obviously respects and likes you. He gave you an inscribed gold watch for your birthday," Paloma assured her.

What confused Hannah the most was how at times Sarra looked longingly at her from under thick dark eyelashes that made him such a heartthrob to the women. When they were alone his words to her were so warm, she nearly had to fan herself. Yet he restrained from acting on any romantic or physical gestures. His goodnight kisses on her cheek were stilted and perfunctory.

"The biggest coward is a man who leads a woman on with no intention of caring for her," said Paloma.

"What is wrong with me? Guys treat me like a sister. Doesn't anyone find me desirable? Will I always be in the friend category?" she asked her roommate in a moment of weakness. Hannah was thinking of both Sarra and Joseph with those questions.

After Joseph returned to the magazine's New York headquarters from his journalist assignment at the Edzna ruins, he had dropped Hannah a short email to establish contact. Afterwards, they chatted online as their respective erratic schedules allowed. No ice had to be broken between messages or video calls. Joseph's notes often dove deep into his insights about world issues and his responsibility to objectively inform the public. Hannah openly shared her experiences and thoughts. She even told him about her Maya noblemen connection.

There were corny jokes and U-tube videos to tickle each other's dry sense of humor. She blushed when he accused her of 'drinking ink', as he called her compulsive reading. She missed him between emails and was happy when she saw a message from him in her inbox. Over the months, a very right and comfortable friendship developed long-distance between them. The rugged journalist grew on her in a way that was both pleasant and worrisome.

Hannah had no idea how difficult it was for Joseph not to sign his mail 'with love' or show other expressions of the deep affection he felt. His aim was to build a solid foundation for their relationship. He took an emotional chance caring for her so much and not telling her. What a toll he paid on the freight of unspoken desires. He uncharacteristically waited in a gray twilight for signs from her first that she was interested in more than friendship. Ironically neither spoke up.

The last thing he wanted was to frighten her with the depth of his feelings, or worse, to find out that she didn't feel the same attraction. He sabotaged himself. His fear of failure defined his limits, making his dreams impossible to achieve. Trepidation became a deviously clever adversary, causing him to waste opportunities for happiness. He would learn the hard way that a fearful present could cause a fearful future.

CHAPTER 42

Ek Balam/Nabalam
1563 A.D.

Yaxche arrived in Ixkunil village near Ek Balam for a long visit with Itz. She encouraged her reluctant niece to accompany her to the regional assembly of artisians and traders in Nabalam at the end of the month.

"Don't let your enemies win. The dangers you face are real, but fear is a choice."

Although Itz was afraid of being in public places where she might run into Tepal or someone who would recognize her, she was soon glad that she accompanied her aunt to the Nabalam marketplace and festival.

Friendly chatter and cooking smoke rose from well-stocked stalls and crowded plazas. The area was known for its trade in salt, cacao, fine cotton and the purest honey. Itz was especially drawn to the embroidered chemises and brightly colored hand-woven cottons. She appreciated quality. The red-orange dye colors of the blood-wood tree from the Kin Pech area cheered her. The town was full of travelers, but that first day there were no *dzul* white men around. To her relief, Itz only saw other Maya faces in the village and marketplace throngs.

"When I was in Izamal, the Spaniards were so funny to watch. They crossed their arms and walked around the sellers' goods," she shared with her aunt. "The braver ones poked and smelled everyday things like tomatoes or chili. It was all new to them." Itz chuckled, "Can you imagine? They'd never seen or tasted maize, turkey or cacao. Such foods were novelties, not mentioned in their Bible book. Some even called them poison."

"They certainly adopted our tobacco and agave beers quickly enough," added Yaxche.

Music and soft chanting rose from the nearby square. Dancers moved to rhythms of clay whistles and drums during post-Lenten celebrations in the plaza. Ceremonies, services and prayers blended conquistadors' Catholic beliefs with the enduring customs of the ancient Maya. Infidel Indios still worshipped their own religion within earshot of Christian rituals. None the wiser, the conquered and conquerors shared the day. At Mass, Spanish priests cried out beliefs of their own making. Followers shouted even louder to promote causes to Indians forced to stand outside in the courtyard.

Yaxche joined several older women in a circular dance. She whistled the tune through her front teeth. When she lifted her skirt a bit Itz saw how rapidly her aunt's sandaled feet moved. Her spryness and stamina were in contrast to her stoop and graying hair. Joy filled Itz from bursts of music and the spirit of the dance.

Itz observed the gathering crowd. What a treat to see native merchants with their bundles of colorful cloth, feathers and other goods spread on overflowing table tops and reed mats around the plaza. The festive sights took her back to better days before widespread intrusions of the foreigners. A wave of sadness swept over her face and heart. Not much was left of her old way of life. But memories sometimes returned, tirelessly spinning their threads to remind her of lost times. Flitting like dreams that cheered her and faded with the dawn.

Across the way she noticed a lively, well-dressed man seated on the edge of a wall by the city portal arch. People gathered around three deep, listening to him as he told a story. Laughter followed some anecdote. It was a sound that was not heard too often. His dynamic manner of speaking reminded Itz of Brother Miguel. The speaker had the same subtle but open dignity and strength, which always appealed to her.

"Who is that man over there by the henequen ropes? Somehow, I think I know him," she asked her aunt and pointed him out.

"Oh good, Kan Ik is here. He is a friend of the family, but I don't think you've ever met him. He is a merchant, a Tico trader from far away lands the Spanish now call their rich coast, Costa Rica. Your fathers were like brothers."

Yaxche pulled her niece over to the group surrounding Kan Ik to introduce her. He looked her way at once. There she stood by her aunt, fresh, like a flower in full bloom. A spontaneous smile creased his youthful but sea-weathered face. His forehead bore a noble slant that flowed down a nose straighter than most. When he stood up, Itz was surprised to see that he towered a head above all the others.

Her aunt and Kan Ik leaned forward and touched each other's palms in the formal greeting of respect. Yaxche turned and introduced her niece.

"I can't believe we never crossed paths. Your father has been like a favorite uncle to me for years. He stood up for me at my *hetzmec*, initiation ceremony," said Kan Ik. He looked at Itz with appreciation and scanned her features for similarities to his dear friend Ko'h.

By the time night had fallen and stars first appeared in a purple gray sky, the three were seated at a table sharing a meal. Kan Ik cried openly when Yaxche told him of Ko'h's death at the Mani burning of the books.

"That was not the death he was destined for. Torture and a tragic end like that at the hands of cruel men offends a certain order of the universe," he anguished.

"He took a stand to the end for the Maya people and his important works," Yaxche noted.

Familiar tears swam in Itz's eyes. She looked up to keep them from falling. It didn't work.

Kan Ik squeezed both women's hands in a consoling gesture. He let go of Yaxche, but held onto Itz a few extra moments. A pleasant warm glow began to move up her arm where it connected with his. Their eyes met and he somehow hoped that she felt the same energy he was feeling at this contact.

"We must be going. It has been a long day of travel and sights. Hopefully, we'll see you again while we're here for the festivities," Yaxche said to Kan Ik. "Your friendship is a blessing."

Yaxche and her niece did not encounter Kan Ik the next day. Itz couldn't stop scanning the crowds for the tall rugged stranger with the easy smile and eyes that sparkled with good humor.

"What if he left town without saying good-bye?" she questioned her aunt. Yaxche saw her niece had an interest beyond work and family friendship. It warmed her heart to see Itz feeling more than grief and revenge for a change.

On the third day of the festival, as Itz sat on a low wooden *canche* stool in front of her pottery for sale, Kan Ik plopped down beside her. He leaned on one elbow and continued their earlier conversation as if there hadn't been a two-day long break.

He admired her multicolored ceramics, "Those hues are as blue as the deep sea or the Spanish Madonna's robes. Show me some more of your works."

Itz unwrapped bundles she brought from Ek Balam and spread out the various pottery wares and a few paintings. Kan Ik was especially impressed with her techniques to make figures stand out.

"Brother Miguel in Izamal taught me how to draw dimensionally." She shared sagas about the good priest and his mysterious disappearance.

"I have been practicing from a sketch portrait he drew of his mother. I add my own colors and touches like this tear."

"It looks like the lily-like scar by the corner of your own eye," he observed as he touched her cheek gently with the back of his hand. "How many tears have run down this beautiful face?" he asked without expecting an answer.

Itz told him about growing up around Edzna with Prince Tepal and his destructive temper tantrums. Just the mere recall of certain incidences left her palms damp and shaking.

"He says he wants to help our people, but I don't trust him."

"When someone demonstrates who they are, like he has, you need to believe them the first time," Kan Ik said.

"I am more afraid of him now that he has allied himself with the Spanish and their Catholic Church. Tepal is always seeking power and ways to control others." Itz felt she could talk honestly and in depth to Kan Ik about anything.

Kan Ik's face creased in concern. He felt a surge of wanting to be close to and protect Itz. But his life was on the seas. He was a trader and courier, gone for months on end. He was the source of rare goods and even rarer news that many depended on. Under the guise of a traveling merchant, he acted as a messenger and vital communication link.

"The exchange of knowledge is a weapon of incalculable potency in the battle for our conquered peoples to protect and raise themselves up. This possibility is what drives my travels and work. The power of truth will effect the changes needed," he told Itz.

Itz listened for hours to Kan Ik's store of tales that led her from one marvel to another. Unfortunately, she had to share him with others. People were drawn to his energy and informative stories from his travels. He leaned into conversations and his alert dark chocolate colored eyes were attentive to whomever he addressed.

Even though Kan Ik tried to treat Itz like everyone else, something about her fascinated him. She had a mixture of serenity and assurance with which she saw herself and her destiny. There were times when Itz did not speak, but her glances were so filled with words and feelings that he thought she'd been talking all the while.

His eyes explored her. She felt herself ripen with color at his gaze and nearness. She gave him a playful nudge and was pleased to find that he felt solid and strong. The muscles on his arms and legs stood out like cords. Strange random markings, unlike any other she had ever seen, covered his body.

"What are those tattooed lines?" she asked, lightly tracing the jagged blue ink under the skin on top of his hand. He hesitated a moment and leaned in close to share his answer.

"Well, I am a merchant who transports goods by boat. I have drawn permanent detailed charts of the seas and lands on my body so I am never without a map," he answered. Then in a whisper he continued, "Don't tell anyone my secret because they think I have special powers, like *Ek Chuah*, the god of trade. It gives me an advantage and keeps me on course."

He shared personal stories of his family, travels and observations of changes taking place since the conquest. They both felt a comfort and trust, like they'd known each other for a long time. It was an emotion too faint to be interpreted or understood.

Night grew dark and cooler, alive with people all around, but where Itz and Kan Ik sat there was only light and warmth and each other. They talked for hours. Itz found his laughter more precious than money and more heart cleansing that any of her tears or prayer.

"I feel guilty being so happy after all that has happened," Itz sighed, as she discussed her feelings with her aunt that evening.

"My dear one, guilt is unproductive. Depriving yourself does not honor the dead or help anyone. It won't make the slightest difference if you allow yourself some joy. A woman in harmony with her spirit is like a river flowing."

"I will miss Kan Ik when we go our separate ways," said Itz.

"Yes," Yaxche answered, "But remember that he is a marinier and merchant, a *pplom*, important as life blood to the people. He needs to be part of the water, the wind and the sky. The stars pull his hair. It is not his destiny to stay in one place too long. Like you, his mission is his life. You must never interfere with his sacred task."

CHAPTER 43

Nabalam, Yucatan
1563 A.D.

Trumpets and drums announced the arrival of Diego De Landa. The Franciscan fathers proceeded through Nabalam's main square and up the local church steps. Leading the group was the Father Superior from Izamal himself. Following him were his minions and a squad of belligerent armed soldiers. De Landa made the sign of the cross in the air over the cowering people along the roadside. Tepal and the other priests did likewise, blessing the masses by waving a hand of benediction.

"Swatting at the air, like swatting at insects, will never cure the ills brought on by the invaders," spat Yaxche whenever she saw priests cross themselves.

Itz and her aunt missed the religious leaders' parade. Unaware of the nearness of their former Maya prince and the prince of the Catholic Church, they continued their day's work and visits with other merchants and friends. They stayed busy selling pottery and medicinal cures in the marketplace. Yaxche taught Itz how to create formulas to deal with the new diseases brought across the seas by the white men. She wrote down the ingredients to later be painted as floral decorations on a plate.

Even though Tepal had taken Catholic vows and wore dark clerical robes, he regularly slipped out of the monastery to be on his own. He dressed in finer garbs and jewels that his vanity felt better befitted one of royal blood. His private excursions and lewd entertainments under the cloak of darkness were anything but religious or monastic.

That afternoon Tepal visited the market to find feathers for a new evening cloak and perhaps a jade bracelet. He reluctantly promised to buy Cimi some powerful drugs to deal with the constant pain in his leg. He felt no compassion for the man's suffering, but needed to keep his old cohort dependent and submissive.

Tepal was dressed in refined local style clothes, but not enough to stand out from the crowd or draw attention to his truancy from the church sanctuary. He strolled among open-air booths to examine goods from around the regions. Tied to his belt were pouches filled with coin of the realm and cacao beans that were better than gold for trading with local merchants. Money he took from the tributes and church poor boxes allowed him to purchase anything he desired. He always got what he wanted, one way or another.

Tepal noticed two young men gathered near a stall buying cups. He noted the long dark eye lashes on the smaller one. His breathe quickened as he began fantasizing about introducing the beautiful male child to the ways of his secret world. Tepal's loins tightened from lustful visions. He moved in closer to get the youngster to come with him and fulfill his pressing needs. Suddenly, he was yanked from his vile revelries when he saw Itz behind the market table wrapping newly purchased wares for her customers.

Tepal drew back behind a piece of hanging fabric to hide himself from view. She looked very different with long braided hair and in dressed in simple peasant attire.

"*No mistake. I have found her. There is her aunt, the witch,*" he scowled. He had been unable to locate her since her escape from Edzna and their brief encounter at the elder council meeting near Mani. Tepal planned his return and how to take her captive for himself. He slipped out of the plaza for reinforcements.

An unexplained chill ran down Itz's spine. She turned, looked around and saw nothing unusual. Not one to ignore intuition and signs, she packed up her few remaining goods for next day's early return home.

Yaxche, Itz and Kan Ik shared a delicious meal of pit-roasted pig at his friend's home just off the plaza. He and Itz were involved in conversations of their own, like they were the only ones on the front patio. The friend and her aunt looked at them together and shrugged knowingly. They were both happy for the young couple.

Itz and Kan Ik walked across the cobblestone square to her temporary market stall. Her aunt's duties as chaperone were fulfilled in that she could still see them in silhouette across the plaza. Neither noticed a shadowy figure skulking between booths trailing them back to her selling space. Tepal decided to come alone to find out about Itz's activities and where she had hidden all those months.

Itz decided to tell Kan Ik about her scribe project of recording the historical books of her father and medicinal formulas of her aunt on pottery to preserve them. She described how she reproduced her father's books onto other hidden pottery and murals. She unwrapped and explained the one piece she had with her.

"This is a cylinder vase I created to portray observations of the astrological passages of the morning star called Venus and of the bright North Star." Itz handed her fine ceramic piece to Kan Ik. Hieroglyphs and ancient symbols were clearly drawn in jet black on a background of orange and red.

'In navigation of a boat, the North Star is my guiding light," he said, and nodded as he admired her accuracy of copying the old texts. "I can read the moon, sky, and date glyphs here, but what is this triadic symbol?" he asked her.

Itz's eyes widened and her forehead creased with questions. She was shocked at his knowledge of the ancient writing system. Only chosen elite, the rulers, were privileged to have training in such literacy skills.

"All the men in my family had tutors for reading and writing," he quietly explained as a part of his well-concealed regal past was exposed. She had trusted him so he chose to trust her with personal information known to very few.

Without words they saw recognition in the other's eyes and realized how both found covert ways to carry out noble duties to their people in spite of the conquerors. An admiration and deep respect developed between the two that moment.

Kan Ik felt a connection, and yet sensed a reservation in Itz he did not understand. She had taken to heart her aunt's disclosure that he must not be encumbered or distracted, and so held back any signs of affection or attraction. It was hard for her to honor his calling when she wanted so much to be part of his life.

Tepal was not close enough to hear their whispered conversation, but he could make out familiar forbidden written hieroglyphs on Itz's pottery. That alone was enough evidence to convict her of heresy and treason. All the leverage he needed to force her to bend to his will or face punishment from the authorities. He cackled out loud at his fortunate discovery as he crept back to the church.

"I'm going to purchase this piece," Kan Ik insisted. "Your secrets will be safe with me."

Itz was not certain if she would ever see Kan Ik again. The idea of him having something special of hers with him pulled at her heart and she agreed.

"It is not for sale. Take it as a gift."

Kan Ik held her in his arms for a brief moment. Their parting was silent. What reassuring words could they say? Neither one could promise another time or place. Greater powers did not seem to take their fateful connection into account. Itz and Kan Ik walked in opposite directions, not looking back.

CHAPTER 44

Nabalam, Yucatan
1563 A.D.

Itz woke at dawn to an astonishing clamor. Tropical birds launched into a frenetic disorderly hymn to the glories of morning. Itz wondered if they sang especially for her, encouraging her to be glad and create. It was an emotion she'd not experienced in a long time. Anticipation of an objective she felt could not be postponed. Everything was packed in bundles to go.

Yaxche was already up, preparing breakfast and food for the journey back to Ixkunil beside the Ek Balam ruins. She squatted on her heels as she tended the fire and pot of maize. Her body communicated a sense of robust power that harmonized with the look of serenity on her face. She wore a spontaneous gap-tooth smile of someone who has experienced enough life to only give importance to what is essential and set aside all else, except for her compassion for others.

Itz savored a bowl of maize and honey-drizzled fruit. She stared at her morning cup of chocolate and wished she hadn't poured so much coconut milk in, because now it was too creamy to resemble Kan Ik's dark brown eyes.

The peaceful moment shattered when four soldiers and a cadre of Spanish priests pushed through the beaded curtain of their shelter. An iron arm seized Itz from behind, pressing against her throat. The action immobilized her and she gasped, unable to speak.

"That is the infidel woman. Bring her," ordered an older priest. His was a graveled voice hidden behind the cowl of dark brown robes.

"What is this about?" cried Yaxche as they dragged Itz outside of the posada rooms.

Soldiers cut open the bindings and unwrapped the women's packs. They scattered personal possessions and remaining pottery around the front of the building.

"I have done nothing," Itz cried out. The soldier's hairy hand closed on her wrist like a vice. The grip did not slacken until she was thrown on the ground at the feet of Father De Landa.

"What do you want? Why are these men searching?"

The gaunt sharp-faced priest responded to everything she said in stony monosyllables.

"A reliable source said you continue to record evil signs of the devil," he finally spat at her. "This is punishable by death."

He grabbed a cane and lashed her back with all the strength he could muster. She fell flat against the stone pavers in throbbing pain. Bloody stripes blossomed on the back of her torn white shift.

Itz fumed in revulsion and fundamental loathing at being accused by the very men who killed her father and enslaved her people. Her mind spun and recalled the people who saw her native scribe works. Recently there was only her aunt and Kan Ik. Neither would turn on her.

Nothing incriminating was to be found in their lodgings or belongings. The guards and priests stopped their shredding and smashing destruction when they found the rolled up portrait of the Madonna she had painted. The Virgin's face seemed to have an unworldly and lifelike glow of its own. Several of the holy men made the sign of the cross and stepped back.

"Is this your work?" asked Friar De Landa.

"Yes, it is the mother of the blessed Christ," she confirmed.

"I will keep this as evidence."

"Evidence that I adore her, the symbol of love and forgiveness," she offered and placed her hands together as if in prayer, hoping to counter the accusations of heresy. It revolted her to do it, but she'd heard that converts had a better chance of survival at the hands of religious fanatics.

The square filled with other people and priests, including Tepal, standing in the back. He became visibly upset that the search and seizure did not produce the vase with hieroglyphs that he saw the night before. His report to the church authorities proved wrong. Tepal, as Brother Juan Guillermo, needed to quickly get back into the good graces of Father Diego.

"Maybe she could be put to work creating art for the glory of God," Tepal shouted out to allow his superior a way to save face. Itz recognized his voice and turned to see him staring at her angrily.

"Indeed, paintings are needed for the new churches. Let the woman go. For now," ordered De Landa with a resigned sigh.

This was not the scenario Tepal planned, but he would find a way for her arrest and even her release to work in his favor.

The soldiers held Yaxche back during the interrogation. When the priests left, she broke away from their rough grasp and lifted up her beaten niece from the ground.

"There is no way I am staying here in his service," Itz choked out through her raw throat. She trembled violently. "Let's go home. I have important work to do."

Yaxche tended to the brutal cuts on her niece's back. They prepared to return a circuitous route back to Ek Balam. Friends would help cover their departure and location. Yaxche repacked what she could salvage of their belongings while Itz rested for the journey. Yaxche went to purchase new food supplies and to the well for fresh water.

Itz heard a tap at the dwelling frame. She struggled up and pulled aside the curtain. Tepal stepped into her space. She took a step back in shock and trepidation.

"You are pleased to see me again. You've forgiven me for this," Tepal said as he reached out and touched her cheek.

"Some scars don't necessarily show," answered Itz as she turned her head away in disgust and fear. "I can not forget or forgive your transgressions against me and our people. Just leave." She walked out the door, pulled him to follow and to get him to go away.

"It looks like your traveling merchant friend spread false information about you at the cathedral before he left town," said Tepal to sow seeds of doubt and win favor.

"That is not possible," shouted Itz defensively. But her head swam trying to figure out how else the inquisitors came looking for her specific work.

"I saved your life over there," Tepal reminded her. He nodded in the direction of the earlier confrontation in the plaza.

"Why? You tried to take it before."

"Remember by all rights you belong to me. You are my subject. We were pledged as children."

"Our star signs are in direct conflict. You and I will never be together. Your family's rule was another lifetime ago," Itz answered with rancor.

"Some things are different now, but I still get what I want," he growled. Tepal grabbed Itz by her neck and bent her backwards. His mouth came bruising down on her lips. She tried to scream but the muffled sound escaped as a high-pitched moan. He pressed himself tightly against her. She put her arms up to push him away, but could not struggle free.

Busy roadway travelers often talked and sang as they walked. Kan Ik overheard someone tell about Spanish soldiers and priests raiding a woman potter's quarters at the marketplace. His heart sank knowing they probably meant Itz.

He asked one of the bearers and the man said, "Prince Tepal stopped the priests from arresting the heretic. Someone said that they were betrothed. She will work for the churchmen now."

Kan Ik fumbled through a jumble of unclear thoughts and emotions. "*Was there more between her and Tepal than she let on? Did she lie or mislead me? Was the traitorous prince the reason for Itz's hesitations?*" he thought.

The unexplained occurrence confused Kan Ik. There was no reason to turn back if she was rescued and especially if she was co-operating with the enemy. His own mission could be in danger. A splinter of loneliness stabbed him, stayed under his skin, and remained in his helpless memory. He returned to his journey with a deeper disappointment and personal sadness than he ever thought possible. Such melancholy took him by surprise. It was not that he seized it, but that it seized him.

CHAPTER 45

Mexico City
Present Day

Hannah was surprised and confused by the kind of reception she received at work that day. As she walked through the Anthropology Museum laboratory to her desk, people avoided eye contact. Like crickets, they made a lot of noise, but when she passed them, they suddenly went quiet or whispered in her wake.

"*What is going on?*" she wondered.

The answer to her question sat on her desk in the form of a magazine opened to a four-page article written by Joseph Comouche about antiquity theft at Edzna. She was excited to see which photographs taken during his three days on site were chosen and to read his published words. Within moments Hannah's hand came up to her mouth and she needed to sit down. She froze, stunned by unmistakable accusations that the destruction of the temple and theft of the stucco sun-god mask were 'likely an inside job'. Hannah felt slapped by innuendoes and lies that filled the magazine pages. Her heart went cold with fear, then anger.

Hannah grabbed her computer and ran to the conference room to be out of earshot of others. Her hands trembled so much that it took two tries to connect on Skype with Joseph.

"Good morning Hannah. What a pleasant surprise to hear from you." His biggest boyish smile flashed across the screen.

"How dare you! What kind of journalist, or shall I say hack, are you? How could you make up a distorted and soul-quenching article like this?" She shouted and waved the magazine in front of the computer.

Joseph actually appeared confounded. Her words cut sharply. He looked at her like she was speaking Mayan.

"I have not seen the final print. I don't know what you are so upset about. I turned in a very favorable report. Let me read the spread and call you right back." In five minutes, Hannah heard the ring and clicked right on.

"Hannah, I swear to you this article was not what I wrote. The editor changed the final version, sensationalizing it to sell more copies. I am so sorry."

His voice and eyes were sincere. But apologies did not alter the fact that thousands of copies were already distributed, insinuating she was a corrupt archaeologist.

"An article even hinting at the appearance of impropriety can ruin my reputation," she cried. "I've seen colleagues ostracized and careers destroyed over less."

"This is not insurmountable," he tried to comfort her.

"You know me. I'd never be involved in the trade of illegal antiquities. How do we undo these lies?" Her voice rose in hoarse emotion.

"Hannah, you are understandably upset and angry."

"My work is my whole life," she admitted. "Everything I love may be taken away or forever tainted by this undeserved scandal."

The muffling weight of unfairness and self-doubt echoed in her trembling voice. Hannah was profoundly frightened. She liked things to be predictable and solid. But this attack proved that nothing was ever certain or in her control. She'd been ambushed and the ground was disappearing beneath her feet. She felt as threatened as she ever had in her life.

"Don't respond or do anything yet. I am going to see the editor-in-chief immediately. He will print a retraction and rewrite. I will do everything I can to undo the damage. I've got this," he promised. Hannah wanted to believe him.

"Printed words cannot be unwritten in people's minds," she lamented. Tears streamed down her cheeks. Joseph was concerned about her. This was not the invincible Hannah he knew.

"I'm taking the first flight I can get to Mexico City. I should see you in less than eight hours. Hold tight."

He disconnected without a goodbye. Hannah stared at the blank screen until it went dark. She felt lost, as if everything she worked so hard for came to an end. Yet time did not stop. She listened to her heartbeat measuring out the seconds. She felt the air conditioner's cold blast on her arms and thirst in her throat, raw from crying.

For the second time in her life, she thought she would die from sorrow. Yet instead Hannah was absurdly alive. She wanted to see Joseph, her friend Tem Chen and face this challenge together. Warm thoughts of the him brought a smile to her face. She scrubbed her tears away with the back of her sleeve and quickly regained her composure.

Dr. Sarra came back from an overseas trip that afternoon and summoned Hannah to his office. They discussed the article and its possible ramifications.

"I spoke to the byline journalist Comouche and he promised a clarification on their website and in the next edition," she told him.

Dr. Sarra didn't appear as upset or pessimistic as Hannah thought he would be over the accusations. Somehow he seemed pleased by an opportunity to be her protector.

"I assure you I don't believe the magazine's thinly veiled

suggestions of dishonesty on your part. I'll make sure you are taken care of my dear," Sarra said. He took her hands in his. "I promise I will defend you."

Hannah figured Joseph would go to her home when he arrived, so she packed up to go home and wait for him there. She and Sarra happened to walk out of the museum at the same time. They paused on the steps down to the underground parking structure to say goodbye. He could tell she was still upset so he wrapped his arms around her and placed a long reassuring kiss on her cheek.

Joseph did not go to Hannah's apartment first. He rushed to the Anthropology Museum. He was coming up to the main building entrance when he spotted Hannah in Dr. Sarra's romantic embrace and stopped in his tracks.

"*They make a striking couple. The director obviously has his sights on Hannah. He can offer her jobs, permits, and special favors. I knew from the beginning that she was an ambitious woman*," ran through Joseph's head.

He stood frozen at the sight of Hannah receiving affectionate attentions from the attractive and powerful Dr. Sarra. He was aware of this ruthless man's reputation and reach.

"*How could I compete with him? I guess I was wrong about Hannah. So very wrong*," he thought.

Love sees clearly, but jealousy sees more sharply because it is love and hate at the same time. The glass through which he saw Hannah became clouded. Joseph's head and shoulders dropped as his usual confidence and energy drained out of him. He turned without a word and careened down the sidewalk in a daze. He grabbed a taxi to the airport and took the first available plane back to New York.

CHAPTER 46

Mexico City
Present Day

Hannah hurried home and tidied up the apartment. She hummed as she prepared her favorite Italian lemon chicken dinner for her favorite Italian-Kiwi journalist. Cooking was one of her hidden talents. She waited for Joseph to arrive. By nine o'clock, she checked to be sure her porch light worked and paced around the living room. Concern and worry lines formed between her brows. A quick check online showed over a dozen flights had arrived from New York.

"*It's been almost twelve hours since we spoke. I wonder what's keeping him?*" Confusion and doubt clouded her inner thoughts. "*Something important must have come up or happened. I hope he's okay.*"

At one in the morning, she placed the uneaten meal in the refrigerator and turned off the lights. She plopped down on top of the bed covers in her clothes and stared at the ceiling. Exhaustion from the doubly disappointing day overtook her and she fell into a deep sleep. Rain beat a constant dance on the roof and tapped sharply on her windows, but did not wake her.

Morning dawned, as such mornings often do after a storm, crystal clear and refreshingly beautiful. Bright light burning through the shutters surprised Hannah awake. First thing, she checked her emails and phone for messages. There were none.

Before leaving for work at the museum, she sent an inquiring message to Joseph, trying hard not to sound too demanding of an explanation or too desperate. When she checked in later that morning there was no response.

"Standing a girl up for a date is one thing, but that article fiasco was a professional crisis for both of us," she said to her father when they chatted at length that afternoon. Hannah could talk to her dad Max about anything. She confided to him about work, Joseph, Sarra and other important life matters. Always able to multi-task, on the side Max called the magazine staff office.

"Honey, I just talked to the magazine headquarters. Sorry to say, but your writer friend Joseph volunteered to be embedded with frontline military troops covering some covert mission. He left at o'dark hundred this morning."

"Without a word? I thought we were friends. I don't understand." Hannah shook her head in disbelief. "He couldn't have been in such a hurry that he forgot our meet up. A quick note and I would have understood his call to work." Secondary realization hit. "Oh my god, he went away to war, in harm's way," she cried out.

"Hannah, right now I know you're probably thinking of your fiancé Stephen who died in Afghanistan. Not everyone who goes to war dies. It will be all right," he tried to sooth his bereaved child who had taken her first love's death extremely hard.

Her rational mind could not override the emotional damage Joseph's abandonment and silence caused. The fact that he was in a war zone, not only frightened her, but also made her angry because of her hatred of war.

"Powers that be may call fighting each other honor or defense, but war boils down to greed and money. No one wins. The soldiers either come back in a box

or return changed forever. Civilians, especially innocent children suffer the most collateral damage," she ran familiar arguments through her brain. No one was listening. She felt helpless to alter present world madness.

Hannah compulsively poured herself into work. It helped numb emotions and anger. She provided her department and Dr. Sarra with detailed documented information about unique Maya sites. She didn't need to get the credit, but she did want to be part of a winning team. He valued her objective and intuitive talents when it came to archaeology. Her resource fountain gave him leads for future projects. He asked her opinions on acquisitions and exhibits.

Hannah possessed a rare gestalt talent for being able to construct the entire tapestry scene after only seeing a few threads. Given only a small clue or puzzle piece, she could reconstruct images and sequences. She trained to recognize ceramic fragments and to deduce the original form, as well as the geographic and time periods they covered. She was like human data bank.

"Dr. Char, you never cease to amaze me. So many of our archaeologists are all antennae and no head," he complimented her.

Professionally they worked well together. But nights at various soirees, she felt like arm decoration, expected to look good and smile. Sam Sarra would hold her hand in public or caringly put his arm around her shoulders. A touch of affection appeared, but passion was absent. End of evening farewells contained no more than a lukewarm peck on the cheek or forehead before his driver dropped her at home.

"You get hurt more than you deserve when you care about someone more than they deserve," claimed Paloma. "My friend, you are a rainbow. Anyone who can't see that is colorblind."

"It's obvious that I've spent too much time in the company of my literary romantic heroes. My expectations and ideals are unrealistic," Hannah conceded to her roommate.

"Optimists like you tend to categorize people as good, bad, kind or cruel based on their public behavior. Trust me, perfection doesn't exist in the world, or in anyone," Paloma replied.

Weeks went by with no contact from Joseph. Hannah quit making up excuses for him. She missed their banter and confidences shared. The loneliness seemed crueler because it was the result of him ceasing communication. She reread their emails, looking for clues to what she might have said or done wrong and for any hints predicting desertion of friendship. Nothing stood out as a warning.

"I guess he's forgotten me. Once again I feel like an option, not a priority in some guy's life." she told Mari over the telephone.

"Even though he told me that he did not write that damaging article, maybe he did slant it on purpose and can't face me," said Hannah. Doubt crept into her voice.

"That does not sound like Tem Chen. Give it time. I am sure there is a better explanation. Hannah, you don't invite robbers into your house. So don't allow thoughts that steal your trust make themselves at home in your head," advised her trusted confidant.

The next day at the museum, dozens of perfect red roses in a crystal vase crowded Hannah's workspace. The attached envelope contained a note from Dr. Sarra.

"I'll pick you up at seven on the dot. Wear something conservative, perhaps your long black cashmere dress I like. Tonight we will attend an intimate gathering of old friends at a widow's home."

His flowers were romantic, but the precise instructions grated on Hannah's nerves as control and manipulation. He was generally right, but she still wanted the respect of making her own choices. He just assumed she was free and would appear, and perform as he wished. Everyone else around him always did.

"At last, Sam seems to be warming to me," said Hannah hopefully, as she dressed for the evening. "Tonight will be different."

"Those are the four most delusional words in your English language," tisked Paloma. "One-sided expectations can destroy you. Please be careful with this man. Being such a trusting Pollyanna is never a blessing," sighed her more experienced roommate.

CHAPTER 47

Mexico City
Present Day

Driving through stately black wrought iron gates, Hannah glimpsed a gleaming white estate--- a manor of otherworld grandeur at the end of a tree-lined drive. Dr. Sarra offered his arm and helped her step out of his sleek gold Jaguar.

The couple paused at the top of the sweeping Carrara marble spiral staircase. Ivory-toned furniture, pale silk carpets, Waterford crystal chandeliers and rare artworks filled the vast space.

A statuesque woman stood looking toward them. "Tina," said Sarra adoringly as he kissed their hostess on both cheeks. Hannah stood behind him. The manor's mistress matched the surroundings. Her complexion was creamy like porcelain, her hair fell in shimmering light blonde waves and she flashed a pearly perfect smile. Cristina Delgado was not at all like the old widow Hannah expected. Her aura and beauty were so powerful they drew everything to her. In stark contrast, Hannah figured she herself would always need to chase and work hard for everything she wanted.

"This must be the archaeologist I have heard so much about," Cristina cooed in welcome. They followed her into a vast mirrored dining hall and greeted over a dozen other guests enjoying samplings of the world's finest wines, pates and cheeses. Freshly baked breads and succulent fruits were available to cleanse the palate between tastings.

All the guests except Hannah and Cristina were men wearing classic black tuxedos and crisply starched white dress shirts. As her glance swept the setting, Hannah recognized Father Frank Dixon, a priest she'd met at other functions. He caught her eye and waved her over to an oversized grand piano he was playing. He patted the bench and she took a seat next to him.

"Pleased to see you my dear," he said in a gentle, but raspy, voice. Hannah admired his work with the poor and felt comfortable in his company.

Over the months she'd heard rumors that as a seminarian and priest, the archdiocese singled him out, educated and groomed him for a leadership role in the Holy Church. They called him their 'five million-dollar priest' because of all the degrees, courses in music, art, languages and travel it had taken to prepare him as a religious prince, their shining star.

Tonight it appeared the good father drank too many glasses of Johnny Walker Black Label, because he began to personally confide in Hannah about his rapid rise to power in the church. He slurred a bit as he told the saga of his grooming and promised future.

"I was the perfect priest on my way to grand things. That was until I met Teresa and fell in love for the first and last time in my life. He continued, "She was a widow I counseled for two years. I couldn't wait for Thursdays when she came for confession and grief sessions. The day she told me she was moving to the United States, I broke down and told her of my feelings. It turned out she was leaving because she couldn't get closer to me or express love she too felt. We held each other." He smiled at Hannah and played the theme from Casablanca on the ivory and ebony keys.

"What did you do? You were a priest, and she a devout follower. How did you two find your way?" Hannah asked, caught up in his surprisingly intimate revelations.

“We discussed what being together would do to our lives. Despite all that stood in our way, I resigned from the priesthood and married Teresa. The church was up in arms over the loss of me, their ‘investment’ as they put it. My two years with her were my happiest,” Father Frank sighed and stared wistfully into the night.

“What happened? You’re back in the brotherhood fold, a priest again. Where is she now?” Hannah’s questions tumbled out.

“Are you sure you want to know? You could enjoy better company than me.” He downed his glass of dark liquor and waved to the waiter for another. “No ice,” he instructed. Hannah nursed her one glass of white wine.

She turned on the piano bench to half face him, isolating his words and emotions from the others. He tickled the keys without cease as he started.

“Where do I begin? Okay, see our hostess, that strikingly beautiful women by the fireplace talking to your beau?” He nodded subtly to Cristina and Sam Sarra. “Let me tell you her story first.”

“What did she have to do with her marriage?”

“You’ll understand soon enough. Cristina wanted more than anything to be a nun. She felt spiritual callings from the age of ten.”

“Her? I can’t picture her taking vows of poverty, chastity and obedience,” Hannah said and scoffed at the idea. “Just the opposite.”

“Mother Superior at Sisters of Mercy turned Tina away several times and admonished her to find another way to serve the church.”

“Was she heartbroken? What did she do then?”

“She told me once that since her beauty caused the rejection, she actually considered pouring boiling water over her head. With scars to show commitment and devotion, they might admit her.”

“No. She couldn’t have been that desperate.”

“Desperate, but in the end, too vain. She came up with a plan of revenge worthy of a Machiavellian prince. Mother Superior’s brother, Dr. James Delgado, was elderly and wealthy. All the family estates were his and he had no children, no heirs. See where this is going?” said the priest. He laughed at the irony.

“Cristina is now the widow of this Dr. Delgado and controls the vast family wealth, which might have been donated to the convent or church if he had not married her,” Hannah guessed correctly. “Sweet! But what about her religious calling?”

“She developed her own way of serving the church.” Father Frank paused and looked around the room to see if anyone stood close enough to hear. He knew that consumption of alcohol made one think they were whispering when they’re not.

“Cristina knew how difficult it was for priests to maintain their vows of celibacy,” he coughed nervously. “So in order to help them remain safe and discrete, she invited holy brothers to her home and gave them a sanctuary. There were parties here, sometimes with special friends or pretty young men. She has entertained and protected an entire generation of priests. We all adore her and would do anything to maintain the freedom she provides us.”

Hannah’s face registered wide-eyed shock and surprise. She’d never heard of such a thing.

“But wasn’t it hard to keep her retreat and services a secret?”

“Priests are trained and take sacred vows to keep secrets of confession,” he reminded her.

“Every story has a however in it,” Hannah encouraged him to continue.

He paused to take a long draw on his drink. “There was a young priest called Manny who fell madly in love with Tina. He begged her to stop seeing her circle of priests and marry him. When she refused, he pulled out a pistol and committed suicide. Right there by the pool,” Frank pointed at the black and white tiled formation across the patio.

"How sad," Hannah said. "Did that expose her?"

"No, she immediately called me and another father to come help her. Actually it was your friend Sam Sarra. You did know he was a priest before, didn't you?" he asked innocently. "Another superstar of the dioceses. Just serving us in different ways now."

Hannah tried not to show the jolting shock that hit her and spread like a glass of red wine across a white tablecloth. But an unintentionally loud "Oh!" gave her away. Her mind flooded with questions and images.

"How many clues I missed. Lots makes sense now, like his austere office, no sensuality, odd friendships and access to unlimited resources and hidden power" she rapidly thought.

"We removed the remains and cleaned up the evidence," Frank continued as if he'd never dropped a bombshell on his audience of one. "We secreted Manny's lifeless body back to his room in the church rectory. We called in a lot of favors, granted penances, and paid off the right authorities to report it as a death by natural causes. Graves hide many secrets."

"Obviously Cristina still entertains, but did she continue to run her own Order of Mercy after that episode?"

"Yes. Every man here tonight, except Sam, is currently a practicing priest," was all Father Frank said for a long time. Wanting to satisfy her curiosity of how this tied into his return to the church, Hannah sat silently and patiently by his side while he played a series of old show tunes.

Dr. Sarra glanced over occasionally and gave her a raised hand salute. He seemed happy that she was occupied so he could mingle on his own that night. Little did he know how many intimate details she was learning about his religious community.

"My wife Teresa was an observant girl," Father Frank began abruptly. "She saw things around the parish that did not make sense to her. For instance, the carnival attendance and income seemed too far off for anything but someone dipping in the till. Rumors of payoffs for altar boys' counseling and silence circulated regularly. Once she saw Tina and the Bishop at the airport boarding an international flight together hand-in hand. Obviously they were not as discrete in public as they should have been."

"Did she ask you about it?"

"Yes, I confided everything to my wife. I pleaded with her to stay silent. She understood and respected my wishes until a new regime of church elders took over the district. She said she felt compelled to report the decadence. That's what she called it, pure decadence."

"Did she? Did she report the corruption and priests' activities at Cristina's house?"

"Never got the chance," he slumped over the keyboard for a moment. She thought that one too many drinks had done him in. But then he took a deep breath, sat up straight and returned to his secret tale.

"One afternoon I got a call from her. She'd had a small accident. Told me the car was not drivable and thought her wrist might be broken. She asked me to pick her up at St. John's Catholic Hospital where the medics were taking her for an x-ray."

"Was she okay?"

"When I got there, she was in a coma. Never woke up. Died that night."

Hannah felt shock and dismay.

"Seems the nuns made a mistake and gave her the wrong injection."

"Oh, Father," Hannah touched his arm gently. "You must have been devastated."

"I couldn't breath. I didn't want to live anymore. I hardly remember the funeral. My church brothers took care of everything. The bishop offered me my old life back. His Holiness convinced me that my vows were to the church first, before my marriage vows. He said they would honor the prior vows, forgive me and take care of me if I would reenter the holy order."

"So you became a priest again."

"Yes, but they got the worse of the bargain because I am a hollow bitter man now. They killed my Teresa," he slurred.

"You really think her death wasn't an accident?" Hannah wondered if his theory was the results of too much liquor and grief.

"I know for a fact they murdered her to keep her quiet. Hannah, never underestimate the evil around you." With that, the sad old priest closed the lid of the keyboard, stood up and staggered out of the room.

CHAPTER 48

Mexico City
Present Day

Sam Sarra drove Hannah home down Reforma. The avenue, wet from an earlier rain, shined like black patent leather. The hour was late so the usual hectic heavy traffic was light. Sarra zigzagged through the remaining cars a little faster than necessary. Hannah was uncomfortable with his speed and tailgating. For a change, he held her hand, but she wished he would use both hands on the steering wheel instead. There was a glazed look in his eyes and she wondered if the usually controlled director had too much to drink at Cristina's party.

She was grateful when they arrived without incident at her apartment. He opened the passenger door and took her arm to help her out. As she stood up, Sarra spun her around backward and pressed her against car. He wrapped his arms around her and pulled her in closer, like right before a couple falls asleep and they spoon. He brushed her hair aside and kissed the back of her neck and shoulder. Hannah felt him sensually moving against her.

"*I just knew tonight would be different. He is acting so loving,*" she sighed.

Hannah twisted herself around, put her arms around Sarra, leaned in and gave him a long romantic kiss.

Sarra opened his eyes in horror and stepped back, as if he'd been awakened from a trance. His furious look darted up and down Hannah accusingly.

"What are you doing?" he asked.

"Me? You started…"

"This should never have happened. It was the wine." He shook his head to clear it and put out an upraised stiff arm to assure she stayed away from him.

"But I thought…" Hannah stammered.

"You stupid naïve woman. If I had been physically attracted to you, I would have done something about it before now."

Hannah stood in confusion and embarrassment at misreading the signals.

"Just go," Sarra ordered. He got into his car and sped away.

After the night at Cristina Delgado's mansion and the hot and cold behavior of Sarra, Hannah pulled back from any avoidable interactions with him. Mostly, Father Dixon's story haunted her. She couldn't be in the company of Sam Sarra without flashbacks to the tales of deception and death she'd been told by the old priest.

Her initial romantic attraction to the handsome director and the shallow glamour of the supposed good life faded daily. All those plastic lives seemed so fake and meaningless. What she needed was honesty and depth in a person. She was not happy in her relationship with Sarra.

"Stop going to the barber shop for eggs," Paloma told her when she shared the car episode.

When Hannah now thought about Sarra, she feared dark and dangerous depths. During their usual morning conference in his office, she felt distracted and longed to be elsewhere.

"Black tie dinner tonight at the Hyatt. My driver will swing by for you at 8," Sarra informed her brusquely. He reached out to take her hand and she jerked back, before manners could stop her reaction.

For the first time, Hannah declined the forceful director's invitation. She offered no excuse and coldly said "No thank you."

Sarra's carved features became tight with irritation. Flaring nostrils and squinting eyes reflected his surprise and anger at losing control over her. He was accustomed to getting his way with others. His charm and money always won over their hesitation. He fumed internally over the rejection. Domination over people and events excited him more than sex and sustained him more than eating.

Hannah could see his anger. She still had expectations of people being fair and doing the right thing. Every violation of that by others shocked her. At first when Sarra was rude or mean to people, she thought his toughness was strength and that strength would protect her. But after a while, she knew it was just meanness. In the same way, she learned that rigid wasn't stable; it was brittle. She left his office without another word and walked back to her analysis laboratory.

Hannah made work-related excuses and canceled the morning coffee meetings with Sarra. Not being his escort was a huge relief, not a sacrifice. Manipulative people need control like others need oxygen. She stood her ground and took his air away. She was finished supplying valuable information, which she suspected he turned over to what he referred to as 'agents'.

"*Were these supposed agents other archaeologists, museums or were they antiquity dealers or looters?*" she wondered. "*If anyone gets to work and preserve the sites or receive credit for finds, it will be Berto and me,*" Hannah swore. Too many recent looters' trenches and priceless historical items from Yucatan already flooded the black market.

"After all I have done for her, Hannah's stubbornness to share is unacceptable. I need that intelligence information. She must be taught a lesson and brought back into line," Sarra told his companion, Father Batz. "I'll show her how the real world treats rebellion."

He sent a cursive note to the human resource department requesting Hannah's personnel file. On his orders, they reassigned her to the dank museum basement to measure and catalogue a skeletal collection from a site called Teotenango.

The old bone hoard was stored in a long windowless room next to a noisy industrial-sized air conditioning unit. Hundreds of boxes stuffed with jumbled bones to sort and analyze were stacked up to the ceiling against ten-meters of back wall in the frosty dark room.

Hannah's cheerful attitude of 'This is great' when she started on the skeletal collection was not what Sarra intended or expected. He saw her bundled up against the cold with a coat and gloves, entering the storage room early every day and leaving late. She was pulling herself out of a crevice of sorrow by a rope, and that rope was constant labor. Her hard work was not always appreciated or noticed. Other staff members chided her about making them look bad. Hannah learned to endure the loneliness that came with the jealousy of her peers.

Despite himself Sarra missed Hannah's company and discussing archaeology techniques and treasures with her. She could take baffling sheets of statistics and point out patterns and trends that others missed, like the colorblind overlook red in a field of green. Hannah, on the other hand, looked quite content alone in the basement and dealt with whatever hardships he placed in her way. She was not physically comfortable in the small basement room, but she loved working with ancient bones.

"*Aside from criminology, archaeology has the highest body count*," she thought while looking at her two-meter high color-coded stacks of evidence. "*Bones tell so many tales.*"

Hannah could look at a skeleton and determine if it was male or female, height, approximate age and weight, and how many times the females had given birth. The indicators were all there to be read. Diet and disease were recorded on bones. She made up stories about the burial individuals assigned to her.

"This was an older man, about forty. Definite evidence showed he'd taken a tremendous blade cut across his forehead and cheek.

He lost his eye, but it healed. Years later he was killed by a crushing blow to the left side of his head," she dictated aloud for the record.

He was probably a warrior, she had deducted. Battle wounds were not rare, but this cranium was almost four times the average width at the occipital base. He had a strong bull neck and hard head like a pro-linebacker, projected Hannah.

One box filled with more delicate bones disturbed her peace. In the report, she wrote, "Female aged 14-16 years. Fractured skull indicates death from blunt force trauma to the right parietal of the skull. Additional fractures appear on the ulna and radius of the left forearm, known as parry breaks. Likely defensive breaks received when she put her arms up to protect herself from the lethal blows that followed."

When Hannah examined the pelvis, she found evidence of tiny fetal bones within the girl's skeleton.

A probable scene flashed in front of her mind's eyes. "Someone probably found out she was pregnant. In a fit of anger he lashed out at the young girl with a staff. First she was able to ward off the attack with her upraised arms, but received debilitating double parry fractures. Unable to evade further wrath, the final blow to the head ended two young lives." Hannah projected sadly.

Even after working through the cartons of skeletons for weeks, Hannah found the challenge exhilarating. She was an archaeologist after all. Measuring and analyzing old bones and clues to put together a life story through fragmented remains was something she reveled in. She loved reconstructing history.

CHAPTER 49

Mexico City
Present Day

"Bones are witnesses to lives lived hundreds and thousands of years ago," she told her dad when they spoke long distance that evening. "I've found non-metric epigenetic changes in over one hundred skulls in the Teotenango collection. Extra cranial bone islands in this group serve as additional markers of genetic groups and invasions." Her voice went up and she talked fast.

"Hannah, you get excited over the strangest things," Max laughed.

"I figured I could suffer or I could create. I chose the latter. I must keep up my spirits and do a competent job so that I can return to the field. Director Sarra can hurt me if I give him ammunition, but there are others who can help me outside INAH. Taking the high road, Dad, like you taught me."

"That's my girl. Whatever situation presents itself, you embrace it as if you'd chosen it. What else is going on?"

"Unusual things are happening in the museum that I find suspicious. People I recognize as antiquity dealers and private collectors blatantly bring in boxes with who knows what inside. Some leave empty handed and others with different containers."

"Have you provided Dr. Sarra with this information?"

"We pretty much give each other broad space now. The trouble is, many of them are coming to see him. I can't confront him without more information and evidence. Besides, he responds badly to being questioned."

"Hannah, when you begin to wonder if you can trust somebody or not, that's when you already know you don't."

"I am at the museum early every day and leave later than everyone else, so I'm going to poke around and investigate."

"Be very careful Hannah. Possession of beautiful and unique items becomes the passion of avid collectors. They find objects that have a history, especially a tragic history, uniquely attractive. I've seen this all too often in the rare book world. In the arena of libraries, we have numerous single-minded collectors infected with bibliomania. They wouldn't hesitate to steal or kill for the chance of possessing certain rare volumes."

"But Dad, many of these people are successful businessmen and millionaires."

"Don't you see, money has nothing to do with it. Collecting becomes an obsession, a compulsion, like that of a serial killer. They can never get enough. I have observed first hand, their driven intensity in the auction houses of the world."

"I am afraid that if a collector laid hands on certain artifacts, they would lock them away in some deep vault, and never consider selling the pieces or letting another person lay eyes upon them again. They rarely let scientists like me study or display the works publically. What could they possibly get out of gloating on their hoard in private?"

"Wealthy collectors are not like ordinary people, baby girl. They become jaded because they can buy absolutely anything they want. It gives them orgasmic pleasure to own something rare or unique that no one else can have. Be cautious with any investigation. You are dealing with a type of fanatic whose disease allows him to stop at nothing," Max warned his daughter.

"They feel they are above the law and therefore can't be punished. Some art thieves and collectors are in cahoots with drug cartels and other serious criminal elements. They use valuable pieces in place of cash or as collateral to fund illegal activities," he said.

"That's what Joseph was telling me. He'd planned to do an in depth article on antiquity theft. From what you say, that type of assignment's about as dangerous as being in a battle zone," she said with a deep sigh.

Her mind wandered back to when she and Joseph shared thoughts and ideas openly. Max could tell his daughter missed her friend.

"If you are finished telling me your news, I have some for you," he said. "I received a call from Joseph this morning."

"What?" Hannah jumped up from her chair and shouted.

"His magazine publisher told him I inquired about him. Joseph called and we chatted for a good half hour. Nice guy. I liked him."

"You let me rattle on about bones and conspiracies when you had information like this? Tell me everything he said, every word," she insisted.

"Well, for one thing, he did fly to Mexico City to clear up the misunderstanding about his article. He felt awful about the way his copy editor slanted it against you."

"He was here in Mexico City?" she interrupted her dad.

"Yes, he went to the museum to get you and spotted you in the arms of some fellow. Guess that might have been when Director Sarra was courting you."

Hannah loudly groaned, slumped to the sofa, and pounded her head on the pillow in frustration. If Joseph saw Sarra kissing her, of course he could get the wrong impression.

"He believed you were in deep with the billionaire, so he backed off," her dad continued.

"Could this get any worse?" she cried.

"Being a gentleman, he thought he should go away. A painful way to say he cares for you, if you ask me. Said it was hard not to contact you so he went where he would be unable to."

"In harm's way! He could have been shot trying to be gallant," said Hannah. "I hope you set Joseph straight on my relationship with Dr. Sarra."

"It's up to you kids to work out those details," Max replied.

"Dad, I love you but I'm going to hang up now and try to reach Joseph. Let's see if we can clear this up."

Hannah immediately shot off emails to both Joseph's personal and work accounts.

"We need to talk. A failure to communicate has caused great misunderstandings," she wrote. Until she went to bed, she listened anxiously for the jingle that announced inbox mail. Nothing came through.

CHAPTER 50

Mexico City
Present Day

Crowds of VIP visitors, accompanied by Dr. Sam Sarra, filled the Anthropology Museum halls. Hannah moved unnoticed past throngs of people and took the elevator down to her dungeon work cubicle. She'd whipped through the skeletal remains quickly. Accuracy did not suffer when she was focused and intent on her work. Within hours she'd have all the bone data ready for statistical analysis. So close to finishing.

As she flipped the switch to turn on the single light bulb in the center of the room ceiling, bright light flashed and popped. The room fell into complete darkness. Hannah walked upstairs to the museum maintenance offices to report her burned out bulb. The secretary finally looked up from her cell phone game and asked, "What do you want?"

"I need someone to change a light bulb in Storeroom G as soon as possible. Please," she added and smiled to cover her impatience.

"An electricians' strike is going on, so you will have to wait."

"I don't need an electrician. I just need a new light bulb."

"Only electricians can handle electrical equipment. You have to wait till the strike is over and they come back to work," the girl told Hannah and returned to her online entertainment.

"When will the strike be over?"

"They've been out about a month now. Who knows when they'll reach a settlement," the girl said with an indifferent shrug of her shoulder.

"I have work to do."

"You get to take paid time off until the strike is over. Lucky you," said the girl without looking up.

"I don't want time off. I want a new light bulb so I can finish my job," repeated Hannah. The young bureaucrat couldn't grasp the concept of a person not rejoicing at an excused break in work.

"Never mind," Hannah said and stomped out of the maintenance unit. Her tolerance at being treated like an ignorant foreigner was in short supply.

She walked to a nearby hardware store and bought a flashlight and a long lasting bulb. Within two minutes of her return to the museum she'd climbed on her desk and changed the light bulb. She went back to work and completed all the skeleton measurements and photographs that afternoon.

As a reward to herself for finishing the arduous assignment, Hannah went upstairs to visit her nobleman figurine. She liked to be near him and meditate on the past, present and future. His glassed dome case stood vacant.

"Empty," Hannah gasped. She felt her stomach plunge. Bitter tastes of disappointment and anger filled her throat.

The curator of the Maya section was in his office. As politely as possible, Hannah asked about the missing figurine.

"I will check our records to see if the piece, which I can't particularly remember, has been moved, stored or sent somewhere on loan. Come back next week and I may have an answer for you."

Hannah was close to the edge with impatience and intolerance for unprofessional attitudes. His behavior reminded her of a common Mexican saying, 'There's always a way out'. It referred to a culturally acceptable exit strategy of finding various ways to not honor their obligations, debts or word.

"Thank you," she replied through clenched teeth.

"Rico," she said in cynical false admiration of the curator's new leather jacket thrown over the back of his chair. Price tags still hung from the sleeve cuff.

Hannah braced herself and went to Dr. Sarra's office. He was in, but the strident secretary kept her waiting for ten minutes before announcing her presence to the boss.

Sarra invited her in. "I was about to summon you regarding the confrontation you staged this morning in maintenance," he began.

"Confrontation? All I did was ask them nicely to change my burned out light bulb."

"That's not how I heard it. You purposefully broke the electrical union's strike line and took it upon yourself to restore power to a storeroom. You were told to wait until a qualified worker could be provided. Did you?" he asked, already knowing the answer.

"I changed a frickin' light bulb so I could finish my project," she shot back. The ideal of being a good and obedient girl no longer seduced her. "By the way, the complete data on the Teotenango skeletons was sent electronically and a hard copy is in your receptionist's basket. Done in record time, I might add. That should make you happy," she countered.

"Don't change the topic under discussion," he said coldly, not letting go of her minor infraction of museum and union rules.

"Hannah, you disappoint me. You can not work in Mexico and try to apply your North American ways to suit selfish needs."

Hannah could not believe her ears.

"How could anyone be upset over my changing a single light bulb rather than taking time off and waiting for strikers to return?" she wailed. "Are you trying to invent some excuse for firing me?"

"No, you are not fired. This time. But don't let your attitude and Yankee ways cost you a job," he said in his constant calm tone. If Sarra ever raised his voice, it would have the same effect as another man's rage. "Go back to pottery analysis and stay out of trouble," he warned.

Sarra picked up a phone and waved his hand to indicate the meeting was over and she was to leave.

"Wait. I came here to ask you about my Maya nobleman figurine. The case is empty, he's gone," Hannah said, trying not to whimper.

"I don't have time to discuss that. Contact the department head. Inventory is not my job."

Sarra turned his back on her. His eyes had already slammed the door behind her. She left the office scolded, shunned and discouraged.

At least she was on assignment back in the upstairs laboratory again. Her workbench was just as she'd left it before being banished to the chilled catacomb full of bones. Having natural light and windows open for fresh air improved her mood. She fetched a crate from storage and unpacked one of the incised and painted clay vessels she'd found during last season's excavation. There wasn't always time in the field to do proper analysis so now she could give the piece the attention it deserved.

Just thinking of fieldwork sent Hannah on a wistful mind voyage. "*I'll work in Maya ruins again,*" she said to send an intention to the universe.

Hannah carefully unwrapped the protective cotton batting from the artifact. She wore cotton gloves so oils in her hands would not mar the ancient pot paints or patina finish.

Hannah filled in the necessary data sheet as she worked. It still felt like dry journaling of an accountant to her. She carried the ceramic piece closer to natural light to appreciate it as a work of art.

"This vase is a masterpiece, created by a genius."

Drawings on the tall cylinder vase were exquisite in their execution. Separate panels illustrated the occasion of a royal birth. Hieroglyphs marked the dates and names of the subjects.

"*A portrait of a noble woman or queen,*" she sighed. "*Not the typical flat profile style of painting. This artist understood perspective.*"

The royal lady was anatomically correct and looked like a real breathing person. She even had a small enigmatic smile.

"*This Maya Mona Lisa is a creation of our mysterious scribe, I would know the style anywhere,*" proclaimed Hannah. "*Yes, a lily mark is on the side.*"

She actually hugged the ceramic piece to her heart. She ran her index finger over the images. "*My dear scribe, I promise to listen and speak for you. Send me more messages and clues like this painted vase,*" Hannah prayed.

CHAPTER 51

Ek Balam, Yucatan
1564 A.D.

Itz held up the vase she was painting to commemorate a prince's birth. She wanted to capture the noble mother's true features and mere whisper of a smile. She adjusted lines for perspective. Then paused with her eyes closed to visualize the next panels and hieroglyphs to tell the story.

The artist had a drive to communicate but realized that passion does not guarantee prodigy. At times she sensed her pottery and illustrated writings were a conversation with someone somewhere in the future, especially because many of her finest pieces ended up buried, hidden from the destructive forces of the conquistadors.

Like legendary Maya warrior queens, Itz planned her strategy and marshaled creative forces. She didn't need to raise an obsidian blade sword against the enemy; instead she wielded her pen and paintbrushes. Wonders of written words and powerful images create potent weapons in the battle to inspire conquered people.

"*I prefer my art work to the Spanish paintings in their churches*," she gloated. "*Too many focus on Christ with bloody wounds in his death agony, or those bland, characterless angels and simpering saints. I find hope and life in the gentler mother and child portraits.*"

Desire to replace representations of suffering with those of grace was why Itz started painting a series of the goddess or, as the priests would call them, Madonna. She chose Maya blue for the Virgin's cloak and cinnabar rising sun red for her gown. Sometimes she drew the blessed Virgin Mary under a ceiba tree, that Itz believed stood at the center of the earth and supported the heavens. The sacred tree symbolized life itself. Itz found it right and satisfying to combine two cultures and religious beliefs into one symbol of unconditional love, maternal love.

"*Christians, whose hearts have grown stiff and stony, need to be reminded of their Virgin Mary's gentleness and compassion. Both Jesus and our Kukulcan embodied wisdom and divine love. Why can't they see and accept that truth?*" she asked the heavens.

A sudden cool wind came through the doorway and wafted her long hair like threads of silk. Strong evening breezes blew bark papers around her workroom. Itz looked out the opening to behold bold brush strokes of pink and blue-gray sunset clouds. Stars came alive on the velvety dusk of the eastern horizon. The moon was several days past full but still bright enough to light up the courtyard. She sat transfixed by the extraordinary beauty of the dying day. Darkness fell quickly. Oil lamps cast a warm light around the room until losing itself in the rafters and thatching of the roof.

After the close call with inquisitors in Nabalm, Itz stayed close to her small compound on the outskirts of the ancient ruins in Ek Balam. Her home and workspaces were set up near the old city wall in an abandoned palace, north of the overgrown acropolis mound.

While clearing rubble from a long room, she discovered an alcove niche in the back wall. Disguised with thatch and plaster cover, it gave her a confessional-sized place to hide. Special items and wrapped bundles of emergency supplies were stored in the back. Never again would she be caught with no place to conceal herself.

"*My life has become one of infinite adapting,*" she mused.

Itz spent the morning transforming the natural elements she'd purchased and gathered into paints needed to create her art. She'd developed new techniques and acquired different ingredients. She mixed white mineral clay with blue dye produced by the indigo plant, *ch'oh*. In one batch she stirred in the bark of chukum to get a darker purple, almost black tone. When she could get them, sea clams from the north coast made a better purple.

She did the best she could with what was at hand. Organic yellow pigment and lime added to blue produced the rich jade green dye shades she loved. She found that different mineral and vegetable colors dissolved in copal gum made pigments stick better to bark paper and stucco walls.

Sharp aromas from boiling tree resin filled her courtyard. Itz concocted long-lasting, blackest of blacks paint by mixing the resin and burnt bone soot. It smelled better than when she boiled *aje cochinilla* insects to extract oil from their bodies. Oil skimmed from the roiling top layer became a polish or base for other pigments. She cut ends of her hair and bound them together around wax tipped sticks to make new brushes of different thicknesses.

Morning bird chatter was rudely interrupted by three long haunting conch shell blasts. Baoooooo, baoooooo, baoooooo rang through the trees as a warning to the small community that strangers were approaching. Many people fled to the caves inside the sheer rock sides of the X'canche cenote well, where the stone stopped and the water began.

Itz glanced around to be sure that she left out nothing of value or incrimination before running to hide in the alcove behind the false wall. Crouched behind the partition, she peeked through a small pinhole overlooking her main living area.

She could hear hurrying footsteps echoing on her stone walkway. Suddenly, an arm yanked aside the cloth door covering and two large male figures stood silhouetted against the sunlight streaming in through the opening. At first the glare blinded her and she could not recognize who they were.

"Itz, are you here?" a familiar voice called out.

With joy she realized that her cousin Etz'nab stood before her. She released her breath and a sigh of relief blew out through her lips. Into his open arms she ran. She buried her head into Etz'nab's shoulder, and then raised it again to look at the second figure standing in the bright beam.

Itz turned and found herself face to face with Kan Ik. She rubbed her eyes. She feared that the sun and shadows played a trick on her. Her confusion continued when he did not react as she expected.

Standing to the side with his arms crossed in front of him, he curtly nodded. He was rude with her to the point of being cold. He acted as if they had never met.

Etz'nab did not notice the discomfort between his friend and his cousin. He broke the tension and spun her around in excitement.

"When Kan Ik brought news that our revolutionary brothers are training for a counterattack against the conquistadors, dozens of us slipped out of the work camp to join them," he said.

"Don't tell me where. These days it is best to not have too much information," she warned. Her cousin nodded in understanding.

"Kan Ik explained that the shipwrecked Spaniard, Gonzalo Guerrero had become a trusted advisor."

Itz remembered the man. He lived in Uncle Tep's coastal city for years, married a cousin, and had three children. He'd been initiated into the Maya ways and proudly bore the tattoos of their clan.

"Gonzalo Guerrero is one of us now. He refused to return to his countrymen's encampments," continued Etz'nab. "He sees how conquistadors destroy our people and he's training us to fight back. We're here to gather recruits and supplies and cannot stay more than a few days. But I wanted you to hear the news from me personally. I also need you to tell my mother that a freedom movement has begun." He could hardly contain his exuberance.

"You were born to this," Itz told her cousin. "I will give you jade to supply yourself and your warriors." Mixed emotions ran through her mind. Itz saw the need to stand up against Spanish tyranny, but she knew war would exact its price through pain and suffering.

"You are welcome to stay here with me," Itz offered.

"No, I will bunk with the troops. In two days we plan to gather at sunset in front of Black Jaguar's temple mound to receive blessings. I hope you will help me get ready and come see us off."

"Of course I will," said Itz.

The two men exited the house as quickly as they appeared and walked through an opening in the wall that once encircled the city. Distracted, Itz wondered if she had imaged seeing Kan Ik. If it was him, his cold indifference was strange and mysterious to her.

To calm herself, she finished preparing her paints and put the new batches into reed and shell containers. She could do little to help her cousin and his friends. But she could make artistic offerings as gifts for them. Three dozen, palm-sized deerskin patches with spirit animals and symbolic verses painted in her brightest colors soon lay drying in the sun along the courtyard wall.

"Talismans provide strong medicine," she nodded, pleased with her simple encouragement tokens.

CHAPTER 52

Ek Balam, Yucatan
1564 A.D.

Itz felt tired after the busy and exciting day's events. She took a hot bath and dressed in her favorite cotton embroidered shift. Resting in the late afternoon sun to let her long hair dry, she remembered her sweet hours in Nabalam with Kan'Ik. But since she thought he reported her work to the Spaniards, her feelings for him wavered between attraction and anger. Two anxieties pulled at her. She feared she would not see him again and she feared that she would.

"*I trusted him. He didn't even stop the next morning to say farewell. Probably because he'd been the one who turned me in to the inquistitors.*"

She trembled at the memory of being brutally forced into the plaza, accused of heresy and beaten by black clad priest.

"*Once they saw the pottery decorated with forbidden hieroglyphs that I'd given him, my life and my mission were in danger.*"

As if thinking of him had the power to conjure him up, Kan Ik stood framed by the corbel arch entry of her walled courtyard. He held his arms stiffly at his side. His icy stare bore a hole into her core. Itz's heart did an involuntary plunge. Their eyes locked. Both remained silent.

"Were you surprised to see me free and alive?" She finally threw the question at him like a dagger. Her hands entwined tightly behind her back.

"I heard about your arrest. I would have come back, but was told that your champion had rescued you and you were released," he said through clenched teeth.

That version surprised Itz. "Just as I thought. You were far away with your reward money after reporting me and giving the authorities my vase as proof."

"Me? Reward? What are you talking about? I still possess your North Star vase."

"I don't believe you. No one else knew of my secret scribe work. You betrayed me," she spat out in anger.

"Don't talk to me of lies and betrayal. I was told that Tepal, that traitor you are betrothed to, helped you and you went to work for the Catholic priests." Kan Ik's voice was hoarse with emotion.

Itz head spun with confusion. "Betrothed?" She questioned. "If you refer to Prince Tepal, he has always been rejected by me." Itz cringed at a host of wretched memories.

"That is not what I heard," Kan Ik responded. Spanish sword steel was not as cold and unforgiving as the look he gave Itz. His mistaken accusations caused a wound so deep in her heart that it did not even bleed. Itz was uncertain how to clear up misunderstandings on both sides.

"Tepal is my enemy. He and I are not promised or together. He frightens and disgusts me. I would never work for those despised church fathers. Trust me on that."

"Trust is something you have to earn," Kan Ik said.

"I trusted you with my secret and within hours I was arrested. If it was not you, then who?"

"I did not betray all you do to help our people save their heritage," he said, desperate for her to believe him. "I can see now that someone is trying to stop our efforts. Who?"

They gradually relaxed their defensive body postures and stepped within reach of the other. Kan Ik and Itz stood quietly, staring at the ground while they pondered possibilities of wrongful impressions on both their parts.

"Too many unanswered questions," she said to break the silence. Her words opened the door a crack, but her eyes remained clamped.

"We can figure this out together," he said, hoping they could unwind the solemn twine of deceit. "I should have known better."

Itz put out her hand and touched Kan Ik on his forearm. Warmth spread through him, like the heated rush he felt after a long swallow of *balche* liquor. It surprised him how her presence intoxicated him.

"I am sorry for doubting you. Truth must be the center of our lives," Itz said. The last vestiges of her anger melted away. "I hope arguing has not harmed our friendship and we can begin again."

"As a seaman, I have never seen a storm hurt the sky."

Itz looked into Kan Ik's lined face and smiled. He reached over and gently touched the upturned corner of her mouth with his callused finger, caressing her with his eyes.

"I've missed you," he said. Unspoken emotions clogged the rest of the words in his throat.

With that simple statement, Itz felt cherished and needed in a way she never had before. A sense of her own worth reflected back to her in the mirror of his eyes. She placed her hand over his, turned his hand upward and kissed its ink-marked palm.

Kan Ik took her chin in his hand and drew closer. She moved into his arms. He looked down into her eyes for a moment, allowing her the chance to step back or push him away. She did not. He kissed her softly, sliding his tongue across her bottom lip. Itz took a deep staggering breath. Waves of heat made her blush all over. Kan Ik smiled and was lost in the warmth of her.

"I want us to be part of each other," he whispered in her ear.

"I want that too," she replied.

Powerful currents swept them away. Their love for each other grew deeper, as did the kisses and caresses. After a moment of sharp pain, Itz joined in his rhythms of movement and pleasure. He made her his own in every sense of the word.

Itz and Kan Ik laid together on the sleeping platform mats and cushions. She rested her head on his broad chest and listened to their blood pumping in unison. The strength and security of his strong arms around her had been long awaited.

"Cycles of time and lives," she sighed. "Our spirits and bodies are now united, bound by a thousand threads."

He held her closer and agreed. "We were meant to be together. The soul does not accept substitutes." They didn't need words to know their fates were now as firmly entwined as their bodies.

Night overtook the remaining afternoon shadows and the courtyard fell dark and silent. From the raised platform they watched the moon rise above the treetops. High in the cloudless isolated air, two birds soared. Almost as soon as the pair appeared, they vanished and left the sky bare. The lovers made wishes on stars shooting anonymously across the abundant sky.

Kan Ik and Itz resisted sleep. They did not want to miss a minute of precious time together. But finally, wrapped in each other's arms, peace and bliss claimed their wakeful spirits.

Too soon dawn gathered in the stars. The faint white moon sank on the opposite side of the sky. The forest grew full of motion and sounds of life. Chirping bird symphonies, without regard to the melody of their voices, woke Itz before Kan Ik stirred. She stayed very still and watched him sleep. His long dark eyelashes rested on wind-burned cheeks. She had to stop herself from touching him and raining kisses all over his body. Itz felt so alive.

"To love and be loved is to feel the sun from both sides. When love comes, it is a tree of life," her aunt told her many times. Now she knew the words to be true.

CHAPTER 53

Ek Balam, Yucatan
1564 A.D.

Kan Ik awoke and contentment filled his eyes. He smiled at his beloved. He wanted to stay, but the new recruits waited. He rose from the pallet he'd shared with Itz to go to them. She understood. "I'll be back later," he said.

Frequent smiles, rare before, now conveyed his newly found connection. He possessed an extra spring in his step as he instructed recruits and took them through drills. They tried their hand at several weapons, jumping from javelins to bows to clubs.

"Focus on one weapon at a time until you are accomplished at it. A man who chases two rabbits will not catch either one," he advised.

Itz went to the encampment to help her cousin pack his supplies. Etz'nab was flushed with the same excitement that ran through the veins of all the young trainees. They bolstered each other's confidence with practice sessions and shouts of encouragement. The young warriors were grateful for the token deerskin patches Itz made for them to carry into battle.

"Symbols instill great belief and empowerment in the mind. Sometimes faith is all one has when facing death," said Kan Ik about her thoughtful gesture.

"Victorious warriors win first spiritually and mentally. Then they go into combat. Anyway, that's what leaders tell us about building up courage," said Etz'nab. "And I want to be a strong leader."

"Then don't try to be the captain of someone else's canoe. Learn to be a good example, a beacon, and others will follow your directions," Kan Ik mentored the young man.

Etz'nab wiped gritty sweat off his brow. He excused himself. "Let me clean up and I will join you at your place," he told his cousin.

When he returned from the sweat room and bath, he found Itz placing flowers and copal at an altar where she had set a clay statue of the goddess Ixchel that she made. Light-winged incense smoke rose upward to ask the gods' favors.

"For the time being, all gods are secondary to the god of war," Etz'nab scolded. "Pray to Cit Chac Coh. Ask for protection for those who fight to free our people from injustices." His voice shook. Itz was not sure if it was from anger or fear peeking out of his false bravado front.

"I know you go forth to defend rights and honor," she began, "but is combat the only solution?"

"Duty to protect the weak and enslaved is the essence of manhood," he puffed up and defended his upcoming actions with rhetoric she was sure had been drilled into him during his training.

"The only option left to us is fighting. We must defend ourselves against a devouring foreigner who wants to destroy us all."

Everyone in camp knew first-hand how the conquerors victimized an entire population and way of life. White men did not talk or compromise with the natives, whom they thought of and treated as less than human. In their minds they had reduced the Maya to a form of evil that must be eradicated.

"I know you are right, but I am so torn. The ultimate price of this rebellion will be borne by a very few, our best and brightest young men like you," she said, choking back and not expressing all her fears.

Kan Ik entered the courtyard where Itz and Etz'nab continued their debate. He'd overheard some of the conversation and could understand both positions. He saw apprehension on Itz's wrinkled brow. He put his arm around her in greeting and comfort.

"War is a cruel thing. It fills our hearts with hatred instead of love," she said. I sometimes worry that the evil we inflict, even though deserved, does irreparable damage to the soul." She looked at the two men she loved and said boldly, "No matter how justified or necessary, war is a crime. It is a dangerous assumption to think that war can bring abut peace."

"Itz, you don't understand this calling. I prepare for battle, not because I want to, but because I have to. It is exciting being part of the spearhead group," he picked up a long obsidian tipped spear to emphasize his statement.

"You always loved your weapons and challenging your comrades, but it is not a game this time," she said.

"I do not love my battle axe for its sharpness. I do not admire the arrows in my quill for their speed, or my fellow warriors for their bravery, I only care about what they defend," he said, searching her eyes for understanding and support.

"Only two alternatives lay before us. Either we can submit and degenerate, becoming more specters of the past than living men, or we can resist and maybe be killed." Etz'nab pulled his shirt aside to expose deep scars he carried from the whip. "I feel duty bound to resist their unforgiveable conduct."

"I don't want any more heroes or martyrs in the family," she said.

Kan Ik, shared the burden of understanding what Etz'nab felt and tried to express. Kan Ik personally knew about war and had already learned its lessons the hard way. He entered into the conversation.

"Now that a challenge has been made, there is only one thing to do. We must fight and win. Subjection to the barbarian invaders would bring worse things than anything that would happen in war," he inserted.

Kan Ik turned and directly addressed Etz'nab. "Never believe that war will be easy. Anyone who embarks on this strange voyage cannot begin to anticipate the storms or be able measure the tides he will encounter. All warriors are tossed about on seas of uncontrollable and unforeseeable events," he warned.

Kan Ik's face was stern and darkly serious. Painful memories played behind those wise eyes. The young man could only glimpse possible horrors for a second, but even that gave cause for quiet and respectful refection.

"We are warriors now, to be feared, not hunted. An army of jaguars," boasted Etz'nab, bouncing back in a louder than necessary voice.

"Warriors are not born or made. You create yourself through pain and suffering, trial and error. Your greatest skill is the ability to conquer your own fears and faults," advised Kan Ik.

"I know little of ways and customs of war, and wish to know less," Itz said to break the tension. "I believe in you and your purpose cousin. If you must go, I will help you prepare."

CHAPTER 54

Ek Balam, Yucatan
1564 A.D.

Itz wanted to insure that Etz'nab had the best equipment and a surplus of supplies. She gave him several pieces of her late father's jade collar. With the stones, he could buy what was needed for an extended tour of duty.

All afternoon Itz familiarized herself with specific items he had to carry with him to training and into battle. She helped him pack. She organized durable clothes, footwear and dried food supplies. She developed a meditative chant she hoped would transform objects associated with loss and injury into items of protection and bravery.

Kan Ik smiled, knowing what she was doing as she used incense to smudge her cousin's body armor stitched with couch shell and wooden panels and sewed tiny totem charms in the hems.

"You take your job of packing very seriously," he good-naturedly chided her preparations for her cousin. Kan Ik loved the nurturing healing essence of this woman.

"*She will be a great mother for our children*," he thought, but kept that dream to himself.

"After he has gone, my job is to whisper into the ear of any gods that will listen, asking them to protect him and make him brave."

"All men are terrified in battle. I know," he confided. "Etz'nab will do well. He is brave enough to face himself when he is afraid, strong enough to know when he is weak," he said to comfort her.

Kan Ik withdrew into his own thoughts while she worked. He worried because the Maya people knew little or nothing about fighting Spaniards, who owned superior weapons of metal and rode horses. His hope was that Guerrero could teach the recruits how to defend themselves against the foreigners' new and different battle techniques. Or better yet, develop supreme war methods of resistance and subduing the enemy, without getting into hand-to-hand fighting.

Kan Ik knew this struggle for independence would radically and forever alter everyone who took part. From his experience, soldiers who fought often found that they not only imitated, but exceeded the brutality of their aggressors. Already other groups of rebels held up examples of Spanish atrocity, and then condoned and labeled their own cruel acts as justice and retribution. War made the vanquished malicious and the victors vengeful.

Young men training to fight the Spanish didn't realize that the conquistadors embraced death as a way of life. Spanish soldiers were masters of war. Foreigners didn't understand that the Maya could never live in peace with them as long as they enslaved and killed innocent men, women, and children. Whereas the newcomers didn't care about death tolls as long as they made a profit off their New World holdings. Kan Ik remembered challenging a captain from Burgos once, telling him, "All the money you make will never buy back your soul."

"You have a worried look on your face. What are you thinking?" asked Itz.

"In commerce or any other trade, men of energy and talent prosper. But in the business of war, they die. Battles never inflict suffering only where it is merited. External and internal wounds last forever."

“But our cause is just and right,” Itz insisted.

“War does not determine which side is right or wrong, it only decides who is left,” Kan Ik responded.

“Those young men practicing in the field are determined and strong like jaguars, according to my cousin.”

“In reality, the peninsula city-states haven’t been united for ages and there’s no true champion leader. I am afraid that Etz’nab’s army of jaguars faces an army of sheep led by donkeys. That is very dangerous. Sheep are inspired by greed, not principles.”

Itz caught something else in his choice of words, tone, and distant look. “What are you not telling me?”

“When forces are at war, the first casualty is often truth. I confess I feel none of the sense of adventure that your cousin is experiencing. I have no optimistic delusions about war, or sense of invincibility like a soldier who has never seen combat. But one thing I know for sure is that it takes the power of information and truth to affect needed changes.” He paused and took a deep breath, “I am honor-bound to accompany the warriors on this quest.”

No!” Itz swallowed the audible gasp that swept up into her throat. Never in her life had words so utterly escaped her. It was all she could do not to burst into tears.

“I have just found love that breathes meaning into my life. Now you are putting yourself in harm’s path.”

She’d heard his stories of how he’d lost his brother, then his best friend in a single fight with the Spaniards. Now he meant to go back into the same conflict.

“Honor is not important to me. You are important to me,” she said.

Kan Ik took Itz into his arms just as her legs buckled under her.

“Distance between two souls is not an obstacle,” he said and stroked her cheeks to wipe away tears.

"Let someone else be the recorder and messenger of the conflict," she begged.

"My cover as a merchant and my prior military experience make me the best one to go."

"I know you must go and do what needs to be done. But, my heart is in shreds. War will separate us and mar the purest joy the gods have ever granted me."

"We may be apart for a while, in distance, but never in heart. Don't be afraid. Our love is stronger than fear."

"How will I survive the wait? Not knowing? How will I survive at all if the worst should happen?" she sobbed into his shoulder.

"You can't lose me. I am part of you now."

CHAPTER 55

Ek Balam, Yucatan
1564 A.D.

"I came as soon as the runner told me my son was with you in Ek Balam," Yaxche said as she hurried through the door of Itz's home.

"Oh, Auntie, Etz'nab and the others left yesterday morning at dawn."

The women fell into an embrace, foreheads touching, like two trees holding each other up against the winds.

"I helped Etz'nab prepare as best I could," Itz reassured her aunt. "My heart was proud and terrified for him at the same time."

"Thank you. I am sure you sent him on his way with courage to do what must be done," Yaxche patted her niece in appreciation.

"I brought medicines and supplies for the fighters. I might have guessed they could not stay in one place too long. I will send my goods to their next camp," she said, pointing to several large bundles carried by the porters who accompanied her. They left the packages by the entrance and departed.

"With a son in battle I am drawn as a mother and healer to be there. But I can serve the efforts better by keeping them supplied."

"I am pulled, wanting to support the warriors while abhorring war," confessed Itz. "I am sorry you didn't get a chance to see him and bid him farewell."

"Goodbyes never said hang like a dark cloud in the back of the mind," Yaxche sighed. "Sometimes I wish Etz'nab had been born in another time. But then I remember there's rarely been a time when men were not fighting one another."

"Come in and rest. You must be exhausted from your long journey. I've slept very little lately myself," said Itz.

After a hearty meal and unpacking, Yaxche shared her thoughts on the situation and her fears.

"War does not bring out the best in people. I worry about the futility of fighting. Even if my son defeated the tyrant's brandished steel advances, he would return a hardened man, not the kind soul I raised."

Itz was equally concerned, but maintained her silence. She sensed that the battle may be won, but the son child would be lost.

"When Etz'nab was a young boy, I would attend all his rough *pok-a-pok* ballgames. Something in me believed that if I were there at his competitions, he wouldn't get injured," reminisced Yaxche. "I cannot provide such a maternal cocoon for him now."

They sat quietly for a long while. In her aunt's expression, Itz could see how Yaxche's memories took her back in time.

"Life has shown me things I never wanted to see. I've been plunged into horrors and sadness deeper than a person should survive. But even if I had known what bitterness the cup of life held for me, I still would not let it pass me by untasted. The lesson is to get up. I always get up."

Itz felt so much love and respect for her aunt. It was terrible to think of her in such angst.

"You were just a child yourself when my precious daughter North Star died from the fever those invaders brought into our lands," she continued. "My little girl left her disease wracked material body to live in *ti chan*, a place of eternal love and happiness. We buried her deep under the palace in Edzna. I wanted to throw myself into the tomb with her."

Yaxche held up her left hand to display a short little finger. "Instead I followed tradition, cut off my finger and placed it on top of her gravestone."

"What terrible pain," gasped Itz.

"The agony of grief was far greater than any pain I felt in my hand. I wanted part of me to stay with her for company. It is very lonely being dead."

"My father's voice still resonates inside my head, especially when I look at his written words. I believe that your daughter and my father's spirits are stirred by feathery touches of our thoughts."

"This concept is something that I have been meaning to talk about with you," said Yaxche. "When I die and all living memory of me ceases," she began. "Especially if my son is killed in this conflict…"

"Oh no, please don't talk like that," Itz interrupted and pleaded. "I am weary of experiencing and worrying about loved ones dying."

"My dear, death is both feared and natural. Even though a person is dead and frozen in time, like insects caught in amber, we can continue to exist," said Yaxche.

"What do you mean? There is no exception to annihilation at the end of one's days," Itz questioned her aunt's direction of thought.

"According to the laws of nature, all living creatures pass away. But you, Itz, possess a kind of power that extends life."

"I am confused. Flesh and bones disappear after death. What can I possibly do to change that reality?"

"Your gift is the miracle of paint on paper and pottery to record significant images. It is your duty to preserve information. Words have great power. The right words together can bend time and space. I want you to continue narrating history and copying my medical formulas. Through your works our voices and knowledge will live on. For years beyond our ken, the light you leave will shine upon the paths of the future."

"I promise to continue my work. I have many pieces finished already. Kan Ik suggested that I build a place to hide my works. We worked on construction plans while he was here."

"Kan Ik was here? How dare he show his face after allowing you to be persecuted by the inquisitor?" Yaxche said in a raised voice and jumped to her feet.

"It was not him who told the priests. He suspects Tepal. Are we at all surprised?" said Itz to calm her aunt, who stood tensed in a defensive stance.

"Was Kan Ik here when Etz'nab and the others came through?"

"As a matter of fact, he accompanied them to Ek Balam for recruitment and preparations. We got reacquainted and …" Itz's deep breath and pause told her aunt more than words could.

"You belong to Kan Ik now. I can tell by your eyes when you speak his name. That is wonderful," she said, truly pleased at a match of kindred spirits. Itz's happiness was important to her. Pairing with a noble man of Kan Ik's quality would bring out the best in each of them.

"Oh Yaxche, he is such a remarkable person and loving," Itz blurted out with a blush. "But now he has gone with the warriors and I am frightened. Afraid for them and afraid to lose him before we have time to make a life together."

"Conflicts are hard on the ones who wait at home. But we will work to make a place they can return to, whatever the outcome," promised Yaxche. "Now tell me about your ideas for this secret storage place."

Itz and Yaxche designed and constructed the extra room by themselves. The fewer people who knew of its existence the better.

They decided to put the addition at the end of a great room in the complex where Itz lived. From outside, unless someone took accurate interior and exterior measurements, one would not notice the four-stride shortened hall.

Plenty of cut stones that the two women could lift, carry and put in position were scattered about the ruined old city. The hardest part was placement of supportive capstones on the upper corbel arch. But ingenuity, perseverance and sapling scaffolding made it happen. No one who passed by, thought anything was unusual about the potter Itz mixing clays, limestone stucco or mortar in her courtyard.

When basic building was finished, niece and aunt collapsed in gleeful celebration. Their hands were cut and rough, their nails broken to the quick. Satisfaction at a job well done helped soothe aching muscles and other pains from unfamiliar heavy manual labor. Later interior plastering and painting seemed like a great joy, not work at all.

Itz was in her element as she sketched designs and transcribed, not only sacred but informative hieroglyphs on all the walls and ceiling. Yaxche brought in baskets full of medicinal plant samples for her niece to accurately reproduce in brightly painted displays. The eastern wall of the hidden room looked like a summer garden in full bloom. The greens that came to life in Itz's landscapes were enough to make the real forest envious.

"Our entire natural world system, our bodies and the universe, are attuned to the same energies and vibrations of life," said Yaxche.

The project kept them occupied in body, but their minds often drifted to Etz'nab and Kin Ik, under their terrible burdens of destiny. No news of the revolution found its way to the Ixkunil pueblo. The Spanish capital of the Yucatan, Merida and large towns like Izamal and Valladolid did not stir with war horns or troop movements. Yaxche assured Itz that no action meant the rebels still prepared and gathered strength before making a move.

Itz woke from a stirring dream early one morning. She hurried to her secret room to add new and different portraits to the wall. Her paintbrushes flowed with natural rhythmic strokes as she spent the week permanently recording her loved one's faces for all eternity. The eyes and smiles of Ko'h, Yaxche, Kan Ik, Etz'nab, Brother Miguel, his Holy Mother and her own favorite goddess Ixchel, came realistically alive. At the last moment, Itz added a detailed self-portrait and her signature lily to the message.

CHAPTER 56

Mexico City
Present Day

"Gringa, pack up. You are finished at the Anthropology Museum," her Mexican laboratory supervisor announced loudly enough for all the staffers to hear. He threw termination papers down on Hannah's workbench. He picked up a clay mask she was restoring and said, "Someone else will complete this project. Maybe. If we have time." He carelessly tossed it down, causing the decorative piece she just glued to break off, taking a large chuck with it.

Hannah's stomach took an elevator plunge ten floors. Although regular meetings with Dr. Sarra had stopped, for the last few months they were again on decent terms. Out of professional respect for each other's archaeological knack, they returned to consulting and discussions of sites and theories. She occasionally accompanied him to museum related functions and fundraisers.

"We'll see about this," she said and stormed out of the laboratory to confront Dr. Sarra upstairs. Even his bulldog secretary did not stop Hannah's determined march into the director's office.

He looked up smugly from his paperwork. "I have been expecting this visit all morning." He motioned for Hannah to take a seat. She decided to remain standing.

"Before you start, your dismissal here is not bad news," he raised a defensive palm in her direction.

"You sent grant proposals to National Science Foundation and National Geographic," he began. Hannah stood with her chin thrust out and arms folded, more defiant that penitent. "Well, they've both been approved. I am obligated to issue the necessary INAH permits for you to work in Ek Balam for the season. We museum directors are always happy to spend other people's money," he smiled.

"I get to dig in Ek Balam?" Hannah could not believe what Dr. Sarra just told her. "When do I leave?" she said, packing her bags mentally before she left the office.

After the looting problems at Edzna, confrontations with museum personnel, and disappointing relationship between her and Sarra, Hannah believed her luck was finally changing.

Ek Balam, the Black Jaguar site, was a vast archaeological zone with unlimited possibilities. The ruined Maya city was the Cupules-Talol empire capital. Earlier excavations uncovered a king's tomb and pristine temple facades with magnificent larger-than-life statues modeled in white stucco. Hieroglyphs and artworks flanked the staircases on each side of the main acropolis tiers. Artifacts of ancient rulers and gods, hidden under tree-covered mounds, awaited Hannah.

Roberto and Mari stood at the site entrance to greet her when she arrived a week later. The archaeologists stayed in Ek Balam village, walking distance from the archaeological ruins. Hannah's Canadian friend Kate owned half-hectare walled grounds with lush tropical gardens that surrounded an underground river-fed swimming pool. The team rented individual rooms and took morning and evening meals at Kate's eco-oasis called Casa de la Paz, House of Peace.

Hannah's treehouse room was dubbed the birdhouse. She climbed leaf shaped rebar steps up a spiral staircase around the massive tree trunk into green branches. Her large room featured a swinging rope bed, open-air shower stall, and patio deck with hammock chairs. This setup was pure luxury after her other fieldwork quarters.

“Even Joseph would enjoy this encampment,” she said. “Probably much better than his assignment station now.” Biting her lower lip, Hannah’s face revealed how hard it was not to worry, both for his safety in a desert warzone and for their friendship.

“Still no word from Tem Chen at all?” asked Roberto.

“Jungle excavation may be hot and dangerous, but at least we don’t have to wear flack jackets and carry heavy packs in triple digit heat or be concerned about bombs in the roads,” he added.

“Not a comforting conversation,” scolded Mari as she put her index finger to her lips to silence her usually more sensitive son.

“People talked about the Maya prediction of the end of the world December 21, 2012. Maybe what the ancients foresaw was not a solar flare or meteorite hitting Earth, but what mankind would become. Look around at the wars, greed, senseless mass murders, cruelty, racism, gluttony, and waste today. Too many folks no longer cherish life or other people or even the earth or the animals and resources put on it,” said Hannah. Thoughts about war brought out an untypical pessimistic mood in her.

Within weeks, excavations at Ek Balam uncovered several significant finds. Clearing away vegetation and centuries of dirt exposed the north wall of matching twin pyramids covered with carved bands of frets and glyphic motifs. The team did a narrow exploratory test trench at the same level as the king’s tomb and uncovered parts of a stucco frieze that once encircled the entire building facade. In an interior rubble-filled staircase, Hannah dug up a seated stone figure, possibly a king’s mother based on what she could decipher from hieroglyphs around the bottom edges. Unknown persons in the far past defaced the head and hands to take away the queen’s power.

The multi-kilometer archaeological zone contained evidence of a network of road systems, huge *chultun* water reservoirs, palaces, semi-public buildings, masonry platforms, and some of the highest temple mounds in the Yucatan. Her favorite find to date was a simple necklace with decorative shells carved like shrimp. It was a totally unique piece for the Yucatan.

There seemed to be no end to the Ek Balam historical site. One was likely as not to stumble on a previously undiscovered group of buildings a few meters off the path into the forest. As tempting as it was, to dig test pits and trenches in numerous locations, the team set limits and concentrated on select areas. Hannah did all she could with the time, money and staff she'd been granted.

CHAPTER 57

Ek Balam, Yucatan
Present Day

Loud shouts of '*Aqui, ven aqui*, Here, come here!' resounded across the plaza from a small complex on the main pyramid's north side. It announced that a worker found something important enough to call a supervisor. Hannah rushed over to inspect.

She joined Roberto and Jorge, a young man from his village. Jorge often helped them with survey work and plot maps. He had a gift when it came to dimensions and space relationships; possibly a young engineer or architect in the making.

Jorge demonstrated how he paced off and twice measured the building end on the outside and then paced off the corresponding corner great room. Unnoticed by all but him, there was a difference of about four meters. So he inspected the interior wall carefully.

Under a build up of old dirt, crumbling rock and bat droppings, the wall appeared to be constructed of smaller stone sizes and different plaster consistency than the other sides. Thinking it might be a false wall, he called over his site leaders to check out his theory.

"Good eye, Jorge," Hannah complimented him. "Observation of anomalies like this are how we discover our best finds."

She found the far wall stucco surface was made of a different texture. A millennium of humidity and centuries of intrusive plant growth left it blotchy and crumbly. Hannah used the point of her trowel to probe between masonry blocks. There was space behind.

"Berto, why would someone go to so much trouble, if not to conceal something of importance?" she whispered. Her adrenaline and imagination went into overdrive.

Even though Hannah's first instinct was to pull down the lightly coated limestone wall and see if anything was hidden behind it centuries ago, she was a professional. The perfectionist in her maintained high standards of excavation and ethical conduct.

"We need to work this discovery carefully, as if the entire scientific world was looking over our shoulders, analyzing and second-guessing every action."

"Oh yeah. After the fact, jealous colleagues love to sit at their desks and tell those of us in the field how it could have been done better," added Roberto.

To keep academic, museum or government peers from picking apart or questioning her work later, Hannah proceeded with deliberate care. Details were recorded in minutia.

Rather than massive and imposing, this residential complex had at one time been a refined and exquisite jewel. It didn't need to reach for the sky like its acropolis neighbor. It was complete and beautiful in its own right. Often living spaces were divided into small rooms. Their size was governed by the fact that they only had corbel arches limited by the stones the masons were able to quarry.

Originally the team had not planned to excavate this building because huge trees sprouted out of several rooms. Portions of the façade had crumbled, covering the ground with stone debris. They changed their schedule and began by stabilizing the main room entryway before starting the interior work.

"Moments like these are why I love archaeology so much," Hannah said as laborers cleared a way into the area in front of the irregular stonewall.

"I can't stop thinking about secrets and objects that wait just below the surface, challenging us to see if we are patient and bright enough to locate them." She sat on an ancient sleeping platform near the doorway, sketching the surrounding area and swinging her feet in nervous energy.

"Since Howard Carter knocked down the barrier wall and walked into the untouched tomb of Tutankhamen in 1922, every archaeologist dreams of finding sealed rooms behind false walls," Roberto said.

Jorge and two other carefully chosen diggers scraped away the buildup of earth and plant remains washed and blown in over the ages. A heavy musky smell filled the air as the team dug through crusty bat droppings. Debris blocked most of the room's end wall. Soil from the preliminary clearing was put aside to be screened, bagged and catalogued for analysis in the lab. Hannah wanted her work here to be a textbook model of accuracy and efficiency.

After much work with small picks and sharp coa blades to remove damp rank rubble, a minimal portion of false stonewall surface covering was removed. Workers moved aside sufficient rocks for the archaeologists to get a look inside the interior vaulted space so long buried in darkness.

"Berto, once we have an opening large enough, you and I will enter to take photographs and make an initial analysis. By the book," Hannah said. She tried to keep the excitement she felt from her voice, but she knew that something meaningful waited in there.

"Let's get started," he said.

The Maya helpers crossed themselves repeatedly. They muttered and stepped outside the building complex into the open plaza, joining others who'd heard of the excavation. Hannah and Roberto were left alone in front of the room opening.

Hannah got down on her knees and put her head through the breech to take a better look. There was no ambient light of any kind in the hidden room. Dim light from behind her penetrated only a few feet into the darkness. As her eyes adjusted, she gradually made out vague outlines and splotches of color. It was frustrating, like swimming underwater, straining to see, vision blurred by a foggy facemask.

"You know it and I know it. This is something big. Let's go inside," she said to Roberto.

They enlarged the opening barely enough to crawl through the narrow entrance. White limestone dust disturbed by their entry hung suspended in the hot heavy air. Hannah used her high-powered flashlight's broad illumination to cut the gloom. Roberto paced out the space of about six meters long and four meters wide. It was no more than the size of a large bedroom.

On the hard-packed plastered floor lay piles of what looked like ropes. These later turned out to be tree roots that long ago penetrated the roof of the chamber, then shriveled up and fell to the floor. The enclosed room's walls and roof remained intact, so at some point the process of decrepitude and decay seemed to have slowed down dramatically. Untold centuries ago it reached an archaeological nadir and froze in time.

They could see solely by the beam of Hannah's light, so Roberto lit his lantern and placed it in the center of the room. They then could make out everyday items on the floor like wooden stool remnants, and a broken stone *matate* with *mano* for grinding corn. Their eyes were immediately drawn up and over to pottery, figurines and conch containers that lined a long shelf bench. Objects appeared and disappeared as light danced over the clutter of artifacts.

Hannah turned her beam upward and scanned the walls and ceiling. Brilliant colored paintings covered all four sides. The effect was striking. In truth, what they saw was far less important than what they felt. The elaborate mural images stretched into the past, into history itself. The art seemed imbued with life and spirits.

In archaeology, as within the study of all disciplines, phenomena sometimes occurred that Hannah was powerless to explain. She hoped that someday her logical mind would find explanation, and perhaps it would. But at that moment, the setting gave her inspiration. Unexplained feelings possessed their own power.

Hannah blinked to clear her eyes. Deep breathing helped to clear her head. She attempted to speak, but no words could describe what she saw before her. She turned to Roberto to gauge his reaction to this incredible find. He simply nodded. Wet streaks marked his dusty cheeks, as if he had wept at first sighting.

They crawled out of the room and removed a bit more of the rock wall to allow better light and motion. None of the plastered sections with drawings on them were disturbed. No one would be allowed to enter the space except the two field supervisors.

Their first helpers stood in wary anticipation with other workers gathering outside the structure. The locals were afraid when anyone uncovered and penetrated ancient ruins. They feared that opening buildings might reawaken terrible old gods who would demand blood from warm beating hearts. Such gods were better left in their sleep of death. Roberto told Hannah that they must immediately conduct a purification ceremony.

She knew that rituals were necessary for protection of the site and to ensure her workers' good faith. Even modern day Maya still believed that ruins were alive with ancient spirits. They were nervous that statues and incense burners might come to life at night. Villagers had been known to deliberately smash artifacts and images to keep them from harming the living.

"Do you believe in ancient ghosts, like they do?" Hannah asked Roberto.

"I will say that I entirely give credence to the power of ghosts. Because unexplained spiritual phenomena can cause the behavior of individuals and societies to become irrational. And whatever possesses such force must be treated as real," he answered.

"Are the ruins' ghosts, or indeed the ancient gods themselves real? Will they come back to haunt or harm?" Hannah asked.

"We can not know or question the powerful influences which motivate human action. Particularly long held beliefs which may trigger actions along the lines that we have witnessed previously in cases like this. We have to treat this seriously," he said.

Roberto, known to the workers as a holy man, smudged the air with a burning bundle of herbs and resin to clear and sanctify the area. He spoke quietly in Mayan to the gathering workers to calm their fears. Together they recited prayers to soothe the souls whose space had been invaded. Those who couldn't read had long ancient chants committed to memory. Blue-gray smoke drifted upward and incantations permeated in the still afternoon air.

"All is well. *Dios and paz*, God and peace," Roberto said in universal benediction. The others repeated his words. He assured them they were safe and the breached building would be respected and immediately returned to its original state.

He underplayed discovery of the room. He did not mention the artifacts or murals. He feigned disappointment and assured those present of the empty and ordinary nature of the place. He needed to stop any rumors of dark magic or riches that might attract destruction or looters. Gossip was a main source of entertainment in isolated semiliterate groups where other amusements were few and far between.

Jorge, aware of his supervisor's ploy, loudly offered to help backfill the hole in the wall before he left. Roberto accepted, hoping their staged interchange emphasized the team's lack of interest.

Site workers were dismissed early for the weekend, glad to be away. Only Hannah, Roberto and Jorge remained behind to process the new find. They had to be completely finished by Monday morning when the crew returned.

CHAPTER 58

Ek Balam, Yucatan
Present day

Hannah and Roberto decided that in this time-sensitive situation, everything would be left in place and undisturbed for later study.

A growing trend among archaeologists called for minimal to zero site trauma. Proponents of zero disturbance thought that any excavation, no matter how subtle or carefully executed, destroyed evidence for scientists who would have more advanced techniques at their disposal in the future. Avid hands-off groupies touted the theory that no historically significant discovery should be physically disturbed. They labeled even the most conscientious excavators as 'artifact whores' and worse.

Hannah could understand the concept to a point, but in fieldwork reality, one could not practice total zero site trauma. The science of archaeology requires exploration, preservation and analysis of the find to reconstruct cultures. To her, the real crime would be to leave a site unexplored and unrecorded.

Yet in the case of the hidden room in Ek Balam, they had no time to properly excavate, so she and Roberto reluctantly adopted non-invasive techniques. They would photograph, inventory and then leave everything as they found it until a future date.

Within sixty hours, Hannah, Roberto and Jorge needed to gather as much information as possible, reconstruct the wall, and backfill to cover their discovery until they could organize a disciplined excavation. Although reburying the room site was an unsatisfactory way to preserve their find, at least it was better than leaving it wide open to vandals and thieves. Hannah's pictures and notes would serve as a basis for her next grant proposal to get funding. She would have to wait.

Hannah took sequence photographs of the room in situ, and surveyed various artifacts without physically disturbing where they lay. Positions of objects were marked on a grid patterned site chart.

The team began their work in the secret room. Shifting dust clouds hung in the air. They cast a luminous light with an ethereal dreamlike quality. Hannah fanned away the thick and gritty air in order to take overviews and close-ups with her digital camera mounted on a tripod.

The expansive murals of the floral and fauna scenes reminded her of the three colorful interior rooms at Bonapak, located in the Mexican State of Chiapas. Those bold drawings depicted royal court life of the rich and powerful, like a thousand-year-old *Town and Country*. Ek Balam's murals seemed more like a walk in a garden with family members arm in arm.

The amount of work, time constraints and the possibility of being discovered left little time for sleep. The trio rested only when their bodies demanded it, not according to the clock. No sense of day or night was present in the windowless hidden room.

Mari joined them briefly and brought meals for the dedicated team. Hannah was surprised to break for what she thought was lunch and find stars shining in the narrow strip of dark sky that showed through the jungle canopy.

Jorge volunteered to stay and guard the area while Hannah and Roberto returned briefly to Casa de la Paz for baths and supplies. He hung his hammock in the doorway of the palace, just to be sure there were no curious or malicious souls lurking about while they were gone.

“It frustrates me that when we make great discoveries, we have to pretend they don’t exist so that they won’t be destroyed.” Hannah reflected their current find and on North Star’s tomb in Edzna. She struggled not to let her enthusiasm for fieldwork leak out through the sieve of reality.

“It is discouraging to work for days to clear a building or free an artifact like the Big Red steale, and then be forced to leave it for a season. Often I have returned and find it more deeply embedded in vegetation than before,” Hannah said.

“Not to mention being unable to find important pieces again at all because the jungle took back its hidden secrets or looters came in behind us and stole them,” interjected Roberto.

At first light on the second day, Mari came to help in their hurried efforts. Mornings in the ruins delighted Hannah. Sounds, colors, and motion filled the whole jungle. Vines twined themselves around the walls of the old palace. Iridescent hummingbirds darted among the flowers. Bright sun burned hotly down out of the cloudless blue. Hannah took a much-needed break and sat on worn steps to eat a bite of breakfast.

Back inside the interior room, Roberto worked with the stone and ceramic artifacts, while Hannah focused her attention on the colorful murals. Fine marl limestone plaster covered all four of the walls and part of the corbelled ceiling. A majority of the cement-like wall covering was applied by trowel. But here and there, Hannah saw markings of palm and fingers pressed into drying surfaces by the persons who constructed their secret room. She stopped and closely studied the limestone plaster walls. Attaching her camera to the tripod, she took careful macro close-ups of several clear sets of fingerprints. In one spot there were two handprints outlined in red. The smaller was missing a digit.

“It is unusual to find clear fingerprints in pottery or plaster. I document them whenever I see them. Human elements remind me of why we are here Berto.”

“We are ultimately studying real people, not just their buildings and artifacts,” he agreed.

Surprisingly, the room's plastered walls and paintings remained in a relatively well-preserved state. In two corners, feathering up from places in the stone floor, orange colored lichens cracked and discolored the wall, partially destroying or obscuring some details. Stucco and paint flakes littered the floor. Hannah mourned over each section of painting no longer intact, beyond hope of restoring.

Artwork and inscriptions covered nearly every centimeter of space on the walls and high roof. Hannah worked deftly and steadily to record the painted decorations in detail. Main themes seemed to be the pantheon of Maya gods, plants and formulas, possibly for medicines. She and Roberto would have lots of work in their laboratory matching the botanical items, deities, symbols, and translating the scribe's chosen hieroglyphs.

Vivid images of old gods surrounded them. Long opened eyes stared from the walls at the foreign intruders and watched them from high overhead. Bands of carefully crafted hieroglyphs recited history of the Maya's existence. Symbols and art extolled the sacrifices and virtues that made the ancient gods love their people.

The artist added realistic free-flowing touches to the naturalist paintings. Hannah loved the use of bright colors, especially verdant greens. The greens captured the sea's hues when calm and springtime trees when first budding. The drawings spoke to her and moved into her authentic heart. All were so remarkable that she felt they might come alive at any moment. Vibrant paintings reflected the fundamental spiritual nature of the world.

"Are you guys getting a bit of *deja vu* with these murals?" asked Hannah.

"From techniques of three dimensional style and realism of painting, I think we have more samples of our unknown potter's work," said Roberto.

"Yes!" Hannah shouted and gave a victory arm pump. "Prayers do get answered. There is a signature lily here on this side wall."

"Serendipity or fate---you were meant to be the one to discover this place," said Mari.

Hannah worked her way methodically around the room taking consecutive shots. Among the last panels in the far corner, she recognized a likeness of the goddess Ixchel immediately. The deity's grasp held a rabbit head glyph, that had been translated by experts as *bah*, meaning portrait or image. In the dark shadows, under the glyph Hannah caught sight of a painting of a woman. Her hand began to shake. She dropped the spotlight she was mounting on her tripod. It crashed to the hard stone floor.

"Mari could you help me over here? Please hold up that light."

Hannah stepped in to get a better look. On the smooth expanse of the stuccoed far wall, a painted face smiled out at her. As she stared, an icy chill trickled from her head to the small of her back.

"Berto, take a look at this portrait. Do you think this might be our artist?" she asked in a shaky voice. "It would be so fitting to finally put a face to the creator of the pottery and artwork."

"All the writing and symbols indicate that this person is the source of this work and information."

"Our unknown scribe is a woman!" Hannah exclaimed. "And next to her is a tattooed man. He looks a lot like my nobleman figure from the museum."

Roberto's head went back and forth several times between the two portraits. "I'll be darned," was all he could say.

"This is centuries old, buried away in the jungle. It is just a fluke," said Hannah, trying to calm down. She returned to scientifically recording the murals.

"There are no coincidences, my dear," said Mari.

Something more, something familiar niggled in Hannah's head. The images disturbed her more than she wanted to admit. Flashes of the nobleman's statue flooded her thoughts.

She couldn't concentrate, so took a break from her work and reclined on the platform near the building entrance. Even though the temperature was in triple digits, she shivered with a strange sensation. She felt like she had circled back, that something was about to happen again, the way the sacred cycles of the Maya calendar predicted. Images flashed around the edges, beyond her consciousness, like forgotten dreams. Hannah sat in a thin zone, a place where certainty shimmered just beyond her horizon of understanding.

CHAPTER 59

Ek Balam, Yucatan
Present Day

Hannah recovered from the shock of seeing the mysterious Maya artist's likeness. She returned to the secret room and photographed the full array of faces in the gallery.

The seven portraits included an elderly woman with laughing eyes and a gap between her teeth; a dignified man with symbols and tools of a scribe; a young man, obviously a warrior in padded armor; the familiar tattooed gentleman; the lady artist; and two others who did not seem to belong in the grouping at all. One of the misfits wore robes of a Franciscan priest and the other looked like paintings she'd seen of the Madonna in Merida's cathedral.

"Quite an eclectic gathering of people," Hannah noted. "Berto, we will have our hands full analyzing this find. Our palace is full of magical things waiting for us to unravel the clues," she said over her shoulder.

"Other mysteries are present in these ceramics too. Come look at this," he requested.

On the back of the shelf, behind detailed clay statues of Maya women, sat a stone box. The rough-hewn rectangular container was encapsulated around the bottom edges in calcified limestone from ages of water leakage. Both archaeologists shared their fleeting thoughts about the contents possibly being codices or texts. With only four documented Mayan Pre-Columbian books in existence, a discovery of new writings would be like finding more Dead Sea Scrolls.

"I know we said we'd leave everything in place, but we can't really examine this special piece in low artificial light and at this late hour. Let's take it back to our lab at the Casa. We'll return everything in the morning before we seal up the room," he suggested. Hannah was in agreement.

After a quick nourishing meal and discussion about their day's remarkable work, Hannah and Roberto walked to their makeshift laboratory shed. Both were mentally and physically exhausted. But they could not rest until they inspected and photographed the sealed box and its contents. They put the odd stone container on a metal lab table. Roberto carefully used a knife to pry open the lid.

Hannah lifted an elongated bundle from the crude limestone box and placed their latest discovery on a cotton pad in the center of the table. From the weight and feel, it was a ceramic piece wrapped in animal hide. A powdery residue of disintegrated leather turned to dust in her hands as she parted the covering. Using a small brush to preliminarily remove centuries-old protective wrappings, she exposed a most unusual vase.

The tall cylindrical painted vase was banded with glyphs and red bands similar to the Codex tradition. A celestial bird sitting in the heavens topped a sky band. Hannah recognized water-lily jaguar and sky dragon symbols. It pleased her that the multi-colors still remained brilliant and alive.

"This series of conventional concentric painted bands of rim text hieroglyphs states that it was created to honor an *ajau*, a divine lord, but the particular name is unfamiliar to me," she said to Roberto, who stood close by trying to decipher the writing.

The first side of the vase she inspected depicted two figures, one male and the other female, seated cross-legged on raised reed mats bending towards one another. Both were dressed simply, no headdressings, jewelry or feathers. They appeared to be common individuals, without the usual markings of high-ranking royalty or super-natural deities.

Bundles of quills next to conch containers immediately caught her eye. A small rabbit to the side of the female indicated that the subject was a scribe. With quill in hand, the lady was dutifully transcribing the other's words. His speech was drawn in curling glyphs rising from his mouth.

That was where the normal Maya depictions ended. The bodies' positioning and realistic facial features were painted with a very free hand, giving movement to the bodies. The art style struck Hannah as more dimensional than the usual flat profiles found in classic Mayan art.

Brilliant blues and greens used on the vase were considered the most precious and beautiful of the pigments. Colors associated with sky, water and jade, were a Maya artist's most valuable material. Green hues also symbolized the maize plant, not only the sacred material from which humans were formed, but maize as the source of food substance and life.

Picking the piece up for closer inspection under her magnifying glass, she studied the portrayed face of the female in detail. A quick gasp followed and her heart pounded.

"Berto, this lady has the same facial markings and distinctive lily on her cheek. It is another painted version of the mural portrait we uncovered in the ruins today."

Hannah quickly turned the cylinder vase upside down in search of any tale-tell marks.

"Yes, this is the potter's distinct signature. Oh my god, I am holding conclusive evidence that the unknown scribe who has been putting books on pots and who painted the hidden room is a woman. This woman!" she exclaimed.

Hannah turned the vase around to see more on the other side. Two bold penetrating speckled sunstone eyes peering back at her. The portrait was of a man, obviously not Maya. His face was rugged but his gentle smile warmed Hannah's soul. The light flesh-toned colors and shading were so realistic they almost leapt from the hard surface.

"This man looks like the Franciscan friar painted on the mural wall. I'll more closely compare the two tomorrow."

"Our scribe's lettering on this side is not the usual Mayan ideograms. Those are old-style Roman lettering and Spanish words," observed Roberto.

He took overall and close-up photographs of the whole process. They preferred to use the Justin Kerr rollout camera technique to produce one flat, continuous scene for analysis. The entire decoration could be viewed at once without having to handle the vessel with its fragile surfaces.

Both habitually paid close attention to detail. The scientists noted the minutia of the unusual artifact. They recorded data on height, diameter, circumference and vase type. It took all the discipline Hannah could muster not to quickly swipe clean the ceramic piece to see everything hidden under the centuries-old buildup and dirt. Years of training kept her from destroying evidence and clues needed to answer questions racing through her head. She cleaned the vase using a dental tool to remove calcified deposits and a fine sable brush to dust off residue.

"Who is this foreign man? How was a priest connected to our artist?" they both wondered out loud at the same time.

"Why did she dedicate such a fine piece of art to him?" Hannah asked as she attempted to read writings surrounding his portrait.

"I can make out something about 'of god, love, kindness' in this area. But over here, in bold strokes it reads, 'disappearance or death by hand of cloth brothers', whatever that means," translated Roberto as best he could under the circumstances.

"Not only does this message seem important to her, but she is using new techniques and two languages to tell the story," Hannah said. "I've never seen anything like it. It's totally unique."

The piece presented more than artistic value or historical appeal. The painting was dynamic, as though the brush strokes still held the passion and essence of its creator.

The communication from the past deeply moved Hannah. Visual works of a past civilization were powerful. Serendipitous finds like this vase fortified her vocation as an archaeologist. A mystical calling to explore and explain the past was not only a glorious gift, but also a huge obligation. This unknown lady scribe had become a significant part of the whole to her.

As exhausted as she and Roberto both were, they knew they had a scientific responsibility to see that this message was preserved and interpreted. Hannah's hands cradled the sacred communication from her mysterious artist. It was her job as an archaeologist to weave connections between the past and her own times. At that moment the past seemed more real than the present.

"Why did this vase have to appear just as we are resealing the room? Tomorrow I have to put it back in its hiding place and walk away," an exasperated Hannah complained to Roberto.

"It is difficult to wait, but more difficult to regret," he replied.

"I wish I could keep digging that palace structure. It is like a time capsule, obviously containing evidence about what happened here as recently as the mid-1500s, after the Spanish came. There are so few pieces from the era."

"This vase of impossible context and content poses more questions than it answers," said Roberto. "It would certainly stir up historians. Sam Sarra, our esteemed museum director and your crush," he snorted sarcastically, "will be especially interested in this latest find. He always discretely asks around for anything to do with early post-conquest works. Pays extremely well from what I hear."

"I have never seen art similar to this cylinder vase," she observed. "And you will not see this again if it is turned in. Over my career, I noticed that artifacts pertaining to the early conquest years tend to disappear very quickly."

"Why?"

Roberto shrugged, "Like a prostitute, the antiquity thief knows there is money in beauty and rarely a shortage of willing customers. Who knows, maybe someone is still burning books and getting rid of evidence."

"I cannot let this special piece end up hidden in a warehouse, vanished into a private collection, or worse yet destroyed," Hannah sighed. Her partner nodded in silent agreement about the loss of unrecorded information.

She held the vase close to her chest like a child. She could not stop looking at it; she did not want to stop looking at it. For the second time in her professional life, she contemplated deception by omission. Hannah quickly, but intuitively, made a decision.

"Extreme circumstances require extreme choices," she assured him as she spoke. "Berto, just like North Star's tomb, we are not reporting the hidden room or its contents, especially this vase, until you and I can research and excavate properly. It may be months or years before we can continue. Once again, I am going to trust my instincts more than my intellect. Will you keep this second find secret for a while?"

"Taking risks is a natural state with me. Instincts have led me into every worthwhile experience I've ever had," he smiled. "What we are doing in this case will justify itself in the end."

CHAPTER 60

Ek Balam, Yucatan
Present Day

Forbidden archaeology is evidence suppressed by the scientific community because it is out of context, too different, or challenges known chronology. Occasionally, a dirt detective finds an out of place artifact, but when the object creates an X-Files moment, field academics often choose to willfully or ignorantly overlook these new bits of knowledge. Many suppress evidence that didn't suit their theories or threatened their credibility. Structured categories cannot admit exceptions or they are not categories.

Hannah's finds of unusual style items, differing historical accounts and overlapping coincidences around her discoveries were adding up. The murals and artifacts had dimensions that seemed to transcend ordinary notions of time and place. She talked to Roberto, Mari and her father about finding the series of oddities.

"Our findings pose more questions than answers. Too many things don't tally up, not in the usual way. I have always thought of myself as a rational conservative person, always coloring inside the lines. How am I going to present raw intractable evidence that contradicts clearly established models and historical records? I don't want to be branded a crank in scholarly circles or scoffed at by my peers."

"The scientific community is not always open-minded," her dad offered. "Archaeologists who push forth unexplainable items or extremely theories find themselves shunned and their reputations ruined." Max had spent his life in academia at Stanford and University of Southern California and saw such smothering actions.

"It's not fair, but scientists are afraid of things they can't explain easily, especially those discovered by coincidence or intuition. Much important research has been crushed," he continued. "Unconventional ideas encounter violent opposition from mediocre minds."

"Don't worry, I won't announce or write about our unusual finds until we have more solid historical backup. We'll hold these truths close in for a while. Besides, we reburied the room and all the artifacts. It has been completely sealed for future excavation," Hannah assured him.

Mari later asked Hannah, "Are you worried over whether you made the right decision about sealing up the mural room and not reporting it to the authorities?"

Hannah nodded in the affirmative.

"Don't assume the universe will punish you for one thing and reward for another. The universe has no fixed agenda," said Mari.

"Just like the Edzna burial tomb, our team is in unanimous agreement about resealing the hidden room." Trying the lighten the moment, Hannah kidded, "See, I told you if I broke one rule, I'd break more. I can hear the string of firecrackers going off now."

"Life is an infinite series of choices. Every decision we make means we sacrifice infinite possibilities that could follow," Mari offered.

"What confuses me the most are the reoccurring thoughts, dreams and insights popping up in my head," she confessed later to Mari. "They force themselves out, like grass pushing through concrete. This is so unlike me. I feel caught between centuries."

Mari, with her Maya heritage, better understood Hannah's uncertainty and questions on circular events and invisible threads.

She encouraged Hannah to tap into that new and different power. "Listen to your intuition, trust it, but never discuss your source with others," Mari warned.

"Berto, you seem to know where to look. Lucky finds and game changing data marked your career. Is it a gift or a curse?" Hannah said, including him in the conversation.

"I have removed myself from the arena filled with battling anthropology gladiators," he laughed. "They may not follow my unorthodox methods, but they seek me out because of my results. Hannah, don't worry so much about acceptance and just do your best. Someday, when the world is ready, evidence will prove you right," he advised.

"Hannah, be outrageously bold in a belief that you will be guided in your decisions, but let go of expectations about how that guidance will unfold," advised Mari.

After sealing the room they did not speak of the murals or artifacts beyond the occasional subtle reference. Hannah observed that the more remarkable and unbelievable events through which a group of people had lived, the less need they felt to discuss it. She thought that the sheer serendipity and inexplicability of such a find would almost require conversation; yet it was those very qualities that made talk unnecessary. Little, if anything, was said about their feelings or discoveries. They each saw what they saw, or believed they did. Analysis or conjecture would require further proof to be obtained at a later date.

CHAPTER 61

Ek Balam, Yucatan
Present Day

By Monday morning, when local workers returned, they found the site directors busy at the opposite end of the plaza cleaning two carved monuments. Roberto constructed a *palapa*, thatched palm canopy to protect the giant limestone columns from dissolving rains and to shade workers from the jungle's penetrating sun.

Hannah worked all day to capture detailed photographs, rubbings and drawings of the stone trees. The three-meter tall chiseled slabs were too weathered to decipher most of the hieroglyphs. However, a portion of a once proud dignitary on the back provided examples of clothing and jewelry worn around 900 B.C.

On the ground, in front of the bas-relief stone, stood an altar. It was shaped like a giant wheel of cheese with an engraved day glyph covering the entire surface. The date must have been of great importance to the kingdom for the residents to erect such a stone.

Hannah worked on a ladder handmade from tree saplings and vines, under the thatched roof. She broke focus and looked around when she heard someone coming down the forest path loudly whistling 'Waltzing Matilda'.

"Joseph?"

Within a minute he stood at the base of the crude ladder. He gazed up at her and said, "It seems communication is our problem. And I believe communication is the solution."

What a reunion they put together at Casa de la Paz that night. Roberto and Mari welcomed Joseph, their Tem Chen, back with open arms. Gloria, a Maya traditional food expert, prepared fresh green cilantro soup, vegetarian lasagna, squash stuffed with black beans and mixed salad. All the ingredients were grown at Kate's nearby organic farm.

"Gloria, this is great coffee. It must be made from magic beans," Joseph complimented the cook, making the tiny lady blush and giggle behind her hand.

Hannah loved the way the Maya staff seemed to be born with good manners and courtesy. Even the way their server handed them dishes on her flat palm looked like a graceful movement in a dance. Everyone finished with Casa's signature homemade dessert, called 'Fire and Ice'. They savored the rich chocolate-cinnamon ice cream with a honey and chili infused topping.

Joseph leaned over and whispered to Hannah. "We have more freedom and material possessions than most locals will ever know. Yet they share and welcome us with such warmth and generosity. I have never seen 'keep out' painted on a Maya gate," he said, humbled and appreciative.

"Poor people are often more generous because they know what it's like to have nothing," said Hannah.

Four other guests sat at a long table by the lodge's front wall. They were pilgrims walking the Camino de Yucatan who took a side trip to see the mystical Ek Balam, Black Jaguar ruins. People from all around the world visited Yucatan's holy and historical places, walking ancient trails from village to village to experience sacred sights, both natural and man-made. The walkers chatted over dinner comparing their current pilgrimage route with the Camino de Santiago across northern Spain. The group retired early to get started again at dawn.

The evening meal conversation was filled with novel-worthy tales of adventures and laughter. Her friend and favorite storyteller had appeared like magic and kept everyone spellbound.

The tall dark journalist looked more attractive than Hannah remembered. Long days in the Middle-Eastern desert sun darkened his complexion. He appeared a few belt holes thinner, but strong. She reveled in his bright intelligent eyes, wide infectious smile and strong jaw that had not felt a razor for a long time.

When they could, Hannah and Joseph left the others and walked into the garden. Two iguanas resentfully abandoned their siestas at the couple's approach. The friends sat with their feet dangling over the edge of the secluded pool. Each told their version of the previous misunderstandings and what happened afterward.

"I made too many negative assumptions," Joseph began, "jumped to conclusions. I've had lots of time to think. Distance and silence are the best truth meters around."

"I am sorry," he apologized. "All the time we have lost…" he put his face in his hands and sighed deeply.

"In French they don't say, 'I miss you.' They say '*tu me manques*' which translates, 'you are missing from me'. That's how it felt Joseph," Hannah said.

Joseph wanted to tell her the same thing, but the phrase 'I've missed you' seemed inadequate to cover the fact that thinking of her was what kept him alive many times in the war zone. Almost as if she'd read his mind, Hannah continued.

"Missing you and fear for you. I never told you, but my first love, my fiancé was killed in Afghanistan. I relived that nightmare when you went off to cover the war without a goodbye."

"I don't say goodbye unless it is final."

"What brought you here?" asked Hannah, for the first time hoping he might take her out of the friend zone.

"You can close your eyes to things you don't want to see, but you cannot close your heart to things you don't want to feel," he said in answer to her question. To lighten up the moment, "That is a quote from Captain Jack Sparrow, one of my super heroes," he admitted shyly, like a kid with a comic book. "You've been such a good friend. I didn't want us to be on bad terms."

"Oh," Hannah's shoulders sank. "Me too." She didn't know whether to be happy because they were friends again or sad because that was all he considered them to be after everything.

As they visited, the last of the day disappeared. Scattered clouds turned slate-colored to match the dark sky. Daylight extinguished itself quickly, without first dimming or apology. Hannah saw one star and then another, until the sky filled with twinkling dots. Venus rose steady and white above the western sky.

"Look, there's the Big Dipper," Hannah pointed upward.

"Do you know all the constellations?" Joseph asked.

"I'm afraid the Dippers and Venus, the evening star are the only ones I can identify. I just don't see stellar patterns that even remotely resemble lions or bears," she admitted.

"Maybe the ancient Greeks took hallucinogenic drugs back then, laid on their backs on Mount Olympus and pointed out star formations to waste away their nights," Joseph offered. He could always make Hannah smile.

They sat in silence and watched shooting stars.

"Well, it's getting late. You have to work tomorrow, so I'll say goodnight," Joseph said. He knew if he stayed next to Hannah in that private romantic setting that he'd probably say or do something that might be taken wrong.

His feeling that they were fated to be together was still as strong as the first time he saw her. He first needed to determine what secrets drove her, and how attached she was to Dr. Sarra and his jet-setting way of life. He also wanted to figure out a way to make their nomadic lives blend. Joseph put his hands on Hannah's shoulders, looked into her eyes and placed a kiss on top of her head.

"Kate put you in the Hobbit room over there by the raised garden, maybe because you are from that part of the world," Hannah laughed.

"New Zealand is not just Lord of the Rings and sheep," he joked back.

"No counting sheep here. But the frogs might keep you awake for a while with their loud pattern of signals. Good night," she said, blowing him a kiss. He missed it because he'd already turned to leave the garden pool area.

CHAPTER 62

Ek Balam, Yucatan
Present Day

At first light the next day Joseph went to work at the Ek Balam ruins with Hannah. He requested that she show him around and tell him about her latest work and finds. He watched her sorting pottery and asked how she evaluated and decided which ones to send to the regional or to the national museums.

Hannah purposefully avoided going near the palace area where the hidden room was located. She'd never mention that discovery to him or to anyone, until after it could be properly excavated and reports published.

Joseph scurried up and down rubble-strewn mounds like a mountain goat. The mysterious stones and ancient shrines of the Talol kingdom captivated him. The past lay right in front of his eyes and right under his feet.

"There are no rivers in the Yucatan, so ancient cities were constructed near natural wells or sinkholes. On this parched peninsula, close-by water was vital. Just look at this grand city in the midst of the jungle with no obvious water source," said Hannah waving over the site with her arms. She offered to take him for a swim in the big cenote later.

When they crossed the main plaza and Joseph first saw the acropolis pyramid, he stopped in his tracks and stared transfixed. There in the middle of a vivid green jungle, stood a grand tribute to a long dead noble lineage and traditions. The temple platform was one hundred and sixty-five by sixty-four meters at its base and almost forty meters high. Another to the right, although covered with trees and smothering jungle growth, stood equally high.

"All these tall vertical mounds and buildings---this must've been the Manhattan of the Maya world," Joseph said.

"Tikal would claim that title," she answered.

"Engineers and architects who designed and built these structures had a vast knowledge of mathematics and astronomy. Their skills reached high levels of refinement while Europe was still in the Dark Ages," Hannah shared. "Incredible as it seems, buildings were aligned with solar and lunar solstices and equinoxes. These axial configurations couldn't be accidental. They are just too pronounced and precise."

Joseph shook his head in amazement. "What stumps me is how they did all this without the aid of wheels, metal tools or work animals."

Together they climbed the uneven worn stone staircase of the towering main monument to access the Mouth of the Jaguar temple entrance. Stucco hieroglyphs symbols flanked the stairs of the tiers they climbed. Vertigo challenged Hannah felt her neck pulse throbbing. She took deep breaths to fight her anxiety.

She pointed out representative sculptures of Chac the rain god and other deities with clicking names. "It took a while, but I eventually learned most of the various deities, their dual personas and relationships to nature," said Hannah.

Joseph turned serious for a moment. "Throughout history people believed that gods were 'up there' or 'out there' in some distant place instead of in the same world as we are. Hopefully someday, images of height will be replaced with those of depth. Spiritual depth," he said. "An inside, not outside god."

"I agree. God is existence." She was pleased that he was not strictly bound by manufactured, organized and political religions.

"Have any of nature's laws ever been changed by men's gods?" he concluded with a final question for them to ponder.

Hannah and Joseph lingered half way up, in front of the pyramid's middle tier façade. A massive jaguar mouth with two meter long white teeth protected the entrance to the Black Jaguar King Ukit Kan L'ek Tok's tomb.

"Like pharaohs in Egypt, kings of the Maya city-states were considered earthly incarnations of the gods. King and deity all in one," Hannah explained.

Large white stucco figures with feathered wings and moveable hands adorned the entrance to the throne room and burial chamber. Hannah's favorite statue of the group was an odd solo person straddled over a bench. The head turned to the side, with an arm casually crossed in front touching the opposite shoulder.

"Are they angels? Who is that lone person in ordinary garb among the king and nobles?" he asked.

"That's what we are trying to discover through additional research. Archaeologists often question and reinterpret earlier finds."

Hannah pointed south to a partially restored series of rooms in the distance, "We call that rounded building a palace. But truthfully, often we don't know with certainty the purpose of many structures. Occasionally we make up names for their cities. If archaeologists can't figure out what an artifact was used for or it shows little daily wear, we label it 'ceremonial'," she admitted.

"I can spend months excavating a building that reveals nothing at all, except that the Maya built the darn thing, which I knew before I ever started."

"I feel a power in these crumbling centers. It reminds me of Ephesus in Turkey, the Roman city where Christ's mother, Mary lived until her death and assumption. Whether all the accounts are true or not, a person can still feel the energy of prayers said by visiting pilgrims over the centuries," Joseph added. "I sense feminine energy here."

"This season we found a stone statue of a seated royal woman. Although defaced, there were enough glyphs to determine her high rank through incorporated motifs usually reserved for male rulers, like symbolic ceremonial bars of authority."

"Are Maya queens rare?"

"Not really. Royal women in Ek Balam, Coba, Calakmul and Palenque assumed high political and military offices, in addition to being noble spouses," Hannah said proudly.

"Do you ever find skeletons?"

"Rarely because the jungle moisture and soil quickly disintegrates skeleton remains. When we do get remains, if they are out of context, no one can distinguish bones of royalty from bones of slaves. Their ability to tell their stories is pretty much lost."

"Ancient Maya mothers used to apply binding devices of wooden splints or wound cloth to the newborn's soft skulls to indent and flatten the forehead and elongate the cranium into a tapered form. Some Mayans would also file their teeth into T-shapes or drill holes to insert jade or other precious stones. The ancients endured unspeakable pain and invested great wealth into their quest for beauty. Such bone and dental markers are one way I can identify older skeletons from modern day ones. Also, Maya craniums are compact, round and wide; with squared cheekbones; u-shaped palatal arches and sharp eye orbits," she explained.

"You're a regular encyclopedia. No need to Google stuff when you are around," Joseph teased Hannah. "Seriously, it takes special qualities to dedicate your life to problems that have no certain solutions and ever-changing answers. You study human behaviors without having any direct contact with the subject. No wonder you have to apply imagination and speculation," he said with more understanding than she expected.

"Yes, sadly sometimes reports have to be tagged only as 'current state of knowledge'," she sighed.

Joseph sat at the top of the acropolis and gazed out over the flat terrain. The tropical forest looked like a riot of frantic green. The jungle stretched to the horizon, broken only by indentations of cornfields and pastures. Small patches of the forest were peeled back to make way for archaeologists and tourists. Overgrown mounds, seemingly flung out in all directions indicated where temples, pyramids and dwellings from the past were located. The great tide of civilization had long since ebbed.

"Ek Balam seems a better setting than where you were digging before," he said. "But, you're still living in the jungle, no more than jaguar bait," he teased. "Words like nosy, Peeping Tom and dumpster diver come to mind when I picture you poking around in dead people's garbage out here," he said with a wink.

Hannah laughed. She enjoyed Joseph's frankness and boisterous joking about her work and environment.

Both his chosen occupational field and hers required adaptability and the ability to tough it out. His equally searching nature struck a cord inside her. In truth, the isolation and lack of stability were harder on her each year.

Hannah glanced over at Joseph. She could see that giving work top priority had a certain down side. After being in his company, she felt a preemptive tinge of lonliness for when he eventually left. Maybe it was time for her to explore new options.

"Archaeology is a painstaking business. Your daily work is contrary to the glamorous image that the popular press foists on the public," he acknowledged. "I can write about realities of your profession to garner more respect for your contributions," Joseph offered.

"That would be great. A person needs to feel they have a mission in life and are doing worthwhile work."

Joseph wondered if she ever considered teaching at a university or curating at a museum, anything to cut back on the dangerous fieldwork aspect of her calling. "Most people are content to live and work in a safe place with lots of modern conveniences."

"I don't want to be most people. Neither do you, obviously"

"Years spent in a cubicle working in diligent dullness would be like having a book and only reading one page," he answered in agreement. "People may criticize us for being different and not living by society's standards or values, but deep down, many wish they had the courage to do the same."

"I always found that my mindset and attitude were indispensible parts of my contentment. I can blossom wherever I am planted," she said. That statement gave Joseph a spark of hope.

Hannah excused herself to finish excavating a test pit in front of the monument where she'd been working when he showed up. Joseph watched her recording stratigraphy and contents on the site bags. Her arduous labors in the jungle heat seemed driven and sustained by sheer will power.

"Hey lady, is it hot down there?"

"Well, a few minutes ago two Hobbits stuck their heads over the edge of my pit and threw in a gold ring," she shouted back with a big laugh.

Where others shirk this kind of duty, she looked happy there in the dirt. It occurred to Joseph that Hannah's work obsession was all she had right now, but he also wondered if that was all she wanted.

Joseph wandered around the ruins on his own. He made quick friends with site workers. "Hey Canul, it looks like you posed for the statues on the temple. Except for hieroglyphic eyes and slanted forehead, it's obvious that you and the sun god were distant kin."

Hannah stopped her digging when Joseph returned. She spoke to three workers, giving them encouragement. "*Malob*, good work," she told them.

"I gather folks still use the old native tongue around here," he said. "How cool that you speak Mayan."

"Not really. Roberto and Mari have taught me a handful of useful words and phrases. It is a very difficult language to learn as an adult. But Mayan is regularly spoken by millions of people in Mexico and Guatemala. It is the only indigenous language in the

New World to dominate that of their oppressors. The Maya are not myths of the past, they are current real people and their culture needs to be respected."

Joseph told her he was on site for a quick personal visit, but took copious notes and photos for an article on her latest excavation.

Cumulous clouds quickly thickened and spilled over the archaeological zone. Dark gunpowder gray skies emptied themselves the way only tropical storms can do. Within minutes the twosome were as wet as if they had fallen into water.

"I love the smell after it rains," said Hannah.

"Reminds me of the Bob Marley lyrics, 'Some people feel the rain, others just get wet'," said Joseph.

Bad weather was a sufficient excuse to call it an early day, dismiss the workers, and return to Casa. The damp earth-laden smell of the rain forest mixed with a strong odor of smoke from field burnings that bordered their narrow trail. Myriads of crickets and frogs, happy with the moisture, vibrated a hidden chorus as the couple walked back to the pueblo.

CHAPTER 63

Ek Balam, Yucatan
Present Day

Hannah and Joseph returned to Casa de la Paz after a day exploring and working in the Ek Balam ruins. Joseph stopped in the front room to chat with Kate. He asked lots of questions about her hundred hectare organic farm on the outskirts of the village. Kate was happy to tell him of her efforts with permaculture. For a journalist, he seemed unusually knowledgeable about soils, irrigation, compost, and grafting.

"Hold on to what's good, even if it is a handful of earth. I like to learn about plants and animals wherever I travel," he explained. "Growing things attaches me to the earth. About ninety percent of the flora and fauna in New Zealand is unique to the islands, so everything here is new to me."

Joseph then sat down on a stone bench overlooking the garden and talked with Mari. "I'll have my mum send you a batch of honey the bees produce from the manuka plant only found on my island." He helped her fold and put away towels for the pool.

"Trust your instincts Joseph," Mari said out of the blue. "The invisible thread that connects certain souls may tangle and stretch, but it will not break. Your heart will not betray you."

He saw the wise healer could read his mind as easily as she did a line of Mayan hieroglyphics. "Are my feelings for Hannah so obvious? I thought I'd lost her to Dr. Sarra. They seem to make the ideal pair. You know, same field of work and all. I tried to forget her and let go, but couldn't."

"Deep true emotions can't be ignored," she offered. "Tem Chen, letting things drift like an unanchored boat invites problems. Don't allow waiting to become a habit," she warned his internal saboteur.

"I worry about Hannah's rejection, so I hold back. This connection I feel is too important to make a mistake."

"Affection not expressed is like having a gift all wrapped up and not giving it," said Mari.

"It's not that I don't want… It's just that I can't decide the best way to handle it."

"Standing on the constant edge of indecision is cowardly. Doubts of any kind can only be resolved by action. Joseph, be brave and take the risk."

Hannah dashed past them and jumped into the swimming pool. She splashed and squealed at the cold embrace of the water.

"Come on in. *Cenote* waters are full of life-force energy." She followed her invitation with double-handed wave splashes that soaked Joseph to the skin.

"Guess I don't need to change into my swimsuit after all." He stripped off his shirt and shoes, down to his frayed cut-off shorts and jumped into the cool underground river-fed pool. He swam in and out of the churning surface like a dolphin. He had legs strong and straight as pillars, with the broad shoulders of an athlete.

For the first time, Hannah saw a tattoo on the bottom of Joseph's foot. "What is written on your foot?"

"Oh that. I don't go for tattoos, but I decided to ink on the latitude and longitude of my home in New Zealand. Reminds me of those I love. Keeps me grounded."

Like children, they played a game of blind man's bluff tag with eyes closed. Instead of calling out 'Marco' and 'Polo', they substituted it with their own 'Aguila' and 'Sol'.

Joseph couldn't help but notice Hannah's shapely curves. Her skin glistened, dappled with late afternoon sunlight coming through the palm trees around the pool. He was startled that brief glimpses of her freckled skin wet with water brought on such intense physical arousal. He looked away guiltily. No one had caused this effect on him for a very long time.

She jumped out and sat on the lounge chair toweling her wet hair. "Are you ready to get out?"

He shook his head, adjusted his swim shorts underwater and decided a little more time in the cold water would save him embarrassment. A sassy glint in her eye made him wonder if she was aware of how she moved him. He was intrigued by the idea.

There was a moment when Joseph looked at Hannah and found she was looking at him in the same way. He gave her a crooked smile, one that without words said, "I know what you are thinking and I'm thinking the same thing."

"Hannah, you said you were taking some things to museum storage in Merida. How about you make it a long weekend and show me around your adopted hometown?"

"Just the two of us?"

CHAPTER 64

Merida, Yucatan
Present Day

"Merida, Yucatan is the longest continuously occupied city in the Americas. The Maya lived here for centuries in a town called T'ho before the Spanish conquered the area in the mid-1500s. Grand pyramids were torn down and those same carved stones were used to build the cathedral, city walls and conquistador Francisco Montejo's home on the main plaza," Hannah told Joseph.

Their first stop in Merida was Mundo Maya Anthropology Museum in the northern part of town. While Hannah conferred with staff and turned over artifacts selected and hand-carried for storage, Joseph explored the facility.

"This is one of the biggest and best museums for displays and interactive exhibits," he said. "How many people work here?"

"About half," answered Hannah.

That old joke got her a dimpled grin and playful push on the arm.

They drove into the center of Merida and checked into the 1901-built Gran Hotel overlooking Hidalgo Square.

"Two separate rooms with views," she requested of Bob at the front desk. She received their keys and a gift basket of fruit from their host.

"That guy seems to know and like you," Joseph teased as they walked up a broad marble staircase. A stained glass window covered an entire back wall and an interior walkway overlooked a peaceful central courtyard.

Hannah told him, "Bob and his family are long-time friends and among the greatest archaeologists to ever work in the Maya world. His brother David cracked countless hieroglyphic codes so we can read the ancient scripts today. Don't judge books by their covers, especially here in the Yucatan."

"Meet you in the lobby for dinner at eight?" he asked. "I want to see more of this city you love so much."

Hannah was delighted with her hotel suite with its century old style. The décor was charming. She detected a hint of eau d' insecticide, so turned on the window air conditioner for circulation. When it remained warm in the room she turned a dial to the coldest setting and held her hand in front of the vent. The air was still not cool.

"*It makes a lot of noise but doesn't work very well. The Mexicans call machines like this 'politicians'*," she laughed.

Joseph's eyes popped as Hannah came down the wide center staircase for their evening out. She wore a shimmery copper-colored full skirt, soft yellow off-the shoulder blouse and matching amber jewelry.

"Wow, those are great colors on you" was all he could muster as he opened the front door for her.

"I know, people think strawberry blondes and redheads should wear greens and blues. I like greens, but never wear blue. Don't like it on me for some reason," she cringed involuntarily.

A nearby restaurant, *Piedra y Agua,* provided breath-taking views of the cathedral lit up against a cloudless night sky. Music, unique to the Yucatan, serenaded them. Two guitars played the rhythm and bass notes, while a smaller type of six-string guitar produced sharp sounds characteristic of local Trova style.

"Romanticism lives in lyrics of these trios, full of soft melodies and poetic words praising a beloved woman and her beauty," explained Hannah.

Songs of love floated on the evening breeze. Even though Joseph couldn't speak Spanish well, on that night he understood almost every word. Talented Maricarmen Perez sang the classic 'Peregrina' ballad. Lyrics begged a departing pilgrim lover, "Don't forget my land. Don't forget my love."

"Would you like to know the history behind this love song?" Hannah asked Joseph. She knew he appreciated a good story, always taking pleasure in listening to other's anecdotes.

"In the early 1920s," Hannah began, "the Governor of Yucatan was a man called Felipe Carrillo Puerto, from Motul, a town not far from Merida. Working hard labor around the peninsula during his youth, he learned Mayan and about the people of his land. There is a lot of urban legend around his life. Rumors claimed he was a descendant of the *Nachi Cocom* dynasty of ancient Mayapan. People called him 'Apostle of the Bronze Race'. Felipe went to prison because he rebelliously translated the Mexican Constitution into Mayan language in defiance to local edicts. Hacienda owners did not want their peons to read or know their rights," Hannah explained to give historical groundwork.

"Against great odds, Felipe was elected Governor of Yucatan. His first speech as Governor was in Mayan. He passed and enforced laws regarding education, voting, land reformation, women's rights, wages and other social reforms to help Indians and the poor. Over thirty thousand families benefited from redistribution of land.

Wealthy hacienda owners thought of him as a meddlesome socialist who was disrupting their entrepreneural efforts and destroying the economy of the region. They relied on plantation-like indentured labor to harvest and process henequen fibers. Landowners believed they were uniquely capable of knowing what was best for the people, so this Governor was not popular with the elite at all."

"You think?" Joseph smiled, "Please continue. So far this does not sound much like a love story."

"Well, Felipe believed that the hacienda smokestacks represented slavery. He wanted people to be proud of their heritage and also to earn good living wages in some type of new industry."

"What did he come up with as solutions?"

"Tourism and restoration of the ancient Maya ruins were among of his answers. He organized a junket of scientists, archaeologists and journalists from the United States to visit Yucatan archaeological sites and cities. The news correspondent for New York Times was a lady named Alma Reed. Her intrepid reputation from California and New York was one of truth-seeking and compassion."

"And now you are going to tell me that these dedicated people from two different worlds fell in love?" asked Joseph. He hoped maybe Hannah would see the parallel.

"Not right away on her part. But she admired his incisive personal force reshaping the world around him. Alma wrote, 'Felipe represented a grand scale synthesis of my own youthful aspirations and feeble crusading efforts toward a better world'," sighed Hannah. "The esteemed North American visitors recognized his compelling personal magnetism, dedication to mission and above all, sensed his inherent right to leadership."

"Sounds like the immemorial Orphic concept of unity that combines the priest, athlete and prophet into one."

"Yes, that is precisely how Alma saw him," Hannah was pleased at Joseph's insight. "Here in this far off corner of the world, an intelligent charming man in a tailored business suit took on impossible tasks of land reform and abolition of slavery."

"Uh oh, that's too much like your Abraham Lincoln. Don't tell me he got assassinated."

"Felipe and Alma fell in love," Hannah continued without answering his question. "They were to be married in December 1923 and planned to work together to make great contributions to life's collection plate. While Alma made preparations in the States, the hacienda owners paid military men to arrest Felipe, three of his brothers and other politicians."

"But he was the Governor. Didn't anyone come to his aid?"

"Several citizens offered, but Felipe knew his defenders would be fighting with machetes against guns. To avoid slaughter of his unarmed followers, he told them not to rise up. He believed his old friend, the President in Mexico City, would send help."

"Did help arrive? Yucatan in the 1920s was still very isolated, only reachable by boat or arduous overland treks, if I remember correctly."

"Soldiers imprisoned Felipe and the others in Merida's Juarez Penitentiary. Governor Carrillo Puerto, his three brothers, and eight other officials were summarily convicted in mock trials by a military tribunal. On January 3, 1924, in the middle of the night, the handsome young Governor and eleven others were taken to Pantheon Civil General Cemetery and put to death by firing squad."

"That's horrible," said a shocked Joseph, who'd seen battle firsthand.

"Those men died against a stone wall among the hissing of bullets. His mother lost four sons in one night," she continued, "Felipe's last words were, '*No abandoneis a mis indios*'; Do not abandon my Indians. He became a beloved legend. There are schools, roads and towns named after him all over Mexico."

"What happened to Alma?"

"She continued journalism and projects around the world. Her last years were as a reporter for an English language newspaper in Mexico City. When she died in 1966, some opposed her burial near Felipe because he had married in the Catholic Church before his relationship with her. He was divorced, but he and Alma, his lady pilgrim, had not yet wed. She had no rights. Finally her ashes were interred in a monument of stone across from the platform and arena where Felipe is buried.

"Is the song "Peregrina" written about her?"

"Yes, during their courtship Felipe asked the poet Luis Rosado Vega to write the lyrics and hired well-known composer Ricardo Palmerin to put it to music. We can visit their tombs in the big cemetery tomorrow, if you'd like," Hannah offered, as if going to gravesites would be a fun outing.

"I'd like to see their memorials," he answered sincerely. "Now I'm going to try this famous Yucatan *pollo pibil*, chicken cooked with spices in banana leaves. Yum."

"Be careful of the green habanero sauce. It's strong enough to cause nosebleeds," Hannah warned.

Joseph studied the beverage menu and discussed vineyards and the best vintage years with the restaurant owner. He ordered half bottles of three individual wines so they could experience differences with their three meal courses. Hannah complimented his knowledge and suitable choices.

"New Zealand has nine wine districts that are coming into their own. Unique soil, climate and water deliver an exciting taste experience. I enjoy wine pairings and how local environment affects flavors," he modestly brushed aside her praise.

"Give thanks to the vine. There's strength and life in every drop," he offered a toast and raised his glass.

After dinner they strolled around the main plaza park in front of the cathedral and conquistador Montejo's house, both built in the mid-sixteenth century.

"That is hundreds of years older than both our countries," Joseph commented with emphasis on the hundreds. Pointing toward the formidable stone structure towering over the square, he continued, "Luther must have had a church like this in mind when he wrote, 'A Mighty Fortress is our God'."

"Morro Castle in Havana Harbor was designed by the same Spanish Colonial architect, Hannah added.

Joseph hailed a horse-drawn carriage, called a *calesa,* and asked the driver to give them a tour of Merida's highlights. As they got inside the buggy from a bygone era, Hannah admired the white silk lilies adorning the canopy. They leaned back and enjoyed views of the backlit grand plaza, Paseo de Montejo with its French-style mansions and the circular Monument of Banderas-flags. People were everywhere, dining in outdoor cafes or casually strolling around town listening to music playing in several venues.

"Look at us, regular touri," said Hannah.

"Touri?"

"My personal plural for more than one tourist," she smiled.

When the carriage turned corners, Hannah and Joseph slid closer on the slippery vinyl seats. Their knees and shoulders touched slightly and Hannah could feel the heat from his body. She scooted back to the other side trying to stop feelings she could hardly avoid and deny. Joseph noticed that she knotted her fingers together in her lap as if she didn't know what to do with them. He smiled to himself at her shyness.

"I love clip-clop sounds of a horse plodding down cobbled streets," said Hannah.

"These horses appear to be well cared for. I grew up in the countryside with horses. Do you ride?" he asked Hannah.

"I was raised in the city, so I'm not much of a horsewoman. From what you mentioned before, it sounds like you enjoy horseback riding."

"Did a bit of competitive riding in my youth," Joseph said, "But it's a costly hobby and now I'm on the road so much."

They walked through the late night city. Old-fashioned street lamps pooled their lemon yellow light on rough stones. A full soap bubble moon brightened their way back to the hotel.

"Even cities have moonlight," said Joseph.

Hannah bid him good night at the entrance of her hotel room. “See you downstairs at seven thirty for breakfast at one of my favorite places.”

She stepped inside and shut the door to her suite. He stood for a moment, staring at the closed wooden barrier, not knowing that Hannah was leaning on the other side, deep in thoughts of their special time together.

CHAPTER 65

Merida, Yucatan
Present Day

The next morning, in front of the Gran Hotel, families strolled around General Cepeda Peraza's statue in Hildago Park. Children chased bright colored balloons and opalescent bubbles. Streets leading to the main plaza were closed off each Sunday morning for bicycles and pedestrians. Music floated on the air from all directions. The atmosphere reminded Hannah of a country fair, a constant celebration of everything and nothing.

As the first customers in Casa del Balam's garden courtyard café, Hannah and Joseph got the best table. Water splashed in the stone fountain while they savored a full breakfast of fresh squeezed orange juice, fruit, and *Huevos Motulenos*, one of Yucatan's signature egg dishes, created in honor of Felipe Carrillo Puerto of Motul.

Joining other walkers, they took a Sunday stroll around the center of town. As they crossed the square, a mass of speckled pigeons pecked at dry breadcrumb offerings thrown down on the sidewalk. The sluggish birds only flapped half-hearted out of the way as Hannah and Joseph scooted by the cooing flock. Joseph clapped his hands to chase them away. They shook their flared tails in indignation and clucked their opinion of his discourtesy. Beady-eyed heads turned accusingly at the intruder. Only a few of the most wary sprang into the air, but immediately dropped down again. He stepped over the resulting frenzy of feathers.

"I don't like pigeons," admitted Joseph as he wrinkled his nose. "They are like rats with wings."

Hannah laughed, "My dad, who adores most animals, feels that way about squirrels. He calls them rats with fluffy tails. His dog thinks squirrels and pigeons are in the same category as tennis balls."

Artists and vendors with handmade crafts lined the square and boulevards. Like a little boy at the carnival, Joseph relished the treasures he saw in the stalls. Asking about their wares, he subjected the locals to his struggling Spanish. They smiled courteously at his efforts.

"I want to get a hand-woven Panama hat while I am here," declared Joseph. "How does this one look?" Piercing blue eyes peeked from under the light-colored brim of the tightly plaited palm straw fedora.

Hannah tried not to focus too closely on those eyes. His boyish charms stirred up feelings she had to subdue. The way he looked at her seemed to ask for something she wasn't sure she could or should give. He never crowded her, but accidental touches or smoldering glances sent her pulse into double time.

Traditional folkloric dancers performed in the square every Sunday. Joseph cheered when dancers in regional costumes swirled around with trays of full glasses on their heads without spilling a drop. Women dressed in brightly embroidered *hupiles* and men in white cotton pants and stitched *guyabera* shirts, proved excellent photographic opportunities for him. Matrons, remembering long ago times as dark eyed beauties, sashayed plump bodies to their own rhythms beside the makeshift dance platform.

"The colorful floral embroidery on their dresses is said to be a reflection of their hearts and connection to nature," Hannah told Joseph. He smiled at that association.

"Merida is like a big white music box. It's wonderful," Joseph said as he tipped his head back and laughed at the cobalt blue sky.

Hannah whisked him past armed guards at the Governor's Office Building. They climbed broad stairs to the second floor ballroom to see a painted history of age-old struggles in Yucatan. Huge murals by Fernando Castro Pacheco, Merida's own version of Diego Rivera, lined the interior terrace walls and ballroom.

"So much cultural activity in Merida is free for all to enjoy," he noted. "I was surprised to see signage in most places printed in Spanish, English and Mayan."

"Over sixty percent of Merida's population is Maya and still speak the old indigenous tongue in addition to Spanish," Hannah said.

They stopped at *Monjas* Church to check on upcoming concerts and visit a handicraft shop next door.

"The name *Monjas* means 'nuns'," explained Hannah. "The convent, originally called Our Lady of Consolation, was built in 1596. Enterprising nuns turned their religious complex, covering many hectares of land, into a self-contained and prosperous production center. Greedy government officials confiscated their property, leaving Monjas as just a church and two courtyards."

They entered the church sanctuary through a small rectangular wooden door cut into a thick iron spike studded wooden barrier. The smell of damp limestone and incense filled Joseph's nostrils and made him sneeze. Vast open space loomed three stories above them. Air swished and hummed like the inside of a seashell held up to your ear. Hannah showed him an antique pipe organ in the upper loft, and the backroom where sequestered nuns sat behind wooden panels to observe Mass, hidden from the eyes of the congregation.

She pointed to several venerated oil paintings. "I once recovered a 16th century statue stolen from this church and returned it to the parish. Churches used to be off limits to thieves, but now nothing is sacred when collectors want certain treasures."

Joseph enjoyed exploring with her at his side. He beamed when her face lit up and noticed how she talked faster as she shared favorite locations and stories with him. Likewise, she felt enchanted by his intelligent eyes, which sparkled with humor, and was taken in by his infectious smile.

They treated themselves and luxuriated in city comforts such as consuming coconut ice cream in a chilled restaurant. "We call it 'borrowing air' when we go somewhere air-conditioned like a mall or movie to escape the heat," said Hannah.

"It really is too bad that some of my colleagues report Mexico as such a dangerous place. Scare tactics about violence are painted with too broad a brush to feed overly fearful imaginations."

"As you see, the city is full of office workers eating lunch in the tree covered plazas, parents walking their children to school, shopkeepers scrubbing their stoops and tourists enjoying delicious meals and local beers in outdoor cafes," Hannah reinforced his observations. "Merida is a safe city; safer than most big cities in the world. I don't ever worry about walking alone at night."

As they strolled down the Paseo de Montejo's broad tree-lined boulevard, a replica of Paris' Champs Elysees, Hannah informed him, "In the late 1880s, henequen millionaires built sumptuous palatial estates along this splendid avenue. Fabulous wealth churned in from their stone-strewn fields of henequen spikes. Sadly, it was wealth built on the backs of their Maya serfs. When plastic came into use and with the resulting demise of the lucrative fiber industry, many stately homes were abandoned until purchased and restored by commercial enterprises."

"I see where some mansions were converted into hotels, banks and tourist shops," said Joseph. "Kind of sad."

"Paseo de Montejo is a faded rose, but has not lost her hue and fragrance entirely," she responded.

Joseph and Hannah passed an antique shop as they returned to the main plaza. The front window tastefully displayed old oil paintings, leather-bound books, stained glass panels, fine china, cut crystal and religious icons.

"I usually cross the street and avert my eyes when I walk near stores known to deal in illegal antiquities. Don't want any association with sinister characters or the appearance of impropriety," said Hannah.

"Like a nun hurrying pass a strip club?" teased Joseph.

"I have heels higher than that proprietor's standards."

At that moment, a stout man inside looked up. His fat chin wobbled as he lifted his head and smiled as if in recognition. He reached over to a shelf behind him and removed an object. His sweat-stained *guayabera* shirt was not long enough to cover the belly that protruded over his pants. He waved a rectangular brown paper wrapped package in their direction.

In the window's reflection Hannah saw Joseph standing behind her slowly move his head from side to side and put his finger to his lips in a shushing signal. He put his arm on Hannah's back, guiding her in the other direction with a bulldozer blade action. He began asking questions about colonial architecture, like he never saw the beckoning man.

Hannah shook the image from her head, thinking perhaps it was distortions caused by the storefront's rippled old glass. Putting his finger on his upper lip was a familiar gesture Joseph often used when he was thinking or just before speaking, she justified.

CHAPTER 66

Merida, Yucatan
Present Day

Only an archaeologist who appreciated bones would think of a cemetery as a good place to take a visitor. For eight pesos each, Hannah and Joseph rode a dark blue local bus all the way to General Cemetery. The multi-hectare location was like a small subdivision made up of mausoleums, tombs and monuments with crisscrossed streets and lanes.

Traditionally, in the Yucatan, when a person died, their remains were buried in temporary graves for two or three years. Natural elements did their job until all that was left were bones. Cleaned and disconnected skeletons got placed in a small box and cemented into the family plot. The eclectic style memorials were crowded together in row after row.

Many of the older mausoleums and wall crypts had not been used or tended for decades. No family members came around to fix damage or care for their loved ones' final resting place. Formerly glorious memorials' cement and plaster cracked, metal gates corroded and tree roots pushed up the stones. In areas of the cemetery, it looked like a hurricane or tornado ripped through and no one cleaned up the aftermath. Headstones and marble statues of angels, saints and Jesus lay shattered over gray cement tombs. The most frequent visitors were packs of cemetery dogs that roamed the grounds and rested in the broad shade of trees.

"You can look into some of these tombs and see old bones. That skull is staring right at us," commented Joseph. He shivered and moved on.

"Look, we are coming up to the graves of Felipe Carrillo Puerto and Alma Reed," Hannah said with reverence.

"Joseph, remember the story I told you last night? Felipe was Governor of Yucatan, an advocate for land reform and civil rights for indigenous Yucatec Maya. Alma, an international journalist, came to report on his efforts. They fell in love, but just days before they were to marry, Felipe was captured and executed by his foes."

"How could I forget a tale like that?"

"As a national hero, Felipe is entombed in a reserved grouping with other reformation socialists, including his brothers who were martyrs like him and his sister Elvia, an early champion of women's rights," she continued as they drew near the spot Hannah wanted Joseph to see.

"Is Alma up on the raised platform or in the wall of honor?"

"No, her grave is across the road. Alma died forty-two years after Felipe. Through the efforts of close friends, her ashes were finally placed nearby inside a stone monument with a record of her greatest lifetime accomplishments etched on the sides."

Hannah removed a dead tree branch that had fallen on Alma's gravestone. She replaced withered flowers in the top urn with a brightly colored floral bouquet she bought from a vendor at the cemetery entrance.

"A few years ago, I came here to find Alma's memorial marker ignored and deteriorating. Tinting in the engraved inscriptions was gone, except where someone badly slopped her name in red. I took an afternoon to scrub the entire stone down and carefully repaint the panels."

"No one stopped you?" Joseph asked. "No one maintains this site?"

"People are only remembered for a generation or two by those who knew them." Hannah sighed and continued, "Often when I am in Merida, especially on the Day of the Dead, I come here to Alma's grave, tidy up the area, place flowers and set up an altar. I sometimes stop by for inspiration and to meditate. If you ever need to find me, I might be here."

Hannah pointed out a crackled marble statue standing beside the lady journalist's obelisk monument. "Last year I bought her this carved angel from a renovated church. The angel was never meant as a grave marker in the first place, so there is something alive about her. Her expression is joyful, and her wings are flared instead of drooped. Her hand rests over her heart, not as a gesture of sorrow or reverence, but I think, in breathless delight. And that's how I see Alma."

They sat in silence for several minutes and shared a bottle of mint tea Hannah had carried along in her woven bag.

Joseph's hand swept through the air, "Being here reminds me of our own mortality. A wake up call that we need to enjoy and live life in the present moment."

Hannah led him a short distance to the stone barrier where Felipe, his brothers and members of his cabinet were lined up and assassinated in the early morning hours of January 3, 1924. Historians left the wall, still pockmarked from bullets, in place. A bust of Felipe sat on a high pedestal with a plaque of his last words, "Don't forget my Indians."

"Yucatan's own tragic Romeo and Juliet," said Joseph, while he checked out the location where the martyrs died. Hannah looked up at Felipe's weathered image. She felt big tears forming.

"Silly me," she waved both hands in front of her stinging eyes, attempting to waylay a swell of unexpected sorrow and emotion.

Joseph patted his broad shoulder, inviting her to a safe place to cry if she wanted. He took a step toward her, closing the space between them. Hannah folded into his arms and placed her head on his chest. She could hear the rapid pounding of his heart, a rushing sound, like beating wings. She took that moment of closeness and breathed him in, a masculine scent that made her flush warm all over.

Hannah looked up in wide-eyed surprise by such a strong physical reaction on her part. She stepped back. Joseph's hand caught her gently behind the neck, winding his fingers into her hair. Hannah stopped breathing as he leaned down.

"To break the tension, maybe we should kiss," he said just before he pressed his mouth to hers. His lips tasted like peppermint, sharp, and cool as winter, but his hand sliding down the nape of her neck, was hot as summer.

That first kiss was tender yet firm enough to be dangerous at the same time---almost unbearably perfect. Dreams, longing and sweet anguish melted away. Electric shivers traveled down Hannah's legs, which were not keeping her standing upright very well at the moment.

He wrapped his arms around her, turned and pressed her between his body and the wall. Hannah could feel the roughness and heat of the coarse stones through the back of her blouse. The contrast of their lifeless cold surroundings and Joseph's warm skin reminded Hannah of just how temporary existence could be.

To be kissed amidst a cemetery full of endings might seem profane, even incongruous to some, but for Hannah, it gave her added appreciation for life and new beginnings.

Joseph drew back slightly for a moment to study her face. Warmth from Hannah's lips lingered on his. She made no effort to move away. Instead, she leaned against him and returned his sensual kiss with another of equal ardor. Trembling, she made a throaty moan against his lips, a small sound, exciting and ripe with possibilities.

He lowered his forehead against hers, trying to catch his breath and slow his pulsating heart.

"Wow. That was…" he began.

“Yeah, what happened just then?’ she asked in a whispered daze.

Joseph stared deeply into her eyes. He grinned, realizing that she’d felt the same surge of energy he had experienced. Something had passed between them so powerful, so incredible there were no words to describe it. Their attraction to each other was as certain and as hard to ignore as magnetism. They were drawn together by invisible forces they couldn’t control, let alone escape.

CHAPTER 67

Merida, Yucatan
Present Day

Joseph flipped the iron latch on his hotel room door, locking the world and time outside. He reached over and pulled Hannah into his arms. A combination of fear and desire churned in her stomach. Her heart pounded with the adrenaline rush of the moment. Joseph leaned down and kissed her softly.

Effects of those first kisses and caresses hummed through them both. His kisses went beyond passion and longing. They overflowed with promises and the beginning of something important between two people who mattered to each other.

Having his body pressed against her, to feel his taunt defined muscles through his shirt and sexual heat rising between them, jolted and swept Hannah away. Every part of her seemed to awaken at once and respond hungrily.

"Lordy, this man's a good kisser," thought Hannah. Then she realized that she'd said it out loud. She buried her blushing face in against his chest.

Joseph's mouth curved up and he laughed heartily. "Thanks. It's funny how we know each other so well and are still nervous as teenagers."

Joseph leaned forward and took her hand. Carefully weaving her fingers with his, he walked to the edge of the canopy bed. He stepped back, put his hands on her shoulders and looked deeply into her eyes. "Is this what you want?" he asked in a voice hoarse with desire and restraint.

"I want to be with you," she whispered, out of breath, "But, you know what? I think I'm getting in over my head."

"Yes, me too. But I'll bet you're a good swimmer." Joseph smiled and kissed her boldly and sensually.

Hannah felt turned on when Joseph undressed her. He obviously enjoyed what he saw and admired her secret lacey underwear.

Soon they lay side-by-side, naked under cool white sheets. Each caress became more pleasurable and exciting. Both had longed for this intimacy since their first teasing kisses in the cemetery. They surrendered to each other, and they surrendered to love.

Joseph's mouth was on hers, alternately demanding and tender. Hannah felt tight anticipation gather in her belly and melt inside her. She shifted her legs when he pressed himself against her inner thigh. He inhaled deeply like he'd been holding his breath under water. Her heart and her body moved toward him in readiness. She couldn't stop herself from anchoring her hands in his hair and guiding him on top of her.

Joseph pushed into her warmth slowly and retreated, pushed and retreated. He set a slow rhythm to extend their pleasure. Her repeatedly contracting around him burned away at his control.

Hannah's world reduced down to the room, the bed, and the incredible man who filled her. She was completely unaware of anything but the two of them. All she heard was her name as he whispered it. She reveled in the love and the need. Pleasure built and tugged at her very center.

Breath came in short gasps. Poised on the thin edge of ecstasy, she cried out his name. Hannah's back curved like a bow as she crested. Her cries of pleasure combined with a gasp of surprise at the intensity. Joseph felt Hannah's surrender. With a shout muffled by her hair, pleasure shuddered through him. It left him weak and stunned. It thrilled her to bring him enjoyment too.

Amazement shone from Hannah's eyes. "*So this is what a man and woman making love give to each other,*" she thought. It was more, so much more than she'd ever experienced or imagined. This intimate connection with Joseph changed her old perspective.

Rolling over to his side and staring into her eyes, Joseph smiled and said, "What just happened between us was beyond lust. This is new for me." She nodded in total agreement. No words were needed to acknowledge that their hearts were as entwined as their bodies.

Hannah and Joseph, in the special communication between lovers made sweet, tender, dangerous and exciting love. Every part was kissed and touched until no bit was left unexplored. Joseph staked a claim on Hannah. He was certain that Hannah was his true mate.

"Fall asleep in my arms. I will take care of you," he told her.

Hannah couldn't stay awake any longer. She curled up in Joseph's embrace and fell into a deep happy slumber. He looked at her golden hair spread out over his shoulder and the pillow. She looked so beautiful. He found it hard to believe that she was really there resting in his arms.

Countless nights he'd dreamed of making love to her. No man ever hated daybreak like he did. Now he couldn't fall asleep because reality was so much better than his dreams. His wishes somehow collided with destiny and brought Hannah home at last.

He was in love with Hannah. He wanted to tell her and shout it to the world. He laughed softly thinking of how the rational lady in his arms would say it was too soon to feel that way. But Joseph knew certain things can't be measured in time.

Hannah woke up first and watched Joseph sleeping beside her. Focused on the energy and essence of his person, she felt connected with his inner self. "*Souls recognize each other by the way they feel, not the way they look. He sees the true me. Maybe that is what love really is, just seeing each other.*"

Hannah shifted to rise, but Joseph stirred and reached out for her. He nuzzled and kissed her. Rough stubble on his chin and upper lip made a sandpapery contrast to the softness of his lips. The lovers started the day the way they had ended the previous one. They teased and laughed a new morning into being.

CHAPTER 68

Merida, Yucatan
Present Day

"You are nobody," Hannah exclaimed to Joseph, as she looked deep into his eyes in sudden recognition.

"That's not a very kind thing to say," he replied looking a bit confused.

"Let me explain why calling you 'Nobody' is my own personal highest compliment."

They sat on the rumbled bed and feasted on fresh fruit the hotel had provided. Hannah took a long drink of water and prepared herself to share a private confidence. There were things in her past that she did not often discuss with others or want to dwell on.

"For decades after my mother's death, folks still recalled her larger-than-life elegant movie star looks and presence. She recited Shakespeare at length, played classical music like a concert pianist, and photographs she took can be found in museums, homes and coffee table books."

"I've never heard much about your mum until now. I want to know as much about you as you are willing to share," he encouraged her to continue.

"Soon after my birth, whether due to dramatic post-natal chemical changes or a family propensity for mental illness, she withdrew into what they labeled back then as schizophrenia and after a while she died. My care was shared among various reluctant relatives.

My maternal grandparents somehow misguidedly blamed me for loss of their remarkable daughter. In their grief, they shunned me. Out of frustration and sorrow, Granny would shout, "Nobody wants you. Nobody loves you."

"That's terrible," Joseph sighed, upset at people for hurting his beautiful Hannah.

"As a child, unknowing and innocent, I believed that 'Nobody' was the name of a real person. At night if I awaken in the dark, I would not sleepily say 'Mommy', I called out 'Nobody. Nobody'."

"That is so sad," he said. Joseph reached over to Hannah, but she stayed where she was seated and continued.

"So when I say 'You are Nobody', it is with long awaited joy. You are a physical body and a separate spiritual soul, a no-body. At last, nobody cares about me, and nobody wants me!" She finished with a smile that melted his heart.

"It's a great honor to be nobody to you." He embraced the small child within the grown woman and held her tightly.

"Thank you for telling me your story. It helps me understand a lot about your drive and need for perfection. Survival techniques created as children take on a life of their own."

"I am turning insecurities and fears around bit by bit. Correcting my positions like a big ship in a harbor," she assured him. "I am giving up things that no longer work in my life and relationships."

"You still seemed puzzled by all this---our connection," Joseph said, pointing back and forth between them. "Like you are trying to figure out the place or the day on your Mayan calendar that laid the foundation for us being together."

"Before I knew it had begun, I was in the middle of it," she smiled.

"My heart recognized you from the very beginning. The attraction was real and I could not turn away," he admitted. "I won't say it was love at first sight," he paused, "It took a whole two minutes."

"It was only a matter of time before I had to admit to myself that I was meant to be with you," she added.

"Our union was postponed too long," he said. Disturbing memories of seeing Hannah being held and kissed by the handsome director flashed across his mind and he frowned.

"I thought I would be forced to give you up when I believed you were seriously involved with Dr. Sarra."

"You're jealous of Sam?"

"Oh, now it's Sam, not Dr. Sarra? Should I be concerned?" he asked with a raised brow.

Hannah hesitated for a couple of seconds before answering. That pause spoke more than words to feed his insecurity.

"Maybe I should say that all I want is your happiness, even if it means losing you to him."

"But…" Hannah stammered to explain.

"Let me finish," he interrupted. "However, I'm just not that generous a guy. I won't give you up. I admit I am jealous. Jealous of every minute you spend with him, every glance, every touch, and every shared thought."

Hannah's face colored slightly. "I confess to temporarily falling under his spell. For obvious professional, financial and physical reasons, he is a most eligible bachelor and could advance my career."

Joseph's face tightened as she spoke. He noticed how her voice took on a different intensity when she mentioned Sarra. He wondered if maybe she was in love with the other man, if he had waited too long, or how he would fare in the face of such strong competition.

"But in reality," she continued, "I fell victim to my own optimism and fantasies. True feelings are either there or not there. Thin love is not love at all. I never felt any spark or connection with him," she said and folded herself into Joseph's arms. "You win. The other guy loses," she playfully announced.

"You have my heart now," he said more seriously, putting his hand on his chest. "So take care of it." Joseph knew himself to be totally in love.

"It's a hard thing to live without a heart. I know. I've tried it." Hannah sighed.

"When my fiancé, Captain Stephen Roth, was killed in the war, I felt like a part of me died with him. It was an act of self-preservation to lock feelings and memories in a box and throw away the key. After Stephen's death, I feared abandonment and pain if I got too close to anyone again. I put a protective distance between myself and others. Working hard was the only thing that took my mind off the grief and void."

"Thank you for also sharing this with me. I often wondered about that part of your life," Joseph said gratefully.

"I came to think of romantic love like I thought of childhood. It was something I experienced once that I shouldn't expect to ever have back again." She blushed, "Until today, I haven't been intimate with anyone since I lost Stephen three years ago."

"Not even Director Sarra?" Joseph asked, wanting further reassurances. "I saw the way he kissed you."

"Especially Dr. Sam Sarra. Some kisses are simply a touch on lips or cheeks, with no more feeling than a social greeting. You can't force chemistry to exist where it doesn't," Hannah assured him.

With that, a relieved Joseph planted a sensual kiss on her lips.

"The same way you can't deny chemistry when it does exist. When it has a life and meaning of its own, like this." He deepened their kiss in the most all-consuming way. Passion rose like mercury in a thermometer.

Every time his hands moved over her throat, her breast, her abdomen, her thighs, Hannah felt as if he were revealing her own body to her for the first time.

The taste of his lips and scent of his skin unleashed a chemical reaction in Hannah's brain. It reminded her of a fifth taste sense the Japanese call *unami.* Certain foods and scents trigger intense cravings, causing people to eat long after they are sated. Hannah experienced the physical and emotional equivalent of that phenomenon. She felt ravenous and could not get enough of him. She'd just have to redefine 'enough', because he was addictive.

Eventually they left the hotel, going across the street to eat and be vertical for a while. Joseph couldn't take his eyes off Hannah, but was careful not to touch her during their interlude in the restaurant. In their state of attraction, even the smallest contact aroused them both. A quick kiss over coffee proved to be their downfall. They did not wait for the breakfast they ordered to be delivered. Joseph threw a fistful of peso bills on the café table. They rushed back to the hotel room.

Both shirts were off before the door was closed all the way. Joseph cupped her breasts in his hands and caressed them with delicate wanderings. Using the doorsill to brace her, he pulled her skirt down and kicked it aside. He threw off his pants. She pressed her hips against him, and felt an erection he couldn't have concealed if he wanted to. He was heavy with a hunger unique to him.

"I don't think we are going to make it to the bed," he laughed.

"That's okay. Maybe next time," Hannah smiled and leaned back to enjoy the sensual recklessness he brought out in her.

Joseph's mouth crushed down on her lips. She threw her arms around him and her lips went wild under his. Hands, demanding and strong, shifted between her thighs. He made only a few circular motions when an orgasm ripped through her, so intense she felt like she would collapse limply to the floor.

"Uh-uh. There's more in there. I want you to go up again," he said. His body pressed her against the wall. Two fingers positioned at one o'clock gently coaxed her passion out once again. Hannah was unable to stop the feral scream that left her lips. Just the way she cried out made desire quicken in him. Affirmation of her pleasure took Joseph over his own edge. He barely managed to hold on to her as they both slid to the cool tile entry floor stupefied.

"Look at us. Whew," he whistled. "Who would have thought the human body could recharge this often?"

"And with such intensity." she added. "I like you a lot Comouche."

Amused, Joseph looked down at their sweaty interlocked bodies, "I kind of figured that out."

They jumped into the shower together. She loved shampooing his curly hair and the feel of slippery soap on his copper skin. Ordinary everyday activities seemed more fun with two. How wonderful to be kissed for no reason or without being asked. They were at ease and peace with one another.

She knew this getaway couldn't last, so she made the most of each moment. Happiness filled her heart, but also sadness. Where one emotion started and the other ended, Hannah couldn't distinguish.

For two days neither brought up the fact that Joseph had a reserved flight back to the States. The finite amount of time together hung over their heads.

"I have appointments with my New York editors and publisher to turn in and consult on several articles and photographs. Then I'll have funds to purchase a ticket to New Zealand. I need to take care of some unfinished business there," he told her as he packed.

Painful separation from him and sudden uncertainty seemed surreal to Hannah. "*Should I tell him how much this time together meant to me*?" she pondered, but said nothing. She refused to mouth the proverbial phrase, 'when will I see you again'.

Hannah closed her eyes and tried to memorize his face, and how his tanned arms looked against his white shirt, and the way his hair curled at the top of his collar.

She stood at the Merida airport. Her vision blurred from the tears jabbing at her eyes as she waved goodbye to Joseph. The moment he disappeared inside the terminal she heard a small, clean sound like the snapping of a twig, as if part of her broke off and went with him.

CHAPTER 69

Ek Balam, Yucatan
Present Day

"You don't have to say anything. I see an awakening of happiness in your eyes and your step," Mari told Hannah when she returned to Ek Balam.

"Our time together was short, but I feel different after being with Joseph. I always believed the old song, *Rosas en el Mar*, that said true love was as hard to find as roses in the sea, but not any more," confided Hannah.

Over chaya-lemonade drinks on the patio, Hannah talked to Mari, "I've heard of traumatic events like war, illness, winning the lottery, or missing a plane changing people's lives, but I am surprised that something so mundane as a chance romantic encounter can have such impact."

"You meet people because you need them to change your life or you're the one who will change theirs. This connection took a while, but the slowest fruit in the garden to ripen, unhurried on the vine, is naturally the sweetest," smiled Mari.

"For the first time, I'm tired of my life being nothing but constant work, no matter how adventuresome it may be. Projecting courage, touting my freedom and trying to prove I can do everything myself seems shallow. I'm ready to lighten up and try new options, especially a personal relationship with Joseph," said Hannah.

"If you don't like where you stand in life, then move. You are not a tree," chuckled Mari.

Roberto joined them as they prepared breakfast in the Casa de la Paz kitchen.

"I've been hiding away in the jungles, slaving to reconstruct long-deceased lives to avoid paying too much attention to my own life. Making career my only priority has got to stop," Hannah said. "Always being in control has gotten out of control."

Roberto grabbed his morning cup of coffee. "An obsessive quest for perfection is an addiction. Constant work only gives an illusion of security. As I reminded you in the past, you need balance for a full life."

"Being stubbornly independent and isolated are modern forms of asceticism. Hair shirts and pebbles in the shoes weren't used in your case, but hard work and loneliness have tortured you a long time, my child," said Mari to Hannah.

"The habit of always struggling is a tough one to break. But, when something no longer serves you, let it go," said Roberto.

"Keep what's worth keeping and with the breath of kindness blow the rest away," said Mari.

"If anyone can learn new ways, it is you," Roberto smiled at his dear friend, relishing her new direction and contentment.

Hannah showed Mari pictures taken during her long weekend with Joseph in Merida. They stirred up spasms of longing.

"These photographs make me miss him so much. But, I don't need images to remind me of our time together. I remember every word he whispered into my ear, every inch of his skin. There was no him or me. It was so intimate that when he fell asleep, my eyes closed. It's the little things, the little moments that matter. I am truly happy."

"What about Director Sarra? Mari asked, hoping that infatuation was over.

"Being with Joseph taught me the difference between 'belonging to' and 'belonging with' someone. My brief fascination with Sarra and his hollow world is finished."

"Anyone who doesn't bring you alive with joy and purpose is too small for you anyway," Mari said.

"Joseph is headed back to New York and then New Zealand on family business or something. It is difficult to think how much we shared, emotionally and physically, only to walk away."

"Often love doesn't know its own depth until you are separated from the person," said Mari.

"What if this was not as important to him as it was to me? If what I consider a whole book is just a chapter to him? What if…"

"Hannah, you misuse your imagination when you worry," Mari interrupted. "Please don't overthink this. Just trust life and welcome the gift of the vibrant, messy, energy-dense romance ahead of you."

"Mari, I have never been with a man like him before, all to myself. He's like a best friend, but also romantic. Of course, I didn't believe all the wonderful things he said to me."

"But he cared enough to say them, that's what count."

"I should have told Joseph I loved him. I guess my fear was that he wouldn't say it back," Hannah confessed.

"When someone loves you, they don't have to say it. You can tell by the way they treat you."

"Life is good. I am going to live it to the fullest," Hannah beamed. "I'll be working in the field lab on site all day. I need to get the rest of the artifacts labeled and ready for transport to the regional museum." She affectionately hugged them both before she headed out the door.

CHAPTER 70

Ek Balam, Yucatan
Present Day

Hannah took a seldom-used gravel path from the pueblo to the Ek Balam ruins. As she walked around the ancient ball court, she heard panting sounds of an idling vehicle engine. The noise sent a quiver of apprehension down her back. A sixth sense that something was wrong prickling her more than perspiration from the heat. She moved closer to the carved stonewall and peeked around the corner.

Over by her thatched laboratory hut near the main acropolis pyramid, she spotted an old battered jeep parked with its tailgate open. A dead deer lay on top, partially wrapped in a dirty blue tarp. She thought maybe the uninvited visitors were poachers until she saw two men loading cardboard boxes.

A tall hard-bitten man in a bright blue shirt, cargo pants and combat boots waved them along and oversaw the operation through mirrored dark glasses. He stood over a bulging satchel of undetermined booty at his feet. Pieces of smashed pottery rejects scattered the ground near the lab door.

On a raised stone platform in front, Hannah recognized Pablo, the lazy son of the village's mayor. He was an unpredictable, damaged teenager. Her team had been coerced into hiring him part-time. He kept his job by virtue of being related to a man with connections. Pablo had been useless as a feral cat. Now he stood and guarded the compound, scanning the area with the point of his hunting rifle. Skin on his sweat-gleaming neck twitched like a horse's.

Reality of the situation struck Hannah hard. Pablo and a gang of marauders were ransacking the site's treasures in broad daylight. Nothing in Hannah's experience could steel her against such a powerful, painful sight. Surprise sent a visceral blow to her solar plexus, knocking the wind out her. She felt physically ill to see looters cleaning out a season's worth of irreplaceable treasures. Rooted to the spot watching, she rocked slightly on her feet in frail astonishment.

"*They're stealing our best pieces. I can't allow these artifacts to disappear.*"

Frozen in nervous suspense that accompanies the expectation of something major about to happen, Hannah thought, "*They will be gone by the time I run back to the pueblo for help. I have to handle it myself. They won't get away with this.*"

Her stomach tightened. Her nerves were strung tight as piano wire, her senses on heightened alert. A flicker of fear wrinkled her forehead, quickly replaced by resolve.

It was fortunate Hannah was still in the habit of wearing her .38 to the field. She pulled it out of the holster and released the safety. She crouched down and ran behind a nearby tree to spy on the robbers. Her throat was dry and the palms of her hands wet against the crosshatched gunstock. A foreboding came over her, but anger at this wanton destruction boiled to the surface giving her courage.

Hannah sprang to the top of a partial wall a few yards from the group and planted her feet firmly. The sun was at her back and in their eyes. Her revolver aimed directly at Pablo, the only one visibly armed.

"Drop your gun," she ordered.

For an instant everyone froze in place, looking around for the voice. Pablo saw her silhouetted in the bright morning light. He slowly put his .22 rifle down on the platform's rough stones and took a step back with hands up. Fear hung like humidity in the air before a thunderstorm. No doubt the clouds would erupt, only a guess of who would be left standing after the tempest. Hannah glared at the man in the blue shirt. He had a long puckered scar down the right side of his face.

"Stop what you are doing. Unload that wreck and get out of Ek Balam," she shouted.

Keeping the four at bay, Hannah motioned at the thieves to remove the boxes and put them on the ground. They looked toward their tall leader for instructions. In frustration he shifted his weight from back and forth, like a dog throwing out dirt with his hind legs. He yanked off his sunglasses to get a better look at his adversary. Seeing that she appeared to be alone and unable to abandon the loot, he whistled sharply to Pablo. The young lackey snatched up his rifle and fired. The shot missed Hannah, but she leapt for cover.

The leader rushed over and kicked the revolver out of her hand. Uttering a vicious hiss, his iron strong hand seized her. She was immobilized. Holding her stiff-armed in front of him, he raised a mallet-sized fist high in the air and brought it down across Hannah's cheek. She automatically brought both hands up to defend herself and doing so pulled away from his grasp.

Looking into the man's cold dark animal eyes, she sensed a deep undiffused nature of evil. She felt as profoundly frightened and threatened, as she ever had in her life.

Then she saw the long stiletto knife he unsheathed. It had an oversized handle bound with scraggy leather. Hannah gasped involuntarily as the blue gray blade shot out in a lunging flash toward her gut. She reacted with an instinctive protective covering motion of her arms. It first struck her left forearm, perforating flesh beneath her elbow and pushed on deeper, piercing under her breast, aimed for the heart. Wild arrows of pain shot through her.

Hannah opened her mouth and tried to scream, but no sound came out. She looked down to see bright red blood rapidly blooming over the sleeve and front of her shirt. The reality of the attack stunned and shocked her, as a mighty warrior might feel transcendent astonishment when the swift heat of an arrow slays him in mid-battle.

The looter smiled triumphantly and withdrew his knife with a jerk. He raised the blade over his head and smashed the wrapped handle into her forehead over the right eye. Blood gushed from the impact. Hannah slumped forward onto the killer. As she collapsed to the ground she trailed a red smear down his body.

"Damn bitch got blood all over my favorite shirt," he cursed and stomped Hannah's crumpled lifeless body.

"Can I shoot her?" asked an excited Pablo, rubbing his hands together in a frenzy of anticipation.

"No. We don't want to make noise and bring others around. She's done for."

The leader and gang moved in the opposite direction. "There are carved stones over by the back side of the pyramid that are on the list. Let's finish and get out of here. I'm thirsty."

CHAPTER 71

Valladolid, Yucatan
Present Day

"*Not today death. Not now.*"

Hannah swam into consciousness through a flickering white haze composed of limestone dust, bright sunlight and shards of memory. She was completely disoriented. Her mind struggled to repel and accept images that flashed through her head.

She wiped away sticky blood running into her eyes. Trying to sit up, she painfully gasped for air and grabbed her side. Remembering the stabbing, Hannah' stomach and hands clenched in fear. Her unblinking eyes searched the area for her assailant.

She stayed sprawled low to the ground, still as a crouching jaguar on the prowl, part of the jungle. Her instinct for survival was followed slowly by the habit of logical thought.

"*They are still here. Over to the north by the small palace,*" she deduced from muffled sounds of voices and flashes of movement through the trees. "*It's good they don't know about the hidden room of murals. Or do they?*" she seized in panic.

"*I have to stop them,*" she thought, irrational in her dazed state. "*Maybe I can disable their get away car.*"

The path to the jeep stretched over a ten meter, wide-open space, broken only by low bushes and a three-step stone platform. Hannah sprang up to make the charge, only to have her knees buckle. She fell back down in a dizzy heap.

Looters chipping at stones to remove them from their ancient niches infuriated her so much that adrenaline kicked in. She ducked down and slalomed her way through greenery, jumped behind the rubble-strewn platform for a moment and sprinted to the backside of the muddy jeep. The effort left her heaving for breath and nauseous. Blood flowed from her arm and forehead, so she used her bandana and over-shirt to apply pressure on the lacerations and bind them. A grabbing pain in her side doubled her over, but she ignored the damage. She crossed and gripped her arms, hugging herself to ward off being sick.

Her nausea came from shock, but also from the revulsion of almost being annihilated at the hands of such a vile person. An unjust undeserved end to her life betrayed her worldview of universal order. More than fear, what Hannah felt was a profound sickening grief.

"*Vamos*, Let's go," a deep loud voice called out, jolting her back to the immediate dire situation. The marauders headed straight toward the jeep. Hannah had no time to disable the vehicle. She could not possibly run without being seen. In a panic, she climbed on top of the jeep, stretched out beside the dead deer and threw the filthy tarp over both of them. The jeep swayed as the robbers put heavy carved stones and crates in the back and got in to leave the scene of the crime.

Hannah's pulse was racing. Even though she lay encapsulated under a plastic trap in the sun, her skin felt clammy and cool. She feared she might pass out. Anxiety and confusion clouded her thoughts of how this risky ride might end.

The overloaded jeep bumped out of the rocky archaeological zone. Hannah sensed vague humming undulations as they drove the rutted two-lane road away from the site and pueblo. After a sharp left turn, she figured the wretched crew must be headed to the town of Valladolid, twenty kilometers south. Hannah heard muffled voices and scratchy rap music from the radio inside. The blue tarp flapped in the wind. She prayed it would still be covering her completely when they stopped.

"Hey, there's blood running down the windshield," Pablo pointed out to his companions.

"That's the deer," the tall leader reminded him. Now that he could pick up a signal he texted someone about their successful mission and arrival.

Being tossed back and forth indicated to Hannah that they'd arrived in the city and were navigating narrow streets to a predetermined destination. The old car's gears ground to a halt. Three horn beeps from the driver acted as a signal for someone to open a gate or come help. Hannah lifted the edge of the tarp about an inch and peeked out. She lay ready to see who took delivery of the artifacts and then escape when an opportunity presented itself.

The jeep pulled in and stopped inside a paved courtyard. Its occupants poured out. Pablo and the two others unloaded the back. They carried boxes into a grand colonial house. Their leader shook hands with an older white-haired gentleman. He pointed to bloodstains across the looter's shirt front and on his leather satchel.

"Someone injured getting this load?" he inquired.

"Just a little hunting incident," the tall man with the scarred face and hard eyes chuckled.

"Come inside. I can't wait to see what you brought this time."

At that point, Hannah presumed the customer for the loot was a private collector or the middleman for a larger operation. Individuals are either in antiquity theft to make money selling or leveraging artifacts or buying items to adorn their homes. They don't care what knowledge is destroyed or lost when sites are plundered. Her assailant was just this fellow's henchman, a tomb robber with no morals or sense of history.

Hannah waited and listened to fading footfalls of the looters and buyer. She could not remain on the jeep roof any longer. She was too vulnerable. When there were no more sounds, she dropped down the side of the vehicle opposite the house. Needles of pain lanced through her as she hit the pavers of the driveway with shaking impact. She trembled and was unaware that she whimpered as she stumbled across parking area. She found an unlocked side gate and exited the grounds.

Stopping briefly out front to note the location, she realized it was only a few blocks from Valladolid's main square. Four blocks isn't really a great distance. But it became very long in her injured condition. To someone in fear, everything rustles, so even ordinary sounds caused her heart to stop.

Hannah raced with reckless speed toward the center of town, heedless of pain, people's stares or obstacles in her path. She was overcome with an animal panic to get away. There was no plan in her mind, but she ended up on Calle 44 where combi taxis took workers and tourists to and from the Ek Balam ruins. Paco, a driver who lived in Ek Balam pueblo, recognized her and hurried to her side. He was shocked at her disheveled condition and blood soaked clothing.

"Take me to Casa de la Paz," she begged.

Without waiting for other passengers, he placed her carefully in the backseat and sped away. Hannah sank into the taxi's dirty upholstery and wept silently. It was over… for now.

CHAPTER 72

Ek Balam, Yucatan
Present Day

"What kind of despicable human stomps an unconscious woman?" raged Roberto as he saw the boot heel-shaped bruise on Hannah's back.

"Unknown to your attacker, his kick may have gotten your body to gasp air and saved your life," Mari commented.

"Ow, ow," Hannah cried out in sharp pain as Mari deep cleansed and butterfly bandaged her lacerations. "That hurts more than the stabbing. I thought he'd just hit me in the chest until I saw the blood."

"Fate stepped in to save you when you put your arm across. The blade went through the lower skin without penetrating an artery or bone. The thick barrier of the arm prevented the knife tip from doing more damage than a shallow penetration and deflection off your rib."

"I am lucky to be alive."

"That cut above your right eye may leave a small scar," said Mari.

"Scars tell better stories than tattoos," added Roberto to defuse the serious moment.

Hannah's hands shook as reality of her brush with mortality sank in. "The shock numbing effect is wearing off and I hurt like hell."

"Drink this special tea and sleep, my dear one," Mari encouraged.

"We have get the authorities over to that thief's house," said a fading Hannah, half-heartedly trying to rise.

"Soon enough," Mari responded as she tucked a sheet around her exhausted friend. "We will do whatever it takes to fix this."

Hannah could not believe she'd slept fifteen hours. Mari often reminded her that a body only released healing and growth hormones while someone was asleep. That was why babies, teens and older people slept so much. It must have been Mari's ancient herbal tea recipe that gave Hannah so much pain relief and needed recuperation time.

"While you were resting Roberto found that house in Valladolid you described," Mari informed Hannah. "He went to the police and they accompanied him there."

"Servants told us their elderly owner left for Mexico City and wasn't expected back for months," he added. "The local police I spoke with were too overwhelmed with current personal injury and property loss to be bothered with ancient item crimes."

"You can't take it personally," Mari said when she saw Hannah's furious reaction.

"I feel violated. These ruins are an extension of me. I am angry with the thieves, police, society and myself for not being able to safeguard the site." Her powerful inner critic poised to attack her.

"It was not your fault and you know it," scolded Roberto.

"Voices of doubt and regret do not require answering," Mari added, hoping to stop Hannah's self-incrimination and anger.

"That's it. I've had it up to here with being responsible and brave," said Hannah.

"The bruises on your soul, like raindrops on the windowpane, are joining up and becoming one. Emotions are high and too big to control right now," nodded Mari in understanding and sympathy.

After a couple of healing days, Hannah declared, "I'm taking a break and returning to Mexico City. Dr. Sarra can use his contacts and influence to track down the buyer and take care of this mess. I'm sure he will help us. I'll also discuss the possibility of getting funding to excavate the palace."

"Regroup and make a plan Hannah," Roberto advised. "When you outsmart your enemy you take their power away and defang them."

"I'm not giving up without a fight. Evil people rely on the fear and acquiescence of good people to continue with their evil. It is time to challenge the old system of corruption."

Hannah hobbled around packing. Even washing and brushing her hair caused her to wince. She looked in the mirror to study the rainbow of bruises on her face and body. The contusion above her eye was subtly lightening from purple to an eerie gray green. At the sight of her injuries, an involuntary rolling shudder of fear ran through her. She took her time getting dressed, resting between each piece of clothing.

Before leaving, she visited Ek Balam ruins one last time. She came face-to-face with the devastating effects of the plundering. The rough Bluto and his gang had ripped the north palace's entrance lintel into bits with chisels and hammers. They tore away individual glyphs to sell on the black market. It was the equivalent of a few select pages ripped from a rare book, leaving messages irremediably lost to the world.

Whoever the thieves were, they knew exactly which antiquities they were after. They took over a dozen of the best pottery and jade pieces. Whether rooted in indifference or greed, the consequences of illicit looting were the same, the wholesale destruction of the past.

"*We can't grow another Maya temple. These are holes that can never be filled,*" she sighed.

Gouging the doorway of the once-intact quarters left the structure destabilized and near collapse. Hannah left instructions for workers to clean and shore up the tattered remains and cordon off the area. She was relieved to see that earlier efforts to reseal and disguise the lady scribe's hidden room were successful. She was thankful the murals, pottery and other artifacts had been left in situ, out of harm's way. They had already waited for hundreds of years. The treasures would remain eminently safe, buried again under tons of rubble, waiting until she could return and excavate properly.

"*My dear sister, thank you for your beautiful offerings. Your art will stay a secret a while longer until I can share your message with the world,*" she communed reverently in a whisper to the mysterious scribe's spirit. Hannah had every intention to make good the promise.

CHAPTER 73

Ek Balam, Yucatan
1564 A.D.

Itz put the finishing touches on her murals and portraits in the secret room. She remembered her father's wise words, "*To be a master at art, one must first be a master in living, because the soul and heart create everything.*"

Shading here and highlights there gave her renderings the realistic three-dimensional qualities that distinguished her works from other Maya artists. She stood, brush in hand, as unique images opened to her. Ideas conveyed only in flashes and hints at first. Through her efforts the messages became intelligible and eternal. Once she finished these last additions, the room would be sealed to prevent the Spanish from discovering her forbidden paintings and writings.

Itz would miss her signature creations of plants, birds, and medicinal formulas. The ancient hieroglyphs telling of her people's achievements in astronomy, engineering, royal lineages, philosophy and history had been faithfully recorded. Every square meter of the limestone plastered rectangular room was covered with detailed information. Her pictorial records conserved the culmination of years of study and knowledge so that future generations could make use of it. She employed her brushes and colors to paint paradise.

"Beauty and design in the natural world are proof of our many gods' divine love," she said aloud.

Lifelike portraits of those she loved especially pleased Itz. Faces of her father Ko'h, her aunt Yaxche, cousin Etz'nab, lover Kan Ik, and a self-portrait all smiled down as she worked. Because one reminded her of the other, like sisters, Itz painted the goddess Ixchel, known as Lady Rainbow next to the Mother of Christ. She'd added pictures of the Madonna and Brother Miguel, her beloved teacher, to the gallery of those who touched her life and made it worth every sacrifice.

"*I inserted symbols that whisper secret knowledge. Many years from now a day will come and my silent testimony will be discovered. These images will be seen by someone with eyes that truly see and understand. Our wisdom will not be forgotten by the world.*"

Painting in her hidden room brought Itz peace and happiness. She sang old melodies while she worked. Feeling an odd tingle, as if someone was watching, Itz looked behind her and around the gallery space.

"*No one is here,*" she laughed softly to reassure herself. "*Maybe the ancient ancestors are letting me know they are pleased with my work. Time to pack up my paints and close this sacred hall.*"

After a last look around, Itz left and stacked stones high into the small portal opening. She threw dirt onto the mixture to make it blend in with the rest and plastered over the false wall at the end of the north palace's main room.

"*You recognize that your efforts have been done out of love, not for any reward, when you know you'll never see their fruition or impact,*" Itz sighed.

She could now rejoin her aunt and focus on other tasks. As she returned Yaxche's residence, Itz noticed the village teeming with people moving hurriedly about. Children ran around her, bouncing like grasshoppers.

"What is happening?" Itz asked her aunt as she entered the dwelling. She worried that they'd received word of another Spanish raid or roundup of Maya citizens for relocation to the grid complexes. Reductions happened more often, where Indians from small, scattered pueblos or farms were forced to concentrate in a town for military, civil and religious authorities supervision.

Rather than an anxious face, her aunt beamed with joy.

"A messenger came. Our warriors return tonight. My son Etz'nab will be here," said Yaxche, radiant in gladness. "Your Kan Ik may be among them."

Itz's face flushed and her heart swelled with excitement. By nightfall Etz'nab and a handful of other fighters entered the village without fanfare and went to their family homes. He told Itz that Kan Ik took a fleet of long canoes out of Pole port with supplies and messages for Cozumel. If the weather held, he should be following within days. She sank down on her chair with disappointment, but was relieved that both her cousin and her lover were still alive. Sporadic news from the battlefront had not been encouraging.

Months of training and fighting left jagged scars on Etz'nab's handsome body, outside as well as inside. He spoke in hushed tones with his mother and Itz about recent scrimmages against Spanish soldiers and the hired mercenaries.

"I can still hear the drone of conch shells calling us to battle, the clash of our obsidian and flint weapons against Spanish metal, and the thunder of Castilian cannons." He trembled at the memories.

"We trained hard, our bodies were fit, but flesh cannot stand up to iron blades and musket fire. How quickly men died; how soon their lives were over. The Spanish slaughtered hundreds. When towns and temples fell, the magic that surrounded them collapsed. The very gods themselves seemed to despair and fall."

The defeated young warrior's eyes filled with moisture. He leaned in for understanding and comfort, as one can only receive in the arms of his mother.

"My tried and fearless son. Cry as you must. It is not a failing or weakness. It is a sign that you have stayed strong in the face of inhumanity for too long." She patted his back and held his head against her shoulder. "Growing pains of the soul are the price of being human."

Yaxche rocked and soothed her grief-ravaged son. Itz slipped out of the room to give them time alone and preserve her cousin's pride.

"After we get medical care and stock up supplies, my company of men leave for *Ich Paa*, the town now called Mayapan, to regroup and return to war," Etz'nab announced. The evening meal of his favorite tamales and frothy chocolate drink had helped to restore his strength and confidence.

"Our people will not give up. As long as we are alive, we will fight," he vowed. "When the enemy yelled, 'You can't fight the storm', I shouted back 'We are the storm'."

Etz'nab continued his tales, "At one point, I was surrounded by four Spanish soldiers. They laughed in my face, thinking I was an easy kill. They didn't know I am an expert archer. My arrows of flint shattered on impact as designed, going through their armor, causing slow painful deaths. By the way Mother, our movement leaders thank you for your *malankanchum* draughts. The plant extract that instantly paralyzes muscles of the heart gave merciful and dignified departures for our mortally injured warriors."

"Everything on earth has a purpose. There is an herb for every disease and a mission for every person. Each of us does what the gods require of us. Be certain of this," said Yaxche.

CHAPTER 74

Ek Balam, Yucatan
1564 A.D.

Itz and Yaxche attended the wounded as they straggled into Ixkunil pueblo over the next few days. Village women restocked food supplies, armor, weapons, and healing herbs as best they could.

"I am worried about Etz'nab and Kan Ik is late returning," Itz told her aunt.

"My dear one, warriors often get broken and sailors get lost. As a woman waiting at home, you must prepare to experience both."

Itz and her aunt were in the main square collecting more provisions, when Kan Ik stepped out of the regional leader's administrative office. He was dressed and coifed in the manner of a wealthy merchant. Intricate woven loin and cheek cloths hung front and back over his lower body. They were decorated with brightly colored geometric patterns. Two jade clasps held his short jaguar cloak in place. Although his bronze colored chest was bare, he wore a pectoral collar of jade and gold pendants inlaid with semi-precious stones. All recognized his vestments as a potent symbol of rank. He had tied his long blue-black hair into a topknot behind the crown.

Kan Ik's poised bearing and cordial dignity, whether speaking to esteemed leaders or humble folk, impressed Itz. When in thought, he stroked his finger across his bottom lip making Itz shiver. She could not stop staring at his mouth when he spoke. She felt his kisses, the kind that arched her body. She decided it was best to quit watching him so closely while they were in public.

Their eyes met across the way. Intense looks held and plunged into each other's depths. Kan Ik found the sparkle in her eyes welcomed him like harbor lights call out to a long lost sailor.

"Greetings, Kan Ik," she said in a calm voice, "I see Ek Chuah, the god of merchant trade, has blown you into our humble village."

"My great cedar canoes are safe. They are as long as ten men and wider than the tallest man. Vast quantities of goods and over twenty people can be carried in one of my sea going boats. I have learned to tie tightly woven squares of fabric to a pole inside and let strong winds push the canoe in any direction I steer it."

Numerous people had gathered around to hear his latest reports and observations. Itz knew the nature of his mission meant she would always have to share him with others. He gave updates from around the region. People lingered a while, especially seeking tales of forbidden uprisings. He peppered the bad tidings with some positive events, but it did not cloud the fact that the Spaniards were victorious in the majority of encounters. The conquistadors punished those who aided the Maya confederation revolution. Eventually the town folks dispersed and Itz could talk to him about her cousin's accounts.

"Etz'nab told me a group of ambassadors who went in good faith to negotiate with the foreign leaders were ambushed. It sounded like a diabolical mix of lies, horror and slaughter."

"Defeated valor lies in the courtyard of the great Santa Elena temple. The ground is made holier by their blood," he said.

"I don't understand how men can return to the horrors of battle," she said as she glanced over the plaza at stricken, limping and damaged survivors.

"Scars mean they lived and were stronger than what tried to kill them. Fighters know that Ah Pech, the death god's shadow, is close behind. Those brave men carry both the fear and the courage to dream of a better world," Kan Ik replied.

In the distance, musicians played a melancholy tune. Clear flute notes rose into the evening sky. The tapping rhythm of a skin drum reminded Itz of far away thunder.

"My cousin appears to be a good warrior and *sajal,* leader of men," she said.

"Yes, in a structure that honors the group as a brotherhood, he is ranked first among equals," answered Kan Ik, proud of his protégée. "He fights, not for gain, but for liberty and his deep love of humanity."

Their eyes and then their hands linked. At last they were alone and free to walk back to Itz's residence. The lovers kissed because they believed that spirit is carried in one's breath and a kiss would unite their souls.

"I am pleased you returned," Itz told him.

"The blood in my body runs toward you as rivers run toward the great sea," he answered.

The sun set as they stood in front of the carved stones framing her doorway. Kan Ik smiled, "Look at that. We cast a single shadow when together."

He placed a fragrant white *plumeria* flower behind Itz's ear. Plumeria represented life, sensuality, and regeneration sacred to Kukulcan, the feathered serpent god. They went inside and left the village to nighttime's somber embraces.

Swept up in the sublimity of sunset and music, they sensed deep joy at the heart of the universe. Itz and Kan Ik's connection was on a profound level and a mystery neither one of them understood. Anticipation fluttered in Itz's stomach. She'd seen moths attracted to torch flames. Her heart beat like the moth's paper-thin wings. She was drawn to this man, an incendiary scorching her soul.

He tightened his arms around her, caressed her round hips and touched her firm breasts. His mouth lowered to hers. Energy surged between them. Their clothing and adornments were quickly in a pile on the floor.

"My heart longs for you Itz," he whispered into her ear. He drew her down to the woven reed mats on the sleeping platform. "You are so beautiful, like a hummingbird."

Kan Ik stroked the hollows and curves of her entire body. Pleasure coursed through her. With every muscle and nerve taut, insistent passions could not be restrained any longer. He lowered himself over Itz and entered her warm readiness. He pressed against her and moved side to side. Their rhythms matched and both were swept away in waves of indescribable pleasure and abandon.

After making love, they lay side-by-side in peace and fulfillment. Itz kissed Kan Ik, tasting his salty skin and drinking in his male scent.

"I made offerings and prayed to goddess Ixchel nightly. I begged that neither desperate times nor deep waters would keep you away from me. I was so afraid of losing you, either in battle or terrible storms at sea," she confessed and held him closer.

"Trust and fear may sail into the harbor of your mind, but only allow trust to drop its stone anchor," Kan Ik told her and continued.

Getting more personal, Kan Ik said, "*Inle kech*, I am another you. You can't lose me. No winds can drive my boat off course from you or change the tide of our destiny. You are bound by a thousand strands to my heart," he said and tapped his bare chest.

"Is this a new tattoo marking?" she asked as she traced raised dark blue lines above his ribs.

"Yes, more maps of places I've sailed. I intentionally inked the Yucatan location over my heart, because it is where you are."

Itz was the woman Kan Ik had been seeking since he could remember. The gods, in their infinite wisdom, gave him love in half. It was up to him to find the other half for completion. Every soul eventually meets itself.

Kan Ik rose on one elbow and addressed his love, "Itz, I want to build a home with you as my life mate, a love to last twenty generations and beyond. Let us marry and pledge our bond. Will you have me as your husband?"

"You are also in my heart forever. Yes. It would be an honor to be the wife of Kan Ik."

Their love and passion were fueled by pledges to each other. Until the planet spun toward morning, the night was theirs.

CHAPTER 75

Izamal, Yucatan
1564 A.D.

An elder who could divine auspicious days for special events examined the couple's astronomy signs to make sure there were no celestial incompatibilities between the respective gods of their birth. The *ajmiats,* holy day keeper felt honored by Kan Ik's request to officiate over their ceremony of union, but recommended they obey edicts and send notice to Catholic Church authorities to post bans in the capital.

"We wouldn't have to be in a stone church or use a Spanish priest to take our vows would we? Neither of us can forego our wish for nature's forests, oceans and sky to be our temple. We cannot embrace a religious creed that forbids people to read or dance. Books and music do no harm to the universe," said Kan Ik.

"No, I can perform a traditional ceremony under the sacred ceiba tree. "By following mandates, foreign authorities might leave you at peace in your marriage. Your notice would be a courtesy, one of thousands in piles, nothing to draw attention," he assured them.

But that declaration proved false. Tepal, in his capacity within the Spanish government and priesthood, had bribed officials and friars to report if either Itz or Kan Ik's presence became known.

The former prince had the marriage ban documents in his hands the same day the church official received them. He crumpled and threw the bark papers across the room. He gut kicked the young messenger in frustration.

Tepal rushed to Ek Balam. Like a jaguar, he crouched, waited and watched. When Itz entered the marketplace near the Ixkunil village well, the prince stepped out of the shadows, accompanied by a squad of minion soldiers.

"Arrest this woman and bring her with us," Tepal ordered harshly. His hard eyes filled with accusation. Anger had become his substitute for love.

"You are coming in for questioning. I know you are a heretic," he hissed.

Itz was beyond stunned at his sudden appearance and false denouncement. She kicked and screamed as foreign mercenaries roughly bound and gagged her. She was tied into a coarse rope line of five other prisoners and forced by spear point to march out of town. Her eyes searched the scurrying escaping town folks for someone to help her. At least signal someone to tell Yaxche or Kan Ik what happened to her.

Tepal rode his black stallion back and forth along the column. When he came near the frightened Itz, he nudged his horse so close that its ironclad hooves almost stomped on her. She tripped over the huge animal's leg and fell, bringing other captives down onto the dusty road. Soldiers unmercifully bull-whipped them back up into line. Blood trickled down Itz's arm and a blotchy red stripe spread across the shoulder of her torn white shift. The sight seemed to delight Tepal. He rearranged his cassock, subtly pushed his arousal down and rode back to the front of the procession.

Izamal's dungeons under the massive church were dark and airless except for one small barred porthole. Itz may have given up if fate had not placed her into a certain cell. Prisoners often scratched last messages on walls. Low on the floor, where guards threw her in the corner, Itz saw a tiny rendering on the edge of a wall stone, a warm smiling face. It was Brother Miguel's mother, the Virgin-like face.

"*Maybe Miguel was here, in this very place. His kindness and strength shall be my strength,*" Itz swore. The needle of fear broke and she breathed in calmness and determination.

Someone in the past had a fire pit in the cell, so Itz took bits of charcoal and drew the three dimensional Virgin Mary over and over again. She recognized some of the larger pieces of charcoal as burnt bone, but pushed aside horror and disgust and worked with all materials available to her. Her fingers throbbed raw from rubbing blackened carbon into stone. Every wall had the beautiful loving mother's eyes staring down.

"Father De Landa sent for you. God rest your soul," a scar-faced guard bellowed. His voice seemed too big for his short stocky body. As he entered the cell to grab her, he stopped dumbstruck with the images that surrounded him. He crossed himself, lowered his head and muttered prayers. His harsh manner subdued. Itz went along peacefully.

"What's this I hear about your quarters being used as a canvas?" asked the surly priest inquisitor.

"See for yourself. Even though I am a new believer, I received a message, a vision," Itz lied. She crossed herself like a nun and looked humbly at the floor in front of her. Itz was not sure if this strategy would save or condemn her. Her inspiration came from a source outside herself. Fate would decide what happened next.

Fortunately for Itz, the Father Superior had heard whispers of his jaded jailer's conversion-like behavior and was curious. He covered his nostrils with a perfumed handkerchief to mask the stench and took a walk to her prison cell. He was visibly moved by the circle of sweet beatific faces smiling down on him.

"Genius. Your work is inspired by the Holy Spirit. We will use your artistic gifts in our church," he decided. "Put her to work in the Chapel of Our Lady. Put a slave collar on her first."

Tepal saw soldiers lead Itz away. She was bent over humbly and wore the shackles of a slave around her thin neck. He gloated over how he used others to punish her.

"*She belongs to me. How dare she consider another? She will be forced to serve me and mine forever,*" he pounded fists against the sides of his thighs.

Itz's only prayers were that Kan Ik would hear of the pictures she painted for the church, find her and take her home. She feared that perhaps he might think she had rejected his proposal and left to continue her book recordings on pots in a more remote location.

Even though Itz no longer stayed in the dungeon cell, she was watched all the time and under guarded as she shuffled to and from a sparse shared women's dormitory behind the religious compound. Never unaccompanied, Itz was unable to send word to her aunt or Kan Ik. At least she did not run into Tepal. The man, who had been a prince, was now a brother called Juan Guillermo who carried messages from one church order to another. He bragged about the fact that he was a trusted favorite son.

"*But even the favorite slave is still a slave,*" said Itz softly to herself.

"How many languages do you speak?" De Landa asked Itz one day as she lay flat on a high scaffold and worked on a painting adorning the chapel ceiling.

"I am adept in three dialects of Mayan and I learned Spanish from one of your priests when he was teaching me the true ways of Christ," she answered.

"Good. In addition to your art, you can serve as a translator. You will accompany a missionary group on a journey across the seas. Gather your tools and belongings. You leave at dawn."

"*All hope is lost. If they take me far away Kan Ik will never find me,*" Itz wailed softly to herself after the priest left the chapel. Her legs trembled as she descended the scaffold ladder. She cried and pounded her chest in front of a crucifix on the church altar.

Wooden crosses, representing the four directions and center, were sacred to the Maya long before being introduced by the Spanish. Izamal's sanctuary cross was carved from the holy ceiba tree. She stood on reused stones from an ancient temple dedicated to the sun, so figured her own gods were still present, just in a slightly different form.

"*What can I do? I have to stay alive,*" she hoarsely whispered and held out her arms in supplication.

"You truly love our Lord and his Holy Mother, don't you?" said Father De Landa, stepping out from his hidden spot behind a curtain. He smiled, reassured that his decision to send the indigenous lady artist to new Spanish colonies in Peru as a gift was a wise choice. She would prove valuable to his superiors---a tribute item that would cause his standing to soar in their eyes.

Itz left the sanctuary without answering him. She loathed De Landa as the wickedest of men for his crimes and now for sending her far away as a slave. At that moment, having learned Spanish seemed a curse rather than a blessing because when hearing his exile orders she had a clear understanding of her situation without the remedy to cure it. Dreams of freedom and returning home seemed futile.

Realizing that day would be her last sights and sounds of her homeland tormented her. Her enslavement and deportation brought on unutterable anguish as Itz bundled her few possessions to board a ship bound for Peru.

CHAPTER 76

Mexico City, Mexico
Present Day

Hannah Char left Ek Balam and went to confer with Dr. Sarra at the National Anthropology Museum in Mexico City. She was a little puzzled by his cool reception. He always acted standoffish when his pal, Father Batz, accompanied him. The priest wore his usual austere black clothes and perpetual frown. Hannah avoided shaking hands with the man and sidled around him, avoiding physical contact as one would with a street dog.

"Well, here you are to report another plundered site," mocked Batz. His voice rasped in her ear like a jar full of wasps.

"Selling stolen antiquities is a global business that's booming. Over three quarters of archaeologists have personal on-site experience with thieves," she defended herself. "To guard everything is impossible."

"Seems you always have bad luck on your sites. Or is it just bad judgment?" the angry priest continued, spitting words full of contempt.

Talking with Father Batz always proved an exercise in patience and self-control for Hannah. She didn't want to show how much he provoked her, but his rudeness pushed her buttons. She reminded herself that sarcasm like Batz's was just a weak person's attempt at strength. She decided not to waste her words on someone who deserved her silence. Arguing with a fool only proves there are two.

Hannah had not been prepared to face such hostile criticism and accusations. She glanced over to Dr. Sarra for support and understanding. There was none forthcoming. His eyes were dark and unreadable.

Father Batz snuffed air through his bird beak nostrils, and held the single expression he used in most situations, a scowl. Hannah felt his venomous gaze boring into her, taunting her with secrets he was not sharing. Hannah's eyes narrowed in suspicion, flitted from Batz to Sarra, then back to the smirking Batz. In that instant, she decided not to disclose anything about the secret room. Not yet.

Director Sarra addressed her coldly, "You have been an asset in the past to the National Institute and Museum," was all he offered. "And I never wanted you harmed," he said, waving his hand in reference to her visible injuries.

"What I suffered does not matter. Information I uncovered and brought to light matters. These latest robbers knew their antiquities and took select pieces. It was like they had specific orders. We need INAH and your help to stop this. With all the systematic looting going on, in another twenty years it will all be gone. There will be no more chances."

"Hannah, a recent pattern here disturbs me," inserted Sarra. "Both Edzna and Ek Balam suffered significant losses under your watch. What concerns me is how and why your sites were targeted for these high crimes," said the director.

"I don't understand the who or whys of those robberies, but I want to move forward. Those misfortunate happenings are bruises, not tattoos. There are still several solid months before the rainy season starts. I need to get back in the field and look for answers before it is too late," she said.

"No. Ek Balam works are to be closed down immediately," Dr. Sarra announced firmly. He symbolically slammed a folder shut.

"Then at least let me return to Edzna and excavate the *stelae* monument, the warrior king I call 'Big Red'," a stunned Hannah requested.

"No, you can't," said Dr. Sarra.

"Why not?" asked Hannah, shocked at both of his abrupt pronouncements and harsh refusals.

"This is why," he said as he threw a handful of photograph over the conference table. They spread out like a colorfully fan.

Hannah picked up the stack and shuffled through it. Her eyes squinted in disbelief and frustration at what she saw. The once beautifully engraved red stone *stelae* was cut off at the base, mutilated by looters. It was obvious they'd used power tools to shave off the most unique carved sections. The front of the stone, featuring the royalty with his plumage headdress and manikin scepter symbol of power, had been thinned with a rock saw to make it easier to transport.

The figure was wrenched away from its foundation. All that remained were sandaled feet and bottom edge of his jaguar robe. Hammers and chisels had chipped out hieroglyphs on the side panels. The ground around the base was littered with fragments of the column and other debris. Careless thieves clumsily destroyed half of what they found. The proud warlord who stood overlooking his forest kingdom for a thousand years was gone.

"They took the best preserved parts," she sobbed.

"That's what you call artistic appreciation," Batz gave a harsh mocking laugh, thrown at her like a stone.

By this point Hannah wanted to smack his thin-lipped smirk so hard that the hair-sprayed wisps of hair over his baldhead would come unstuck. "Your opinions are neither required or desired," was all Hannah said to him.

"Don't you see an obvious connection between all these thefts?" asked Dr. Sarra to bring her back to the point he wanted to make.

When she did not answer, he continued, “It seems whenever that journalist was around, a site got plundered, items went missing.”

“It can’t be! Joseph is my friend. He would never be part of such desecration,” Hannah defended him.

“Suspicious how objects you professionally authenticated as rare and valuable invariably ended up on his radar and disappeared,” Sarra continued.

“That red warrior figure will sell in the six figure range, especially in its pristine condition. Money changes people,” he said.

“But Joseph lives frugally on his salary. Material things are not part of his lifestyle,” Hannah told them.

“Hah!” Batz cawed. “Missy, you should go on line and look up your special friend. He just happens to own several award-winning vineyards and raises a stable full of horse each year for the Olympics. Hard to do without somehow supplementing his reporter’s pay, I’d say.”

He cackled and swung a laptop around displaying pictures that showed Joseph by a champion horse in the winners’ circle. Click. Another featured him in a glossy magazine article, smiling and describing artwork behind his newest wine labels.

“Seems your writer friend loves money.”

“Wasn’t he with you in Edzna and Ek Balam before the robberies? Where is he now?” Sarra asked. Instinctively Hannah slouched down, as if to avoid the reproachful gaze of the museum director.

“He went to New Zealand to take care of family business.”

“Where exactly? What kind of business? When will he be back?” Batz asked in rapid succession.

“I don’t know. He didn’t tell me.”

“Beware of a man who keeps secrets and isn’t bothered with details. He used you, my dear,” Dr. Sarra stated bluntly.

Hannah was shocked. Was anything about the way Joseph represented himself true? Truth was sacred, like a Holy Grail to her. What passed between them seemed so real, but so were the accusations and insinuations she was hearing. They showed her concrete evidence of a side to Joseph she knew nothing about.

"*If he withheld all that, what else was Joseph hiding*," she wondered.

Her faith in him began to fracture. It was like driving on the highway when the car in front kicks up a little rock and it hits the windshield. At first the chip is tiny and almost invisible. Eventually the miniscule spot begins to spider and spread into cracks that compromise the stability of the whole. Another blow to the broken windshield of her trust might cause a total collapse.

Hannah looked at the stolen *stelae* column photographs again. She wanted to find anything to prove the two men in the room with her wrong. The air crackled with tension.

"What is that?" Sarra asked, pointing to an object beside the shattered monument base.

"It might be the walking stick Joseph lost."

"Lost? It looks like a red signal marking a location to me."

Hannah's head was spinning. "I can't believe he would do this. I trusted him."

"Self-delusion knows no boundaries," Batz mocked her, his obsidian eyes ablaze.

Odd suppressed sights and questions flooded into her mind, sticking out in her memories and rubbing like a pebble in a shoe. The universe never liked secrets. To uncover the truth, it set traps that can't be ignored or avoided. Everyone talked about how truth will set you free, but at that moment Hannah strongly suspected what Sarra and his cohort proposed as possible truths, in this case, were going to destroy her faith in love and in her own judgment.

"Your discoveries at Edzna and Ek Balam were near genius, and of great value. However, my superiors were never pleased that a

North American led the teams. From now on if anyone excavates in that arena, it will be a Mexican national, not a foreigner, especially a woman," Dr. Sarra announced.

Weight of disappointment and doubts crushed down on Hannah. She felt sudden despair descend over her like a dark veil. A host of inherent fears and real dangers surrounded her. Everything seemed out of focus. She grabbed the edge of the table to steady herself.

"Most importantly, your lack of discretion could cost our institute its reputation and funding. That might get expensive. Not expensive like champagne, but like mistakes in a hospital, a doctor's error. I can't afford to have such a liability on my staff." Dr. Sarra looked Hannah right in the eye and said, "You're dismissed, fired."

CHAPTER 77

Los Angles, California
Present Day

Back in Los Angeles, California, Hannah told her father all abut her disastrous encounter with Dr. Sarra in Mexico City.

"Weaving tall tales like Indians weave baskets. The fewer the facts, the stronger the accusation. That's what I think of Sarra's version about the thefts in your ruins and the museum," said Max.

"Sarra could have thrown me down the stairs and I wouldn't have been as surprised or hurt as I was at that moment," Hannah confessed.

Max looked at Hannah and saw her devastation. "The only taste of success some folks have is when they take bites out of others. All his so-called evidence sounds speculative. Finger pointing at Joseph, meant he had four other fingers pointed back at himself. That fancy-pants director was on your site and had inside knowledge of the treasures too. Ever think of that?" he offered to comfort her.

Hannah had known she would feel better and make some sense of the last days of confusion once she got back home and talked to her wise father.

"Of course, there could be other explanations for the lootings. I shouldn't listen to just their version. I still find it hard to believe Joseph was behind the thefts."

"You'd better clear the air. Mistrust becomes a self-fulfilling prophecy," he advised.

"He was my best friend and more. I physically hurt inside, Dad. Not with the stab injuries, but with doubts and regret."

"Nothing will stop that gnawin' ache until you find out the truth. Joseph is a great guy. Listen to his side of things."

"But he lied to me about a lot of things with words and with silence. I can't understand why he kept me in the dark and misled me about his personal life. "

"Are you forgetting the Law of Parsimony I taught you? The simplest explanation is usually the best. The solution to your confusion is easy. Ask Joseph."

"What? Just call him up and confront him about the thefts? And say, oh by the way, what's really going on in New Zealand?"

"Sure, direct communication is the only way to straighten out this mess and get you some peace of mind."

"Funny, that's what Joseph said before. 'Communication is the problem and the solution'," she recalled fondly. It was the first time she'd smiled since returning to stay with her father in LA.

It was strange being in the United States again. Los Angeles shocked her senses. It was more than a huge city. Some labeled it a hundred suburbs looking for a city. It hummed day and night like a hive with human industrious action. For a change, she enjoyed the newness of the buildings and the roads. The people were even newer. Nearly everyone was from somewhere else. How could she not be entertained by a place that treated palms, nature's comic relief, as a serious tree.

The hardest chore was to switch her brain back to thinking and speaking in English all the time. Hannah would have a simple thought and find Mayan, Spanish and English idioms competing inside her head to express it. When preparing her resume, cover letter and application for employment at the Natural History Museum of Los Angeles County where she worked before, she actually had to look up a word in English.

While she waited for their response to her inquiry, Hannah helped her father in the university library's bookbindery. She had learned restoration of books and paintings at his knee as a young girl. Fixing books was one of her favorite things to do. Working with leather, linen, papers, oiled parchment, presses and dyes kept her mind active. It was great to have dramatic before-and-after results by the end of a day's work. She savored the feel and smell of a solid book in her hands. She cherished printed words on a page and was reminded to appreciate the broad margins of her own life.

"Dad, I brought you Mari's best beeswax for your book oil," Hannah announced. "Let's cook a batch of leather dressing today."

Max had studied bookbinding and restoration with masters in England and learned Vatican techniques of preservation. His five hundred year old book dressing formula, a concoction of wax, lanolin and natural oils, gave new life to parched leather covers.

People sent their rare books, manuscripts and family heirlooms to him from all over the world for professional and caring restoration. He was not one to rip off the old bindings and put on new covers. He salvaged as much of the original materials and incorporated them into the renewed book spines, headbands, and cover boards. After his skillful touches were applied, they were good for another two hundred years or more.

That first week back in LA Hannah helped him evaluate and repair books from the State Supreme Court's rare books section. It was amazing how often otherwise competent librarians, not caring or not knowing any better, stuck duct tape and kindergarten paste on covers and pages of archival tomes. Hannah and her father had their hands full trying to de-acidify papers, replace broken spines, shore up corners and reconnect the backs to precious academic and literature treasures.

Hannah used the bookbinding tasks to distract her from worrying so much about what happened in Mexico. She was also upset and confused about Joseph. She knew that anger was just sorrow's companion. She was sick with heart pain and he was the cure.

"Running away from your doubts and fears is a race you'll never win," advised Max.

So Hannah worked up the courage to contact Joseph. She sent him a simple email asking him to call her in California as soon as possible. She didn't know if he had attempted to reach her in Mexico City or not. Two minutes after she sent the message, her computer chirped with a response.

She read the words over and over until she had them memorized. "*I tried desperately to locate you. I will Skype you from home tonight eight o'clock your time. Love, J.*"

When they connected online both started to talk at once. Hannah insisted, "Please listen and answer my questions first."

"Okay," he answered curiously. "God, it's good to see your face. I have several questions of my own."

"First, I lost my job at the National Institute. They suspected collusion between us and blame me for allowing you in the archaeological ruins. The director believes you are behind the looting of Edzna and Ek Balam."

"What the hell…"

"Let me finish," she continued, happy at his believable shocked denial of sorts. "I want the truth. Did you have anything to do with the plunder of my sites?"

"Absolutely not. I swear Hannah, I would never destroy or jeopardize your ruins or career," he said, leaning forward toward the computer screen, as if being closer where she could look into his eyes might help her believe him.

"Big Red, the *stelae* monument I showed you at Edzna was carved up and stolen. They say your walking pole with the red handle and stone cairn by the road were used as locators."

"No way! That was your prize project. I am so sorry," he frowned and shook his head in disbelief. "This news makes me ill. I can't believe you have being dealing with so much trauma and loss. I wish I was there to hold you and help."

"I have another mystery for you to clear up. It was obvious the antique dealer in Merida knew you and had a package for you. What was that all about?"

Joseph smiled. "I was hoping you didn't see him waving at me."

Hannah's held her breath. Maybe she had uncovered something she'd rather not know.

"Remember when you told me that reading Stevens and Catherwood's accounts of their travels in the Yucatan started your love of Maya archaeology? Well, before I came out to Ek Balam I asked the antiquity storeowner to locate 1843 first editions of the two volumes as a surprise gift for you. Just didn't have time to pick them up. We got a little busy with other matters, if you recall." They both blushed.

"Mr. Comouche, I believe you had nothing to do with the thefts. I'm sorry I gave any credence to their accusations. You're hardly the tomb robber type," added Hannah.

"Truth is generally the best antidote to slander. Thank you for trusting me again," he said.

"Not so fast. Why did you lie to me about your personal life? You're not just a poor journalist living an itinerant lifestyle."

"Let me explain…" he started.

"I almost didn't let you buy dinner and wine in Merida for fear it would dent your budget. Now I find out you own vineyards and raise prize horses," Hannah inserted. "Why couldn't you trust me to share those details?"

"Hannah, my family…"

"Yea, the family you said had a modest printing company. They turn out to be the largest publishing firm in the Southern Hemisphere."

"About that," he stammered. "I am the oldest son, but never wanted to run the family holdings. I legally turned all that over to my brother and siblings. My life work is independent photojournalism. I wanted to make it on my own merits.

"I can understand that," she conceded.

"I made a few investments in areas of agriculture and husbandry that interest me. With good managers, they have been successful even in my prolonged absences. Maybe because of it," he joked. "Possessions and money don't define a person---they tend to be encumbrances."

"Most importantly," Joseph continued slowly, "as trite as it may sound, I wanted to be loved for who I am, not the social circle I came from or my net worth. You seemed to like me for myself."

"That I did. Tattered jeans, scruffy beard and all." Warm memories and dreams stirred once again. Listening to him, she realized the diverse aspects of Joseph were not in conflict. His various qualities merged like an orchestra's instruments integrating into harmony. They both sat quietly for a moment.

"Look at me, a journalist who can't find the right words. So please accept my heartfelt but unspoken apologies."

"Now, what were your questions?" Hannah asked.

"Certainly nothing quite as serious as yours about antiquity theft or bank accounts," he teased. "I couldn't locate you. It drove me crazy. I just wanted to hear from you about what happened when Ek Balam was robbed. Were you wounded badly? Are you in Los Angeles for a visit or what?"

"Slow down. One thing at a time."

"Okay, start at the beginning and tell me everything. Not just facts, but those inner thoughts and insights you are so good at," he said.

"My dad's right. Telling the truth really creates the possibility for more truth around you."

Hannah and Joseph chatted and laughed through the evening until her battery was blinking with 5% of power left. She'd lost her charger in the quick return to the States.

"I am recharged, but can't say the same about my old laptop. We will continue this conversation tomorrow," she signed off.

"Hannah, I am relieved you are safe. I hope you get the museum job. I am going to be stuck here in New Zealand for a while tying up some difficult loose ends. When I finish I will come to Los Angeles to see you. You are in my thoughts and my heart."

"Good night," she sighed and touched his face on the screen. Hannah felt reassured, knowing that her presence and absence both meant something to Joseph.

Hannah hugged herself with joy. "*Maybe one day I will have something in my life to warm my soul, besides a pot of green tea and grandmother's quilt.*"

CHAPTER 78

Los Angeles, California
Present Day

Dr. Hanna Char was hired and began her tasks at the Natural History Museum of Los Angeles County.

"Bones never forget or lie. Skeletons are not just inert objects, they are witnesses from the grave," Hannah told her new intern. She reached out and respectfully touched one of the bones displayed on her metal laboratory table.

"Each one still contains the essence and character of its owner. We can reconstruct much about life long ago from what the remains reveal to us forensically. Different bones tell us age, race, sex, height, and whether they were left or right handed. If the bones are from a female, they let us know if she had children and how many. They can even reveal the cause of death."

The reluctant student looked down his nose disapprovingly at the skeleton, which he saw as unsanitary and morbid.

"How can you tell whether bones are human or animal?" he asked.

"Human bones are more porous. The tongue will stick to them," Hannah said and demonstrated by touching a fragment to her mouth. "Here taste this," she offered a different piece to the shocked young man. He covered his mouth with both hands and exited the room.

"*Probably going back to study business law the way his parents wanted in the first place,*" thought Hannah. She shrugged and returned to analysis of the pre-Columbian skeletons, which she found a fascinating subject of inquiry. She loved reading life histories in the bones.

Holder of a new ID badge, the laboratory, elevator and office keys, her own desk space and a museum computer, Hannah fell right back into step at the Natural History Museum.

The archaeology staff consisted of three fulltime people and an array of students and volunteers. The director of the department, Dr. Michael Rose, had a pale plain face topped with thin closely cropped hair. He always wore a simple gray suit and white shirt. He appeared no more or less distinguished than others she passed in the hallways. His meek demeanor led people to underestimate him.

Dr. Rose taught at the state university occasionally, but preferred conducting research and museum department management. He traveled every summer to various archaeological digs and conferences. His expertise was highly praised and advice sought.

Hannah worked for a field season with him in the California desert ruins. She'd read all his published books and papers. Whenever they discussed past and upcoming work, her belief in his brilliance was confirmed.

She felt awed to be in the presence of a genius like Dr. Rose. Awareness of his remarkable achievements and his own direct manner made her want to abandon small talk. Half of what people said was some sort of filler anyway, to be polite and agreeable.

She wished she could ask him if he was lonely living in a world full of mediocre people who were usually intimidated by his intellect, and ask when did he first sense he had an extraordinary gift. Instead she was happy to listen and always learned something new from her mentor. She'd bring him hot coffee, which he appreciated. She discovered that he sometimes used cream, but never the powered stuff in small packets.

Hannah's museum projects included challenging work on bones, mummies, pottery reconstruction and analysis, the authentication of antiquities and arranging public exhibits. She savored every minute of being on staff again at her former museum.

"Hannah," shouted Dr. Jay Risna from across the lab. "Welcome back." The department's resident Egyptologist ran towards her like a long-lost cousin and swept her up in a big hug. He was a barrel-chested bear of a man with a grand Tom Selleck moustache. She knew it wouldn't take long for Jay's teasing, playful banter to begin.

For years he had unsuccessfully tried to convert her from New World and Meso-American archaeology to studies of the Middle East. He was an ardent admirer of everything Egyptian, so much so that his custom car license plate read 'Hotep', an abbreviation for the ancient pharaoh Amenhotep.

Despite their different loyalties, Hannah and Jay enjoyed great rapport. This modern day Renaissance man impressed her with his eclectic areas of expertise. Jay collected Persian miniatures, classical Verdi records, and world leaders' signatures. She imagined he'd probably developed a few new interests since they last saw each other and she looked forward to learning about them. He pillaged life for funny ironies. He could make her laugh until she snorted at his wry puns and imitations. They shared a vocabulary and devotion for archaeology.

"A new shipment of pieces came in on loan from the Cairo Museum. It contains some of the last bits salvaged before revolutionary mobs reeked havoc on their own heritage centers. I'd like your help unpacking the crates," he requested. "I've already cleared it with Director Rose," he added, knowing what a stickler Hannah was for rules and departmental protocol.

They opened the wooden containers carefully and unwrapped treasures only seen in history and art books. Hannah murmured in awe as they uncovered one priceless artifact after another. Numerous containers held inscribed vases, official seals, and gilded furnishings. She especially admired a tightly wrapped mummy in his enameled sarcophagus. An assortment of amulets, funeral masks from long forgotten royal burial chambers reminded her of

Maya tombs. The various crates also held dishes and vessels decorated with precious metals and stones, illustrated papyrus books, objects of lapis lazuli, and boxes of ancient jewelry. The latest of the items dated from 100 BC, the twentieth dynasty of the New Kingdom.

Looking over the Egyptian treasures before her, Hannah said, "Even the greatest civilizations were not invincible."

Jay confirmed what the science of anthropology taught them both, "The Egyptians, Sumerians, Greeks, Romans and Maya were all once powerful dynasties and empires. But now their cities lay in ruins and their creations buried or in museums and collections around the world,"

Small ibis statues with eyes of white crystal and black onyx watched over the two archaeologists all afternoon long as they catalogued and organized the collection for exhibition.

"Being able to see and actually touch such incredible objects is one of the perks of working in a museum," Hannah said.

"Step over here for a minute and turn around," instructed Jay. He encircled Hannah's throat with a heavy bejeweled necklace collar. He added two cuff bracelets and a golden tiara from the tomb of an Egyptian princess. The black turtleneck sweater Hannah wore was the perfect backdrop for displaying the royal relics. She felt beautiful and empowered. She believed there was truth in myths about objects and their energies.

From a hidden cache, the ever-resourceful Jay produced a bottle of red wine and filled two of the ancient goblets.

"Here is to you and all your hard work, Dr. Char."

"And to you Dr. Rizna," she chimed back and flashed a broad smile. "I can't tell you how much I appreciate the opportunity to be included once again in this community of liked-minded scholars."

"Mountain peaks see one another, while the valleys do not," Jay raised his golden vessel and toasted her. "We are proud to have you back, pooling our abilities for the advancement of science," he said.

His deep contagious guffaw followed and Hannah found herself laughing and content. Her days at the LA Museum posed sharp contrasts to attitudes, dangers and harsh difficulties she'd experienced in the field and at the Mexican National Institute of Anthropology and History that she'd left behind.

CHAPTER 79

Los Angeles, California
Present Day

Over evening dinner, Hannah discussed recent museum projects and revelations with her father. He'd prepared a dinner of vegetables from his summer garden.

"Happiness is green tomatoes turning red," he beamed, showing off his latest crop. Max campaigned each year for changes in legislation to put gardens in schools, on each city block and rooftops. One of his most dog-eared books was 'All Hell Needs is Water' on irrigation. He loved the Cicero quote, "A library and a garden are all one needs."

"Dad, this time with you and working at the museum, emphasizes how unbalanced my life had become the last several years. My field work grew into an all-consuming obsession, an addiction."

"Yep. At times you seemed to be a machine that knew nothing but how to run," he agreed. "The glorification of busy, I called it."

"I've been the sort of control freak who could not distinguish between unnecessary details and essentials," Hannah admitted.

"Now I hope you finally realize that you don't have to be perfect to be excellent," Max said.

"You are so right. I have learned to be more flexible and not so hard on myself. Mari and Roberto and the thrill of unearthing new information from the past remain the best parts. But I am finding satisfying new ways of contributing to archaeology. I enjoy working at LA Museum but would also like an opportunity to do further fieldwork in the Yucatan. I have unfinished business there."

"How's your extra-curricular work going on the Mayan scribe who put books on pottery?" he whispered from behind his hand, even though just the two of them sat at the backyard patio table.

"Even though I seem to be banned from working in Mexico right now, I will never give up on looking for examples of her works with the lily signature. As much as I can, I go through physical collections, books and online catalogues for more clues. Absence of information tells me as much as the presence of the pieces Berto and I discovered. I want to return to Ek Balam someday to discover the answers. There are just so many obstacles in my way."

"Dreams don't have expiration dates. I'm certain that when the time is right you'll get back at it and solve the mystery," Max said.

"Do you really believe that will happen?"

"Does it rain in Oregon?" he nodded up and down.

Hannah had disclosed details of the unusual artworks and secreted mural room to her father. She stressed and he understood the need for strict confidence. He insisted that she make a complete record of her notes, photographs and theories. She assured him she had backup copies locked in a personal safety deposit box, as well as a second set hidden in the safe at her museum office.

LA Museum was a vast complex of buildings. Most areas were equipped with modern security systems, but sometimes the older, tried and true methods proved as effective. One alternative method to safeguard collections was the use of Dobermans. When canine acute hearing picked up the slightest disturbance, they responded with speed and voracity. Trained guard dogs roamed the halls after dark until their handlers called them back each morning.

Hannah had adjusted to working regular 9 am to 5 pm hours. But one evening she straightened up from analyzing a recent delivery of Inca bones and rolled the kinks out of her tired neck. She was surprised when she looked up at the skylights in her laboratory and saw pitch-black night.

"It must be later than I thought. I'd better head home," she said out loud.

Hannah grabbed her sweater and opened the door to a darkened hallway. Before she'd taken two steps, she heard the scratch of running claws on the smooth marble floors.

"*Oh no, they've already let out the guard dogs.*" Hannah jumped back in the lab and slammed the door just as the ferocious creatures came bounding around the corner. The canines pawed and whined at the door, making her exit impossible.

"*Surely, a guard will hear and pull them away.*" She looked around for a telephone to call the security station. There was none. She'd left her purse and cellphone in the main offices.

An hour later, it was clear that the dogs were camped outside her lab door for the night. Hannah was trapped until morning. She found bottled water and an energy bar in her desk drawer. She decided to go back to work until she couldn't keep her eyes open. Navaho blankets from the Native American exhibit stack made a decent pallet for sleeping. So she settled in for the night.

The next morning, Hannah was the first person in Dr. Rose's office. She told him about her misadventure of the night before. They both found humor and lessons in her crazy situation. He advised his workaholic employee to come up for air more often when she focused on projects in the future.

"I'd like a clock and a telephone in my laboratory, please."

"Of course. We'll make those needed changes. Now go home, rest and I'll see you tomorrow," he chuckled over her disheveled appearance.

When Hannah arrived at her workstation the next day she was greeted by a skeleton model dressed in her white lab coat. It was positioned seated at her desk with a pen in its boney fingers working on a report.

Dr. Rose and Dr. Rizna jumped out from between nearby shelves, hooting at their joke. Hannah laughed until stomach hurt.

"This prank is the best. You guys are such characters," Hannah hugged her co-workers. Life lessons are often learned through humor.

CHAPTER 80

Los Angeles, California
Present Day

Dr. Rose wholeheartedly supported Hannah's theory of Maya books being transferred to pottery. He granted her admission to museum networks and archives in the depths of their rambling facility. Unlimited access to database reports, collections that were not on display, inside information and professional resources helped her research Maya pottery sequences.

"I will do everything in my power to ensure the mysterious artist's works are not forgotten," she told her father. "Mari wrote to me that our friends Marianne and Jim who live on Calle 56 in Merida found a rare 1600s volume called *Yucatan People of Interest.* It was hidden high atop an antique bookcase in their colonial home. Berto said it mentions an indigenous portrait artist named Clara. He is following up on that clue."

During breaks and on her own time, Hannah wandered about in immense underground and attic storage rooms. Honeycombs of high shelves filled with thousands of artifacts rose up around her.

She whistled, "*I could create an entire new chain of museums just from the overflow in here. Less than five percent of any museum's holdings are placed on display or loaned at any one time,*" she had remembered reading.

"Accumulations such as those could benefit my search for additional pieces. Now if I could only find the needle I want in this vast haystack."

Acquisitions were coded and catalogued by interns and staff. When Hannah started in the profession, she hand wrote information on index cards. Card catalogs were the Google of her era. Nowadays graduate students and interns entered data into computers. Hannah accessed and studied whatever her museum and other institutions held in inventory. It wasn't a perfect or complete system, but better than roaming warehouse stacks and personally visiting other distant depositories.

"Too bad unknown and finer Pre-Colombian pieces remained secreted away in private collections," she lamented to Dr. Rose.

Rumors of large superior quality collections in private homes and offices constantly circulated. In the antiquities and art world, everyone knew about private collections. Dealers and curators follow, as best they could, who collected what, where and how much they paid for their pieces.

Museums regularly reached out through the grapevine asking to anonymously see the artifacts and study them for science. While the museum generally refused to buy undocumented items, on rare occasions principles were sacrificed to expediency. If curators believed the art was surreptitiously obtained, they promised confidentiality in exchange for an opportunity to examine the item.

"We have been granted permission to photograph another estate's private collection," Dr. Rose announced at their Monday morning conference. "Hannah, since it is reputed to contain a majority of Maya pieces, I will send you to record the inventory."

"As much as it disturbs me, I have to face it. Pre-Columbian art has become fashionable," sighed Hannah. "When and where do I go? Shall I drive?"

"No, the collector insists on remaining completely anonymous. He will send a driver. You may be taken there in a car with blacked out windows or blindfolded so you won't know where the hoard is located or who the owner is."

Hannah agreed to the owners' terms. "That's paranoid, but I will go along with just about anything to get glimpses of lost troves."

"In exchange for access," Dr. Rose continued, "if you spot any forgeries, you are to let their agent know. Even though serious collectors generally deal with reputable people, they sometimes end up with frauds. That's part of the reason they allow us to view their antiquities. You won't be asked for an expert, museum appraisal."

"That's good," said Hannah, "because it would be difficult for me to help buyers of stolen art. However, telling a collector that he got taken in with a fake would delight me."

"Hannah, I know how strongly you feel about plundered artifacts, but this information exchange is a time-honored symbiotic relationship. Remember, if we did not meet private collectors half way, their pieces and insights of knowledge would be hidden from us forever."

The driver indeed blindfolded Hannah. He drove great distances and in circles so she couldn't reproduce her journey. Collecting antiquities and artworks without proper provenance or documentation, like most illegal activities, generated a clandestine environment of deceit and intrigue.

Her eyes needed a moment to adjust to the light once she was inside and the thick cloth eye-cover was removed. She stood in a climate-controlled room with no windows. Over three thousand square feet of space was loaded with beveled glass cases, which in turn were filled with some of the finest pre-Columbian art Hannah had ever seen.

Obviously someone with sufficient power and enormous wealth gathered this vast collection of antiquities. Treasures had been locked away in a hidden vault where no one but the owner could lay eyes on them and fondle his precious artifacts in private.

Craving and hoarding rare possessions was more than a passion. It was comparable to compulsion, like a serial sociopath who could not stop himself. Max's strong words about wealthy collectors' obsessions manifested in this private museum.

The unknown owner provided his own on-site curator to assist Hannah. At first the female overseer looked at her like a madam might regard a nun invading a brothel. Then when they made closer eye contact, Hannah sensed that there was something vaguely familiar about the lady curator.

"*Was she a former student or intern at the museum?*" wondered Hannah. "*I'd hate to think we trained someone only to have her turn to the dark side of the profession.*"

Soon the two settled down into a silent routine of recording the art. Wearing white cotton gloves, she removed selected artifacts from their spaces and positioned them on a black velvet draped tabletop for Hannah's inspection and photographs.

Hannah took measurements and digital pictures of the various invaluable pieces and thought, "*Don't they understand how plundering the grave this bowl came from destroyed the context and all the information surrounding the burial, not to mention destruction to buildings and other artifacts?*"

"Another orphan without a pedigree," Hannah let slip out loud as the assistant placed a rare ceramic plate before her. The curator seemed embarrassed by the excess and cringed at the remark.

"*What they promoted by obtaining this piece is immoral and illegal,*" Hannah fumed internally. She dared not speak her mind as boldly as before. But the curator, as another woman, appeared to read her facial expressions and body language.

At the end of their long session, the helper brought out one last object. "This is our latest acquisition, a bas-relief limestone and stucco door lintel piece," she stated as she placed the heavy stone carving on the table.

"From the north palace in Ek Balam, Yucatan," said a stunned Hannah. In front of her sat one of the glyph fragments stolen from her archaeology site the day she was stabbed.

"Just how do you know that?" asked the dubious curator.

"It was in situ the last time I saw it."

CHAPTER 81

Los Angeles, California
Present Day

Hannah gave Dr. Rose a complete report on her assignment at the private collector's secret museum. She expressed her dismay at how many illicit items made it into the country without detection.

"How do antiquity thieves accomplish this level of importing?"

Two days later he invited her to his office for some insights to her query. Grainy surveillance video showed a man held in airport customs. Seated behind an institutional metal desk, a uniformed officer jabbed his insistent finger at pages in a discolored regulations book and yelled at the person.

"Infractions of the law," he pronounced in the offender's face. "You're looking at years in jail and disgrace for trading in artifacts."

The well-dressed courier calmly crossed his arms and waited.

"But…" the border official said, "For five thousand dollars, perhaps we can forget about this unfortunate encounter."

The gentleman took bank-banded cash out of his coat pocket and slid it over the desktop with two fingers. Without looking at it, the officer stealthily pushed it into a convenient manila folder.

He continued, "And for another five thousand you can have your bags back." The antique dealer left the airport security area with all his stolen archaeological goods that same hour.

"That footage should answer your questions about how the private collector might have gotten some of his looted goods into the country," Dr. Rose told Hannah.

"Hannah, I want you to meet Officer Lauren Sullivan of the U.S. Customs Service. She has requested our help in stemming the flow of illicit antiquities across the borders."

"From what I've heard, it sounds like we are on the same page about stopping the sacking of other nations' history," said Lauren.

"No major artifact or artwork ever crosses a county's frontier without at least two laws being broken," replied Hannah. "I'm tired of unconvincing arguments that antiquity theft can only be stopped at the source. Grave robbers in Guatemala are called *esteleros*; in Peru *huaquers*; in Italy *tombaroli*, but around the world, the terms all signify the same thing---those who plunder the past."

Lauren pointed out, "The smuggler in our surveillance tape was a professional carrier who knew what he was doing. Various other sources include people with foreign diplomatic cover who bring pieces in via embassy pouch," the customs agent told them.

"That's how the U.S. Consul Edward S. Thompson shipped hundreds of artifacts back to the Peabody Museum in the United States. He dredged priceless items out of Chichen Itza's sacred well in the early twentieth century. Some say he felt he was protecting them from being sold by corrupt local officials," Hannah said.

Lauren reported further, "Dealers assure collectors, 'If you want, we can get export permits. We have a friend at the museum'."

"Who is that museum friend?" Hannah interrupted.

"We don't know. Yet." Lauren continued, "Other importers are tourists and customers who are advised to take pieces with them on planes and ships. 'Mix it in with other souvenir junk. Nobody will look at your bags. Why should you worry?' they are told."

"Some antiquities in the country are legit," Director Rose reminded them. "People come here to the museum wanting to sell or donate items that have lawfully been in this country before there were antiquity laws. Vases and figurines were legally brought across the border by someone's grandparents. Be careful not to assume judgmental attitudes concerning items gathering dust in an attic or parlor for over half a century," he said.

"Thank you for the cool down," Hannah teased the boss who knew how her mind worked. "But you know this is not who we need to target. It's the masterminds who pay tomb robbers and sell stolen objects to private buyers. After what I saw the other day, the money is definitely with the wealthy collectors."

"Looting of sites is not a new phenomenon. It was as lucrative in antiquity as it is today, in spite of UNESCO Convention agreements," said Lauren. "Over eighty-five percent of countries with prime archaeological locations report active ransacking. US Customs officers work heroically to help countries protect their national heritage, but poorly written stolen art legislation and pressure from special interests, makes the judiciary arm unwilling to prosecute," Lauren sighed in frustration.

Dr. Rose stepped in to relate his experiences. "Buying, selling and exporting cultural properties from the country of origin is illegal, but that fact seems immaterial to traffickers I encounter," he commented. "Recently the internet has become a powerful sales tool in the antiquities market."

"Artifact theft is real. It's not scare monger tactics of field archaeologists like me, accused of over-exaggerated imaginations and harboring thinly-veiled preservation agendas," said Hannah.

"The law rarely stops the spoiled rich from getting what they crave. The collection you observed yesterday focused on pre-Columbian treasures. It has gotten out of hand," Lauren said in agreement.

"Officer Lauren, how can we help you?" asked Hannah.

"Show me and my agents what to look for in shipments and how to tell fakes from the real thing."

Hannah prepared and taught a morning-long condensed class on spotting authentic versus fraudulent artifacts. Her lecture included tips such as noticing paint runs, patina, thickness of the clay, natural color pigments and indicators like firing techniques and tool marks that didn't exist in ancient times.

Hannah's instruction time paid off. In the first week she received a call from Lauren about two cases marked 'handicrafts' stopped at Los Angeles Airport. Based on Hannah's classroom descriptions, the inspector did not think what he saw looked like modern day artisans' work. He was right.

Agent Lauren seized the items and called Hannah to authenticate the artifacts. The team of two set up in a small low-ceiling room. Cases, sealed with yellow U.S. Customs tape, sat on wobbly folding tables. There was only one electrical outlet in the room. Hannah borrowed a long extension cord so she could keep her computer next to the work area. Their assigned storage facilities were not designed for electronics. It was a real dead zone. Between them they had three computers and two cellphones. In the final analysis, only two devices worked through the whole process.

The seized ceramics and stonework had been shipped in rough wooden crates, packed with newspapers and old clothes. Hannah made detailed inventories of the stolen collection in preparation to return them to their country of origin.

"Of course, the person named on the shipping label did not come forward to claim the cargo after they were confiscated," Lauren informed Hannah. "The business destination address was found deserted. Another dealer was thwarted, for now."

Hannah found it delightful to work with Agent Lauren. She seemed unafraid, incorruptible and matched Hannah's enthusiasm and dedication. Finally, someone in an official position to stop antiquity thefts was working with her; a person who put archaeological interests ahead of her own personal interests.

After verifying that some of the confiscated goods were indeed antiquities, the U.S. Customs made contact with Guatemala's embassy. Officer Lauren worked with them to start the process of repatriation. The recovered cultural heritage pieces would eventually go into a new museum. National treasures placed on display for all to see rather than sold piecemeal to private collections.

“Now those artifacts can be publically enjoyed, showing the glory of ancient Maya art and the infinite possibilities of human creativity,” said Hannah, as she thought of her Ek Balam artist with the lily signature.

CHAPTER 82

Los Angeles, California
Present Day

"Dr. Char, I need your assistance in selecting pieces to take to auction," said Leo Newton, the Natural History Museum's Board of Director President.

"For sale…?" asked Hannah.

"Our museum prefers to use the term 'de-accessioning' when they sell objects from their inventory overstock," he explained.

"I thought a museum's major tasks were acquisition, conservation, and exhibition. Aren't we here as caretakers, holding things in trust for future generations?" asked Hannah, a bit too sarcastically.

"Of course, to a certain point. But museum administration's first obligation is to our public. We need to provide new, captivating pieces for them to see. There is a national demand for star quality. Attention around newly purchased rare art means better attendance and funding. Competition is fierce."

"I never realized museums both sell and buy so regularly." Hannah said to confirm his statements and intentions.

"No auction hammers go down at the world's great art dealer

houses like Sotheby's or Christies without at least a few pieces on the block from museum collections," he said.

"Or without some museum representative raising the bid paddle in his pudgy hand to buy," said Hannah.

"Our museum only purchases legal pieces with solid provenance documentation," Newton answered too quickly and defensively.

"Guess one of the charms of being a public institution director is that you can vicariously acquire great works of art using other peoples' money," Hannah retorted.

The Board President squirmed in his seat at her accurate appraisal. This debate was an old conflict between museum curators and field archaeologists. Archaeologists accused museum folks of being unquestioning collectors. And in turn, curators criticized archaeologists for being high priests that hide their finds and knowledge away from the public in the name of scientific analysis.

"The auction houses and dealers we work with are reputable specialists, dedicated to scholarship," President Newton continued. "They only feature antiquities with proper permits."

"You know as well as I do, the majority of certificates of origin attached to such artifacts are unreliable. Falsification and laundering of papers is a routine business method among dealers."

"Our museum system can not be responsible for another nation's failure to enforce its own export laws. Often countries of origin make a lot of money off smuggling. They may scream and yell, but then turn a blind eye and allow it to continue.

No American law is broken when artifacts are sold and bought. It may not be ethical, but it is legal. Besides, most judges, dealing with backlogs of homicide cases or recession-causing white collar fraud, don't think that stealing an old vase is so bad."

"Why can't museum systems declare a moratorium on acquisitions and just stop buying? A unilateral agreement between all museums that they would not purchase any antiquities unless they came with impeccable pedigrees might discourage theft and fraud," she said.

"Hannah, compare our museum's situation to the world disarmament problem. If we stopped buying antiquities for our exhibits and if everyone else continued, it puts us at a great disadvantage. If we don't acquire a special piece, the treasure would be purchased by a rival museum or vanish into private hands."

"Pressure is palpable to continuously provide outstanding art for the public, I understand that," she said. "However, new works could come from imaginative loans or swaps arranged between museums. Thousands of pieces gather dust in storerooms around the country. Bequests and gifts could provide further resources," Hannah argued. "I also think the IRS should refuse to allow tax deductions for charitable donations of antiquities without documentation of legal export." She was on a roll.

President Newton was not ready to be a pioneer in museum methods of acquisition and de-accessioning. Other battles called.

"You are right about cultivating rich patrons and contributors as sources. Curators and staff often provide expertise and guide purchases of wealthy buyers. Every collector is a potential donor."

"So people with outstanding collections are personally assisted and unashamedly courted?" Hannah asked.

"Of course," he answered in a frigid huff.

Her brow wrinkled in a puzzled crease. This frank admission of a museum's catalytic role surprised and disappointed her. She wondered if any institute held to high standards of research and ethical conduct. The over-the-spectacles pursed-lipped look on the Board President's face silently conveyed that he thought she was being childishly naïve and argumentative.

"As a matter of fact, one of our premiere benefactors is visiting today with some pieces. I want you to work with Dr. Rose to accommodate her." Tired of ethical confrontation and rusty arguments, the Board leader got up and left their meeting.

CHAPTER 83

Los Angeles, California
Present Day

After Hannah's disillusioning confrontation with the museum Board President, as instructed she went to meet with Dr. Rose and the patron who wished to make donations.

Margaret Haynes was already in the curator's office when Hannah arrived. She was a sweet elderly lady with perfectly coiffed hair, colored faintly blue like skim milk. Her attire and demeanor were elegant and bespoke of immense wealth and breeding.

The three shared a high tea of cucumber sandwiches, Earl Grey tea with double bergamot and English shortbread cookies. There was a pleasant exchange of introductions and conversation.

"Mrs. Haynes…" Hannah began.

"Please call me Margaret."

"Margaret, may I examine the artifacts you have so graciously brought to us?" said Hannah, smiling and playing the curator-donor game.

Hannah had not wanted to appear too eager, but she glanced furtively at art objects Margaret had laid out carefully on a felt-covered tabletop. Her collection was like a dealer's bag, not from the same site or cache, just things thrown together.

It was clear to Hannah that many items could only have been unearthed in clandestine operations. Educated scrutiny, even from across the room, told her that the largest piece was not genuine. The prevalence of frauds is the curse of illicit trade. Hannah thought that collectors getting duped was just punishment for bad judgment and obsessive accumulation. Replicas by good forgers were more a problem for private collectors than museums or archaeologists who knew how to spot reproductions.

The three moved over to Margaret's display of pre-Columbian treasures. Hannah and Dr. Rose picked up various pieces and studied them.

"I wanted your museum to have first choice. I'll donate these three on the left for a tax write-off, but would like to sell the rest. Of course at a greatly discounted price for you Michael, my favorite curator," Margaret nodded graciously at Dr. Rose.

"Those four items have been in the family for decades. Some were recently purchased, like these two cylinder vases I acquired last month. They aren't as colorful or impressive as the auction house catalogue made them appear," said Margaret with a dismissive wave of her bejeweled hand. Hannah discretely rolled her eyes at that reason for disposing of eight hundred year old Maya art.

Dr. Rose taught Hannah to watch and listen carefully, because there would always be a backstory behind each artifact. He wisely advised, "You can buy the piece, but never the tale."

Dr. Rose was like a Bridge Master who never lost a hand. After the first bids were out, he would know exactly what cards Margaret held. He was aware if she tried to bluff, because he could out-bluff anybody. Hannah loved to watch him in action.

"I'll need time to study the pieces further and consult with others. You know we are not allowed to accept donations or buy items here illegally or ones those that come with questionable documents," he reminded the owner.

"You'd turn down my hundred thousand dollar gifts?"

"Yes, if the provenances were questionable," Dr. Rose answered firmly but politely.

"As one of our esteemed board members, you'll also understand that budgets are tighter than usual this year," the curator explained and continued to flatter the lady patron.

The two went through ritual bargaining motions while both calculated in their heads what the other wanted. Hannah stepped forward and examined an impressive jade mosaic funeral mask.

"Margaret, could you enlighten me about the origins behind this particular piece and share some information on the dealer?"

The donor hesitated, like she'd been caught having an illicit love affair. Collectors thrilled in the similar atmosphere of secrecy and deception. It was not normal protocol or good manners to delve into specifics and provenance so directly. Hannah's request threw Margaret off for a moment, but she recovered and replied.

"I bought that mask at a reputable auction house in New York City last year. I have all my paperwork and receipts with me. The dealer assured me of its provenience."

"Provenance, from the French word *provenir*, means 'to come from.' It is very different from 'provenience', which means ownership origin, source or place of manufacture," Hannah informed her.

"I didn't know there was any difference," said Margaret.

"It's not your fault. Auction houses and antiquity dealers find it to their advantage to blur the subtle distinction between the two words. When a piece has a dubious history of discovery or ownership they rely on the fact that civilians think the words are interchangeable. Dealers advertise the artifact's provenience to be 'pre-Columbian Mexico' or 'Olmec style' or 'from the collection of XYZ, known to buy the finest pieces', thus increasing the asking prices and their bottom line."

Dr. Rose broke the tension when he told them about a major Ohio museum that named its new restaurant 'Provenance'. "It was an ironic choice, knowing their reputation, like so many other museums, for not taking documented origins seriously."

"I only asked about your special mask because genuine pre-Columbian artifacts like it are covered by Memorandum of Agreement," said Hannah. "There is no way a shipper sent it to the United States legally. I am pretty sure this particular piece is on a current international list of stolen archaeological material."

Hannah pulled out her computer and retrieved various websites with photographs and descriptions of the very object she held in her hands. It was on the 'Ten Most Wanted' list.

"Yes, here it is again," she said and showed the surprised patron another high crimes illicit trade lists. Margaret gasped and asked for a glass of water.

"But I was told everything was in order. I paid a fortune for that jade mask," she whined. "What do I do?"

"I will contact my friends at group, facetiously called Loot Busters, right now by telephone. They can assist you in getting a refund and negotiate an amicable return of the piece to its country of origin. Like you, a majority of collectors and auction houses co-operate when told they have stolen goods," said Hannah. "No one wants to be cheated or ruin their reputation."

"So I'll get my money back and not be embarrassed or dragged into court over this honest mistake?" asked the frightened lady.

"This foundation group has a policy of strict confidentiality. There is no 'gotcha' attitude among these folks. They keep a low profile and help parties sort things out quietly."

Hannah's contact went out of her way to help and reassure Margaret. The recovery organization found that letting the collector voluntarily return items, get refunded, and take credit for a good deed always worked better in the long run. The welfare of art is an international responsibility and lost art foundations' concerns were for the irreplaceable pieces.

Hannah made a fast friend in Margaret after helping her identify the stolen item and recoup her losses through intercession by the amicable repatriation group.

Margaret kissed Dr. Rose on both cheeks in the European manner. She handed the curator and Hannah engraved invitations to a cocktail party at her Beverly Hills home. “I’d love for you to see some of my favorite art in a proper setting,” she said with pride.

CHAPTER 84

Los Angeles, California
Present Day

A week after helping Margaret recover her money from the dealer who sold her a stolen artifact, Hannah and Dr. Rose accepted the invitation to her party. They talked about the antiquity theft situation and possible solutions as they drove up winding Coldwater Canyon and turned onto Mulholland Drive.

It wasn't difficult to locate Margaret's large rambling estate overlooking the San Fernando Valley on one side and the Santa Monica Mountains on the other. The immense Frank Lloyd Wright style mansion merged seamlessly with the natural setting on three different levels, with stunning views in all directions. Her parking area was larger than the museum's entire lot.

Margaret enthusiastically greeted Hannah and Dr. Rose at the entrance. She acted delighted that they'd accepted her invitation. As the trio moved toward the front room, a tuxedoed waiter handed them crystal flutes of champagne from a silver tray.

"Come see my newest acquisition," Margaret said, as she turned, fully expecting them to follow in her wake of expensive perfume.

"There it is, on the marble pedestal over there, with a spotlight on it. Isn't he the most exquisite example of manhood you have ever seen?" the hostess boasted.

Hannah took three steps forward, just to be sure she was seeing correctly. Her normally light complexion went a shade paler, but she did not let her emotions show. She froze in place and grabbed Dr. Rose's arm for support. Under a brightly lit glass dome stood her beloved Maya nobleman figurine from the Mexico City National Anthropology Museum. She'd shared the story with Dr. Rose about its surreal impact on her and its mysterious disappearance.

"Margaret?" she whispered.

Her gracious hostess saw the questioning look on Hannah's face.

"Oh no. That statue is totally legit. It comes with tons of papers and stamped certificates. I bought it from the most popular and reputable source around. As a matter of fact, the seller is right over there by the fireplace at the end of the room. I will introduce you to him," Margaret said reassuringly.

Hannah turned in the direction Margaret pointed. A sophisticated gentleman stood chatting with three grand dame society ladies. The gentleman was Dr. Samuel Sarra.

Hannah gasped involuntarily and turned away before he could spot her. She and Dr. Rose both suspected Sarra might be mixed up in more than he let on, but this confirmed their worst fears.

"There aren't many things as devastating as mistaking an enemy as a friend," Hannah said. Any feelings of respect, trust or otherwise that she harbored were now gone completely and forever. It was like a soul leaving the body after death, quick and final.

"Let's get out of here right now," said Dr. Rose and guided her through the main door. Margaret looked back and saw the two were not accompanying her. They were nowhere in sight, so she shrugged her shoulders and conversed with other guests.

Hannah's car had not been there long enough for the valet to park it, so they reclaimed the vehicle and drove away.

"The tragedy of betrayal is that it never comes from enemies. He is the worst kind of dealer, catering to the upper tier of wealthy collectors. The type who is very selective, choosing only art treasures of the greatest value, priceless artifacts," said Dr. Rose.

"Director Sarra has the whole National Museum and all of Mexico's archaeological sites under his supervision to pick from," Hannah seethed. "A pirate who has stealthily taken over a great ship. People kill to supply his greedy business." She touched the scar on her ribcage.

CHAPTER 85

Los Angeles, California
Present Day

The next morning, Hannah, Dr. Rose and U.S. Customs Agent Lauren Sullivan sat around a conference table at the museum and brainstormed strategies to stop Sarra's illicit pipeline of antiquities.

"Trade in stolen art is the fasting growing crime in the USA," the agent told them. "Smuggling is a very lucrative business for those who do it well."

"Many great classic archaeologists of the past, like Carter in Egypt and Schliemann at Troy, started out as collectors and dealt in artifacts," said Dr. Rose.

"Their objectives were treasure first, history second," interjected Hannah.

"Archaeologists today try to distance themselves from that image with the passage of ethics codes and international antiquity legislation, but it still occurs," the curator reminded the team.

"What really ticks me off is how Sarra dared to fire me as a person of suspicion and accuse Joseph of being behind the lootings. I guess I got too close to his secret network," Hannah fumed.

“Speaking of networks,” said Lauren, “there are dangerous parallel trafficking networks of illegal objects smuggled alongside antiquities by the same gangs. Arms, drugs, rare plants and animals and people are regularly traded by a single organized cartel.”

“We can never stop all looting, but to prevent large scale plunder like what we’ve uncovered, we must disrupt whatever organization brings the antiquities to market,” said Hannah.

“To build a strong case against Sarra and his cohorts, we need to collect information from officials, informants and surveillance operations,” said Lauren, thinking like an officer of the law. “We can assume his source is the National Museum and INAH archaeological sites. No doubt his revenue comes from illicit sales to private collectors and other museum buyers.”

“Perhaps we could plan a sting, where our museum puts out the word we are looking for specific type items. Maybe something like the large *stelae* column stolen from Edzna,” offered Dr. Rose. “When Dr. Sarra and his thugs bite, you arrest them and put them out of business,” he suggested enthusiastically.

“For this all to work, someone must penetrate his network. I will go undercover and set up the sting,” offered Hannah.

“Hannah, this is not a ‘Tomb Robbers’ movie. Traffickers are hardened criminals who think nothing of killing anyone who gets in their way or interferes with their business,” Lauren warned. “I believe a qualified agent would be better on this assignment.”

“I’m an archaeologist by training. I know the players and the objects they seek,” Hannah supported her offer to assist.

“Seriously, you have identified one mastermind, Sarra. You are acquainted with him and might be able to get close enough to gather intelligence. I may need your help at the beginning of this case,” Agent Lauren admitted.

Dr. Rose’s face creased with a deeply concerned look. “The museum is in. We will do whatever it takes, but I don’t like the direction this conversation about undercover work is going. Hannah, you are set in your field, you are golden. I don’t want you getting involved in something illegal that could tarnish your reputation, not to mention the grave danger involved. As much as we all want to stop major antiquity theft, it doesn't make sense for you to take personal risks."

"Don't worry. I won't take any unnecessary chances."

That statement deepened Dr. Rose's concern. He knew Hannah was engrained with the Mexican sense of fate. She was really saying, 'if something happens there is nothing we can do about it, so there is no point in worrying about it.'

That night over a spaghetti dinner, Hannah brought her dad up to speed on the discovery of Dr. Sarra as a key dealer in the antiquity smuggling activities.

"This treachery grates on me in so many ways," she fumed.

"Think of Sarra like sandpaper. He may scratch and hurt you over and over, but when its done, you'll end up polished and he'll end up useless," Max declared.

She told her dad about the plan to lure the thieving director into a trap so U.S. Customs could shut down his trafficking network.

"Be very careful. Dr. Sarra is a smart man, even if the bent of his genius is a very crooked one. Don't jump into this dangerous venture without a good strategy and backup. 'Saddle your plans before you ride them' is probably what Joseph would tell you. Have you talked to him or Roberto and Mari about this?"

"I emailed all of them from the university library, not my work or private computer. I don't want to put too much about our secret mission in writing. No answer from anyone yet. Joseph is at his remote valley vineyards. Like in my fieldwork, sometimes there is little or no satellite connection for long stretches of time. Hopefully when he calls or comes for his visit next month, we'll celebrate a successful operation," she told her dad.

"I agree with Dr. Rose. I am concerned about your safety. I know you want to be part of the sting and blister this scoundrel. But don't pick up something you can't put down, baby girl."

CHAPTER 86

Los Angles, California
Present Day

In their strategy meeting at the museum, Agent Lauren began, "Art is currency. Cartels use valuable art and artifacts as collateral for loans to buy drugs, weapons and operate their illicit trafficking businesses. Stolen antiques are easier than suitcases of cash."

"The avid collectors, like the bibliopiles my dad told me about, accumulate immense wealth to acquire whatever they want. But on top of that, all of them have specific visions of their ultimate collection. This single-minded obsession drives them," Hannah added to the profile.

"If we find out what Dr. Sarra or his clients want the most, we can use that knowledge to lure him into dealing with the museum. When he does, we will come down on him," promised Lauren.

Dr. Rose spread out his arms with a sweeping motion around their setting. "As the first step of your agency's sting plan, I can extend an official invitation from one museum director to another to visit this place. When can you be set up with surveillance?"

"It can't be complex or Sarra will spot it a mile away. Something simple in your office or the laboratory," calculated Lauren.

During their planning session, Dr. Rose called Dr. Samuel Sarra. He accepted the curator's invitation to a private lunch and tour of the renoun Natural History Museum.

The following Friday Sarra arrived early and walked through the exhibits with the curator. Rose could see his colleague from Mexico was impressed with the quality and extent of the collections and their presentation. A catered lunch in the terrace sunroom outside the executive office went well. Topics ranged from museum training to more specifics about recent acquisitions.

Once their plates had been cleared, Dr. Rose leaned forward to Sarra and confided, "We have a major exhibit coming up this fall. We'll feature current and recently purchased pre-Columbian Maya artifacts," the curator shared. "However, I need a focus piece with punch," he sighed. "You understand how important it is to wow the patrons and public. That's how we keep our jobs and get more donations." Sarra nodded in collusion as one executive to another.

"Ideally, I am envisioning something like a magnificent carved monument, right in the center of the main hall." Dr. Rose was making bold hand gestures to indicate the size and awe he wanted. "Something with feathers and glyphs and jaguar markings," he said with mounting excitement. Director Rose was really getting into his part of subtly asking for Hannah's 'Big Red' statue from the Edzna ruins without saying it directly.

"We sold some of our overstock and could pay generously for such a piece," he said, hoping Dr. Sarra would take the bait.

A large smile filled Sarra's face as he counted on the six-digit figure he could ask for the Edzna stelae. The stone statue was already in his Los Angeles warehouse. Now he wouldn't need to search for a private collector or sit on it.

"I may have just the thing for your dramatic showing. I will forward some photographs and descriptions. This will be a high ticket item, but well worth it, I assure you," Sarra promised.

Dr. Rose was pleased that his performance drew a positive response and possible recovery of the stolen warrior king statue.

"Whatever your price, I can get it," he further encouraged Sarra to reveal his possession of the missing treasure.

"Did you say the museum was selling some of its inventory?" inquired Dr. Sarra, always on the lookout for more products. "I'd like to see if there is anything of interest for our National Museum of Anthropology."

"Certainly. Let me call Dr. Char. She is in charge of the archaeology department's de-accessioning this year."

Dr. Rose rang Hannah and invited her to his office. That was her cue to renew acquaintance with Dr. Sarra and, if possible, once again get inside his confidences for information.

Hannah's feeling for the man had deteriorated from admiration to disgust. But for their recovery plan to work she would act as if all was forgiven and well between them. Her hands felt clammy and her stomach did somersaults, but she put on a smile and joined the two museum directors in Dr. Rose's large office.

"Dr. Char, Hannah Char?" asked Sarra. "Delightful." He'd not heard she had relocated or that she worked at the LA Museum.

"*Our association and working relationship may have ended on a sour note, but like the other times we disagreed I am confident I can charm her back into helping me,*" he thought. He gloated at his good luck of having Hannah in charge of a major museum's inventory. He was already thinking up ways to use her to get what he wanted.

"My dear Hannah, you look more beautiful than ever," Sarra said as they walked down the museum's marble halls to the storage rooms and between stacked shelves. In the past he convinced her to believe herself privileged to be at his side. But that was when her heart and head knew no better.

For a moment Hannah wasn't sure she could go through with the charade. She almost visibly cringed when he put his hand up to touch her shoulder. She felt like screaming or running, or both.

Thankfully, the mischievous Dr. Jay Rizna purposefully brought scores of pornographic Inca ceramic pots forward. Lining row after row on the shelves rested ancient men grabbing their oversized phalluses and lovers coupling in various positions. This inside joke kept Hannah from fleeing and made her laugh.

"It seems our South American collections grow larger each year," she punned.

"My family has extensive land holdings in Peru and Columbia," Dr. Sarra informed her. "There is renewed interest in those countries' archaeological findings."

Knowing that Dr. Sarra favored, and even coveted pre-Columbian Jaina Island burial figurines, Hannah intentionally led him over an aisle and lingered near a spectacular example of Classic Maya ceramics. The chosen lure was a sacred ball player, posed in his semi-squatted position. The statue's detailed clay muscles were taut and he looked ready to slam rubber balls down court. Bright blue and red paints still clung to the lifelike player's uniform.

"Now this specimen catches my eye," said Sarra.

The team figured it would and placed it in his path on purpose.

"Something so remarkable would be a 'must have' for the finest collection. But, it is one of the museum attendees' favorites and not for sale," said Hannah. She enjoyed watching the man passionately lust over something his money could not buy.

"I want this piece. Certainly, in your position, you could influence decisions and let it return to Mexico with me," Sarra said. He raised her hand to his lips and kissed it.

His touch felt creepy, like spider webs on her skin that she wanted to brush off immediately. She forced herself to endure the cold grasp of his fingers entwined with hers.

"Well, I don't know…" she played him along.

"Maybe this will help you decide." Sarra took a double strand diamond and emerald bracelet out of his suit pocket and placed it around Hannah's trembling wrist. She looked down at the glittering jeweled band.

"What kind of man carries a diamond and emerald bracelet in his pocket?" she blurted out.

"One who is ready for any opportunities to acquire what he wants," Sarra smiled.

"*One who might need to make a fast get away is more like it*," whispered Hannah under her breath.

"I told you I have connections in South America. Columbians have the best emeralds, don't you agree," he said, turning her arm so that the deep green stones sparkled in the light. Hannah knew for the sting operation to work, she had to accept his attentions and favors graciously no matter how undesired.

"We will discuss arrangements regarding payment and shipping of your new art piece, Dr. Sarra," Hannah said as pre-arranged.

"*Yes, he took the bait*." She hoped Jay and the customs agent, hidden behind boxes a row over, got recordings and photographs of the whole proceeding, especially the blatant bribery.

"Let's seal our deal over dinner tomorrow night. I have been invited to a fundraiser and insist you be my date. Wear your new bracelet, darling," added Sarra as they left the antiquities collection storeroom.

Hannah nodded outwardly, but internally cringed at his assumption that she would go with him and do whatever he asked. She had never been one of those codependent women who thought that controlling behavior was sexy. In fact, when he ordered her around, it had the opposite effect. He utterly turned her off. But for this assignment she would play along like an obedient girl, smiling to stay in his good graces.

"I'm so glad we can put past misunderstandings behind us and move forward. I'm sure you understand the pressure I was under to dismiss you. Nothing personal," Sarra said as they parted.

Hannah just nodded. "*How can he almost destroy my career and life and then casually dismiss it by saying 'nothing personal'? This narcissist mistakes my faked co-operation as forgiveness*," she fumed as she waved goodbye.

Officer Lauren congratulated Dr. Rose and Hannah on their first encounters with the target.

"Trained archaeologists working with our criminology department seems just what this operation needed," Lauren said, pleased with the outcome.

In spite of the success, Hannah looked distraught. "Do I have to go out with him tomorrow night? I don't know if I can keep up the false front. I loath the man and all he stands for," she wailed.

"You don't have to do anything you are uncomfortable with. We can find other ways to track his movements and identify his contacts. But, I worry that at this point strangers might spook him," cautioned Lauren.

"Okay, I'll go tomorrow night. I'll see if I can get you any leads to follow up on." Hannah said. "He invited me to a big society gala at the Beverly Wilshire Hotel. What a woman has to do for her country and career," she joked, trying to bolster her courage.

The hotel ballroom was packed with Los Angeles high society, movie stars, and others who flew in from all over the globe for what was touted as the party of the year. The Who's Who and Blue Bookers were in attendance. Paparazzi cameras flashed all night.

Customs Service had outfitted Hannah in a stunning floor-length dark green St. John knit gown from their seizures and forfeitures department. It matched the emerald bracelet she'd been instructed to wear. Dr. Sarra looked like he just stepped out of the pages of GQ in his Armani tuxedo. They made a striking couple.

Hannah played her role as arm decoration to the handsome director as she had in the past. At one point he leaned over and kissed her lightly. Hannah noticed that his eyes were open and wandering. Mari warned her "never trust a man who looks anywhere else when he kisses you."

Dr. Sarra seemed pleased to show her off to acquaintances and business associates. She overheard him mention her credentials and position at the museum, probably using her prestige to solicit new clients for his nefarious trades.

He mingled and worked the room in his usual fashion. He both expected and responded to adoration and flattery. Sarra talked to practically everyone but Hannah. By the end of the evening, if she had asked him, he would not have been able to tell her one new thing about herself or her thoughts. Yet, he commented on what a wonderful time they had and insisted she join him the next night for dinner in his private suite. It fascinated Hannah how ego distorted facts.

CHAPTER 87

Los Angeles, California
Present Day

"Hey, you looked great last night," whistled Jay Rizna. "I saw photos of you and Sarra in an LA Times' spread about the gala."

"Seems everyone has. I received several emails with comments. Here's an odd one…" she said slowly as she read.

"Oh my god!" Hannah shouted through clenched fists over her mouth. Her eyes stood wide open in shock.

"What is it?" asked Jay. He scooted his chair over and read the message out loud. "*Looks like you each dodged a bullet. Now you make up two perfect couples*," the subject line read.

Two photographs were attached. One featured Hannah and Sarra arm-in-arm at the ball. The second picture grabbed Hannah's attention. It showed a newspaper photograph of Joseph and another woman on horseback looking adoringly at one another. The New Zealand news header caption said "Italian Stallion and English Thoroughbred to be wed. Joseph Julian Comouche and Mary Rose Drake…" The society column article cut off in copying.

"Mary and Joseph, for christsake!" swore Jay. "Isn't or wasn't that your boyfriend?" he asked a stunned Hannah.

She couldn't believe what her eyes saw on the screen. She punched copy and printed out the email and attached photographs in color.

"Whoever sent that message to you also copied Joseph," he noted. "So your Italian Stallion is probably having the same sort of reaction about being replaced by Dr. Sarra."

"But I'm not dating Dr. Sarra. This is just undercover work. Joseph should know better."

"How would he know? Have you talked or emailed since this covert operation started?

"I sent him an brief update but couldn't very well give confidential sting operation details away online. Besides, he's working in remote locations. He was supposed to be back last week. I guess he's still out of touch."

"Oh really? Out of touch?" said a skeptical Jay. "Sounds like an excuse to avoid telling you what is really going on down under," he dropped his voice two octaves on the last two words.

A thousand thoughts ran through Hannah's head all at once. When one has no solid information, one imagines stuff to fill the void. Most of Hannah's inventions were not positive. She needed to talk to Joseph and clear this up. Despite time differences, she dialed his cell. It rang and rang, out of range. The message box was full. She sent him an email to contact her as soon as he returned.

She went back to her computer and pulled up the complete online article about the engaged couple. Even referring to him in those terms made her hands shake and her stomach tighten. The society page tidbit was the usual gush about how the purebred bride's family felt to be uniting two outstanding New Zealand bloodlines.

"Too many similes about horse breeding for my taste," Hannah joked with Jay to lighten the serious darkness enfolding her. "I just want Joseph to answer and tell me what is happening."

She took the grainy photograph she'd printed and folded it in half, with Mary tucked under. She studied Joseph's face and traced his profile with her trembling finger until it smudged the ink.

Hannah wondered why he looked younger in the picture. "*Maybe he's happier and more relaxed at home.*"

Hannah tried to focus on work but stared out the window or repeatedly checked inboxes and telephone for messages.

"I'm going home early to prepare for my last evening with Dr. Sarra. I must become an actress playing a role, because I don't want to be myself in his world. As much as I dread the deceptions, I want more than ever to beat him at his own crooked game," she told Dr. Rose.

At home she confided in her dad and showed him the emailed announcement and photo of Joseph with Mary.

"Doesn't feel right. Something is off. It's not an official announcement, only society gossip. Don't believe all you read in the papers or online. Verify first," Max advised.

Hannah joined Sarra in his hotel suite. It contained more square meters than her dad's whole house. He'd ordered room service and they dined elegantly on pressed duck, wild rice, and sautéed vegetables. Flamed crème brule was served as dessert.

Hannah usually enjoyed a glass of cold Sauvignon Blanc wine. But tonight it blazed a fiery path down her throat. The drink did not relax her or remove the rancid taste of fear from her mouth.

After dinner, Sarra brought out numerous papers for her to sign regarding his purchase of the Maya ballplayer figurine. She played along as instructed.

"Transfer of funds will follow to the account noted on the documents. I must insist on certifications on museum stationery, you understand," he said with a businesslike handshake.

Completing purchase of a coveted piece put Sam Sarra in a festive mood. Wine began to flow. He swept Hannah up to dance to a musical series of Latin beats piped into his quarters.

"*Being in his arms is the last thing I want tonight. Any physical contact reminds me too much of Joseph. Why doesn't he call?*" Hannah fretted.

Sarra did not notice her distress or reluctance to celebrate with him. She was relieved when he got a call and took it in the far back bedroom behind closed doors.

Upon arrival, Hannah had noticed several boxes and crates stacked against a wall in the second bedroom. She slipped in and carefully pulled back a blanket covering the stash. Two of the longer crates were labeled 'dry fish'. She doubted the director could eat that much fish in a year. They were sealed so she couldn't see the contents, only some shipping labels. Hoping that was enough, she snapped photographs on her phone. She recovered the boxes, went into the bathroom, and emailed them to Lauren.

Hannah used the facilities and washed her nervous sweating hands twice before she exited. Sarra was standing right by the door.

"Are you alright?" he showed concern. Whether it was for her or his property, she could not tell.

"Sure, just a bit too much wine after a long day at the museum. Speaking of the museum, do you want to see some more artifacts? I put aside other outstanding pieces you might like." She needed to distract him from her presence in the same room as his loot. She didn't look at the crates as she took his arm to exit the bedroom.

The next morning at the museum, Hannah, Dr. Rose and a group of U.S. Customs officers held a strategy session.

"I am not cut out for cops and robbers action," she confessed to Officer Lauren. "I was so nervous, I thought I'd faint or get sick."

"What you sent us last night helped immensely. It gives my agents the element of surprise for raids on the address label destinations. Good job, Hannah."

"Steady on," Dr. Rose advised Hannah. "Your assignment is to bait the trap, not to spring it."

Lauren prepared Dr. Rose and her officers for Sarra's promised delivery of Edzna's *stelae* monument. They had his signature on incriminating documentary evidence already, but wanted to nab him in person. U.S. Customs didn't want anything to go array.

Even though so much else was going on, Hannah monitored her emails several times a day. She'd received no response from Joseph all week so decided the wedding announcement must be true. She reluctantly grew to accept the fact that he moved on, for whatever reasons, and she would have to let him go. Disappointment and disillusion seemed to have a penchant for taking her by surprise.

She spoke to Mari on a Skype call. It comforted her just to see her dear friend's face and hear her voice.

"Mari, he won't even answer my messages. It is tearing me apart inside. I found that a breaking heart isn't loud like shattering glass; it is as quiet as a falling leaf. And the most painful part is that no one really hears it except me," Hannah sobbed, in need of Mari's motherly hugs.

"It is okay to cry. He is worth crying over," Mari said. "Every tear will wash away some of the pain."

"I can't forget him. He gave me so much to remember. I will always be faithful to Joseph---if that is the right word for saying that he will be the standard by which I gage any relationships I may have in the future. My only regret is that I believed he loved me."

"Joseph loved you and still does I'm sure. Deep feelings like his for you can't be erased. There is more behind this story than we know."

"I'll never see him again," Hannah wailed.

"There is no 'never', my dear, just long periods of 'not yet'."

"I promise I will not cause problems or try to win him back from Mary. Any plan that involves hurting others frightens me off. I could never base my own happiness on someone else's sorrow. To want the best for him whether it includes me or not will be my final expression of love."

"You will get through this bump in the road and be stronger for it," Mari offered soft words of comfort for Hannah's wounded spirit.

"Oh Mari, my dear healer, when I fell down you gave me sour orange for the bump on my head. Where is the sour orange balm for my heart now?"

Hannah sent a farewell and final note to Joseph. "*Congratulations on your nuptials. I wish you only the best. I will never regret what we had or loving you. Forever, Hannah.*"

CHAPTER 88

Los Angeles, California
Present Day

The Maya, like the Chinese, believed jade thwarted the corruption of death. Sarra called and asked Hannah to bring him the extremely rare carved jade necklace he'd seen during their tour of the museum collections.

The next morning she left work with the precious artifact and drove it straight to his hotel. She arrived about fifteen minutes earlier than arranged. Noticing the suite door was not all the way closed, Hannah slipped into the living room. About to call out and announce her presence, she spied Sarra and Father Batz through a crack in the master bedroom door.

The priest massaged the neck and shoulders of his friend. Leaning against the other man's back, he seemed consumed by the nearness and touching. Hannah stayed quiet and pressed against the wall to avoid being seen.

The two men moved over to a work desk. An antique cracked painting lay spread out, corners held down by four books. Hannah inched closer to get a look. Her eyes widened at the distinctive style and natural colors used by her lady artist that sprang from the canvas. A lily symbol in the corner confirmed it to be one of the series she'd been searching for. Depicted on the old pigment painting were the artist's distinctive Madonna and a likeness of the fair-skinned Franciscan monk Hannah remembered from murals and pottery in Ek Balam. The three-dimensional faces were the same, no mistake.

"Our brotherhood is proud of you Samuel. This is the third artifact of this type that you alone have uncovered. Finds like this are the reason the church trained you and supports you in your current position. You have been chosen for a sacred task," Batz said as he fingered his gold crucifix.

"This painting is so beautiful. It is almost a shame to destroy it," said Sarra. "This incident happened almost five hundred years ago. What harm could evidence of the martyr's story do at this point?" he asked.

"Don't go weak on us now. Consider the uproar if the world learned of this saint, this possible second coming. And, God forbid, accusations that our faith's own inquisitors and priest killed him. Think Samuel!" Batz shouted. "It would shake the foundations of the church and all we hold dear." He was angered by Sarra's hesitation and recent doubts, so he continued.

"Imagine the repercussions on religion and our control of the masses," asserted the priest. "The Virgin of Guadalupe appeared in 1531 near Mexico City to announce a messiah's coming in the New World. This holy man in the picture had his ministry of kindness and healing ended by De Landa. All evidence of his existence and death by priests' hands must be eliminated."

To emphasis his point, Batz flicked open a razor-sharp box cutter and slashed at the Madonna. Hannah almost cried out. The gaping downward cut on the painting looked like a teardrop on the Virgin's face.

"Our brethren have received reports of other portraits and script in Peru," said Sarra. "We can't suppress them all."

"We will go to South America or wherever to take care of any evidence. Anything can be easily destroyed or hidden, especially the truth." Batz ended the discussion by lifting up the director's hand and kissed a signet ring on the little finger. "We are servants of a great cause."

Hannah silently backed out of the hotel suite. She mentally sorted through all she heard and caught her breath. She knew for certain that her decision to rebury the pottery and mural paintings she'd discovered at Ek Balam was well founded. It was more important than ever to protect these items.

But right now she had to pretend for another day. When the hooligans were arrested, she would return to work in the Yucatan and report the whole truth. She tiptoed back to the suite entrance. The two men came out of the bedroom, surprised to see her standing there.

"I'm here. I brought the necklace you wanted to see," she swung about and said in as innocent cheerful a voice as she could muster.

Batz announced, "I was just leaving." He gave Hannah his coldest up and down stare, nostrils flaring like an animal on the prowl.

"Give my greetings to Christina when you see her," she said to the departing back of Father Batz. She couldn't help herself to get a dig in before he left. She should've known better than to insult a jaguar before she was out of his jungle.

Conversation between Sarra and Hannah seemed more stilted than usual. He visibly brightened when she removed the ancient jade necklace from its velvet container.

"Model it for me," he ordered.

Hannah put the heavy stone collar around her neck. It felt cold to the touch, but soon pulled in her body warmth. Sarra moved toward Hannah like a man in a trance. As he stoked her throat and the ancient stones, he swayed and moaned softly. Pieces of greenish blue jade, engraved with floral patterns and glyphs by carvers who had been dead for a millennium, excited him more than the live feminine woman who wore the jewels. Hannah dared not move until he returned to his senses.

"I definitely must own this treasure," he informed her. She removed the jade necklace slowly and put it into its satin lined box.

"I will prepare documents as you like them. Dr. Rose can turn this prize over to you when you see him on Monday," she said to further entice him to step into the sting trap.

"I am going to wash up," said Hannah, wanting to scrub off his touch and compose herself after the strange revelations.

"Certainly, my dear. Stay for a celebration brunch with me."

Hannah didn't respond. She wanted to get away as soon as she could. While in the restroom, she realized her phone was in her purse on the sofa. So she picked up the room extension receiver to call Dr. Rose regarding the necklace and her progress. Men on the line argued loudly.

"She knows too much," a raspy voice insisted.

"I can handle her," replied Sarra.

"Too late for that. We will take care of her like we did Teresa. No one will ever suspect. Another accident---the hand of god."

Hannah covered her mouth to stop an audible gasp. "*Father Frank was telling the truth. Churchmen murdered his wife*," she realized. "*I am next on their hit list.*"

"We will take care of this problem immediately."

"Bring me the jade necklace," was Sarra's only response to the contract on her life.

Hannah took three deep breaths to calm down and walked quickly toward the front door.

"I can't stay after all. See you Monday," she said over her shoulder. She couldn't face Sarra, knowing that predatory animals sensed if you were weak or frightened. She was both.

She scurried for the elevator, punching the button several times. On her way through the lobby, she could have sworn she saw the tall robber who stabbed her. Not waiting to check this disturbing fact, she walked faster down to the parking garage. She had her keys ready to get away. She put the car in reverse. Suddenly a hand reached through the open window and grabbed her arm.

"You aren't going to leave without a good-bye kiss are you?" Dr. Sarra said with a charming smile.

"Sorry," replied Hannah and leaned over to receive the first real kiss he'd ever given her.

Hannah sped away from the luxury hotel into a perfect southern California sunlit day. She couldn't wipe her mouth enough to get that kiss of Judas off her lips and off her mind.

CHAPTER 89

Los Angeles, California
Present Day

Hannah's head was spinning after overhearing Sarra and the mystery voice agree to kill her for knowing more than she should. She took an alternate route, longer than normal to throw off any possible tail and have time to think up a plan. She dare not go home and bring danger to her father. It would be among the first places they would look for her.

"*I'll probably be safer in the bustling halls of the public museum. Maybe Officer Lauren will be there to protect me,*" she pondered her options.

When Hannah arrived at the museum, she parked in a different lot and took a back entrance so noone would see her enter. Dr. Rose and Lauren were not in. The secretary said they'd gone to the Customs office downtown. Only Jay sat at his desk translating Egyptian hieroglyphs etched on amulets from a mummy wrapping.

Hannah ran up to him and blurted out what happened at Dr. Sarra's suite. The whole story, with all the crazy details about the saint and priestly brotherhood destroying evidence, and a hit contract on her life gushed out in high-pitched rapid fire.

"Are you hysterical? I'm not keen on slapping women," said a stunned Jay. He'd never seen Hannah in such an agitated state.

"I'm just trying to tell you everything at once. This sting isn't about antiquity theft alone. They want to kill me for knowing too much about church corruption, the 1500s saint's appearance in the Yucatan and their involvement," she cried out.

"Unbelievable. I mean I believe you. It isn't out of the question for the Vatican to find a way to get rid of any witnesses or written proof of a martyr they neutralized," he agreed.

"We need to stop them from destroying evidence. Set the record of what happened back then straight," she said frantically.

"The record is never straight," Jay replied. "Victors always rewrite the record of history anytime it doesn't suit them. To force them right now would expose you and your loved ones for nothing. Hannah, you should have stuck to digging up old bones instead of old sins."

"These people after me are every bit as dangerous as I was warned. They have seemingly endless resources to accomplish their ends."

Jay nodded, "What can I do to help?"

"I have to get away and hide until these guys are caught. Please take me to the bank for my passport and cash. I will put more documentation in the safety deposit box. In case I don't escape, their sins will be exposed one way or the other," she pledged. "If anything happens to me, all the specifics of crimes and corruption are to be sent to authorities, archdiocese, newspapers, and social media," she instructed Jay.

"Please book me the next flight to Mexico. Use your credit card and I will pay you in cash. I finally get a ride in your fancy sports car with the Hotep plates." Hannah tried to sound casual, but she was terrified. She left Jay her phone with the chip removed, computer, keys, and cards.

"Hide all this in the museum stacks till I get back. Tell Dr. Rose and Officer Lauren all the situation details. They will have to find a way to cover my disappearance. I don't want to jeopardize the sting operation. Last, but not least, please check in regularly with my dad and see that he is okay."

At the bank she put the coveted jade necklace into her safe deposit box just for spite. "*Sarra will never have this.*"

Hannah used Jay's phone to call her dad at the university library. She tried not to sound as frightened as she felt. She briefly told him about the latest developments. "The information about the thefts, corruption and abuse of power is written out and in my bank box. I can't tell you or anyone else where I am going until it is safe again. Dad, I love you bunches."

"Why do insist on taking the hardest path?" Jay asked as they drove to the airport.

"Why do you assume I see two paths?" Hannah replied.

By afternoon siesta time, Hannah had stopped at Berto and Mari's home in Merida to discard her city clothes and jewelry. She retrieved some of her belongings left there and purchased other basic field goods to see her through a forced retreat. She told them all about the sting operation, what she'd heard regarding the Franciscan friar, and the death threat against her.

"All the museum's and my efforts to help the U.S. Customs Agency will probably stop or put a big dent in Sarra's antiquity theft network. That feels like a big win," Hannah gloated.

"And this new information gives us insight into his various reasons for plunder and the church's drive to destroy evidence of a saint killed during De Landa's inquisition. This incident is one of the secret messages our Maya artist repeatedly sent to us," Hannah said. "More so than ever, we have to preserve the articles we found and then tell the world about them."

"The truth alone about the martyred priest could cause the church irreparable harm. Of course they need to stop it," added Roberto.

"I could see Sarra's loyalty waiver for a moment between his God and his Church," said Hannah.

"They are not necessarily one and the same you know," said Roberto.

"Then Sarra buckled under and agree to have me eliminated to protect their secret and his way of life," she lamented. "My enemies are more wicked and powerful than I thought."

"Right now you just need to stay hidden and safe," advised Maria. "Evil may set out to corrupt, but in the end it is ultimately self-destructive."

"As many tentacles as the Vatican may put out, they will never bury or destroy all the evidence or witnesses to such a truth," said Roberto.

Her friends' dedication to preserving true history and their faith in a victory of good over evil comforted Hannah as she boarded a bus for Valledolid and then on to Ek Balam pueblo. When the sun dropped below the horizon she was swinging in a hammock at Kate's off-grid, organic farm.

CHAPTER 90

New Zealand
Present Day

Joseph finally returned from his most distant vineyard. His boot treads were caked with mud. Green vegetation marks stained his work shirt. His trip took much longer than expected. He wanted two things, first, a long-overdue hot bath and then to talk to Hannah. After washing up, he called but got no response. Next he checked emails. They'd really piled up in his three-week absence. He took the dispatches in chronological order. Several long ones had arrived from Hannah up to two weeks ago, then nothing.

"That's odd," he puzzled. Her first batch chatted about enjoying museum work, fun stories about staff, helping her dad with bookbinding projects and his garden, disappointment at museum policies on purchases and sales, and then something cryptic about covert efforts to stop antiquity theft. It came from a different return address at her father's university library. Hannah's notes were filled with intimate memories and signed off with love. Just reading her correspondence made him long for her.

Then Joseph noticed an email marked with a red urgent flag. It had been sent to both Hannah and him. Curious, he began reading, "*Looks like you each dodged a bullet. Now you make up two perfect couples.*"

A newsprint picture of Hannah and Sarra arm-in-arm appeared at first glance to be vestiges of an old flame rekindled. It felt unreal to him. But when he saw the four-year-old photograph of himself and Mary Drake on horseback with the caption "Italian Stallion and English Thoroughbred to be wed," Joseph went berserk.

"*What are Mary and her conniving mother up to? I am not marrying her, as much as our neighbor's wife would wish it.*" His mind spun in panic thinking of Hannah seeing this lie.

Joseph grabbed the phone to call his family and try Hannah again to straighten the mess out. But hung up when he decided to finish reading messages, hoping to see that this disaster had resolved itself while he was away at the vineyards.

When he finally talked to his dad, he told him the engagement announcement was retracted. The family had made it clear to Mary Drake and her mother that Joseph would not be part of anyone's social climbing scheme. His father had understood. But then the confusing miscommunications only got more tangled.

"*Who sent the false and damaging message to both of them? Why?*" banged around his head without answers.

He went back to his inbox full of messages. Hannah's last letter tore his heart out. She wrote to congratulate him on his marriage. Although unspoken, he could tell by her short note it was her greatest sacrifice to let him go. As if that was what he wanted. She loved him, he was sure.

"*But, if she believed I was getting married, could she rebound with Dr. Sarra? Would the glamor, money or career move to continue excavations in Mexico tempt her?*" all ran painfully through his head. "*There is something going on and I am going to find out what,*" he vowed.

A long call to Max had Joseph packing as they talked. The situation was worse than Joseph could have imagined. Max told him as much as he knew about the U.S. Customs' sting operation she'd gotten involved in. Hannah, with a threat to her life, had intentionally disappeared, not even telling her own father where she was going into hiding.

"Max, I can't bear the thought that she is out there alone, in danger and believes I married someone else. I am on the next flight to Los Angeles."

It frightened Joseph to realize how quickly things could go wrong.

CHAPTER 91

Ek Balam, Yucatan
Present Day

Hannah's escape was guided by principles of mobility and improvising. She chose to protect herself by returning to the cocooning green depths of the jungle. Raw, primitive elemental isolation safeguarded her in the tropical rainforest of the Yucatan.

She camped on Kate's two hundred hectare farm in a small house built out of handmade adobe bricks. The casita consisted of one rectangular room. Inside only had space for Hannah's hammock and mosquito net for sleeping, a rickety plastic folding table and two low wooden chairs. Clothes and a backpack hung on pegs or ropes suspended from ceiling rafters.

Most of the time she sat under the attached covered patio, writing at a table made from an old wooden door and three saw horses. An outhouse stood in the far corner of the clearing. When she wanted a bath, she sat on a stool and dipped water from a large plastic pail. She had two practical white cotton *huipiles*. She would wear one wash one. This worked well in the jungle heat and did not require much effort on her part.

"My own Walden Pond, but without the pond," she'd jested with Kate when she got permission to stay.

Hannah cooked on a propane single burner camp stove. When she felt hungry, she walked through the plentiful organic gardens to gather beans, squash, corn, lettuce, tomatoes, chaya, herbs and various natural produce. Fruit trees provided fresh oranges, papaya, avocados, limes, coconuts, and her favorite, mangos. Chickens and ducks pecked away in the front yard of her hut, but Hannah couldn't bring herself to kill them, not after she'd given them individual names. An oversized cooler kept insects and dogs away from the food, but was a far cry from refrigeration. Hannah hung dried foodstuffs in woven straw baskets suspended from the beams of the open-sided patio.

There was no electrical service on the remote property. When building the casita structure, Kate had placed clear glass bottles filled with water and chlorine, to keep them from getting cloudy, in the ceiling and walls at intervals to provide small tube skylights. The roof bottles were the equivalent of forty-watt light bulbs. It worked fine during the day, but when the jungle night fell as quickly as it always did, Hannah relied on lanterns and candles. A noisy diesel generator turned the squeaky windmill, which pumped more than enough well water for her use and to irrigate the gardens, trees and animals.

Life on the remote farm was minimalist but safe. Hannah helped the local day laborer with watering, weeding and transplanting as needed. She especially enjoyed caring for two mischievous burros named, Frida and Diego. Scrawny rescue dogs, with free run of the place until Kate placed them, accompanied her everywhere.

An independent orange cat visited occasionally. The scruffy feline wouldn't take Hannah's food offerings. Instead it hunted for rodents and reptiles, taking its prey to the privacy under her porch. Hannah burst into laughter when she saw the cat with a lizard's tail hanging like an old shoelace from its mouth.

Hannah had gone into total isolation. Kate came by each week or so to harvest food for the lodge and bring basic supplies. She'd briefly report world events, but carried no news of happenings in Los Angeles or from Hannah's loved ones. Kate wouldn't contact them or do anything that might give away the secret location until Hannah felt it was safe to reach out. Her father and others had no way of knowing how to find her. They did not even know of the existence of this hideout. She planned to stay away for at least a month before asking her friend to test the waters.

"Hopefully, Sarra and his trafficking network guys will have been arrested and called off their hit man. I want to go home," she told Kate during one of her farm visits.

Alone on the farm, Hannah had too many hours to fill each day. Time oozed slowly like honey. No matter how rapidly she shook her hands, the sticky days would not drop off or evaporate. Insignificant hours wouldn't cooperate. Smothering time stuck like a swarm of Mari's bees to a tree trunk.

The natural flow of days forced Hannah into a non-workaholic state of mind. A day without clock hours became calming. Most of her life she'd gone to school fulltime and worked, so living without schedules, assignments or deadlines seemed foreign to her brain. She missed having a strict sense of purpose and direction. Routines and rituals helped her feel secure.

To avoid curling up in a shell of boredom or loneliness, Hannah busied herself by exploring the lush jungle forest grounds. Once she followed a deer down a trail until it narrowed to nothing. Overhead the trees closed their arms and blocked out the sun. Steamy, wet-earth smells of the tropical forest filled her nostrils. She tripped over a gnarled root that hugged a carved stone. It was just Hannah's luck to discover archaeological ruins near the back property line. Discovery and excavation were as natural to her as water on a frog's face. Over the next few days she roughly surveyed the dilapidated residential structure and attempted a small test pit. Anything to keep her hands and mind occupied.

Growing up in America, the feminists of her era said, 'You can be anything', but Hannah heard the message as, 'You have to be everything'. In the past, she'd pushed herself to be meticulous and compulsive about everything, but being reflective alone in the jungle, she analyzed her motives and insecurities. She realized that a life in overdrive was all about fear. Hannah had feared making mistakes, failure, or disappointing others. Imperfection, rejection or abandonment had been entwined serpents for her.

Trying to maintain her perfectionist ways in such a chaotic natural setting was a sobering lesson. She learned the difference between healthy striving and the perfectionism that had been sold to her as a virtue. Now she was okay just to do something until it was right. Flawless was not possible, mistakes were part of being human.

Hannah read every book Kate brought to her, twice. She even read a children's book of fairy tales. It appealed to her, not because she thought dragons were real, but because it helped her believe that dragons and bad guys could be defeated. But life didn't have the neat and happy endings she found in most books. The traumas and heartaches that the heroines in novels went through and survived were just words on print paper. In real life Hannah's emotional pain hurt more than the stabbing the looter inflicted. But recent assaults were not deflected by bone.

Hannah's neatly kept world that she'd cherished had reared up to confront her with reality and all its irrationality, and messy emotions. She played mental reruns, as though viewing an unending triple feature of the magic and also the unutterable disappointments she'd experienced the last year. Scenes of her field and museum work, time undercover and her love affair were the best and the worst episodes to review. The mind replays what the soul can't delete.

Hannah knew that duality was central to Maya beliefs and this had proven to be the case with Joseph. He had given her the deepest joy, infiltrating the secret fibers of her heart. She had changed just from knowing him. When she least expected it, opposite memories jabbed her with their sharp edges. His absence left a space nothing else could fill and a void inflicting the deepest most painful wound. Loss served as a transforming teacher. Hannah let both positive and negative memories and feelings come and go like visitors.

"*I've experienced both happiness and suffering. Maybe it's not about getting a happy ending; maybe it's being lucky enough to have lived the story. There is no true loss as long as I have memories and knew true love,*" she decided. "*I'll be more serene when I quit hoping for a better past and a different endings.*"

Time and distance also gave Hannah more insight into the illicit antiquity trade and psyche of the criminals she had encountered.

Attempting to understand the motivations and behavior of the others was frustrating, like trying to smell the number red. She realized that good people like her lose because they play by the rules and the bad guys don't. Wicked people lured others in and then mercilessly blindsided them. First she wanted to get even, to destroy them. But following that, she found that her perception had been blurred by vengeance. Angry revenge would make her like the very people she was fighting.

"*The conflict between good and evil is not as straight forward as I once thought. It is more a confrontation between two irreconcilable worldviews. But in our hands always lies the power to choose good.*"

She now had some understanding of why Dr. Sarra's office was so bereft of objects and intimate details. It showed an external emptiness that reflected his internal void. There were no paintings of places or family photographs to bring back memories because he was pledged to turn the past into a blank slate. With lies he got ahead in the world, but he could never go back. People can't be fixed once they are broken in certain ways.

After seeing him hesitate to destroy the painting of the saint, she had remembered what a competent scholar he could be. "*No one is all good or all bad. Everyone moves in and out of light and darkness their entire lives,*" she thought. "*Besides, people can only meet others as deeply as they have met themselves.*"

Knowing that the Catholic Church leaders had their talons deep in him since youth, she saw that many of his choices had been taken away. It made him a little harder to hate. "*Everyone has a chapter in their life story that they don't want anyone to read.*"

Hannah tried to understand Sarra, but she still found it impossible to forgive her old colleague. "*The man coldly approved an order to have me killed. When he kissed me goodbye at my car, he had a chance to warn me, but didn't. He chose evil. So to hell with him!*"

Hannah found 'what ifs' and remorse to be among the heaviest things in the world. Even looking back at the good times made her weep. She indulged in howling rage and what she called 'ugly cries'. But Mari was right, tears were healing and soon they stopped.

"*It's time to create a new way of life*," said her heart.

"*It's about time*," replied her soul.

The present moment and future were given priority after that insight. She decided to deal with the scars of loss in a more proactive way. Her thoughts about future plans were emancipating.

Hannah's focus turned to sketching, making notes, and analyzing details she could remember about her excavation at Ek Balam. She wrote up detailed theories on ancient Maya knowledge and codices being transferred to pottery. She outlined all the scientific evidence she'd found and told the scribe's story as best she could.

"*Forbidden archaeology and threats from the established church be damned. I will expose the hidden secrets. When I return, my purpose will be to present all the solid evidence we've found and let others decide*," she pledged in firm resolve to implement her brave decision.

Kate came out to the farm and spent an entire day with her. It gave Hannah a chance to discuss some new insights and ideas with her world-wise friend.

"As much as I love fieldwork, I can see how being a museum curator or university lecturer would allow me a more balanced life. My experiences with Agent Lauren make me consider forming an antiquity criminology unit. Maybe my knowledge and efforts could impact the looting of archaeological and historical sites and discourage illicit trade in cultural properties." Hannah found goals to be like magnets that attract things to make them come true.

"Being a field archaeologist, you can approach antiquity trafficking from new angles. Maybe you'll even come up with some workable regulatory responses to this problem," Kate affirmed the new options Hannah explored. "Sometimes in the wind of change you find your true direction," she said, sounding like Mari. "You are only a decision away from a different life."

"You know, many times when I thought I was being shut out from something good, I've actually been re-directed to something better. Still I'm a little frightened of change…"

"Don't be scared. Those feelings mean you are about to do something really brave. Reality will move if you just give it a small push." Kate said.

"I'll never forget the lessons these experiences have taught me. I want this hiding exile to be over. I'm ready to get back and move in new directions," Hannah declared.

CHAPTER 92

Ek Balam, Yucatan
Present Day

The day after Kate's visit, Hannah woke up sick, with grabbing pains in her stomach. Her pulse felt more rapid than usual. She hugged herself against small shivers.

"*Maybe a little flu or food poisoning. I've had my shots and took malaria tablets. I'll be better in the afternoon.*"

She drank chamomile tea and rested. By afternoon, she was burning up with fever and her body shook with chills. The sequence went for several days: fever, sweating came on, followed by a few delusive hours of wellbeing, and again the fever with spasms of shivering. The muscles in Hannah's legs knotted up and she'd walk out the cramps. She ached all over, especially her joints. A rash with small red dots developed around her elbows and knees.

It was the splitting headache and distinctive pain behind the eyes that disabled her the most. She couldn't face bright light or lift her head from the hammock without excruciating pain.

"*This must be dengue fever or chikungunka from a mosquito bite,*" she concluded. "*Those stinging devils took loud but invisible tours of my room every night. Kate will be here tomorrow or the next day to help me. I don't even know what day it is,*" she whined through chattering teeth.

Hannah forced herself to eat a few bites of food and drink water to stay hydrated. Her temperature spiked over a hundred and two. She wiped her nose and found it bleeding. She had a day of promising recovery and then again the fever. She couldn't get comfortable. Yet there were times when she woke up and realized she'd slept deeply through the entire day and into the night. Feverish perspiration left dark splotches on her hammock lining sheets.

Hannah was haunted by strange dreams about the lady scribe. The artist's face and beautiful art works swirled through her head like vivid movies. During the day, Hannah sat at the wooden door table and drew the visions and a profusion of symbols on her tablet.

On the eighth night, when the full moon woke her, Hannah stumbled out of her hammock onto the patio. Dizzy and disoriented, she grabbed the edge of the table for support. Something vague inside was pulling her to Ek Balam. Despite her delirium, she pulled on her white huipile, shoes, and her weathered canvas hat. By the fading beam of her small flashlight, she found her way and left the secluded farm.

Hannah staggered down the rutted dirt farm road to a paved section of highway. Two dogs tagged along, but turned back when they felt unfamiliar asphalt under their paws. It was another four kilometers to the archaeological zone. Heat waves rippled off the blacktop. Hannah could feel warmth radiate through her shoes.

The moon with its calm composed face shined boldly, lighting her way. She hypnotically reeled onward, feverish and swaying down the middle of the empty road. Not a single car went by in the night. They would have thought her lost and drunk. Trees along the roadside were watchful and silent, their limbs reaching into the clear moonlit sky. Bats stitched through the still night air. Distant sounds of pueblo dog packs and other things that came out at night in the jungle to hunt did not distract Hannah from her march to Ek Balam.

At the entrance to the official archaeological ruins, Hannah climbed over the rusty chain linked fence. She knew where she had to go. Heading directly for the small noble residence with the hidden room, Hannah walked through tangled vines, tall grasses and over jagged rocks. She seemed oblivious to scratches and bruises on her feet and legs.

When she reached the rubble-strewn north palace, she collapsed on the sleeping platform by the entrance. The building was as dark and empty as she was. She began to tremble violently. Hair was fever sweat plastered to her face and neck. She used the hat to fan herself and then as a flat pillow. Hannah fell asleep from exhaustion.

She woke with a start when the rising sun's milky light showed through the damaged doorway. Rather than return to the farm, she stumbled to the back of the long main room. Hannah used her shaky bare hands and a large shard of broken pottery to dig and remove marl plaster and stones placed there to disguise the entrance to the hidden room. With a hole just large enough for her to fit through, she crawled on her stomach into the chamber. The close space embraced her with its four walls of colorful art.

"*I'm home. I will be safe here,*" Hannah whispered in feverish delusion.

She lit a beeswax candle they'd left on the shelf and stared through blurred eyes at the wall murals surrounding her. In dim light, the same ancient faces that first greeted her when she discovered the sacred room, smiled back at her again. The young lady noble's likeness held her gaze.

"Elegant face, tragic eyes, there must have been many who loved you. *Bix a k'aabe*, what is your name?" Hannah asked in Mayan. She put her hand up to her throbbing temples, "I could just sit here quietly studying your art until the end." she said with shallow breath. Hannah frowned when thoughts of death crossed her mind. She could hear faint heartbeats measuring out time and felt thirst in her throat and hunger growing in her stomach.

"I'm alive, but so very tired." Her eyelids closed in surrender.

A soft rustling sound rousted Hannah. Her red-rimmed eyes fluttered open. Hannah spotted shadowy movement at the end of the room. A woman in a brightly embroidered shift like hers stood on tiptoes, reaching up to paint the walls, to implant the ancient words. A strange song echoed through the room. Hannah shook her head knowing what she saw and heard was a hallucination or fever dreams. But it seemed so real, and not frightening at all. Hannah sensed that the past and present were occupying the same space and time. It was like circling back in time, as the Maya said all things did.

The artist hummed and chanted as she painted. She stopped and looked over her shoulder in Hannah's direction, smiled but said nothing. The lady gathered her paint pots and brushes and left the room. Hannah thought she heard stones thudding into place, closing where the passage had been.

"If I have to die, this ancient chamber would be a good place to be spend eternity. Buried like a Maya queen surrounded by beauty. Birds and flowers and…" Her hands felt cold; the blood seemed to have left them. She slumped sideways and fell unconscious. Soon the candle flickered out and the room went black.

CHAPTER 93

Xcaret, Quintana Roo
1564 A.D.

Spanish soldiers escorted Itz to the ancient port of Xcaret. They treated the translator artist with respect and let her rest and share a meal under the thatched shelter with the ship's passengers rather than in the wooden corrals holding the other slaves bound for southern destinations.

Prince Tepal watched the travelers' shore gathering from afar. He painfully ground his teeth and kicked a hole in the sand in frustration. When he captured and brought Itz to the church authorities, he expected her to be unmercifully tortured, killed or at least shamefully enslaved. Instead, high-ranking priests praised and rewarded him for discovering such a devoted talent. In private he pulled his hair and screamed to the heavens. Cimi took the brunt of his anger and bled in her stead. Tepal wanted Itz to feel pain and death, not be valued and washed in admiration.

In order to survive, Itz had become masterful at acting pious and cooperative around her captors. She hid her anguish about being separated from her family, true work and love. She wanted to go home. Even as Tepal watched her, she subtly glanced about looking for a way to escape before being forced aboard the ship.

She found an opportunity to slip away from the gathering and walked straight toward the mangroves. In front of her a flock of blue herons started up in fright, then settled back down again. She reached the edge of the clearing. Her knees and hands quaked, afraid the embarkation group would see her fleeing.

Like a black ghost appearing from nowhere, a hand grasped her forearm and spun her around. Chills ran up into the center of her chest. Fear made her heart go cold. Without raising her head up, Itz knew Tepal had her in his gripe. She glared up into his eyes. Taking Itz by the shoulders he shook her so hard her hair came loose from its topknot bun.

"If they won't kill you, I will," he threatened.

He pulled a double-edged obsidian blade from his waistband sheaf. The morning sun reflected off the deadly 'hand of god' dagger that had once been used for sacrifice in the old temples. His eyes were dark pools of hatred and lust combined.

"Today is the solar equinox. The gods will be pleased if I offer them such a gift on this auspicious sacred calendar day," he gloated. He started an ancient slurred chant.

Itz felt the shock of vivid memories of blood-smeared priests who had almost sacrificed her in her youth. She wrestled from his grasp, dropped to the ground and rolled over and over out of reach. This odd action surprised Tepal long enough for her to crawl, and then run back to the beach and waterfront. People turned toward the disheveled Itz approaching. Tepal dared not follow to complete his fatal mission.

"I will find you and kill you," he swore as she sprinted away.

Itz stood trembling close to the water's edge. Gray-green seaweed bounced in the sunny shallows. Waves hissed as they rolled across the sand and dissipated before washing over her feet. Sadly, getting on the ship was her only way to escape certain death at the madman's hands.

Questions about Itz's rush from the mangrove forest were interrupted by the hustle and confusion of boarding. The ship was loaded with passengers in time to catch the winds and outgoing tide. Weathered sailors pulled up massive iron anchors and shouted. Their voices competed with the shrill calls of circling seagulls that screamed their disdain at the world in general.

The vessel strained and groaned against strong cross breezes and surging channel currents. Itz watched tearfully from the upper deck of the wooden sailing hulk. Heaven's blue bridge of the sea arched toward the unknown. Her Yucatan homeland faded in the horizon. Nothing but water was visible in any direction. They sailed resolutely over vast turquoise expanses onward to a world absolutely foreign to her.

At one point she saw faint outlines of finger-like barrier reefs to the east. Kan Ik had told her stories about shifting sand bars, narrow channels, strong tides and other hazards on this route.

Itz missed her sea captain, her mate. She could only hope that the paintings she left behind and news of her transport to Peru would reach the ears of her beloved.

"*I can't bear it if he thinks that I chose to leave him. He must know my heart remains true,*" she lamented.

The vessel's journey south was Itz's first time on the Great Waters. The undulating ocean delighted and disturbed her. The first day's waves, taller than a man, crashed over the bow onto the deck. The ship groaned and creaked as it pitched side to side and up and down. She relished the salty taste on her lips from misty sea spray splashing up as they rode the rolling ocean swells.

When they sailed past the island of Cozumel, tonal base sounds of conchs reverberated in the air. She remembered stories of how the island's low buildings had these shells embedded in the seaward walls. When winds reached a certain speed they blew through the seashells and sent warnings to the residents of an impending storm.

The ship's crew awed her with their nautical skills. They raised and lowered cloth sheets they called sails. Fabric tied to a pole caught the breezes and pushed the heavy vessel forward. A strong northeasterly wind caused the sails to billow, smack and crackle with ominous sounds. The experience brought her closer to understanding and sharing the seafaring part of Kan Ik's world.

She struggled to remember and identify the passing landmarks and shorelines tattooed on his body. She closed her eyes and traced similar inked patterns she had memorized from his chest, arms and legs onto the rough wooden rail where she stood every day. The memories in her heart and mind were clearer than the realities of the dangerous voyage. She did not suffer from nausea like many other passengers. Her love of the wide-open sea and sky overrode the physical difficulties of the long journey.

Itz looked up at the stars and prayed. She asked for suffering to be taken away and for protection against anger and rage of emotions. She hoped her own actions could somehow guide sacred decisions and determine her fate. She believed that people, animals and nature were imbued with powers and spiritual potency.

"*After all, as much as we people depend on your graces, my gods, you also require humans like us for prayers, offerings and attention to sustain you.*"

The Maya people believed heaven and earth were linked. Life energy flowed in both directions. This connection and process of reciprocity between gods and man seemed too radical a concept for the Spaniards to comprehend. The conquerors viewed their one God as complete unto himself, transcending creation and not needing humans to survive.

Itz had been taught about a universal cycle. Her teachers told her that the gods needed to be fed the substance of life so they would be strong enough to provide for humans. Without the exchange with people, world order and the very existence of the gods were threatened.

Maya people believed that nourishment flowed in both directions, like a sacred umbilical cord, connecting gods and men. In the people's eyes, when the Catholic priests forbid ancient rituals, they essentially severed the cord and placed the whole nature of the universe in jeopardy. Religious restrictions were at the source of the angst and rebellion against the religious practices of the conquerors.

Even thought the old gods remained silent to her requests, Itz believed that her capacity to love gave meaning to the indifferent universe. She made the choice to see life as beautiful and treat this new reality as an adventure and opportunity.

On board ship, the boundaries and distinctions between Spanish and Indians were blurred for the sake of manning the vessel and cooperation for survival. But Itz never forgot that she was nothing more than trading goods and a gift to be presented to new masters at their destination.

At times she felt helpless, drifting like a ship without wind in its sails, but then she learned to divert currents of her thoughts into deeper, swifter channels. Itz took control of her situation and found ways to make it less frightening. She grew adept at masking trepidation and sorrow, turning negatives into positive actions. She spent hours sketching and perfecting her unique techniques of portraying human faces and spirits through art.

Left behind, Tepal had raised both fists in ragged frustration at Itz's departing vessel. Infuriated by his failure to humiliate or eliminate the woman scribe, he decided to follow her to Peru and finish the task. Tepal renewed his rage against Itz for a long time after the reasons for it had died. In his eyes, killing her became his only passion She had to die if he was to ever feel any emotion at all.

"She must be sacrificed to the gods for me to be free of her curse," he told the battered Cimi. The older priest had again been useful to receive Tepal's cruel outbreaks.

To fund their excursion to South America, together the two stole rare jewels, precious metals and treasures from both hidden ancient temples and Spanish church coffers. Tepal refused to travel without his usual comforts and diversions.

"I will not stop until I find and destroy the witch," Tepal swore.

CHAPTER 94

Lima, Peru
1565 A.D.

Itz had disappeared from Ek Balam's Ixkunil village without a word or trace. Kan Ik had not seen her for days. When her aunt also pleaded concern and ignorance of her whereabouts, he was tormented by uncharacteristic doubts and fleeting notions. It seemed as though Itz had changed her mind about their union. But memories of her face and her essence caused powerful surges of love to rush through him and banish any doubts he had. He and Yaxche asked around the pueblo and area for clues to explain the disappearance. Aching weeks passed with no news.

"I saw the pottery lady pulled behind a giant Spanish dog," a small girl finally told Yaxche.

"A horse?" asked the worried aunt. "Which way did they take her?"

The child pointed toward the main road.

Kan Ik prepared a trading mission as his excuse to visit main towns on the peninsula. His purpose was to look for Itz in every Spanish compound. Simple white cotton pants and shirt helped him avoid unwanted attention. As he traveled, he asked reliable sources along the route about any recent siege of prisoners. The accounts of arrests and kidnappings were too frequent an occurrence to warrant special notice anymore. No one could tell him anything significant to his quest.

In the outdoor chapel of Izamal, Kan Ik overheard a friar teaching Indians about the Virgin Mary. The priest talked of a life-like picture that showed sacred light and love coming from the Holy Mother's eyes. For the first time since leaving Ek Balam, he felt hopeful. What the priest described so specifically could only be one of Itz's drawings.

Kan Ik rushed up the grand staircase of the Franciscan church on the city's highest mound. He ran down the center aisle of the semi-dark stone chapel. Above the altar platform, to the right of the wooden crucified figure, hung a realistic picture of a holy woman, clothed in traditional garnet red and blue. Her gentle face turned forward. A translucent aura seemed to surround the figure of Mary. His attention was drawn to a familiar loving smile and eyes that gazed into the distance, as though contemplating something far away. The virgin's portrait was definitely Itz's work. Her signature lily formed part of the crescent moon and floral border depicted below Our Lady.

Gratitude and powerful pangs of love overcame the once aloof warrior. He sobbed and fell on his knees at the altar in thanksgiving for finding a life sign. In front of the painting were vases of fresh flowers and flickering beeswax candles left by devoted converts.

"Queen of heaven and earth!" he shouted to the rafters.

De Landa, leaving his post in the confessional booth against the back wall, saw Kan Ik at the altar. He had been about to call for soldiers to remove the brown skinned native who had the audacity to enter the main sanctuary of the church. But the Maya man's religious devotion and fervent outcry of faith stayed his orders.

"My son, I am touched by your love of Mary, Mother of Christ," the Father said as he walked forward. He made a sign of the cross and placed his hand on Kan Ik's back.

Kan Ik sprang up instinctively at the touch. He nodded silently in response. Kan Ik did not want the priest to suspect him. He needed information and help locating the artist, his betrothed Itz.

Keeping in mind that all life and deities came from one Great Spirit and that the spirit takes on many guises and forms, Kan Ik could, in good consciousness, acknowledge the Virgin Mother. She was the most precious to the Spaniards and they drew inspiration from her essence. He did not compromise his beliefs by bowing down to an Ixchel-like goddess in her new form. If pretending to worship their version of the mother deity would help him find Itz, then he could look like the best convert that monastery had ever known.

Monks readily shared information with Kan Ik, the new Christian. They told him of the native artist woman they christened and renamed Clara. All were in awe of her skills at portraying the various saints and Holy Mother.

He was shown her works. He reached out to reverently touch the surface of the paintings, knowing that she recently touched them herself. The priests were convinced that he was a most devote native, one who truly understood the salvation they offered. The most informative, but disturbing fact he gathered from the brotherhood was that Father De Landa had sent Itz as a gift to the Viceroyalty of El Peru.

Kan Ik knew from experience how arduous the sea and land journey could be. He prayed zealously to the gods for her safe passage. He planned to go to Peru as soon as possible. Kan Ik sent word to Yaxche of Itz's situation and his solemn pledge to find her and get her home. He knew the warriors, including Etz'nab, would return for the planting season and care for Itz's elderly aunt. The noble merchant prayed openly in front of the Spaniards as if all was up to God, but privately believed that it was all up to him to bring Itz back.

Walking through the Izamal marketplace, Kan Ik saw a disheveled cross-eyed woman with what appeared to be her last worldly possessions spread before her on a straw mat. Everything was for sale. He noticed an amulet made of amber with silver borders, similar to what Itz had described as her mother's power stone. He purchased it to give to Itz, when, not if, he next saw her. The talisman symbol made his reunion pledge seem solid and possible.

Without reveling his motivation, Kan Ik told the Father Superior and others of his skills and experiences as a navigator.

“Brothers, I am willing to assist with the next excursion to Ciudad de los Reyes that you call Lima in El Peru.”

“Do you know the ways of the seas and most direct routes to the southern hemisphere lands?” they questioned him.

“Like the back of my hand,” he replied, biting his lip and trying not to smile about his hidden tattoos. “I have sailed as far as the Gulf of Hondurus and know of the Darien area, Panama.”

Recently several Spanish ships had sunk in seasonal storms. Messages and cargo needed to reach their brethren and military command to the south in order to maintain their control on local populations. The powerful Inca state of Piru or Peru, meaning ‘land of abundance’ was a jewel in the Spanish crown and must be held. The conquered country’s silver and gold filled both royal and religious coffers.

When De Landa waved farewell at the launch of the next sailing vessel, Kan Ik stood beside the Spanish sailor at the helm, guiding the ship out through the channel and into the vast ocean.

It took several weeks on the sea, arduous weeks slogging overland through the Darien and several becalmed weeks in the opposite ocean to reach Peru’s new Spanish capital in Lima. The party lost a third of its crew to sickness, desertion and marauders. These morbid statistics left Kan Ik in grave fear over Itz’s similar trek three months before.

CHAPTER 95

Lima, Peru
1565 A.D.

After anchoring in the natural harbor of Callao, Peru, Kan Ik was among the first ashore. The priests believed and excused his haste when he told them, "I must offer prayers of thanksgiving to the Virgin for our safe arrival."

It was a half-day walk to Lima, built in the coastal desert plains next to the Rimac River. He hurried through the perpetual mist and low clouds, down the cobbled streets to the Baroque Cathedral of Lima. This basilica of worship, like so many of the New World churches, was built on the ruins of an ancient indigenous temple.

He began his search for Itz in the city's most massive stone fortress church, the main cathedral. He ran through the intricately carved front portals, not caring if there were rules against the presence of Indians in Spanish places of worship. Stone statues of Catholic apostles and saints silently watched his entrance. In spite of himself, Kan Ik was awestruck by the physical dimensions of the central nave vaulted ceilings and the numerous ornate side chapels. Above him was a painted depiction of sinners writhing in the flames of hell. That horrific scene and the gaudy gold-plated main altar with bejeweled decorations jolted him back to reality and disgust. The spell was broken.

After months of exposure to the Spanish male priest hierarchy in the Yucatan and onboard ship, he recognized the clergy as a heartless, bloodthirsty gang. They talked about saving souls, but real human who perished while building their new kingdoms had no value to them. Their institutions and personal lives were driven by greed, aggrandizing of their cult and self-preservation. Pompous ceremonies used to enforce rules, made common people rely on priests as the only emissaries to their one paternal god figure. He found no balance in Catholicism of the male and female spirits, no acknowledgment of nature, and no personal responsibility for one's spiritual path, like that in the Maya ancient beliefs and practices.

It was within Kan Ik's lifetime that the soldier adventurer, Francisco Pizaro landed in Peru with his one hundred and eighty heavily armed men and thirty horses. Historically, timing worked in the Spaniard's favor. The mighty Inca Empire had been embroiled in a civil war. Two half-brothers, Atahualpa and Huascar, joint heirs to the theocratic throne battled for sole control. Pizaro showed an uncanny ability to turn the war of succession to his own advantage. The Inca kings' conflict against each other left both their indigenous defenses weakened. Alahualpa defeated his brother, but soon after was taken hostage by the Spanish. The Inca populous paid the conquistadores with rooms filled with gold and silver as ransom, but the Spanish executed him anyway.

The leaderless kingdom was left wide-open to subjugation by the conquerors. Between military conquests and diseases, within a decade the Inca people had been decimated and enslaved. Survivors and resistance forces took refuge in high peaks of the Andes Mountains. The conquerors dealt ruthlessly with Inca commoners and forced them to labor long hours in the precious metals and mineral mines. Fortunes in gold and jewels were sent back to Spain.

The Spanish took over the fertile Valley of Cusco, the jungles to the east and the coastal plains. They forced native slaves to built colonial cities for the endless flow of new European settlers.

Kan Ik wanted to find and rescue Itz from this world and return to their beliefs and way of life. He attended Mass several times a day, knelling and praying in different churches and chapels in search of evidence of his beloved's presence in Lima. He refused to entertain the idea that she did not survive the journey. He could not ask the padres outright about the artist Clara for fear of suspicion about his connection or motives.

Weeks after his arrival in Lima, Kan Ik carefully lit a beeswax candle and burned the last of his copal incense in a small chapel near the rear of the main cathedral. He meditated with closed eyes, knowing that others could not see where his inner thought took him. He could return to the arms of Itz in her soft-lit rooms of Ek Balam or ride turquoise waves in his cedar canoe off the shores of Cozumel Island. Memories of bouncing jolts over the sea suddenly felt too vivid and real. Kan Ik opened his eyes to see the paved floor buckling and objects falling around the chapel.

"This must be caused by angry gods shaking the world. These are the earthquakes I've been told about."

Covering his head with his arms, he ran into the monks' private sacristy to avoid the shower of plaster and stones coming from above. He pressed his back to an outside wall and waited for the powerful upheaval to cease. A large canvas picture in a gilded frame crashed beside him. He frowned and pushed it aside with both legs. Through the dust he saw the crumpled face of the Virgin mother smiling back at him.

"Itz!" he jumped up and shouted with uncontained joy and relief. "You answer my prayers. Stop this tremor so I can find you."

He embraced the torn portrait of the Holy Mother. Three priests came into the room in time to observe this act of devotion. At that moment the earthquake ceased. In their pious view, this Indian's faith called on the Virgin and she stopped the shaking earth. Word of this miracle spread among the church leaders and worshippers.

Itz's portrait of the Virgin Mary, with the glowing aura about her beatific face, was moved from the priests' private preparation room to the main chapel. Miracles were good for drawing people into the church, good for business. Lima's Bishop called on their gifted artist Clara to make repairs to the canvas and repaint damage sustained in the fall.

Kan Ik hoped this would happen. He waited quietly in the shadows by the main altar each day. Then Itz appeared. His heart beat wildly at the sight of her. She paused briefly half way down the aisle and touched her chest. Images of Kan Ik flashed before her eyes. They filled with moisture and longing.

"*My tears are prayers that travel to the gods when I am unable to speak*," she lamented.

Itz slipped into a pew and knelt on the lower padded bench to steady herself. She hoped the strong energy flow that overtook her as she entered the basilica was not a bad omen.

"*Universe, Ixchel and all the gods, protect my true love. If the cycles of life will it, let us be together as we were destined.*"

Itz both sensed and felt that someone was nearby. She could not move or turn around. She was frozen in place fearing her mind was playing tricks on her or worse. Time stood still during that life defining moment. A hand touched her forearm. Her head lowered and she glanced down at undulating blue lines over bronze skin.

"Your prayers are answered," a rich baritone voice from behind her called out in her own Mayan tongue.

"My love, you are really here," she swooned.

Kan Ik joined her in the pew and folded her protectively into his strong arms.

"Destiny binds us. We will find a way to be together and return home," he said, touching his forehead to hers.

"But we will still have to hide. Tepal will kill me," she blurted out.

"According to a Spanish priest I sailed with, your Prince Tepal and his evil friend are on the run themselves for theft and desertion of their posts," he replied with a smirk. "They are the known criminals. For a change they are the hunted ones."

"The white man's Bible says, 'Put not your trust in princes', so who are we to question the holy word of their sky god? Tepal's revenge terrified me, but I would be foolish to let him harm me anymore that he has. No more limiting myself in fear," she said with deep relief and resolve.

"This might help," Kan Ik slipped a silver chained necklace over her head. The amber pendant rested on her chest, returned to its rightful owner.

For the first time in months Itz could breath and relax. She nestled into the embrace of her twin spirit. His nearness filled her with ecstasy and hope.

"Itz, we may have to stay in Peru while I arrange for passage or get my own boat. Every day I learn more about new methods of sea faring. I teach others. Even men from places with strange names like Genoa want to know my nautical secrets and copy my maps."

"Perhaps we are here for a purpose," she said. "I have discovered that our conquered Inca brothers speak Aymara, but have no written language, no books as we Maya do. They used oral traditions and *quipu* knotted cords to keep track of accounting figures. I could record true Inca history and wisdom in pictures and words as I used them to preserve the soul of our own people."

"As we have seen in our homeland…until the deer learns to write, every story will praise the hunter," Kan Ik smiled.

"Truths must survive. My art and writings can serve that purpose," offered Itz.

"We both have rightful callings wherever we are. Being alive and together is by far the most important thing, my wonderful lily. No matter what fate may hold for us in the next months and years, our love has prevailed. Such binding unity force lasts forever. Repeating cycles of life may allow it to be reborn within other lovers in the future long after we have returned to source."

CHAPTER 96

Ek Balam, Yucatan
Present Day

Soon after daybreak at the remote Ek Balam farm, Kate arrived with supplies for Hannah. Her friend was nowhere to be found. The day worker said he'd discovered the gate slightly ajar and dogs outside on the trail nearby. Kate looked for signs of a struggle, but there was nothing to indicate Hannah left any way but on her own. Her walking shoes and the battered canvas hat she always wore were gone. Crumpled sheets on the floor, empty medicine packets and general disarray so unlike Hannah indicated that she'd been sick. Stacks of scribbled notes and odd drawings filled the archaeologist's open tablet. Kate knew how dengue or other tropical illness led to disorientation and confusion, so she took Hannah's absence very seriously.

After searching the grounds and finding no sign of her, Kate gathered up the scattered paperwork and returned to Casa de la Paz to call Roberto and Mari. She told them of Hannah's reclusive stay and the current unsettling findings. Her voice sounded near panic over Hannah's disappearance. They immediately drove from Merida to the lodge in Ek Balam to look for their friend.

"Page after page of pictures in her notebook are copies of mural art from the palace room," said Roberto. "Notes indicate she was having obsessive dreams about the artist. She was probably drawn to the ruins. That's where we'll start," he said and rushed to the car.

The trio sped to the archaeological zone and entered through the nearest side gate. Roberto ran down Ek Balam's causeway, through the entry corbel arch and into the main ceremonial center. A ballet of buzzards circled above the stone plaza. He called Hannah's name over and over, until his voice grew hoarse. As he neared the palace he stopped. He closed his eyes, took deep breaths and tried to prepare himself for whatever he might find. Mari and Kate caught up with him.

"Let's look around here. Be careful of the rubble. The doorway is unsupported and dangerous after the looters removed lintel stones," he warned.

"That's Hannah's hat on the platform," Mari cried out. "At least we know she was here."

"But where is she now? No one is around," said Kate.

As the group started to leave the ruined palace and continue their search, Roberto swung his flashlight across to the end of the darkened main room one last time. A tiny pile of rubble and rocks in the corner caught his eye. They looked recently disturbed.

"I want to check this out."

He knelt down and saw where a patch of plaster and stones had been removed. He recognized the eighteen-inch square opening they'd left partially sealed for later access. It led into the chamber.

"*Only Hannah, Mari and I know there is something behind this wall. Would she have returned to the muraled room?*"

"Hannah," he called out. There was no answer. Roberto stood up to leave, but his instincts told him he should remove a few more stones to be sure. He lay down on the hard-packed dirt floor and stuck his head, shoulders and flashlight through the enlarged opening. Against the far wall was a heap of white fabric. He first thought it was part of the drawings on the walls. Then he noticed a burned out candle.

"Oh my god, it's her," he gasped. "Hannah, we're here. Are you okay? Wake up!" There was still no answer or movement from the body in the ancient chamber.

"Mari, Kate, I found her," he screamed.

Roberto took a stick and rapidly dug away more plaster covering. He threw stones aside as quickly as he could to make the opening large enough for him to crawl through and get to Hannah.

Hannah was unresponsive. Roberto scooped her up in his arms and passed her through the opening to Mari and Kate. He carried her to the car. As he drove her lifeless body back to Casa, he pleaded with all the gods of the universe to save her.

Mari immediately went to work. She called on her medical skills to revive Hannah. She felt the entirety of the person was too often lost in modern medicine, so she also closed her eyes and visualized emerald green healing light surrounding her other child of love. Mari sought the body-mind balance. The others paced and prayed for signs of life. No one spoke.

Hannah felt someone touch her forehead with a cool cloth. A lavender-scent filled her nose. She floated into consciousness and opened her eyes as much as she could. Mari's concerned face appeared through the haze.

Hannah's throat felt parched, her lips cracked. She swallowed, opened her mouth to say something but was unable to speak. So she simply nodded and smiled at her tender caretaker.

"There you are. Waking up. I'll get you some water," said Mari.

Hannah drank the cool liquid in tiny sips. Mari put in a touch of honey and papaya leaf to help her scratchy throat. She saw Roberto and Kate hovering near the end of the bed.

"What happened…?" Hannah strained to ask.

In two strides Roberto was beside her. He squeezed her limp hand in his rough paw.

"You are very ill. We're taking you to the hospital in Merida. Everything will be alright," he assured her and himself.

"They'll kill me at the hospital, like Teresa," she cried out in fear.

Roberto, Kate and Mari looked at each other, confused by her outburst. They thought Hannah was still delusional with fever.

"We'll be there to watch over you," Roberto assured her. He gently put his finger to her lips, signaling Hannah to keep silent and rest.

Leaving Ek Balam, a change of weather blackened the skies before their eyes. Winds kicked up, causing tree branches to bend and sway. Restless skies let loose a resounding crack of thunder from an anvil shape cloud mass growing on the horizon. Chains of lightening continuously flashed from all directions.

At first, large raindrops splatted on the windshield, then the low and dark sky opened up with tumultuous fury. Shimmering sheets of rain pounded the car and pavement in front of them so hard they seemed to be driving underwater. Windshield wipers beating their rubber wings could not keep up with the downfall. Navigating the narrow road was slow and treacherous. The flooded tarmac wound through the jungle until they reached the main highway. Mari feared they might have to stop or turn back if the storm did not cease. But Hannah desperately needed medical attention, so Roberto pushed on through the deluge.

All the way to Merida, Hannah was oblivious to the soaking downpour and slept with her head in Mari's lap in the back seat. Check in at O'Horan Hospital was quick and her doctors provided immediate professional care.

"It is good that you got her to the hospital when you did. If this virus is not treated, it can result in liver and kidney problems and sometimes causes death," said the attending physician.

The hospital staff ran blood tests and started Hannah on transfusions to remedy low platelet count symptoms. Bed rest and plenty of fluids to rehydrate her system were mandatory the doctor told his patient and her friends.

CHAPTER 97

Merida, Yucatan
Present Day

After a week of treatment for her virus at O'Horan Hospital, Hannah felt somewhat revived. She found lying about in bed all day to be boring and stifling. She heard about the Saint Vincent de Paul Albergue north of the hospital and asked a nurse to take her to visit the shelter. She considered volunteering to pass the time.

The good nuns of St. Vincent ran a sort of Ronald McDonald House to provide a place to sleep and food for hospital patients' family members who could not afford lodging while staying in town. This allowed them to be at the bedside of their ill relatives. Most people at the shelter came from the poorest pueblos and primarily spoke Mayan. The big city and hospitals frightened them. The nuns provided temporary sanctuary and helped them navigate strange systems.

"Good food is good medicine," said the elderly blue-eyed Mother Superior, as she gave Hannah the requisite orientation speech. The old nun's beaming smile lit up the room. The nurse who took Hannah to Saint Vincent's told her that this hunched over angel with the rusty walker had been the darling of high society circles in Merida during the era of the elite 'Divine Caste' henequen millionaires. When the heiress felt the vocation to join a convent, she asked for the order to place her in a South American nunnery where no one knew her, to avoid differential treatment. At ninety she returned to Merida. All the people she'd known were dead.

Two Maya laywomen, Dona Maria and Juanita, ran operations of the St. Vincent Albergue like a strict ship. There was no compromise on cleanliness or timeliness. In physical stature, the two supervisors came only to Hannah's shoulder, if that. But their hearts and spirits were huge and embracing.

The staff made do with random supplies donated by the community, yet created three meals per day, three hundred and sixty-five days a year. They fed an average of sixty or more hungry people at each sitting. Sometimes eggs, beans and tortillas were all to be had. Other days they feasted on plates of meat and vegetables. Everything depended on the generosity of donors, suppliers and availability of day-old or discarded goods.

"I am still too weak to help regularly or for very long, but I will do what I can," Hannah offered.

"There is no act of kindness too small," Juanita advised. "These people have nothing and yet are grateful for everything. They make sure all others are served before they even touch their own food."

Hannah was happy to don an apron, hairnet and mask to cook and serve. She saw people shyly glancing at her while she set tables, stirred cauldrons of boiling food, scrubbed or did whatever task was necessary. For some it was the first white woman they had ever seen up close. To have her helping them was living proof of scriptural teachings about giving of oneself to others.

"Mother Superior said, "Service is nothing but love in a work apron. The fragrance of the rose always remains on the hand that gives it."

Even though she only served two hours a day, Hannah's time in the St. Vincent kitchen took its toll physically. Her joints ached and it was hard to close her left hand all the way.

Weakened after a particularly hard afternoon, she rested in her quiet dimly lit room. A knock on the door woke her.

"Thank goodness you are here and safe," began Mari. "Yesterday two priests came to our place asking after you. I told them nothing. Today when I returned from the market, the house had been ransacked," she said. Anger welled up in her eyes. "The only thing missing is your engraved gold watch from Dr. Sarra. This tells me that he knows you are here in the Yucatan."

"I wouldn't do anything to put you in jeopardy. I must leave and return to the farm," Hannah exclaimed in a trembling voice. "I have a treatment this evening I can't miss. Then I'll take the night bus back to Ek Balam." Hannah put a few possessions in her weathered gray backpack in readiness. She dressed in a loose yellow shirt and her brown cargo pants with all the zippered pockets, putting pesos in the deep front slot. She had to return to her hideout to keep those she cared about out of harm's way.

CHAPTER 98

Merida, Yucatan
Present Day

At the back of the St. Vincent de Paul chapel, Sister Karin droned on with her confession. The priest visited the albergue's order every Thursday. He found it difficult to understand the nun since a stroke melted the right side of her face in paralysis and garbled her speech. He tapped his fingers impatient to return to his quarters and belt back the top of a new bottle of scotch purchased that morning. But the confessor sat up and paid closer attention when he heard the old sister tell him about a new kitchen volunteer, a North American at O'Horan Hospital for treatment.

"I confess my sin. I was judgmental. I didn't think I would like her at first, but now I acknowledge that she is humble and good hearted," the nun rambled on.

He made a rolling motion with his hand, meant to get her to the point and end her confession. The Father had recently received confidential notices that church leaders were looking for someone who fit that description. He knew he'd receive a reward and accolades if he turned over the hunted woman. He ended the session in the confessional abruptly with terse instructions for penance---nine rosaries and one day of fasting. He sped to the cathedral to make calls to change his finances and placement status.

Hannah dozed in the wheel chair used to bring her back from treatment. Her eyes flew open in alarm when the hospital room door banged open, hitting the wall with a thud. Bright lights from the corridor blinded her and she shielded her eyes. A needle jab stung her neck. She was too stunned and drowsy to shout or fight.

Two men grabbed her arms on either side and lifted her bodily from the chair. They pulled her out the door and down the hallway. She could see they wore black slacks and white shirts. Their shiny patent leather shoes held her dazed attention. Then her vision shattered and collapsed into shards before her eyes. She passed out in the midst of her drugged exit from the back of the hospital.

Hannah awoke with the morning light. She looked around, alarmed by her predicament. She lay face up, bound to the corners of an antique four-poster bed. She tugged on the ropes around her wrists and ankles. The constraints were the strong braided type used to string up hammocks. They would not loosen. Struggling made them tighten more and caused pain.

Stained glass windows at the end of her narrow room had thick wooden bars. The heavy metal entrance door was closed and presumably locked.

"*The priests found me*," she groaned. "*No one will come looking for me. Mari and Roberto think I took the bus back into hiding last night.*"

Hannah heard voices coming. They unlatched her door and looked in. She pretended to still be unconscious.

"How much of that stuff did you give her, Brother John?"

"She is probably better off knocked out. Our superiors are arranging 'an accident' for her," he said, using his stubby fingers to make quotation marks in the air. "Until word comes, we just have to keep her secured." Hannah heard them bolt the door. Indifferent to her plight, as they walked away, they argued about the soccer game they watched last night.

Sometime later a nun in an old-fashioned floor length habit came into Hannah's confinement room. She untied the bonds so Hannah could use a porcelain bedpan and drink some water. Hannah ignored the cold greasy plate of unfamiliar foods placed on the table, but did drink all the water.

"Why am I here? Where am I?" she questioned the elderly nun. She hoped for a show of compassion. The woman could perhaps tell her something and help her.

"You offended some very powerful people, holy men," the nun scolded and wiggled her finger in front of Hannah nose. "Where you are now is unimportant. It is where you are going when you die that matters. You need to pray for your immortal soul." Her boney old finger pointed toward the damp rough stone floor. Hannah realized the ancient crone expected her to drop to her knees that instant and plead for salvation. She sat up and tried to play along but her legs felt too wobbly to move.

"I hoped that…" Hannah began.

"Hope is for fools who refuse to recognize the truth," interrupted the nun.

"How did they find me?"

"Your friends and family were no help. One of them, a man named Max died under interrogation. He would not give up your whereabouts."

"My father? Dead?" Hannah collapsed back onto the hard bed and curled into a ball sobbing. Her face twisted into a mask of tragedy.

"Have you no faith? You may see him in heaven. You are Catholic aren't you?"

The sister hissed, crossed herself, and clacked her tongue disapprovingly when the prisoner did not answer in the affirmative. The nun didn't bother to retie Hannah's restraints before she left. She figured that the devastating sorrow she saw in Hannah's eyes had immobilized her sufficiently for the time being. She turned the key in the deadbolt though.

Hannah felt defeated like never before. She could hardly breathe through the dull gray emotional pain. She felt fear slink in and bore under her skin. The armor of hope she'd always worn like a cloak unraveled and the last speck of her will faltered.

Deep regrets flooded across her mind. The missed life opportunities crushed Hannah like heavy limestone blocks falling from a Maya building.

"*I should not have worried so much about things that didn't matter. I wasted precious time on work that could have been spent with loved ones. I can't deal with all this loss,*" she cried out.

With her beloved father dead and Joseph out of her life forever, a sobbing grief below grief overcame her. She felt as if something inside her had splintered into a thousand pieces. She could not move, not even to open her eyes.

Hannah had ample reasons to be fearful and heartsick. But from somewhere within she found that she also had many reasons to rise up and take action. Determination broke into her consciousness. In a snap, Hannah stopped crying, not a tear left in her. She opened her eyes wide. She pushed down that initial fear, pushed back her first impulse to quit, and pushed through feelings of helplessness.

"*I must make my father's sacrifice count. He protected me so I could stop those murderers and thieves, and by god I will,*" she said in defiance.

CHAPTER 99

Merida, Yucatan
Present Day

Hannah's resolve to live crashed through the barriers thrown up by her pain of loss. The devastation she felt turned into a drive to defeat the men who attempted to break her. She knew that dark discouragement was the enemy's favorite tool to put out the light in someone. She was determined to fight back even though she was afraid. Like the snake she found in her boot one time, it took courage to toss it and the fear out so she could move on.

Hannah swung her legs over the bed's edge and stood up. While she steadied herself, she listened for voices or other telltale signs of guards and heard none. She pushed a chair over to the window to inspect the bars covering the stained glass panes. They appeared to be made of old wood with dry rot. One quickly gave way when she pulled it back and forth. Like the refracted sunlight bouncing off the colored glass, Hannah had a quick glimmer of hope. She used the first wooden bar to pry others loose. She worked as quietly as she could, looking over her shoulder for thugs in black and white who might try to stop her.

When she'd cleared away enough wooden barriers, she unlatched the colorful window. She saw that it opened to an interior courtyard garden. Hannah sighed in nervous relief, slipped through the narrow space and dropped to the ground. She looked around for ways to escape the compound. A truck carrying large containers of drinking water for the building drove in a side gate. She exited through the same delivery entrance to an outside sidewalk.

For a split second Hannah felt free but froze when she observed Father Batz and his henchman standing on the edge of the narrow residential street. The priest saw her. Their eyes locked. Something feral and cold came over his squinty cruel stare and scowl. Wounded animals often bare their teeth. He pounded his fist on his car hood in rage. The hard-bitten man who stabbed Hannah sprang at her in pursuit. She bolted away from him.

Hannah deduced that her captors must have confined her near the hospital, because within a block she emerged onto bustling Itzas Avenue. Noisy growling buses, belching plumes of soot and fumes, caught her eye. She still had pesos in her pocket, so she ran along side and jumped into a moving bus headed south. Bodies, crushed together like so many department store manikins, concealed her somewhat. But her red-blonde hair and yellow blouse didn't help her blend in.

Batz got his car in gear and along with her pursuer followed the bus. At the stoplight, Hannah saw the tough minion get out and try to come aboard. She worked her way through the people-packed center aisle toward the back. Thankfully the bus lurched away with high-pitched grinding gears. Her predator was left pounding on a moving closed door. The priest's car wove in and out of traffic never losing sight of Hannah's transport as it slalomed down Itzas.

At the bus stop near Aurrera supermarket, she exited with a scurrying crowd of shoppers. Even hunched over, she still towered above the group and stood out like a beacon. She sprinted past the store entrance and through the parking lot to a back street. A stack of wooden pallets and cardboard boxes hid her while she peeked out to see if the priest and his hired hand caught her escape route. Their black car circled the lot. Maybe, if lucky, she'd have a few minutes lead to slip away. Timing was of the utmost importance. While trying to decide when to start her dash through the back loading area, a smelly trash truck pulled away from the store. It hid her long enough to run down the alley.

Merida's General Cemetery was only a couple of blocks away. Hannah ran through the iron gates as fast as she could. She ducked into gravestone paths off the main entry road and zigzagged around monuments and statues to stay out of sight. Her legs shook with exertion. Sweat trickled down her back. She kept rubbing the stinging red marks on her wrists where she had been bound. She was unfettered but she would not be free until she lost her pursuers.

"*If I could hide near Alma and Felipe, their spirits will protect me. I need time to catch my breath and come up with a better plan.*" She was still woozy and confused by the drugs.

When she reached Alma's memorial, she touched it with reverence like a talisman. She sank down behind the marker with her back against the overhanging tree. Hannah's pounding heart measured out the seconds, skipped a few beats, and then painfully raced to catch up.

"*No cavalry coming. I am on my own. What should I do?*" she fretted. Time to think was not in her favor. The slow moving black sedan loomed up across from Felipe's raised platform memorial. It stopped and both men got out of the vehicle.

A succession of gun bursts rang out. Hannah flung herself flat on the ground as bullets hammered the grave monuments around her. Plaster from a statue showered Hannah with fragments. A splinter cut her cheek. Fear made a statue of her too, but she knew she had to move. She scrambled to her feet again, ran down the row and crouched behind a marble angel holding a stony finger to her lips. Tense with premonition, Hannah crouched down like a runner at the starter's block.

"Give it up Hannah," Batz shouted. "Or not. Who would look for a corpse in a cemetery?" he cawed like a crow.

She heard the hollow sound of his approaching footsteps on the broken cement walkways. Panic hovered around her like a hummingbird. Frantically, Hannah dashed across the main road toward the wall where Felipe Carrillo Puerto was assassinated. Bullets whizzed by, close to her head and pinged off pavement at her feet. The next round grazed her calf. She stumbled. Hannah's stomach tightened with fear. Her movements slowed and became mechanical, like in a nightmare. She flung herself behind the martyred governor's pedestal. She was cornered. Escape seemed futile. Adrenaline prickled her skin and dread clung to her bones.

Batz must have called for backup because she saw a second car rapidly coming through the entrance and approach. Another person got out and searched in her direction.

Her body shook with pain and fear. But more than fear, a fierce anger surged. It was because these punks had it in their power to end her life. She felt a fundamental revulsion at a death by such vile hands. Most of all, the nature of their evil unsettled her. Her plans did not include dying like this, at this time. But death has a perverse habit of making his own appointments.

"Aguila," A deep voice rang out loud and clear over the large graveyard.

Hannah, without thinking of any association, automatically shouted out, "Sol."

The rapidly approaching third man was coming in her direction. Behind him a stream of police cars entered the cemetery grounds with lights flashing and sirens whooping.

She looked out to see Batz and his cohort bolt away from her hiding spot in an attempt to escape the authorities. Batz reached the black vehicle first and sped out the Calle 66 side entrance, leaving his partner in crime chasing behind on foot. Two policemen grabbed the priest's muscle man and wrestled him to the ground with a fierce body slam. He was instantly in handcuffs.

Hannah tried to rise from her huddled position, but couldn't. She knew Batz had fled and his henchman was in custody, but she couldn't see the newcomer anywhere. The light changed as the third man's shadow crossed over her.

"Who's there?" she whimpered and cowered down.

"Nobody," sighed the approaching stranger with a familiar voice.

Hannah looked up into Joseph's blue eyes.

His face, creased with concern, relaxed with relief when he saw that she didn't appear to be seriously harmed. He sank down beside her, placed an arm around her shoulder, pulled her toward him, shrouding her body with his own. Hannah collapsed in his embrace and began to cry between stuttering breaths of air.

"You are not alone, I'm here. It's going to be alright." he comforted her. She calmed and they sat in silence for several moments.

"They shot me," she said, as if just realizing it.

He saw the torn pants leg and bright blood stains. Joseph took off his shirt and then his t-shirt so he could use the second's soft fabric as a bandage. He tied it securely around Hannah's calf.

"Oh Joseph, they killed my dad," she wailed.

"No, your father is bruised but alive. Thugs tried to get information out of him, but he faked a heart attack and they left him for dead. When I went looking for you in LA, I found him and got help."

Hannah couldn't speak.

Joseph held her close and continued, "He insisted I should come here to locate you and make sure you were safe."

"How did you find me?"

"I contacted Mari and Roberto. We deduced that you did not leave the hospital voluntarily. Your pack and hat were still by the bed. I remembered you told me this is where you come when in Merida," he said to lighten the moment and with gratitude for blind luck.

Hannah sighed with deep relief. She wiped her teary eyes, looked at Joseph, and whispered, almost not wanting to hear the answer, "You're here. I thought you got married."

"I'm not married. That was a vicious rumor. I want to spend the rest of my life with you. And I want the rest of my life to start as soon as possible. It will take some doing, but we'll find a way and it'll be worth it."

"I could do with a different kind of excitement than I've had these last few months," Hannah admitted frankly. "I'd be content to work with museums and investigate antiquity thefts."

"I heard Dr. Sarra got busted because of your work with the U.S. Customs. That loser headed to South America to avoid facing prosecution," Joseph said with an undisguised smile over the fate of his rival.

"Father Batz will probably be right behind him after today's fiasco," said Hannah. "I may have to follow their trail to stop further desecrations."

"We'd make a good team in that effort---astute reporter and dedicated archaeologist," said Joseph.

"I thought it was over for us," said Hannah as they stood up.

"Circumstances certainly threw up roadblocks, but I always knew we'd prevail and find our way back to each other. Real love stories never have endings." He moved closer, the movement opened his cotton shirt.

"What's that mark on your chest?" she asked.

"It's 20 degrees 58 minutes by 89 degrees 57 minutes, the latitude and longitude of Merida. I had a small tattoo put over my heart to remember where I found my true love," he said. "This is the spot where we first kissed," Joseph whispered.

Hannah leaned against the rough cemetery wall. Joseph held her and kissed her. Their breath and spirits intertwined. The invisible strength of their binding union would be like others that last through the ages. Energy and time flow in circles.

The End

Made in the USA
San Bernardino, CA
06 January 2017